ALLY ALDRIDGE

SKY HEART

The Soul Heart Series: Book Two

To my friends,

Thank you for being there for me during the hard times,
and being part of my adventures growing up.
Things change too quick ;)

Us5 Forever, Ally x

CHAPTER 1

Y NAILS DUG INTO MY PALMS as I clutched the soggy red dress Jace had handed me before walking out of my life. I shivered as I stood on the porch. My hand rose to my mouth to stifle a sob, powerless to do anything as I watched him leave.

He was in a rush to be gone like he couldn't get away from me fast enough. His words had been brief. The interaction was only a few seconds long. His words rang through my head, drawing out the agony of being dumped. I collapsed against the door frame with the shattering pain of my heart breaking, choking on a lump in my throat. My tears faded him out like the closing of a film.

"Kiely!" Mum called.

Hearing my name made me gasp with internal pain. I wasn't ready to face anyone. I couldn't let her see me like this. My shoulders slumped as I closed the front door.

"Who was it?" she called from the kitchen. We'd been making mince pies together before I left to answer the door. My fingers were sticky, and spices clung to my clothes like a festive perfume.

I didn't trust myself to speak without crying and didn't want to talk about it either, so I ran upstairs before Mum realised something was up.

Passing the string of Christmas cards hanging in the stairwell full of love and well wishes made me rage. I tugged the thread at the top. Freeing the folds of cardboard was satisfying to watch as they slid to the floor, undone and depleting into a gratifying mess.

I heard Mum grumble about how clumsy I was as she swept up the pile. Their messages were insignificant, their thoughtful meaning lost, defaced into a mocking joke. They didn't match the mood of my shattered heart.

On the gallery landing, a cheap-and-cheerful, plastic, happy Christmas picture hung on each bedroom door. A *'Ho Ho Ho'* and a picture of Santa adorned my parents' door. My brother Murray's room had a picture of a beaming reindeer and the phrase *'Jingle Bells'*.

My room was the smallest in the house, and it's always irritated me, but tonight, it felt fitting. I wanted somewhere I could tuck myself away from the world. On my door was an image of a fairy with the words

'*Magical Christmas*' written in a pretty italic font.

I didn't feel like laughing or singing, and I certainly wasn't having a magical Christmas! I ripped the fairy from my door and threw it across the hall. I flung the door open with the same force as the venom festering inside me and slammed it shut behind me.

I'm not a Scrooge.

I don't hate the Christmas holidays.

Normally, I loved the over-the-top extent my mum went through to ensure we all enjoyed the celebrations. I loved choosing gifts, wrapping them up, and placing them under the tree. These days, I got more excited thinking about the recipient opening my gift to them than I did about receiving my own. I enjoyed crafts with Mum, making Turkish delight, decorating a gingerbread house, and the big roast dinner she'd prepare on Christmas Day that would take us days to eat. But, right now, I wasn't me. A part of me had died, and the rest of me that had somehow survived didn't like what was left.

Whilst dumping me, Jace had returned my red dress. I'd leant it to his best friend Mariah. I'd tried hard to get along with her. I really did. But she was my boyfriend's *female* best friend.

I tossed the dress across the room into my laundry basket, wrinkling my nose at the smell of chlorine radiating off it, killing any remaining Christmas vibes. The smell took me back to that night of the Mistletoe Disco, my last date with Jace. Murray had taken Mariah, so we'd been double-dating. I felt sick as I realised there'd be no more dates. It was over.

Murray was always watching me, being overprotective. But, for the first time, he left us alone together. Not exactly alone, as the room was full of people, but it'd been nice to not have *him* looking over my shoulder. I'd hoped this would be it. The moment Jace and I would finally have our first kiss.

We'd wanted this for ages, but once the opportunity arrived, I'd been giddy with nerves. We'd slow-danced, pressed up against each other. My heart thudded as I plucked up the courage to do it.

Just do it.

We had stared into each other's eyes whilst I willed him to make a move. His mouth had been so close to mine that I felt his rapid exhales. Then, I realised he was as nervous as me, so I did it. I kissed him.

It had been awkward. A messy snog that was over too fast.

My heart fluttered at the memory, and then I came crashing back to reality with a fresh wave of heartache. Ex-boyfriend. I flung myself back on my bed and bumped my head hard against the headboard. I didn't care. Nothing could hurt as bad as this.

The ceiling blurred above me. *I wouldn't cry!* I vowed to myself. No more tears.

I turned on my music app and cranked up the volume. I didn't care what came on. I needed enough noise to drown out the sound of my thoughts.

I rolled over and buried my head in my pillow, took a deep breath, and let it all out in one pitiful scream. Lifting my head, I gasped for breath, relishing the cool air pricking my sweating forehead. I felt a little better, but not by much.

I reached for my mobile and bashed out a text to my girls. They were going to find out sooner or later anyway, and I'd much rather tell it once. Besides, a text message was far less personal than telling them face-to-face, and I liked how it kept me separated from them. It was easier to stay in control of my emotions that way.

Kiely: I got dumped for Christmas.

Almost as soon as the text was sent, my phone rang. I cringed at the irritating Christmas song I chose when I'd been in high spirits. I put the phone on silent because I couldn't deal with talking to anyone right now.

Pretending to be fine as we opened presents, ate Christmas dinner, and sang Christmas songs, exhausted me. Our relative in Ireland gifted Murray UNO, and he insisted on us all playing together. It was easier to join in than to stand out by declining.

As the evening darkened, I felt relief knowing I could soon retire to bed. Dad was flicking through the on-demand movies for something we could watch together, whilst Murray microwaved packets of popcorn for us.

"I'm taking Aero out." I said. He was a good dog,

but he was getting restless. The fresh air would do us both good.

Aero started wagging his tail with excitement as soon as he saw his lead in my hand. He was a gorgeous chocolate Labrador and always sprang up with excitement at the prospect of walkies.

"I'll come with you," Mum said, pulling on her coat.

I couldn't suppress a noticeable sigh.

"What is it? What's wrong with you?"

"Nothing." I shook my head and got my coat on. I clipped the lead to Aero's collar as we went out the front door.

Mum was silent beside me as she fiddled with her gloves, tugging at each finger as if they weren't in right. Then, she began tugging at her scarf, which sat against her neck.

I kept my focus on Aero as we crossed the green and headed down the steps onto the beach by our house. I unclipped Aero so he could run.

The sea was noisy, and the wind was rough and bitter. It was too cold to have a long walk, but Aero didn't care. He jumped in and out of icy waves, barking at the splashes. He loved it. Seeing his daft antics made me smile for real, for the first time.

"There you are," Mum said.

I'd forgotten she was there. Red hair stuck out under her black woolly hat and blew around wildly in the wind.

"You've been miserable all day. Not my happy little Kiely."

I swallowed a lump in my throat. "Of course, I'm happy. It's Christmas."

"You can fool your dad and brother, but not me. A mother knows. Something is off with you."

The corners of my lips tugged down. My heart was heavy and tired from hiding my heartbreak. "Jace dumped me."

My promise not to shed another tear over him shattered as they came pouring out. Mum pulled me against her, wrapping her arms around me. The wind, the sea, my tears, it was all too much. Mum mumbled soothing words into my hair. Despite not hearing what she said, they brought comfort and made me feel loved.

As I calmed down, Mum faced me and said, "You'll be okay."

"It hurts." I stifled a sob as the pain welled up again.

She squeezed my shoulders. "It gets easier. I promise. If you ever need to talk, I'm here for you."

I nodded and sniffed, annoyed by the snot running down my face, making me feel gross. Mum pulled out a packet of tissues from her pocket. I took one and blew my nose.

Aero was at our side, looking all worried about me. I rubbed his head to reassure him I was okay and clipped his lead back on. By now, the cold was biting the skin of my face and had seeped into my bones.

As Mum linked arms with me, we started walking home, deciding to watch the Grinch and eat popcorn.

After finding out about my breakup, Murray invited me out in his new car to get McDonald's via the drive-through, insisting this was a rite of passage for a new car. My dad shared his secret stash of toffees with me, and Mum kept fussing over me. It was sort of nice, but also a little too much.

Back in September, Fallon had her sweet sixteen. She'd wanted us to get drunk with her, which sounded like fun. But, when my parents saw the state of me afterwards, they banned me from any future parties at her house. Tonight, however, Fallon's family was having a New Year's Eve party, and I'd been invited. I hadn't told my parents because they would have said no. A part of me wanted to go. The other part realised Arizona, our mutual friend, was away visiting family. I wouldn't miss much if I didn't go. Still, the urge to go was bigger, and as I felt ready to face my friends, I called Fallon.

"Keily, about time! Have you been ignoring me?"

"No. I've just been – you know…"

"I can't believe he dumped you! Tell me everything! When? How?"

I felt a sharp pang in my chest as my mind flashed back. With a shake of my head, I got rid of the feeling. A lump lodged itself in my throat, and my voice came out as a croak, "To my face."

Everyone says it is the honourable way to do it.

Only a coward would do it by phone, text, or email. It hurt all the same, and there's nothing honourable in breaking someone's heart.

"What did he say?" Fallon was fishing for details.

My jaw tensed as I remembered what he had said. "He's a complete bastard, Fallon! It's not what he said, but how he said it! He was—" I searched for the right word, "—eager." I thought for a bit, trying to figure out how to explain his odd behaviour. The way he blurted it out and hurried off. "He seemed happy and in a rush to get somewhere."

"Did he say why?"

I grunted and mimicked his voice. *"It's not you; it's me."* I let out a bitter "Ha!" rolled my eyes and continued, "He acted as if he was doing me a favour!"

"He has."

"What?"

"He *has* done you a favour. Come on, Kiely, you know you can do so much better than Jace Walker! I never got what you saw in him, anyway."

I wasn't feeling as if I could do any better than Jace. Plus, I didn't want to do any better. All I wanted was to have him back. The need felt unbearable, suffocating, crippling almost. We'd only just had our first kiss, and I yearned for so many more. I felt robbed before we'd even begun.

My eyes welled up, and I sucked in a deep breath to stop myself blubbering.

"Look," she hesitated before continuing, "We're having a house party for New Year's Eve. Come over?

But not if you're going to be all mopey. You're hot! You're sexy! And we should be finding you a new man! A real man."

That was easy for Fallon to say. She wasn't short of interest from guys at school. She was stunning, with her gorgeous blonde ringlets that dropped into natural waves. Plus, she had an insane amount of confidence. Fallon had broken many hearts, and despite her vicious side, they'd all forgive her in a heartbeat to get a second chance. But Fallon wasn't into 'school boys' she was chasing older guys, *'real men'* as she liked to refer to them.

"Don't worry, I'm not moping," I lied, thankful she couldn't see me. "I'm going to have to sneak out. Mum and Dad are still mad at us for getting drunk at your birthday party. They think you're a bad influence."

"I am a bad influence," Fallon said with an air of pride. "That's why you love me. See you later."

CHAPTER 2

THE MUSIC BEAT FROM FALLON'S HOUSE like a battle drum. I jutted out my chin to feign confidence. The pebbles shifted beneath my feet, ruining my strut and causing me to wobble in my heels. All I wanted to do was cry, but I swept my blonde hair over my shoulder and adjusted my black Lycra dress. Now that I was here, it felt too short. I felt too exposed and wanted to go home and change, but I also didn't want to incur Fallon's wrath.

My chest tightened as a group of drunk lads spilled out of the house. Seeing me, they jeered 'Happy New Year' and passed by. I returned their well wishes and made my way into the house, wanting to get inside and find Fallon fast.

I was late, but I had to wait until it was a suitable time to go to bed otherwise my parents would've got suspicious. I squeezed my way through the crowded hallway and mumbled, "Excuse me," and, "Thanks." I searched for a familiar face. I felt like I stood out on my own, as everyone else was in groups. My arm folded across my chest as I held my elbow. My eyes raced around the room.

Fallon, where are you?

I spotted Scarlet, Fallon's older sister. She was almost a mirror image of Fallon with the family's trademark golden curls, slight tan, and green eyes. I hadn't seen her for a while, as she'd been away at university, but her eyes lit up with recognition upon seeing me.

"Hey Kiely, you alright? Fallon's in the conservatory." Everything Scarlet did oozed confidence, even the little nod afterwards to check I'd heard her before returning to her conversation. Fallon idolised her. She was about the only person Fallon did.

I cut through the kitchen to get to the conservatory. On my way through, I bumped into Fallon's older brother, Nate, Budweiser poised at his lips. Running a hand through his short blond curls, he leaned back against the counter, giving me a cheeky wink that would make any girl flush red.

The 'gorgeous' gene that ran through the Rein family was undeniable, and didn't they all know it? Everyone fancied Nate, but we all knew he was off-limits. I remember Arizona making the mistake of admitting she had a crush on him and Fallon flipping out. Since then, Ari hadn't shown an interest in anyone else. She might be over Nate, but she wouldn't dare admit it if she wasn't.

In the conservatory, Fallon sat on a wicker frame sofa that used to belong to her nan. The thinning weave had faded, as had the floral pattern. She was watching two older lads playing Guitar Hero on an old console. Her face brightened when she saw me, and I got the distinct impression that she'd been bored prior to my arrival.

"Kiely! You made it. I thought maybe you weren't coming," she cheered and got up from her chair to embrace me in a hug. I could smell alcohol on her breath.

"Are you drunk?"

"Not yet, but I'm working on it." She reached into a crate of Smirnoff and passed me a bottle.

"Jim!" she yelled over the noise and waved her arm to get someone's attention.

In response, one of Nate's mates made their way toward us, eager to help. I couldn't help but snigger. His cool guy swagger came off more as a dorky limp. He dug into his pocket and pulled out a key chain with a bottle opener on it.

"Ours have all gone walkabout." Fallon shrugged.

"No worries," Jim croaked. He took my bottle, opened it, and handed it back to me, all without taking his eyes off Fallon.

Fallon swished her hair around as she turned her attention back to me. I caught a waft of her perfume. It smelled new, so I guessed it must have been a gift for Christmas. She leaned back into the chair, with one arm dangling across the back, and stretched her free arm to get a selfie of us together.

"Don't post it. I'm not meant to be out!" I reminded her.

"Don't worry, you know I like to edit it first, anyway."

Jim returned to stand next to Nate in the kitchen. He stood in the doorway, appearing to take part in their conversation, but he kept stealing small glances at Fallon, willing her to look. But Fallon never turned his way again.

"He's into you, you know?"

"You think?" She rolled her eyes. It was clear this was old news and way too obvious.

"Do you like him? You like older guys. He's eighteen, isn't he?"

Fallon gulped her drink and wrinkled her nose as if it tasted bad. "Yeah, but he's also my brother's mate. Remember the rule."

I nodded. We couldn't date each other's brothers or our own brother's mates. Fallon had made the rule and made sure we never forgot.

Fallon leaned close to me and added in a low voice, "Also, ew, I don't want my sex life out for public consumption. I've heard Jim talk about other girls, graphically."

Jim was so into Fallon I was sure he wouldn't do anything to ruin it if he was ever lucky enough. But, instead of telling her that, I swigged my drink and watched the air guitar show play out in front of me. One guy fell to his knees in victory, leaning back, sticking his tongue out, whilst strumming his guitar controller.

"Yeah, that's how you do it!" he gloated, head banging like a rocker.

"This is way better than that lame Mistletoe Disco!" Fallon's voice was calm again, and she smiled at me. Fallon hadn't even gone, so she didn't know whether it had been lame. She was having a dig at me for going.

I nodded in agreement, even though that disco had been my first and last kiss with Jace. My heart pounded at the mere memory of the closeness and anticipation before our lips met. Since then, he'd been distant and even blanked me on the bus. Guess I should have seen it coming; all the signs were there.

I downed the rest of my drink before daring to ask, "Do you think Jace dumped me after he got what he wanted?"

"You slept with him!" Fallon's eyes went wide. "Shit! I didn't know things were that serious between you two!"

The game was quiet whilst the lads chose the next song to compete. I saw them exchange a look and laugh. I cringed.

Tugging on Fallon's arm to pull her down towards me, I whispered. "No. We just kissed!"

Fallon glanced over at the lads and whispered back, "Has anyone else dumped you after you kissed them?"

I knew where this conversation was going. "You

know he was my first."

Fallon shrugged and sank back into her seat, her bottle poised at her lips. She raised an eyebrow at me. "But not your last."

"You think I can get him back?" My heart raced with the idea.

"Of course, but why waste your time on him? I'm thinking we get you some practice, build your confidence back up, then upgrade to someone way better than Jace."

"I don't know…"

"He's just knocked you down," she said, lost in thought. "First, we need to sort out some practice for you."

"Practise?"

"Yeah. We could make out, and I could give you some pointers."

"I don't think…You know, I'm not into…"

Fallon laughed. "You need to lighten up a little. It's just a kiss, not a marriage proposal. FYI, I'm an amazing kisser, so you're totally missing out."

I folded my arms, the bottle still in my hand. The cool glass chilled me through my dress. "I'm sure you are."

"Shot or dare?"

I couldn't risk a repeat of how ill I got after her birthday. "Dare."

Fallon leaned into me. "I dare you, when they do the countdown, to snog the first guy you see."

"Oh no. I can't. Shot. Get me a shot."

Fallon cracked up. "Too late. You said dare."

"What about you?" I asked.

"I'll do it too. Make it fair."

I groaned. What had I got myself into? I knew Fallon was trouble, which was why my parents had banned me from attending anymore of her parties.

My heart thudded as midnight neared. If I chickened out, Fallon would never let it go, so I started drinking more, forgetting all about how I would regret this tomorrow morning. Scarlet called everyone out into the garden with the promise of fireworks.

Fallon took my hand, and we followed the crowd outside. A projector played live footage of Big Ben. The people in London gathered around like us, waiting to see the new year in.

10

9

8

This was it. I was pretty sure I was shaking. As Fallon let go of my hand, I focused on the screen.

7

6

5

I didn't dare look to see who was nearby. I didn't even want to even think about who I would be snogging any second from now.

4

3

2

1

Fallon was to my right, so I turned left.

"Happy New Year!" Nate cheered and dipped down to kiss my cheek.

I can't.

It's Nate.

"I dare you." Fallon's whisper echoed in my head.

He's so hot. Who wouldn't?

But, the rule…

Before I could talk myself out of it, I moved so his lips were pressed against mine.

I did it! We were kissing. All around us, people were cheering. Auld Lang Syne erupted around us and fireworks exploded above.

As I relaxed into the kiss, I realised he was kissing me back. His rich scent was intoxicating, making my mind go soft and mushy. I wanted this warm, tingling sensation to last forever.

"No," I moaned as his lips left mine. I blushed as I realised I'd said that out loud. Cool air filled the space between us, and my heart thundered in my chest.

I hoped he hadn't heard that. *Please, let it be noisy enough that he didn't.*

I dashed into the house to get away from him. My fingertips brushed across my lips, trying to hold on to the sensation of his touch. I wanted more. I needed him. In that heated moment, his kiss had made me forget Jace. I wanted to feel that good over and over. I couldn't bear that he'd stopped, but he wasn't Jace. He was Fallon's brother.

My heart was racing and sweat prickled my body. Was that the alcohol or his kiss?

"Kiely!" Fallon catches up with me. "Nate?"

"It was just a kiss…You dared me."

Fallon groaned. "I meant anyone but my brother?"

"Sorry. Who did you kiss?"

She rolled her eyes. "Jimmy. Funny how he made sure he was there. Totally *not* a coincidence."

"Was he any good?"

"Eurgh, let's not exchange details. Yuck."

My head was swimming. I was still hurting over Jace, but the warm sensation that Nate had triggered in me was addictive. The idea of falling for someone again scared me. I wasn't ready to move on, but in his presence, I could forget.

Fallon was excited by her new project. "I think we need to rebuild your confidence, then get you a real man. I'll draw up a plan. When Ari's back, we can meet up for yoga on the beach, and strategize."

Fallon continued telling me all her ideas to help me, but I wasn't with her. I was thinking about her off-limits brother, and how I wanted to kiss him again.

I woke up with a splitting headache and the sound of my family bustling around downstairs. Dragging myself out of bed, I headed for the bathroom cabinet and foraged for paracetamol, but discovering the empty packet made me feel worse. I groaned as I tossed it in the bin.

I continued my search, but the best I could find was some painkillers, once prescribed for my dad. He'd been reluctant to take them, claiming they were dangerous. But, when the pain got too much, he gave in and took some.

Unlike Dad, I didn't feel cautious. I was desperate. It wasn't the headache that bothered me, but the dull ache left by Jace. It made me feel heavy like my life was sludge and I was dragging myself through it. The hangover was simply adding to it.

I swallowed two pills and washed them down with water straight from the faucet. Dropping the packet into my dressing gown pocket, I made my way downstairs.

Mum was busy working on the roast, and the smell filled the air and turned my stomach. Sweat prickled my brow, and the bile rose up my throat. I raced as fast as I could to the downstairs toilet, falling to my knees before it. My muscles contracted as I emptied myself. My throat burned and tears filled my eyes.

Mum quickly joined me, pulling my hair back and rubbing my back. "Oh, Kiely honey."

I retched again. Mum waited with me until we were sure I had stopped. There were too many smells making me gag.

"Let's get you back to bed." Mum helped me up and rubbed my back as she returned me to my room.

I laid on my bed, feeling pretty sorry for myself. "Sorry, Mum."

"It's okay. It's not your fault. Not the best start to the year, but it can only get better." She placed a hand on my head. "You feel clammy. Did you know you were unwell?"

I shook my head. I couldn't tell her I'd snuck out and drank too much alcohol.

"I'll get you a bucket and a glass of water." Mum quickly went to get what she promised and returned.

"You rest up and if you feel better, come and join us. I'll check in on you throughout the day." She kissed my forehead. "Usually, these bugs pass quickly."

She left me to continue working on the family meal. I turned to get comfortable, but nothing felt right. I sat up and glimpsed myself in the mirror. My makeup was smudged under my eyes and my hair stuck to my sweaty face.

Maybe a shower will help freshen me up.

As I crossed the hall, I glanced across to Murray's bedroom and saw the most bizarre thing. He was sitting on the edge of his bed, staring down at his hands. They appeared to be lit up with a white glow, but I couldn't tell where the light was coming from. It shone up into his face, and his eyes looked odd. When he saw me, the colour drained from his face, but it was quickly replaced with anger as he kicked his bedroom door shut.

I blinked. Dad was right, those pills were strong. Even after bringing them up, they were still powerful enough to make me hallucinate. Or, maybe it was the alcohol still in my system. I gagged and swore at myself for my stupid choices.

CHAPTER 3

"Y**OU KISSED NATE?**" Arizona's dark brows folded in and her bottom lip jutted out. She'd slicked her afro down to pull into a hairband, and she wore a sweatband to stop the curls from escaping.

I blushed and stretched out into the downward dog pose. "It was a dare."

Arizona twisted her head to face Fallon. "But you said—"

"Nothing has changed. He's still my brother," Fallon interrupted and turned to look at me. "Don't ever kiss him again."

Fallon changed position, lowering her body and wrapping her leg around. We copied her into pigeon

pose. "Kiely thought Jace dumped her for being a crap kisser."

"Is that what he said?" Arizona gasped.

I was burning up, and it wasn't from the workout. I mumbled, "No." I was not enjoying this well-being exercise. It left me dreading what would be next in Fallon's plan for me, realising I didn't want to be her project.

"Doubt it. Nate gave her top marks." Her eyebrows bounced with mischief. Then she gave me a serious glare. "I reminded him of the rule, so there will be no more hanky-panky."

I blushed.

"Next step is to get you back out there. Goodbye, silly boys. Hello, real men."

"Oh no, Fallon, I'm fine," the words rushed out. "I don't want a boyfriend. Not right now, anyway." Not unless it was Jace.

"I'm not talking about a boyfriend. Just a bit of fun. Flirting, snogging, and definitely no commitment." Fallon got up into the tree pose, standing on one leg, and her hands pressed together like in a prayer.

Arizona was sulking. She'd only missed the party because she'd been away visiting her family. Ari gets major FOMO, and knowing I wouldn't be going was the only thing that had comforted her. Now, it looked like I'd betrayed her and gone behind her back and snogged Nate, who I still suspected she had a crush on. I felt awful.

Fallon didn't acknowledge Arizona's scowl. "I'm

thinking we should go clubbing this weekend. I've already sorted it."

I sighed, knowing that once Fallon had an idea, there was no way to change her mind. "Okay, I'll try."

"Find a way. We're doing this for you," Fallon said, and it almost sounded like a threat.

I dreaded going back to school after the holidays. I'd woken early to curl my hair the way Jace liked it. I'd taken extra time to get my makeup flawless. Fallon wanted me to move on, but my heart wasn't ready to give up. He had dumped me out of the blue, and if I could figure out why, I could get him back. I feared he'd blocked me as he hadn't read my messages.

We were waiting for morning registration. Arizona and Fallon were busy chatting about what to wear for our night out. My elbows rested on the desk, and I sunk my head into my palms, propping my face up.

I didn't want to look, but my eyes sought him out. All I could see was the back of his head. It felt deliberate, like he was punishing me, but I couldn't fathom why. I hoped his coldness would pass soon so we could work things out.

Maybe he wasn't speaking to me because he thought I didn't want to speak to him. I tried to think of something to say to break the ice.

Hey Jace. Nice to see you.

It sounded sarcastic considering our last meeting was him dumping me.

I'm sorry for whatever I did wrong.

Did it even count as an apology if I didn't know what I was apologising for?

Are you free for lunch?

It was too out of the blue, and I could already envision the excuses he'd make.

Do anything interesting over the break?

My mind instantly thought about my kiss with Nate. I hoped Jace hadn't heard about it or kissed anyone since our breakup. My cheeks flushed.

Everything that came to mind made me cringe, sounded desperate, or led to a conversation I didn't want to have.

A teacher entered the room. It wasn't our usual homeroom teacher. She was plump, with ugly square-toed shoes and glasses on a string hanging around her neck. She set up her things on her desk and, as she went to sit down, her elbow caught a stack of documents. It was like a domino effect, the way they toppled over, crashing into her mug, which fell to the floor, spilling its contents. She scooped the papers up into a messy heap and returned the empty mug to the desk. She pulled tissues from her handbag and got down on her knees to mop up the brown puddle of what appeared to be a caffeinated drink.

"Talk about making an entrance!" Fallon said, and laughed.

The woman's head kept bobbing up like a rabbit from a burrow, wary of a predator close by. My heart stopped when I recognised her. It was our form tutor from first grade. She'd left to work at another school, but I'd heard rumours the students there had made her life hell. It was almost uncomfortable to see her jittery nature. If she didn't pull it together fast, her teaching profession would be over.

"It's Mrs Fancy. Give her a break. She was good to us," I whispered to Fallon.

Fallon's jaw dropped in shock as she stared at the woman, who appeared to be searching the room for something. I wondered if she remembered us. She must have met loads of students since.

"What happened to her?" Fallon said in a low tone.

I rolled my eyes and elbowed her to be quiet, which made her giggle.

Mrs Fancy approached a girl sitting near the front of the room that we hadn't noticed. She mumbled something to her. The girl's head was bowed as she worked on something, perhaps a drawing. Her dark hair was like a curtain, concealing her face from us.

"Yes, I'm the new girl."

Mrs Fancy lifted the steel-framed glasses from her chest and pushed them up the bridge of her nose. Big, magnified eyes met those of the new girl. As she raised her head, her hair fell back, revealing a pale, pretty face, almost gothic looking.

"Ah, Briar. Welcome to Stowe High."

Mrs Fancy moved to the front of the room and puffed out her chest as she addressed us all. "Seats, everyone!"

Arizona's twin brother, Phoenix, fell into the

seat next to Briar. Jace and the other lads took the surrounding seats. Everyone was in their usual place, except the lad who'd lost his seat to Briar. His eyes darted around searching for somewhere new to sit.

Briar acknowledged Phoenix next to her. Like Arizona, he was gorgeous, with his dark skin and strong jawline. I saw him acknowledge her and wondered if this could be the start of him moving on from his forever crush on Fallon.

Fallon had never shown even a speck of interest in Phoenix, but she enjoyed the attention, knowing he'd do anything for her.

Briar took in the rest of the room. Her eyes met with Fallon's, and I saw the frosty exchange.

"What's *she* doing here?" Fallon snarled.

"The new girl? Do you know her?" Arizona asked.

"Unfortunately."

"I'm not sure you'll remember me, but I'm Mrs Fancy. I remember some of you though. I'll be covering for the rest of the term. I hope you all had a lovely Christmas break and are ready to get back to business. Please, give a warm welcome to the newest member of the form, Briar." She extended her arm out toward the new girl and smiled at her. "I see you're making friends already. Phoenix, take good care of Briar. Make sure she doesn't get lost."

"I'll make sure Phoenix takes good care of her," Fallon said under her breath, with a smirk.

"Okay, let's get this register done," Mrs Fancy announced. The room began rolling off their names in alphabetical order.

"How do you know her?" Ari asked.

"She's that bitch who cut off my curls," Fallon whispered through barred teeth.

Years ago, Fallon came to school with her ringlets gone and her hair cut short. She claimed her nan's neighbour's daughter had done it when she visited. I'd always thought Fallon made it up because she'd wanted to cut her hair for ages, but her mum said no.

"That's her?" Arizona gasped.

"I need a plan to get her back. I might need a favour from her buddy."

I felt sorry for Briar but was relieved by the distraction it presented from Fallon's other project *get-Kiely-a-real-man*. Now I could move on with my own plan to get Jace back. I wasn't sure how I'd do it, as he was making it obvious he was ignoring me by refusing to look my way.

The bell rang overhead. We gathered our belongings and made our way to class to head to maths. We were all in different classes.

Phoenix was quick to leave the room, abandoning his chaperoning duties. Briar stood at the door with her timetable in front of her, seeking some form of direction. Fallon shoved her as she went past, causing Arizona to laugh. I positioned myself in Arizona's way to prevent her from copying Fallon. I gave Briar a sympathetic look as I went by and hoped she'd make friends quickly and keep out of Fallon's way.

I trailed behind, hoping Jace would catch me up.

Then I could casually say hi and he'd have to speak to me.

But, he never came. He must have taken a detour to avoid me. My shoulders slumped.

I spotted Briar walking in the wrong direction.

"Briar!" I called out, but she didn't hear me.

I hurried after her. Maybe this detour would lead me to Jace. Or, perhaps, I should accept that we were over.

As I reached the stairwell, I realised I didn't know which way Briar had gone. To the left was reception, and to the right were the doors leading outside.

I was about to go when an arm slipped around my waist and pulled me under the stairwell. "Hey, gorgeous."

"Nate!"

"Now we can talk without getting in everyone's way."

"What's there to talk about?" I shook my head.

"My sister."

His fellow sixth formers made their way out of the doors, disappearing behind him. We may not have been in their way, but I still felt too visible. Everyone turned to see what we were up to.

"What about Fallon?"

"She'd be mad if she caught you sneaking off with me."

"I'm not sneaking off with you." I folded my arms across my chest.

"That's not how she'd see it." The corner of his

mouth lifted in a smirk.

He was right. Fallon always jumped to conclusions first and wouldn't bother asking questions after. Then I remembered I was only here because he'd brought me here.

"Are you done? Sounds like I ought to get going before Fallon finds out about this."

"She's not going to know because we're not going to tell her."

The last bell for lessons rang, and the corridors emptied fast. We were alone, and I was going to be late for class.

"There's nothing to tell her." I looked at Nate as if he'd lost it.

"That's right." He moved closer, causing my heart to race. I could feel his breath against my skin as he lowered his voice. "Meet me here at first break. There's more *'nothing'* I want you not to tell her."

I looked confused as he stepped back, which only appeared to amuse him. The cool air enveloped me as the door opened and he made his exit. He glanced back over his shoulder to give me a wink, and I pressed my back against the wall for support. I tried to make sense of what had happened as I rushed to class, not even pausing to catch my breath.

The whole maths lesson, I kept my head down. I knew the teacher wasn't impressed by my tardy entrance, and to make matters worse, I couldn't concentrate, no matter how hard I tried.

Nate had definitely been hitting on me, but I didn't want to get hurt again. I still hung on with the hope that I could get Jace back. My heart kept remembering our kiss, and if it wasn't for the rule, Nate would be an option. It didn't feel like a smart move to reveal that to him when I needed him to back off. My brain was scrambled by the breakup. I didn't need to add anything else to the mix.

No good could come from dating Nate Rein, and that was exactly what I'd tell him.

My maths paper was filled with doodles of flowers and swirls instead of calculations. I dreaded the bell ringing as I wasn't a fan of confrontation or upsetting people. This wasn't a conversation I wanted to have. Then again, this could be another little game. Fallon may have told him to test my loyalty to her.

When the bell rang, I took my time packing up my things. I was the last to leave the classroom. I tracked across the school to the meeting point, but I couldn't tell if Nate was there until I passed the stairwell and reached the red brick alcove underneath.

"Hey, gorgeous," he said.

I hoped the greeting would die a death before Fallon heard it.

"Hi." I slid next to him.

"Are you okay?"

I fidgeted with the strap of my bag so I didn't have to see those green eyes that had a crazy effect on girls. Other girls. Not me. I didn't dare risk it. "Yeah, I'm fine."

"I was hoping to catch up with you. Fallon said you're hung up on Jace, and I thought you might struggle with the first day back."

I felt my face crumple. It had been hard seeing Jace again, especially as he was getting on with everyday life as if I'd never existed, treating me like I was an invisible void. Three months of flirting and dating had led to that one kiss under the mistletoe, and then it was over. All of it for nothing. I dreaded people thinking it was because I'm a crap kisser. The gossip would spread like wildfire, and then I'd become an Undateable.

His breath tickled my ear as he leaned close. "You can talk to me, Kiely. Think of me as your mentor, your confidant, and... your lover."

I gasped and backed away. "I can't, Nate! It's not just Fallon, it's Jace, too."

Nate was laughing at my reaction, and I realised he was winding me up. I punched his arm and folded my arms across my chest. My stern look sobered him up.

"We can keep it a secret." He brushed my hair away from my face. His fingers made my skin tingle as I remembered our kiss.

My eyes widened. Maybe he wasn't joking. "But, it's wrong."

"What is?"

"This..." I blushed and waved my arms around me

to show our close proximity.

He smiled. "What is this?"

I could tell he wasn't getting it on purpose. I was burning up, trying to explain what hadn't actually happened yet. Why couldn't he ask me out like a normal guy? Then, I could at least turn him down without all the awkwardness.

"You," I mumbled and moved his hand from my cheek. "This. Touching me."

He pulled his hand away. "Okay, I'll stop. I shouldn't tease you, but I wanted to show that I'm here for you. I thought you might need someone to talk to. Someone that understands what you're going through. Like a therapist."

A therapist! I laughed.

Nate blushed. He ran his hand through his blond curls and stepped back. "I do know how you're feeling. Sort of. I went through it when Em and I broke up. I thought you might appreciate a fun distraction or someone to talk to who gets it."

I softened. I'd forgotten about Emma. He was cut up when he found out she'd cheated on him. He'd refused to come out of his room for days.

"Please, let me give you my number. You can call or text if you need me. Or not, if you don't."

He pulled out his mobile phone and clicked on the screen to bring up his number. He turned the screen so I could see.

I shook my head. "I'm fine."

"I'd feel better if you took it," he insisted.

"I already have it. Remember when Fallon broke her phone and basically commandeered everyone else's?"

Nate chuckled. "Yeah. I remember that."

He scrolled through the contacts on his phone. "I don't think I've got yours saved."

"Nate, you know I can't go out with you…"

He caught me with those stunning green eyes I'd been avoiding, causing my heartbeat to jump. His attention returned to his phone with a smirk on his face. "Just as well. I'm not asking you out. Now, call my mobile so I can save your number."

I shook my head. "No. You'll just have to wait and see if I *ever* call you."

"Fine, but you will call me, and when you do, I'll be there for you."

He was so sure that it had a sexy appeal to it. If only I could have an ounce of that to get me through the day. Maybe Nate *did* know about these things and could teach me to heal. The pain of my loss came to the surface, and I felt that desperate urge for someone to take it away.

Nothing felt safe anymore. Nate was forbidden, and I couldn't help but feel this was part of a game. A game I would lose and get hurt in.

Fallon's plan for the weekend came to mind. She could be right. Going out and getting wasted sounded like a good idea. I wanted to forget everything and be free. I didn't want to be Nate or any guy's amusement again, not unless they were amusing me too.

"Thanks, but I don't think I need your services. See

ya. Don't want to be late for class again."

I pushed past him, back toward the main corridor.

"You will need me!" Nate called from behind me.

Turning my back on him gave me the sensation I was in control.

His comment amused me.

Sounds more like it's you who needs me, Nate.

CHAPTER 4

"So, mine at 8:00 pm." Fallon gave us a stern look until we both nodded. We were sitting on the back of a bench, our feet on the seat, discussing our plans for the weekend. This was our usual lunchtime hangout spot, as it provided excellent views of the guys playing football.

I wasn't enjoying it as much as usual because my ex-boyfriend was having too much fun with his mates. I'd suggested we try somewhere different, but Fallon felt it best he saw I wasn't bothered. This made me more enthusiastic about clubbing than I might have been, but at least it stopped me from thinking about Jace.

"Can I stay over? There's no way Mum'll let me stay out that late," Arizona begged Fallon.

"Sure. What about you, Kiely?"

"I snuck out on New Year's Eve. I'm sure I can do it again," I said, casting them both a smirk. Since being dumped, I'd found a thrill in rule-breaking. The darkness and rebellion were new; even though I fought it, I couldn't deny the allure. I could get into trouble, but it felt good to be bad.

Bright red hair and loose curls bobbed along the sidelines. Mariah had never come to watch Jace play before, but now they ran up to each other. He cheered his best friend's nickname, "Freckles!"

I wanted to puke. The other lads all taunted and jeered, picking up on the change in their relationship. It was so obvious, like a hard slap across the face. It took all my strength not to march over there and rip her hair out. My blood chilled. I couldn't keep up my fake smile any longer.

"Oh, my god! He's not seriously seeing her?" Fallon spat.

Jace swore they were just friends. When he told me she didn't own many dresses and had nothing to wear to the Mistletoe disco, I lent her mine. I let Jace pick it out, and he returned it when he came to dump me. It was soaked and reeked of chlorine like she'd worn it for a swim in the pool. Now, I regretted my generosity. Look where it got me.

They used to be neighbours, but after Jace moved, he was upset that they didn't get to see each other as often. I felt bad for him and tried not to be annoyed when he cancelled dates for her... only for her to steal my boyfriend.

The darkness reared inside me, begging for an outlet for my fury.

My jaw tensed, my fists clenched. I held my breath to stop myself from crying in front of everyone. I didn't dare move. All my strength was being used on holding myself together as I watched Jace place a kiss on Mariah's forehead. My breathing came in short bursts.

"How dare she! She's gonna get what's coming to her. Don't you worry!" Fallon pushed herself up off the bench and started making her way over to Mariah.

My nails dug into my palms as I watched Fallon confront Mariah. I couldn't make out what they were saying, but I prayed Mariah would say something stupid. I wished with every bone in my body that Mariah would piss Fallon off.

Go on, Mariah, give Fallon a reason to pound your face in.

I relished the thought of her missing teeth. A crooked nose. A swollen eye.

"Are you okay?" Arizona whispered.

Her kindness was like fire licking across my eyeball, forcing me to acknowledge the pain of my losing battle. I jumped up from the bench and grabbed my bag, racing into the school.

Arizona chased after me, calling my name. It made me run faster. I didn't want to talk. I needed to forget. All I wanted was to be lost in a kiss that took the pain away. For a moment, my heart filled with the idea of Nate and what he could do for me.

When I reached the girls' toilets, my hand rested on the door, and I hesitated.

This would be the first place Arizona would check, and I didn't want to be found. Instead, I pelted out the side doors and off the school grounds. Then, I ran.

Once I was free from the building, I stopped and drew in a long breath.

My hands shook with fear at the thought that a teacher could catch me. I wasn't the sort of student that bunked off. I'd never left school midday without a good reason, like a dentist appointment. Shame followed the adrenaline rush.

I'd never wished someone pain, and as much as I hated Mariah, I was ashamed of my cursed thoughts. The anger was like a poison turning my soul sour. The infection spoiled all that was once good. It left me feeling sick. Sick of everyone, and especially myself.

I was a fool. Deep down, I knew they liked each other. That was why I kept asking Jace for reassurance. I saw they were more than friends, but convinced myself that it was paranoia or jealousy. I wanted to believe Jace when he told me I'd nothing to worry about. If I dug deep enough, that was the real reason I was mad. How stupid I was. Too trusting. If I could kick myself, I would.

Now, I didn't know what to do with myself. *What do truanting kids do all day?* Maybe they had good reasons for not going to school, maybe they were hurting too, and I wasn't so alone, after all.

I decided to text Murray, as I knew he was always

there for me, but when I looked at the screen, I saw I had a text from Nate.

Nate: Found your number. Promise not to text anymore, unless you want me to. x

I recalled Nate's parting words, *"You will need me!"*

My lip quivered and my fingers ran across the screen, typing out a reply before I could even think about what I was doing.

Kiely: I need you.

I made my mind up. I wasn't going back to school, not today. My feet were moving, heading home. My phone beeped. I glanced at the screen.

Nate: Where are you?

Kiely: Walking home.

My feet had felt light, as if they'd grown wings and flown me out of the school. But now they felt heavy and wrong, like elastic bands tied around my ankles, pulling at me to return.

The further I got, the more they tugged, and the harder it was to press on. My pace slowed with the effort.

I wrestled with my inner conflict; not wanting to return to school and not wanting to skip school. I felt trapped in some limbo where I'd lost all sense of myself.

I didn't want anyone to see me, so I turned into the back alley where some businesses had workshops and garages. My heart thudded as I walked past the open doors. I saw men in overalls, hard at work. I expected one of them to look up and question what a young girl was doing out of school. No one did. As it turned out, they were too busy to notice or care.

My phone rang. It was Nate.

I took a deep breath and answered, "Hi."

"Where are you?" he panted down the phone as if he'd been running.

"Down Bridge Road alley."

"I'll meet you at the far end."

"Thanks." I ran a hand through my hair.

"See you in a minute."

"Okay."

The bumpy track became more uneven the further I went. At the end, it twisted to the right and narrowed so only pedestrians could access it. Sure enough, at the end, I saw Nate's concerned face. He pulled me into a hug. I hadn't realised I was cold until I felt his warm body engulfing me with his.

"It'll be okay, Kiely. I'll make sure of it. You can trust me." Nate rubbed my back and squeezed me tightly against him. As I relaxed into his arms, I could feel the tears peppering my eyes.

I couldn't cry! Not here.

My body went stiff. My internal shields shot up. His words felt eerie familiar to his sister's, and it put me at a slight unease, regarding us being together. But I wanted to trust him. I wanted to get back to my normal self.

He held me at arm's length, holding my upper arms. "Can you do that for me?"

I nodded, unsure what the question was, but I couldn't speak. The tears were waiting to run free, but I wouldn't let them. His closeness and comfort made me feel like I could share my pain with him.

"Good." Nate smiled and loosened his grip on me. He then ran his hands up and down my arms. "You're cold?"

I was cold, but that wasn't all I felt. So many emotions bubbled beneath the surface. The frustration and loss, the anger, and stupidity. It all rose inside me, choking me, and making it difficult to swallow. "A drink?"

Nate had taken off his jacket and attempted to wrap it around me.

I shook my head.

"Come on, you're cold. Plus, your uniform is a dead giveaway that you should be in school."

He was right. I didn't want to get caught. I slid my arms into his jacket. The fleece lining was still warm from his body heat.

"There's a cafe at the end of this road. I'll treat you."

We headed out of the alley.

He looked back over his shoulder and winked at me. "I'm going to help you. Just trust me, and do as I say."

There it was again, his request for my trust that

hadn't yet been earned. I'd always been so trusting before, but now there was fear. Fear that if I let anyone get as close as Jace, they'd hurt me again. My walls were up and even though I could listen and do as he said, I wasn't sure I could ever trust anyone again.

We made it to the cafe before the darkening clouds poured. We sat at a table in the back with views over the spa gardens. The rain thundered on the roof of the extension, reminding us how fortunate we were to be inside.

Nate treated me to a hot chocolate. Ordinarily, I would love it. But today, it had a bitter taste, making me incapable of enjoying anything right now. I'd taken the seat in the corner, so I'd be less likely to be spotted.

"I'm glad you called me, Kiely."

"I don't know what I was thinking."

"I'm thinking you want someone to talk to." Nate reached over to squeeze my hand. I didn't pull it away. The warmth was comforting.

I shook my head. "I really don't want to talk."

"How about I talk, then? Do you remember Emily?"

I breathed a sigh of relief as the pressure lifted. I met Nate's expectant gaze and gave a slight nod to show I remembered Emily.

About two years ago they'd dated, and she was always at the Rein house. They'd broken up just before their exams. There was talk that she'd cheated on him, but she stopped coming over and I never saw her again.

"I don't think I'll ever get over her, and that's okay. It took me a long time to accept that. I remember how hard it was, and that's why I want to help you."

I took a sip of my bitter chocolate and glared out at the grey sky, blending in with the horizon of the sea. My heart was heavy. It was refreshing to have someone accept that I didn't have to get over Jace. Everyone kept telling me to do better, to move on. His words alleviated some of the pressure the expectation had placed on me.

"Have people said it's his loss, and you can do better?"

I rolled my eyes, and Nate laughed.

"I heard it all, too. People just don't get it, but I do. You can call me, or text, any day, any time."

I sighed and said, "I just…"

I paused, unsure of how to explain the need for Jace to want me, and the lack of control over the situation. I felt like a failure for not being able to hold on to him tightly enough. How foolish I was to not see that there was more between him and Mariah. My eyes peppered, and I pressed them shut.

"And, you don't have to talk about it if you don't want to."

"Can we talk about something else? Anything but exes."

"Deal." He nodded and maintained eye contact whilst taking a long sip of his own hot chocolate.

The school had rang mum to notify her I had been absent from my afternoon classes. As soon as I got in, she was ready with the questions. There was no point lying. I told her what happened and how I needed to get away. Mum hugged me. She'd told the school I was struggling with my first breakup. They suggested that if there was a next time, I should go to the reflection room to relax, rather than skip school. I promised I would try that next time.

When Murray got home, he suggested we take Aero out for a walk. We hadn't gotten far before he decided to ask me about what happened.

"Mum said you bunked off school today."

I shrugged. "Guess so."

"That's not like you, Kiely."

"I know." I couldn't look at Murray, so I kept my eyes on Aero.

We walked across the green toward the steps. We headed down to the beach and let Aero off the lead. He started his usual antics, running in and out of the sea.

"How are you feeling?" I asked. The focus had all been on me and my heartbreak, but I wasn't the only one who'd been hurt.

"Me?" Murray's eyebrows shot up.

"Well, you and Mariah. And now she's with Jace." I swallowed down the sickening feeling that always came when I thought of them together.

"We weren't really a thing. I liked her, but she wasn't into me."

"Because of Jace?"

"I guess so." He picked up a pebble to toss at the sea.

"Are you upset?" I copied him, but the waves were too rough to try skimming. It felt good to throw as hard as I could and hear the splosh when it met the water.

"Nah. Plenty more fish in the sea." He tried to sound dismissive, but it wasn't convincing. He still liked her.

What was so special about her?

"Did you know about her and Jace?"

Murray turned to me and frowned. "No, of course not. I suspected she liked him. I even asked her on the bus but she said they were more like brother and sister."

I huffed. I'd been told the same by Jace. Liars. Both of them were liars.

"They won't last," Murray said.

"What makes you say that?" I asked, and my heart felt a whisper of hope.

"They're not right for each other." He shrugged.

Aero ran up to us, shaking himself, and covered us in a light spray of salty seawater. We both laughed and screamed for him to stop.

"Cut it out," Murray yelled as he wrestled Aero to put his lead on. "No more sea for you."

Murray straightened up, but where his hand gripped the lead, his skin shimmered in beautiful shades of blue, green, and silver. It looked like fish scales made of jewels, but had to be a trick of the light.

"Look at that?" I pointed at Murray's hand.

Murray saw what I was pointing at. His face flushed, and he rubbed the back of his hand against his coat. "It's nothing."

He was acting strange. "What is it?"

Putting his gloves on, he said, "Nothing. Stop acting weird."

He walked back up the steps. Moving so fast that I had to jog to keep up with his strides.

"Show me your hands, then."

"Cut it out, Kiely!"

"No. You're acting weird."

We were almost home when he stopped. He closed his eyes and took a deep breath as if my badgering was getting on his last nerve. Then, he removed his glove and showed me his hand. There was nothing there. Nothing unusual.

"Satisfied now?"

"Sorry." I swallowed a lump in my throat. This was the second time I'd seen something strange involving his hands. I needed to get a grip on myself. I was losing my mind.

CHAPTER 5

WE WERE HANGING OUT in Fallon's bedroom. Outfits were littered across her bed, with choices for our upcoming night out. Some from her own wardrobe and others borrowed from her sister's.

"I don't think it'll fit." Arizona's brow wrinkled as she held up a sparkly black dress. She sucked in her lip and turned to Fallon for some reassurance.

"It fits me," Fallon gave a warm smile.

Arizona looked at the dress and pulled a face, appearing unconvinced.

"Try it on." Fallon encouraged her.

"Okay." Arizona began taking off her clothes to put on the dress.

It fit her like a glove and hugged her curves in all the right places. She had no idea how lucky she was and seemed to want a figure like mine. Which makes no sense as I'm hiding my small boobs in a padded bra to try and create some shape.

Arizona turned to the mirror and screwed up her face. "It clings to my fat."

"You're not fat, you're curvy," I said, shocked that she didn't see herself as I did.

"Easy for you to say, skinny minx."

"She's right, though." Fallon backed me up before closing in on Arizona. "You are beautiful, healthy, womanly, and any man - or woman - would be lucky to have you."

Arizona rolled her eyes at the 'or woman' part. Instead of arguing, she turned her attention to the mirror. "Perhaps I could make a pretty glitter eyeshadow to make my eyes pop."

"Have you started your online store yet?" Fallon asked.

Arizona sighed. "I'm not ready yet. There's so much to learn and with our exams… It's a lot. Plus, I have to be eighteen to set it up because of taxes, so I'll have to enlist my mum."

Fallon hugged Arizona from behind. "When you do, I'm going to be your number one customer."

"You'll be first to know when I do."

"Just nipping to the loo." I excused myself and headed down the hall. I made sure I was quick. When I opened the door to return, Nate was standing there waiting. "Sorry." I moved out of his way to let him pass.

But he didn't go into the bathroom. He leaned against the wall and gave a slight smile as if I'd done something amusing. "I was waiting for you."

My skin prickled, and my heart raced. I licked my lips and looked down the hall toward Fallon's bedroom. Before that kiss, this wouldn't have meant anything, but now it felt like the air was thicker between us.

"Not now," I whispered. My eyes widened as I pleaded with him.

"Meet me tonight?"

"Where?"

"The summerhouse."

"What about Fallon?"

"I'm not inviting her. Just us."

I rolled my eyes. "That's not what I meant."

"Go home. Come back at midnight. Don't tell her anything." Nate pushed off the wall and headed downstairs, while I returned to his sister's room to sit amongst the dresses. Neither of them noticed my return. If they had, they may have detected the telltale blush in my cheeks.

Dad picked me up from Fallon's at 10:00 pm, so I didn't have to walk home. He thought I was being good, ringing him and getting home on time. He wouldn't be as pleased with me if he knew that instead of revision for our upcoming exams, we'd been planning to sneak out and go night clubbing.

On top of that, I was considering Nate's proposal.

"How are you doing?" Dad asked, not taking his eyes off the road.

"Fine." I shrugged.

"Do you want to talk about that boy - um, Jace?"

"No, Dad. I'm fine."

"You can talk to me though, you know."

"I know," I said with a sigh, unable to help myself.

"I'm just worried about you."

"You don't need to be."

"You could help your mum out at the café sometime. It's good to keep busy."

Mum was always asking for help at the café. Although she paid us, it cut into our weekends, so neither Murray nor I wanted to help unless we were saving up for something.

"I've got to revise for my exams, otherwise I would."

"Of course." Dad pulled into the driveway. "It's good to see you taking them seriously, but if you need me, I'm here for you."

"I know. Thanks, Dad."

"No more bunking off school," he added more sternly.

"I won't."

"Good, because I don't think I can deal with you *and* your brother going wild."

"Murray?" I laughed. He was the perfect child, obsessed with swimming, and it paid off. He'd been bringing home medals and making our parents proud since he was eleven, giving them bragging rights. Not like me. I did nothing spectacular.

"The school doesn't want him representing anymore since he got that damn tattoo."

"A tattoo? Of what?"

"Not really of anything. He called it a burn tattoo. It's barbaric, like something out of the dark ages."

"Why'd he do that?"

"Because he's an idiot." Dad pulled into the drive and looked at me. "No body modifications for you. No piercings. No tattoos of any type. None of that stretching ear lobes or making lumps under your skin stuff."

"Okay Dad." That wasn't my scene so he didn't have anything to worry about.

We got out of the car, and he unlocked the front door. Inside, we hung up our coats. I stood on my tiptoes on the bottom step and placed a kiss on my dad's cheek. "Thanks for picking me up."

"No worries. You're my little girl and I'll always come get you." His eyes wrinkled at the corners.

"I'm going to head up and get an early night."

Upstairs, I went through my usual evening routine, visiting the bathroom to brush my teeth, and running the water as if I was washing the makeup off my face.

Meet Nate or stay home?

I got clean pyjamas out of my drawer but didn't put them on. I paced around my room, contemplating what to do. Going felt like crossing a line, but curiosity was winning.

I stuffed pillows under my covers to make it look like I was still home sleeping and switched off the light.

It was convincing enough should anyone check on me, which they wouldn't. They never checked on me. I was being overly cautious.

I climbed out my window and sat with my legs dangling over the edge. Sitting here made it feel like a big drop but it wasn't far. I rolled onto my belly and dropped onto the slate-tiled kitchen roof that sloped off beneath my window. On tiptoes, I reached up to push my window closed so it would appear shut.

Now I was out, there was no turning back.

Walking along the sloped tiles was a little tricky, and I ended up crouching and sliding along on my bum. The tiles were filthy, and I hoped I wasn't picking up bird poop on my clothing. As I reached the lower end, I listened carefully to the sounds of the kitchen. The light was on and I could hear the faint sound of my parents talking. I could just make out Mum's concern that I'd gone to bed so early and my dad reassuring her I just needed time to get over 'that boy', and at least I didn't have a dumb tattoo. The fact my parents cared was a conflicting comfort. It made me feel guilty that I was sneaking out. But at least I wasn't getting a tattoo.

The light from the window went out, and I identified the darkness as the signal it was safe to go.

There was no simple way down. I hung my legs over the edge and took a deep breath. Here goes.... *thud*... I landed in a crouched position in my back garden. I dusted off my arse.

Being out without permission felt more dangerous. As I hit the streets, I felt as if people were watching and knew. I expected someone to step out of the shadows, grab my wrist and march me home to my parents. I took a deep breath to calm my nerves, but the fear was relentless. A niggle told me I was being watched. Following my instincts, I glanced in the direction where I thought I sensed someone. I hadn't expected to see anything, but to my surprise, shining through the darkness, two bright yellow eyes stared back at me, causing my heart to jump.

But as quick as it was there, it was gone.

Had I imagined it?

Do cat's eyes glow yellow? I thought their eyes were green.

There was something unnerving about the eyes. Something that didn't feel natural. Predatory. As much as I tried to hush away my fears, my pumping adrenaline was making me sweat. My pace quickened, and I soon found myself running to get to Fallon's house faster.

I could see Fallon's house up ahead, but tonight I turned into the alleyway that ran behind the row of houses. The dirty track allowed them access to their back gates and was often in use on bin day. I moved quickly, checking over my shoulder, expecting the yellow eyes to be following me. Nobody was there. I was just being stupid. Once I reached Fallon's back gate, I reached my arm over to undo the bolt and let myself in.

"Hey, gorgeous!"

The sound of his voice scared the life out of me, but

as soon as I realised it was Nate, I gently punched his arm. After freaking myself out, his welcome had made me feel caught. My heart thudded in my chest.

"You alright?"

"You just made me jump."

"I can't believe you came." Nate leaned back to let me pass. His lip rose on one side in appreciation as his eyes ran up and down my body.

"Me neither." My fingers combed through my hair, needing to keep my hands busy. The adrenaline was still pumping through my body and the way Nate was looking at me wasn't helping.

"Are you cold?"

In my haste, I hadn't thought to grab a coat, but that wasn't why I was shivering. "No. Just nervous."

He looked baffled. "Nervous about me?"

"No. Scared of getting caught," I confessed.

"We won't." He leaned close and placed a gentle kiss on my lips.

Nate led me into the summerhouse. Inside was set up like a small lounge with a leather sofa and a flat-screen TV against the opposite wall. There was a dresser against the far wall and a rug in the middle. In the corner was a black leather futon. Nate sat on the sofa, making himself comfy. He patted the seat next to him.

The sofa was literally one step away, but it felt like a big distance to cross. Even with Jace, we'd never got time alone. We'd spent months agonising over a first kiss, but Murray or Mariah were always there. Being alone with a boy felt like a big deal.

Maybe I wasn't the first girl he'd invited to the summerhouse. His green eyes met mine, and he had that playful smirk on his face. I felt butterflies erupt in my stomach as I wondered what could happen between the two of us, hidden away from the world. I couldn't stand by the door all day, so I joined him.

"Now what?" I wondered.

"We keep each other's secrets. You can tell me anything and, as your therapist, I won't say a word." Nate looked intently into my eyes.

"What secrets do you have?"

"You." His cheeks flushed.

I raised an eyebrow and looked at him with a puzzled expression. "Me?"

His head dipped, causing his blonde curls to drop forward, and he combed them back with his fingers. "I've liked you for ages."

"What?" I gasped. My mind raced as I tried to recall any hints he'd ever given that he was into me. I'd followed Fallon's rules and kept out of his way. We'd both stayed in the background, and it wasn't until the New Year's kiss that I'd ever felt seen by him.

"Surely you knew? That's why you picked me at New Year's Eve?" He raised one eyebrow, and looked slightly bashful.

Damn Fallon, and her stupid dares.

"No. It meant nothing." My face flushed hot.

"Nothing?" He rubbed the back of his neck.

"Not like that. I mean because you're off limits."

"Ah, the rule; Fallon doesn't go out with any of my mates, and vice versa. It was my idea to protect her. That's back fired for me." Nate dipped his head at the last part.

I didn't believe what he was saying. It didn't make sense. How could Nate Rein be into me? But, I wanted it to be true. His words made me feel desirable and wanted, and it eased the pain Jace had caused me. But, at the same time being here felt wrong, like I was breaking some girl code by meeting him behind Fallon's back.

My broken heart had put my walls up and I couldn't help but question Nate's intentions. Was this part of his plan to help me get over my ex or was there more he wasn't telling me? He stared at me like he was waiting for me to say something, but I had no words. The long silence was awkward, so I was relieved when Nate creased up.

"Okay, this is awkward. So, you didn't know."

I shook my head.

His head dropped forward as he peered up at me. "I probably shouldn't admit that I overheard the dare."

"You did?" My mouth felt dry. My head spun at his revelation.

"Yes, I did. Let me take you out for Valentine's Day?"

"We can't," I whispered, thinking of Fallon. The New Year's Eve kiss was one thing, but right after, she'd scolded me for kissing her brother of all people. I was confident she'd not be okay with me dating him, and that sounded a lot like a date.

"Let me rebuild your confidence. If I achieve more, that's a bonus. But first, let's get you over that dickhead."

"How do you propose we do that?" My heart thudded in my chest. It felt like I was daring him to offer himself as my rebound guy, and daring myself to accept. To be honest, I wouldn't be opposed to the idea. Nate was hot, but I could feel my walls creeping up in defence. I didn't want to get hurt again.

"Let's start by talking."

"Talking?" I sunk back into the sofa. That wasn't quite where I'd hoped this was heading.

"Let's start with where you are at with Jace. How are you coping?"

Hearing Jace's name brought it all crashing to the surface, but it felt different now, like Nate had invited the pain into our hideaway. It invaded the place where I was safe from the outside world. No matter how much I clenched my jaw, I could feel the pain stabbing at my eyes. Nate wrapped an arm around me and pulled me into him.

"It's okay, Kiely. Let it out."

Slowly, his captivating scent changed from something I feared to be caught by into something that soothed me. The tears I'd held in for too long found their way out. I cried through crushed eyelashes whilst Nate held me, rubbing my back and telling me about his breakup with Emily. Distracting and soothing me until I calmed down.

"I'll get you a tissue." Nate left the summerhouse.

I stood by the window, watching him return to the house. I listened to the sounds of the garden. Not far away I could hear trickling, and guessed one neighbour must have a water feature. I could hear the wind and distant traffic. In the distance, I could hear music playing and wondered if someone was having a party.

Near the back gate stood an animal with the strange glowing eyes I'd seen earlier. My body froze. It was bigger than a cat, more like a dog. Its fur was pure white. It stared in my direction, watching me and unafraid.

"What do you want?" I asked.

The creature leaped over the fence, leaving the garden as it always had. It was so brief I wondered if I'd imagined it. I waited to see if it would return, but it didn't. It reminded me of a wolf, but bigger than I thought they were.

What would a wolf be doing here?

The longer I stared into the darkness, the more I doubted I'd even seen it.

Nate returned with cans of fizzy orange pop and a toilet roll.

"We don't have any fancy tissues." He passed the roll to me. "But the packet says it's double quilted."

"Sounds luxurious." I accepted the roll and turned so Nate couldn't see me. It was gross enough that he could hear me blowing my nose without seeing it too.

When I turned back, he was holding the can out to me. "Are you feeling better? Ready to talk?"

"Can't you go first? Jace still feels too fresh." I swallowed a lump in my throat.

"Fair enough." Nate nodded and sat down next to me. "You know Emily broke my heart, but I hadn't really told anyone what happened. I found the texts on her phone. She said it was just flirting. Like that made it okay. Then I caught her with him. In her bed. I didn't say anything. I just left and felt stupid."

"She denied it, of course. She even got mad at me, accused me of being jealous and seeing what I thought rather than what was. I apologised like a muppet. Thought it was my fault. Then she dumped me and got with him. She still denies she ever cheated, but I know what I saw."

I remembered seeing them together, but I hadn't known the details of their breakup. I listened. He needed to get this off his chest. It made me think about the red flags I'd had regarding Jace and Mariah, and how he'd assured me that I had nothing to worry about.

Nate's voice dropped to almost a whisper. "Part of me still misses her. The Emily I thought she was. You know, before I knew who she was. A cheat."

Something tickled my cheek. His fingers ran up and down the side of my face, stroking me. It felt nice and soothing. "I see similarities in how Jace treated you."

I met his green eyes, feeling seen by him in a way nobody else did.

"It hurts. The betrayal. I get what you're going through 'cause I've been there too, but I promise it gets easier. I'm gonna be here for you."

The conversation felt heavy, and I needed a hug. Nate was there, offering to help me. I snuggled into him.

It was only a hug. Just a friendly hug.

Within his embrace, the darkness inside me hushed. My eyes shut and I felt peace for the first time since Christmas. I felt heavy and drained from holding everything inside.

As I relaxed, my breath deepened. Curling into Nate more, I enjoyed the peace his arms provided. I relaxed, and my body felt heavy as sleep claimed me.

CHAPTER 6

DAZED AND CONFUSED, someone shook me. It took me a moment to realise I wasn't at home in my bed. I had fallen asleep in Nate's arms and his hot breath warmed my neck as he said, "Oh, Kiely, don't make this difficult. I need to get you home before your parents report you missing."

"Mmm," I cooed sleepily. Heat rushed to my cheeks as I realised what I was doing. I let him go and sat upright. "Sorry."

He got up. "Keep teasing me like that, and I'll give you what you want."

"And what do you think that is?" My heart fluttered as I waited for his response.

Nate got up and pulled me up with him. He stood

close, his lips almost touching mine. "Enough about what you want. You're not ready - yet. Let's focus on getting you home."

I breathed the same air as him. I wanted to kiss him so badly and I could tell he felt the same. Maybe this was for the best. After all, I was still healing. I blushed and turned away.

Based on my recent experience with Jace, I didn't understand why Nate would even care whether I was ready? *Aren't guys like that just doing what they want because they can?* Look at Jace with Mariah. He didn't care that he was hurting me, flaunting their 'togetherness'.

Nate put his fleece jacket over my shoulders. "Here you go."

Probably all my crying put him off.

The cold outside helped wake me up. The sky was half-lit, a warm red as the night ended and the early January sun made a start. Nate locked the gate behind us. Once in the alley, he reached for my hand.

At first, I wasn't sure and froze. I saw the slight panic flash across his eyes.

"Is this too much?" he asked.

"No, just different." I shook my head.

He gave my hand a reassuring squeeze that helped me relax. We didn't speak, but we began walking. At first, the silence was nice. It gave me a chance to gather my thoughts about the evening we'd spent together. But the longer it went on, the harder it was to speak, and there was one question that thundered in my mind.

"Why don't you want to kiss me?"

As soon as the words left my lips, I regretted it. I was burning up, my hand sweating in his. I worried he could feel the dampness, which only made it worse.

The corner of his lip curled in a half-smile. "Why do you ask?"

"Maybe I want you to," I mumbled, lacking the confidence I'd intended.

"I see," he said and shot me a grin.

"I do." I threw my head back.

"Sounds like rebound?"

"It's not." I frowned.

"Maybe, I will."

My heart raced at the thought. "Are you worried about Fallon finding out? I won't tell her."

"More like Murray."

"My brother?"

"Don't you ever wonder why a hot girl like you doesn't get more interest?"

"I'm not hot." I bowed my head, causing my blonde hair to cascade around my face.

"Your brother hated Jace for dating you. I wouldn't be surprised if he didn't have something to do with your breakup."

"No, he's not like..." Although it made sense; his insistence on chaperoning all my dates, bringing Mariah - a girl that was so not his type! Now, he wasn't interested in Mariah, and she was with Jace.

No! He wouldn't have fake-dated to help her get Jace and break my heart. Would he? My brother?

"He's made it clear that no one is to touch his sister. He'd deck me just for saying you're hot."

"No way. That's not fair. He goes through girls faster than hot meals!"

"I don't blame him. I'd be the same with Fallon, except with her I wouldn't have any knuckles left."

"She's not that bad." Fallon wasn't like that. It wasn't like she tried to attract guys, they just fell over themselves for her. She never returned their attention. She wasn't into school boys and had set her heart on meeting an older guy.

"I know. My rule is to hurt anyone that hurts her, but so far she's doing all the heartbreaking."

Poor guys. I knew how they felt now. I'd never given them a second thought before Jace.

The light, giddy feeling Nate gave me turned into a heavy lump in my throat. I wanted comfort; a cuddle, a kiss. Was this what rebound felt like? A desperate need to feel loved and touched again by someone, anyone. Was that all Nate was - a somebody? We turned onto the high road that followed along the cliffs.

It wasn't fair to treat Nate this way when he was being so kind. I felt bad for using him. I tugged my hand free of his and folded my arms across my chest. "I can walk myself home."

"Don't be silly."

We were nearing the cliff tops, and the wind picked up my hair. The sea was dark and looked hard and cold except for the warm reflection of sunlight glimmering like hope in the distance. Perhaps everything wouldn't be so bleak once the day was here.

"It's pretty, isn't it?"

"The sunrise?" Nate asked, following my gaze.

"Yeah."

He hummed in agreement. "Maybe, next time you come over to the love shack…"

"Next time?" I giggled at the thought of this becoming a regular arrangement. "And please don't call it that."

"Only if you promise to visit again."

We turned the corner to follow the cliff tops along to my house. A bike riding on the pavement almost crashed into me. Nate pulled me out of the way, up against his chest. The rider slammed on their brakes.

"Watch it!" Nate snapped.

"Sorry," the rider apologised.

My heart recognised the voice. He had a paper round bag over his shoulder. My body felt prickly, and I pressed my lips together.

"Oh," Jace said as he registered me standing wrapped in Nate's protective embrace.

Why did everything go wrong for me?

Jace frowned, and there was a long pause as we all stared at each other.

Awkward.

Confused.

Jace's proximity stoked my need, making me want him, and wish Nate wasn't here. I needed to explain that this wasn't how it looked. Before any words came to me, Jace nodded and peddled away.

"You okay?" Nate squeezed my hand. This time, the gesture didn't provide any comfort.

My body felt like Death himself had crawled over me. The corners of my mouth pulled like a heavyweight and I knew I wasn't *okay*. Nate's chat had opened me up and made me vulnerable. With my walls down, I was no longer in control. Hot tears warmed my cheeks. I wanted to stay cold; I wanted to be numb.

"No!" I pulled my hand away from his and ran, batting the tears from my face.

I didn't want warmth or love or anything like that ever again because afterwards, all that remains is pain. How could I have forgotten that? The emptiness was sickening, burning in the pit of my stomach like bile. I wanted to take a knife and cut it away from me; amputate my heart, feeding the poison to my body. I couldn't take it anymore.

Rough hands grabbed me and as I tried to shake him off, I fell forward onto the pavement. Nate toppled down with me, gripping my shoulders. He rolled me over. I saw red and shoved him off me. He reached for me again, trying to pull me to my feet.

"I'm sorry, Kiely. I didn't—"

"Get off me!" I screamed and pushed myself up onto my grazed palms. "Leave me the fuck alone!"

The prickling sensation of being followed returned. This time, I knew it wasn't some strange animal with yellow eyes. It was Nate. And I wanted him as far away from me as possible. "For goodness' sake, don't follow me!"

I marched home with my head down, not looking back. I tugged the hood to cover my face. Taking huge breaths as tears continued to roll down my face from my hollow pit of a body. I was alone at last, but still wanted Jace; nobody else would do.

I wished for a piece of him to fill the gaping hole in my life. I wanted to be important to him, to matter. That's when I had the strangest thought.

Imagine if I was pregnant with his baby.

I wasn't ready for sex, and nowhere near ready to be a mother. But, as I rubbed my stomach and comforted myself with the idea of a tiny piece of him growing inside me, it made me feel better.

A piece of him I could keep forever.

I knew I was being crazy, but the idea soothed me. My tears stopped, and a silly smile filled my face as I got lost in my daydream. It was just a story I could tell myself to ease the emptiness I felt. A fantasy where Jace and I got our happily ever after.

Unlocking the front door, I crept inside, shutting it carefully behind me so as not to make a sound, and tiptoed up the stairs to bed.

I snuck in, trying not to wake anyone, but I failed. Aero noticed. He wagged his tail, banging it against the kitchen cupboard, creating an excited tempo.

"Shh," I hissed at him like he might understand me.

He bound up to greet me, and I buried my face in his neck. He smelt good - not a nice smell, but his familiar smell. I led him up to my room. We weren't meant to have Aero in our bedroom, but his company felt like what I needed. I sat on my bed, and he jumped up to lay down beside me.

His big brown eyes seemed to ask what's wrong. A lump rose in my throat and I shook my head. Everything was such a mess, I couldn't explain. The tears came, and he pushed his head into me, as if trying to hug me in his own way.

Ping!

Ping!

My notification woke me up. I still felt miserable, and the text messages from the girls filled me with dread. This wasn't what I needed.

Fallon: Don't forget, tonight is Project-Get-Kiely-A-Man!

Ari: Can I stay over?

Fallon: Of course.

Fallon: Kiely. U wanna, too?

Ari: Can I borrow something to wear?

Fallon: Always ;)

Fallon: Kiely?

I was definitely not in the mood for a night out.

Kiely: Sorry, I can't. I've got a funny tummy.

They tried to call, but I ignored them. Right now, my maths homework was a ton more appealing. I didn't want someone new. Plus, as far as my friends knew, I might be so sick I couldn't get to the phone.

In a way, I was sick. Not physically sick, but I was sick of myself. I kept breaking down and crying. It'd all caught up with me. Everything felt like too much effort. I cursed Nate for getting me to open up. I felt heavy, exhausted, and frustrated at myself because I couldn't snap out of it. My mind kept forcing me to relive the once happy memories, but now they broke me down, reminders of what I'd lost.

I remembered Jace and I standing in a gap between a batch of lockers as he showed me a picture on his phone. We were so close. The echo of noise carrying in the busy corridor surrounded us.

The mobile lit up his face, making him look godly. Godly and hot. My body prickled with our proximity. I wanted him to turn his head, for his lips to meet mine. The longer we waited for our first kiss, the bigger a deal it felt. He smelt so good and it made me want to breathe more deeply, to inhale him.

"Look." He turned the screen towards me and showed me the black-and-white neonatal image of his mum's pregnancy. He'd gone with her after school the other day to check everything was going well. "It's like magic. That tiny life.

So perfect."

It looked like an alien to me, with a massive head and partially formed limbs. Jace zoomed in on its features to show me the tiny blob of hands and its patchy face. He was so proud. He couldn't wait to be a big brother.

For a moment, I let the memory evolve. I imagined the picture was ours, that we'd been sharing our little miracle. As a virgin, it would've been a miracle, and my damn brain kept reminding me of that. No longer was my fantasy baby providing the same comfort it had the night before.

My mind kept forcing me to acknowledge it wasn't true and never would be.

He didn't want me.

My maths homework was due on Monday, and it wasn't working at taking my mind off my breakup. It was about angles. When was I ever going to need to know about angles again in my life? It was only homework to prepare for the upcoming exams. It felt like useless information and that made me less motivated to do it. Making little progress with my assignment, I'd taken to drawing circles on my page with my compass.

I pressed my thumb against the sharp spike. I liked the way it felt. A little red blob rose to the surface. It hurt, but it was like releasing a tiny drop of my heartache. Something compelled me to scratch a heart on the back of my hand. I liked the way it felt hot, like fire. It left a pink line against my skin. Across the middle, I drew a jagged line like a lightning bolt. My broken heart is there for all to see.

If people could see how I hurt inside, maybe they'd understand how I'm suffering.

Then, I cringed.

I didn't want anyone to know I was broken. Freak, they'd call me. I licked my finger and rubbed over the pink rawness to soothe it, praying it would go away.

But it didn't.

It was still there. I pulled my dressing gown sleeve over it. It shouldn't take long to fade.

It wasn't a deep cut, but it was embarrassing.

Cancelling a night out was like committing social suicide. I knew exactly what to expect as I knocked on Arizona's front door. They wouldn't admit to my face that they were angry I cancelled, but they'd punish me by insisting they had the best night out ever. They wanted me to know I missed out.

What they didn't know was that I wouldn't have been any fun to hang out with. My thumb rubbed over the back of my hand, tracing over where I had drawn my broken heart. It was barely visible today, which was a relief.

Seeing Jace out of the blue had knocked me. After I gave up on my maths assignment, I spent the rest of the day in bed, sobbing.

It surprised me when Fallon greeted me. Her brow wrinkled as she asked, "Are you feeling better?"

I nodded, feeling a tad guilty for lying. She led me into Arizona's home like it was her own, and I followed her. Fallon sat down next to a candle, where she held a needle in the flame. Arizona sat at her dressing table, painting her nails.

"The entire night was a disaster," Fallon said, as I sat down on a beanbag.

The slouched position suited my mood. This welcome wasn't what I'd expected at all. I tried to sit upright.

"We got in the club, then the police arrived to do an ID sweep." Fallon paused for my shocked reaction. "We got behind the bar and out the backdoor without getting caught, but there was an officer with a van parked there!"

"Did you get arrested?"

Fallon shook her head. "No. We ran so fast I thought I'd die."

The words rushed out of Arizona's mouth. "We got to the gardens and hid in some bushes, and this officer shone his torch right at me. It was so bright I couldn't see. I thought I was done, but he moved on."

"He didn't see you?"

"I've no idea how he missed us. We sat in those bushes for most of the night," Arizona said, and glanced up from her nails.

Fallon touched my upper arm and added, "Once we realised we were safe, we couldn't stop laughing. It was so funny, Arizona wet herself laughing - literally!"

"Oi. You promised!" Arizona's cheeks burned as

she glared at Fallon.

Fallon bit her lip. "I didn't mean to tell you that bit." She mouthed 'sorry' to Arizona.

"We were home by ten! How lame is that?" Fallon finished.

"Sounds like a night you'll never forget."

"Yeah, and we met this guy, Brad. He'd be perfect for you."

"Oh Fallon, no," I complained.

"I told Fallon you wouldn't be interested." Arizona blew on her nails.

"Wait until she meets him."

I rolled my eyes and leaned back. I wasn't sure how to free myself from being Fallon's project. A random guy named Brad, whom neither Fallon nor Arizona fancied for themselves had zero appeal.

"I've changed my mind," Ari said.

Ari shook her hands to dry her nails. How had she gone from Brad being perfect for me to changing her mind about setting us up together? I hadn't even started putting up an argument.

Ari was shaking her head at Fallon, who was messing around with a needle in a candle's flame. That's when I realised this wasn't about Brad.

"What are you doing?" I asked Fallon.

"Arizona wants her ears pierced, but her mum said no. So, I'm doing it."

Arizona chuckled. "I'm not sure that's safe."

"It's fine. My sister does her friends' earlobes all the time. Use the ice lolly to numb the area." Fallon got up and approached Arizona with the pin.

Arizona then held a wrapped ice lolly against her ear and tipped her head to the side. Fallon brushed her hair away. I got up to have a closer look. I couldn't believe Arizona was going to let Fallon do this.

Fallon marked a dot on her ear with a felt tip and then went to push the needle in.

Arizona squealed and jumped up. "No! No! I can't do it. It hurts."

"What? I didn't even touch you!"

Arizona paced around the room like a boxer does their opponent. She wouldn't take her eyes off Fallon in case she jabbed her unexpectedly.

Fallon shook her head and sat back on the bed. "Don't be so dramatic. I didn't force you. You said you wanted it."

"I do, but I can't."

"I'll do it." My voice surprised me, as I'd not intended to volunteer my body to be impaled by Fallon's Hodge-Podge Piercing Studio.

Fallon grinned. "Give her the ice lolly."

Arizona handed it over, and I held it against my ear. The cold wasn't pleasant.

The pen tickled as Fallon marked the spot. Holding the needle against my lobe, she asked, "Are you sure?"

"Yeah. Do it."

There was a quick pain. It was like someone had pinged me with an elastic. Then, my ear lobe was on fire.

"It's done," Fallon announced and moved around

to do the other side.

Arizona held out some pretty imitation diamond studs. "I guess you'll need these."

"Thank you. Are you sure?" I said as I took them with my free hand.

Arizona nodded. "I can't use them. Consider them a prize for your brave stupidity."

I felt the sharp sting, followed by the warmth.

"You're all done."

I got up to take Arizona's seat at her dressing table and added the earrings to the fresh new holes in my ear. I liked the throbbing sensation. Having a real physical pain distracted me from my internal agony.

"Beautiful," Arizona said, looking at me in the mirror as she stood to my right.

I loved them, but I'd have to wear my hair down. Dad wouldn't be pleased I'd done this after how he reacted to Murray's tattoo.

Fallon stood on my other side, admiring my new piercing in the mirror. "We're going again this weekend."

I looked at my friends via the reflections. "The club?"

"No excuses." Fallon gave me a knowing look.

CHAPTER 7

WE SAT ON THE BENCHES, watching the lads play. When we spoke, our words came out in little puffs of cold condensation clouds. They were still talking about the night out I'd missed.

"I can't believe you told Kiely! Please don't tell anyone else. I'm dying here!" Arizona screamed at Fallon.

"Chill. It's between friends. I wouldn't tell anyone outside our group," Fallon promised, taking Ari's hand. "If anyone ever made fun of you, they would die. You know this."

Arizona pressed a hand to her chest. "I know."

"We don't keep secrets from each other." She looked between us. My heart sped up as I worried she

was giving me the opportunity to fess up about Nate and already knew about the other night. If she didn't, there was no reason to admit to it because after what happened the other night, I had no intention of seeing Nate again. The nights at the summer house were over.

"Have you guys thought about work experience?" Fallon asked.

I sighed with relief at the subject change, although the new topic wasn't one that excited me. We'd been told during the school assembly they would allocate us a time to speak to the career adviser about our futures and they'd support us in getting a placement, although they encouraged us to find one ourselves. I'd not given it any thought.

"No idea," I admitted.

The only future I'd wished for was one where I was back with Jace and the crazy notion of having his baby. I was pretty sure 'stay-at-home mum' wasn't a suitable career choice that the school would support me with.

Jace was on the pitch, busy playing. I wondered whether he felt jealous of seeing me with Nate. Did he think we were together? Had he told anyone? I needed to speak with him and let him know it was nothing. Maybe if I could speak to him, we could work things out and get back together.

"I want to work in a lab, developing cruelty-free beauty products," Arizona said proudly.

"Are there any labs around here?"

"I've been looking, but can't find any. The school will get me to assist a science class or work in a shop selling beauty products."

"Probs." Fallon shrugged. "They're so lame. My sister wanted to be a fashion designer so they sent her to work at a nursery as they do 'drawing'."

We all laughed and shook our heads - our careers adviser was creative at finding a way of bending a job to fit the skills we needed for our career goals. "That's why I'm going to sort out my own."

"How?" I asked. We all knew that Fallon had her heart set on getting into law. In particular, she wanted to be a judge.

"You know that awkward lad - Ryan Kenned?"

We both nodded.

"His dad is the founding partner of Kenned Law in town. I'm going to see if I can get in via Ryan."

My friends were so focused on their futures, it made me feel stupid that all I'd done was get my heart tangled up over Jace. My plan was just to get through each day, maybe pass some exams. It was all too much with my heartbreak. Plus, how was I supposed to concentrate on anything when Nate was a ticking bomb of information I didn't want him to tell Fallon? If she discovered I'd been with him behind her back, she'd be after my blood.

I sighed.

"What's up?" Arizona leaned close. Her dark brown eyes, warm and full of comfort.

"I just wish I had your vision."

"Come over tonight. I'll give you a manicure with my new homemade nail polish, and we can hash out some ideas," Arizona offered.

"You make nail polish now?" I asked, impressed.

"Well, Kiely will be my first guinea pig," Arizona said with a laugh. "I'm serious about starting my own makeup line."

The bell rang, and everyone began making their way back inside the school

"I'll be your biggest fan," Fallon promised.

"I'm going to create a limited edition shade just for you." Arizona told Fallon as they linked arms on their way in. "We could call it Super Fan Fallon."

"I think I need to help you with the shade names," Fallon said, laughing.

I slowly collected my things from the bench to put in my bag. I was taking my time to allow Jace to reach me so we could walk in together just like we used to, and talk. As he passed me, I jumped up and increased the speed of my footsteps to match his.

"Hi," I said as I reached his side.

He looked at me awkwardly. "I'm with Mariah."

"I know, but I thought we could talk."

"I'm not interested. Try Nate." He jogged the last few yards into the school to create a distance between us. My eyes darted to Fallon to make sure she wasn't in earshot. My heart raced as I worried that Jace could have told someone about Nate and me.

I tried to catch him at lunchtime, but as soon as he saw me, he skipped lunch and headed out to the playing field. The other lads surrounded him, immersed in the game, making it impossible for me to reach him.

During the last break, I waited under the stairwell.

I was going to try the trick I'd learnt from Nate. When Jace walked past, I grabbed his arm and pulled him out of the crowd.

"What are you doing?" he snapped.

"Nate is just a friend."

He shrugged. "You're not my girlfriend. Go out with whoever."

"We're not like that."

"I don't care." He shook my hand off his arm. "Leave me alone."

"I can't!"

"Please, Kiely, don't make this harder." He looked at me with pity as he joined the swarms of students and disappeared out of sight. Leaving me alone. His words slammed into my gut. I felt suffocated by my pain. People walked by on their way to class, oblivious to my inner turmoil. I felt trapped at that moment, the darkness blinding me. I sunk to the floor and as the corridors quietened, the only sound to be heard was my broken sobs.

I felt sick and rested a hand on my stomach. I remembered my fantasy baby, which grew like the darkness inside me, filling all the places Jace had left me hollowed out and empty. I wanted to hurt him back. I revelled in the possibility and wiped the tears from my eyes and smiled.

How dare he look at me with pity!

I hadn't wanted to go to Arizona's house. I wanted to stay home and wallow in my self-pity, but I was sick of that too. So I'd forced myself, against my will, to take her up on her offer.

We sat on cushions in her front room on opposite sides of the coffee table. She had my hands soaking in a warm bowl of water whilst she got her stuff together. The scratches on the back of my hand had healed, which was a relief as I didn't want Arizona to see what I'd done.

"Did you seriously make this yourself?" I asked.

She smiled and held up a little glass bottle. "I made this shade with beetroot and purple sweet potato. It will be this season's colour."

"Yeah, but how did you make it into a polish?"

Arizona sighed. "Well, I don't have all the ingredients so the base is a clear polish I bought, but the colour is all mine."

She lifted one of my hands from the bowl, dried them. She massaged my hands with coconut scented moisturiser. "Do you want to talk about Jace?"

My jaw tensed. Everyone kept prying and fussing when all I wanted to do was go back to how it was. I wished to pretend we were still good. I shut my eyes and saw his pity face.

"I'll take that as a no then." Arizona put my hand down. She picked up a clear base coat and began painting my nails. "Anyone new you like?"

"Do we have to talk about boys?" I snapped.

"No," Arizona replied. "Have you any ideas for

work experience?"

"Not that," I groaned.

"How is your exam revision going?"

"Oh Ari, you are full of light-hearted conversation." I coughed a laugh. "Crap, everything is crap."

She tilted her head. "I'm worried about you."

I shook my head. "Please, don't give me the pity face."

"Sorry." Arizona blushed.

"You know what?" I asked, but didn't expect an answer. "Fallon is right. This weekend I need to get wasted, have fun, and move on."

"Yes," Arizona said with a grin. "That's the spirit."

"But I'm not looking for love. I'm done with boys, boyfriends, and all that. I want to be wild and free."

Arizona placed my hand under a UV lamp to dry the colour. She unscrewed the bottle of polish she had created and showed me the deep violet-purple colour. "I was going to call it 'Heartbreak' and dedicate it to you, but…"

"Call it 'Heartbreak', but I'll be the one breaking hearts from now on." Like food spoiling, my love for Jace went from something sweet to something that burned in my gut.

Arizona sang, "Watch out guys, this new Kiely's fierce and unstoppable!"

Yes. I'd make Jace suffer.

My hand shook. Deep down, I knew what I was doing was wrong but I couldn't shake that look of pity Jace gave me. It circled my mind on replay, driving me mad. Nate's words added to the toxic cocktail. All those double dates had been no coincidence. I could see it now and it boiled my blood.

It didn't help that I could hear Murray chilling in his room listening to his music. He wasn't sad about things not working out with Mariah. She'd left him for Jace, and he didn't seem bothered. She had just been another one of the many girls he messed with. How dare he interfere in my love life.

The idea Murray would betray me hurt more than being dumped. Once again, I felt naive and stupid. It made me want to mess with them both; Murray and Jace. All my anger had brewed into wanting revenge and now I stood outside his bedroom door, my right knuckle poised to knock with one simple lie to ruin them both.

I knocked and entered.

He muted his music and swivelled around on his computer chair. "What do you want?"

He didn't know I knew.

I sat on his bed. "I'm in trouble."

"What's up?"

I'd been thinking about what Nate had told me about my brother interfering with my romantic life. The only reason I could think he'd do that was to protect me from getting hurt, but it didn't make it okay. His actions had caused me to get hurt and now I knew, I wanted him to suffer too. Using his overprotective nature against him, I would use him to get my own back on them both.

"Jace won't speak to me." I looked at the floor.

He placed a reassuring arm across my shoulder. "His loss. You'll meet someone better when you're twenty-one."

I looked at him confused. "Why twenty-one?"

"Finish university before you even think about dating."

"What about you?"

"What about me?" He leaned back in his chair and lifted his foot into his lap.

"You're always fooling around with girls."

He folded his arms across his chest and chuckled. "I'm no role model."

This conversation wasn't going in the direction I needed it to go. I pretended to cry. "I need Jace."

"Cut it out, Kiely. You know I'm no good with crying. I'll get Mum for you?" He stood up.

"No!" I said. "No-one must know. Not until I've spoken to Jace."

The colour drained from his face, and he swallowed. He ran a hand through his hair, as he crouched down in front of me. "Kiely, you're frightening me. Talk to me."

Murray took my hands in his. I focused on my 'Heartbreak' nails as I couldn't look at his face for fear he'd see the lie in my eyes. "I'm pregnant."

"What!" Murray dropped my hands in my lap and stepped back.

There was a delicious sensation saying it out

loud and having someone believe me. Almost like an incantation, making it real. I chewed the inside of my cheek to stop myself from laughing at his reaction.

He paced back and forth. "How did this happen? No - don't answer that, I don't want the details!" He stopped in front of me. "You have to tell Mum."

I rushed to grab Murray's wrist before he could leave the room. "Please, no, I should tell Jace first."

Murray shook his head. "Is that why you were sick the other day?"

I nodded. I hadn't thought of that, but it played nicely into my story. Much better than the truth.

He sighed heavily and his shoulders dropped with the burden of my news. "You've got twenty-four hours to tell Jace, then we have to tell Mum."

"He won't speak to me," I reminded him. "Can't you... please, Murray, I need your help."

"I'm going to kill him," he growled.

Yes. I chewed my lip to prevent myself from smiling. I wanted to jump about and celebrate that Jace was about to get what was coming to him, for my plan to work.

"We're going now!" Murray grabbed a hooded jacket off the plastic chair by his desk and headed out the door.

I swallowed a lump in my throat. "Go where?"

"To tell him."

Dread filled me as I realised the magnitude of what I was doing. My plan was in action. There was no turning back.

The stress played tricks with my eyes; it looked like Murray's eyes flashed silver. The room spun. What I was doing was wrong, but the way Jace blanked me was wrong too. He'd lied about just being friends with Mariah when now it was obvious that he'd been cheating on me. And Murray was no better. He'd blocked guys from dating me and made me think something was wrong with me. They both deserved this. It was time for them to both get played.

"I can't face him," I pleaded in the hope he would let me off and go alone. I needed him to confront Jace, and for Jace to deny it - which he obviously would as we'd never had sex - and then Murray would punch him.

"Mum, or car?" He held the door of his car open as I considered his ultimatum.

I got in. My lie was big enough already without involving anyone else.

Murray's lack of driving experience and rage made me bite my lip. I put on my seat belt and my fingers clung to the base of my seat. The thrill made me want to wind Murray up further. I wanted Jace to suffer so I asked, "Does it bother you that Mariah dumped you for Jace?"

His jaw twitched as he clenched his teeth. "We weren't together."

He didn't realise what he'd admitted. His confession made my blood turn cold. I wondered if it'd been his plan to help her steal my boyfriend or only to cause Jace and I to break up. Yet, he looked upset about it.

More upset than the initial idea that his sister was pregnant by a guy that wanted nothing to do with her. Maybe I'd misread this, and he was hurt over Mariah. My jaw jutted out as I sulked and watched the houses flash by. What was so special about Mariah that drove my brother and Jace crazy?

"So, it doesn't bother you?" I pushed him to test my theory.

He ignored my question and pressed harder on the accelerator, and turned the radio up.

The brakes screeched as we pulled into Jace's driveway. Murray jumped out of the car without bothering to shut his door. I got out of my side, fully aware that we weren't here for a friendly chat. The wind picked up and blew wildly around us, as if the air was filled with the energy of what was about to happen.

Murray hammered on the door.

"Can you calm down? You're not making this easier."

"What do you expect from me?" he snapped. "Why drag me into this and then expect me to play nice?"

My brow knitted as the reality of what I was doing came crashing down on me. A wave of nausea washed over me.

"We should go. He might not even be in and his mum's pregnant."

Murray stepped back and took a long breath to calm down. He moved away from the door. "Sorry, you're right. I'll behave, and be here if you need me."

Jace opened the door wearing a gentle smile, but

once he realised it was me, the smile vanished. He looked over my shoulder at Murray and raised an eyebrow. "Why are you here?"

"I need to talk to you," I began, but wasn't sure what to say. My stupid heart still sang in his presence and pretending to be pregnant was going to kill off any last chance of us getting back together. He'd think I'm crazy.

Perhaps, I am.

Glancing over at Murray, I realised I couldn't back out of this. His face was getting redder waiting for me to tell Jace. But, now I was here, the lie felt stupid. Instead I said, "I need to know what I did wrong. Why we can't be together?"

"Kiely, this is…" He stopped and looked over at Murray. He shuffled and ran a harassed hand through his hair. "You know I'm with Mariah. You've got to move on."

"Tell him," Murray said, stamping his feet as he joined my side.

"Tell me what?" Jace looked from Murray to me.

"I- I—," I couldn't say it. This was a bad idea. I just wanted Murray to punch Jace's smug face.

"She's pregnant!" Murray yelled.

No! No! No! There was no backing out of this now.

"What's that to do with me?" Jace asked.

"It's yours, you muppet!" Murray yelled. He stepped up onto the porch and got right into Jace's face. "Show some responsibility."

"It can't be!"

Murray's fist swung up and undercut Jace in the jaw. Jace stumbled back into his house and then tried to slam the door on us. Murray stuck his foot in the way and howled in pain as the door crushed it. He snarled.

"Get out here, you coward!" He pushed his body against the door to force it wide.

Jace held the door to. "We never had sex! Tell him, Kiely!"

Murray pulled his foot back and let go of the door. It clicked shut. Murray glared at me. "Kiely?"

"He's lying," I squeaked. My face was burning red.

Jace's voice sounded wobbly. "If she's pregnant, it's not mine. We kissed once. That's it! I think I'd remember."

"Is this true?" Murray's eyes flashed silver, and I thought I saw sparks of lightning flickering off his fists. I needed to sit down before I passed out from the stress. I rubbed my temples.

Fuck! I'm seeing things again.

The breakup stress was too much. The dam of built up tears burst. I threw myself at the closed door and wailed. "Give me another chance!"

"For Christ's sake!" Murray swore. He dragged me off the step and toward the car.

Seeing another pity face caused my shoulders to collapse in on themselves, and I choked out the tears. This wasn't the revenge I'd hoped for. It'd backfired and now everything was a hundred times worse.

What had I been thinking? Stupid, stupid plan!

"Kiely? Seriously?" Murray opened the passenger

door. "You can't make shit like that up. That's not how you get a guy back. He'll think you're bat shit crazy."

I sobbed even louder.

"Damn, Kiely." Murray held me by the shoulders. "You're so messed up. Stop hiding in your room and talk to Mum. Please."

He sighed and let me go. I got in the car and as he walked around, I could hear his words ringing in my head.

"You're bat shit crazy!"

"You're so messed up."

He was right. I hung my head in shame.

Murray got in and leaned over to get some tissues out of the glove compartment for me. The drive home was slower and in complete silence. We pulled into the driveway. He turned off the engine, but didn't get out of the car. We sat together and waited until I calmed down.

"He's not even that special." Murray broke the silence.

Feeling braver, I looked at him. "Sorry."

Murray smiled. "It felt good to hit him."

I managed a brief smile, relieved he'd forgiven me.

"A word from the wise." Murray looked me dead in the eye. "Never make stuff up like that. Promise."

I nodded. He was right. This wasn't the way to get Jace back. The pain I felt as I realised I would never get him back now was confusing, as I wasn't even sure I still wanted him back.

CHAPTER 8

WE HUDDLED TOGETHER for warmth while queuing outside the club, wearing skimpy dresses that left little to the imagination. Fallon's older sister had told us dressing this way would distract the bouncers from asking for our ID. I could see how that could work for Arizona and Fallon, as it was hard not to look at their ample busts, but next to them, mine looked tiny. I'd spent a little longer on my makeup and added some false lashes that I was now worrying might come unstuck and the wind kept blowing my hair into my lip gloss.

"What if the recent visit from the police makes them more thorough?"

"They won't be." Fallon tossed her hair over her

shoulder and pushed out her chest.

"They might," I agreed with Arizona.

"Trust me. We'll be fine. Confidence is key." Fallon strutted forward, and we joined the queue.

I could see the tension building on Arizona's face. Her big, brown eyes darted around and she twisted a curl around her finger. She was making me nervous. I reached for her hand and gave it a squeeze. "If any of us don't get in, then we all don't go in."

Arizona gave us a weak smile and tried to relax.

Fallon rubbed Arizona's shoulder. "You're my wing woman. My lucky charm. You're going to help me find Brad for Kiely."

We moved forward, and the bouncer unclipped the rope to let us through. My heart thundered as we walked past to the kiosk. I kept expecting a hand on my shoulder, but they barely gave us a second glance. We were in. We paid and headed for the bar where Fallon insisted on us doing shots.

"Kamikazes all round!" she cheered as the bartender placed three little glasses in front of us. "And three double vodkas and lemonades." As the bartender made the additional drinks, we lifted our glasses, and Fallon counted to three. We threw our drinks back, and all winced. It was sweet, but I felt the kick of vodka burn at the back of my throat.

The bartender gave Fallon the price, but the music was too loud to hear. She swiped her mum's debit card, which I wasn't sure she'd got permission for. We took our glasses and followed Fallon to a corner.

I gingerly sipped my drink, whilst a plant with sharp leaves poked the back of my legs. I tried to move away, but a wall of jostling sweaty bodies held me in place. The drink made my face screw up. It tasted like more than a double. I didn't want to get drunk and risk spilling my secrets. They didn't know about Nate and me meeting up, or how I'd ruined things eternally with Jace. I discreetly shared my drink with my leafy nemesis.

"Can you see him, Ari?"

Arizona shook her head.

Fallon leaned into me. "I can't wait for you to meet him. He's a god, and you are going to worship the pants off him."

"Oh, there is!" Arizona squealed and started pointing.

I grabbed her erect arm and pulled it down by her side. "Don't. He might see you!"

The guy looked over with a puzzled look on his face. Fallon feigned being bashful as she dipped her head and fluttered her lashes. I could tell she was secretly pleased Arizona had drawn his attention to us.

"Oh my god, he's coming over," Fallon squealed, squeezing my hand. "You can thank me later."

"Hey ladies." A guy sauntered over.

"Hi, Brad." Fallon stepped forward.

He appeared younger than I'd got from Fallon's description. He had a clean-cut, boy band look, with dark hair and a piercing in his right ear.

"You left before we got a proper chance to get to

know each other. I was going to buy you a drink."

"That's sweet." She turned and looked at me. "Isn't that sweet?"

He turned and looked at Arizona. "Can I make it up to you? What would you ladies like?"

"We're drinking double vodkas and lemonade." Ari raised her glass.

"Wow! You girls aren't taking it easy." He said, echoing my thoughts.

"Thanks." Fallon took it as a compliment.

"Find somewhere to sit and I'll bring your drinks over."

Fallon reached for his arm. "Could you get Kiely a drink, too?" She tilted her head toward me.

Brad looked at me for the first time and smiled. "Hi, Kiely."

"Hi, Brad," I said and blushed. I couldn't believe Fallon had told him to buy me a drink when we hadn't even met. I began fiddling with my hair and found a sticky strand that added to my humiliation. "You don't have to worry about me."

"It's no problem." He shrugged and turned to Arizona. "Do you mind giving me a hand?"

"Okay," she said.

I saw Fallon's smile drop as Arizona and Brad headed off to the bar. Fallon turned to me. "Are they flirting?"

I shook my head. "No, Ari's not like that, but Brad may have taken a shine to her."

Fallon threw her head back and groaned. "Why are

men so stupid?"

I shrugged. "Don't get mad at her. It's not her fault."

"I know," Fallon stuck out her bottom lip at me. "But I wanted him for you."

"I'm sure there are more *Brads* out there."

Fallon threw her arms around me in a clumsy hug. She loosened her grip and drew back, resting her forehead on mine. "That's the spirit. I love you, Kiely."

"Come on you drunk tart, let's dance." I slipped out from under her arm and reached for her hand. We pushed our way through the crowd of bodies until we found a suitable spot to dance.

Fallon and I were having a laugh with silly dance moves. It wasn't until Arizona appeared between us, looking unimpressed, that we stopped. She grabbed Fallon's hand and dragged her off the dance floor. I followed them to a marginally quieter part of the club.

"Why did you leave me? With Brad?" she wailed.

I bit my lip and laughed. "Did something happen?"

Arizona looked worried and shot Fallon a look. "Why didn't you stay?"

I gasped and covered my mouth. Something had happened.

Fallon sighed. "I get it. Brad likes you. I'll find someone else for Kiely."

"You knew!" Arizona's jaw dropped in disbelief. "And you still left me with him."

Fallon giggled. "Why? What happened?"

"He tried to kiss me. I said no, of course! I knew he's meant for Kiely."

My hand fell around her shoulders as I giggled. Her horrified face looked so funny.

"It's fine. If you like him, you can have him." Fallon shrugged.

Arizona's face flushed, and she raised her voice. "I don't want him! He's not my type!"

"What is your type?" Fallon raised an eyebrow.

My hand slipped away from Arizona's shoulder and rubbed the back of my neck. Fallon had a weird obsession over who Arizona was into. Perhaps she suspected Arizona was still crushing on Nate. It reminded me that it wouldn't go down well if Fallon ever found out about Nate and I's secret rendezvous. My mouth felt dry at the thought.

"Don't start this again!" Arizona shook her head and backed away.

"What about me? Am I your type?" Fallon flicked her hair as she stepped into Arizona's space.

Arizona pushed Fallon away and took off.

"Did you see that?" Fallon said with a grin.

She moved to chase after Arizona, but I grabbed her arm. "Leave her alone."

Fallon shook off my arm. "You're not the boss of me. Nobody is."

"Then do a better job at managing yourself, because you're being a bitch."

Fallon took a deep breath. Her shoulders dropped. "That's not what I want. Me and my stupid mouth."

"Just give her a moment."

"I can't. I've got to fix this."

Fallon hurried off to catch Arizona. I leaned back against the wall and closed my eyes. I wasn't sure I had the energy to deal with Arizona and Fallon having a falling out and all the drama that went with it. It'd taken most of my strength to pull myself together to join them on a night out. The club was hot, and the music was thumping.

I didn't want to be here.

I opened my eyes to discover that Brad had joined me.

"Hi, Kiely?"

"Hi," I groaned inwardly.

He handed me a drink. "Vodka double?"

"Thanks." I accepted it and looked around for my friends. I couldn't believe they'd wanted this guy for me. I sipped the drink and pulled a face at the overbearing taste of vodka.

"I think I upset your friends." He handed me another drink. "That's for Fallon."

"What makes you say that?" I took another sip and gagged. I wanted to spit it out, but didn't want to appear rude or immature. Brad stood too close. I tried to back away, but there was no space. I sipped the drink.

Eurgh, I wish I'd stop doing that.

"She said I wasn't supposed to be into her, and Fallon was gonna be mad." He laughed. "If I had known, I would have… you know. I mean, I like Fallon too. Can you talk to her and see if there's still a chance?"

Oh wow! I really had dodged a bullet.

I turned to face him square. "Are you serious? You

came here to persuade me, to persuade my best friend, to be your second choice?"

"No, it's not like that."

"Fallon is a queen. If she goes out with anyone, she's going to be their first choice, their only choice, their whole fucking world." I spat the words out.

He raised an eyebrow and smirked. "Is that a no? You won't help me?"

"No! That was 'fuck off'. Nicely!"

"I guess there's no chance I could get your number?"

My jaw dropped. There were no words.

He laughed. As he left, he looked at me over his shoulder and gave me this creepy smile and a wink. "Enjoy your drink."

I looked at the glasses in my hands. There was something disturbing about his smile, like he was making fun of me. The hairs on my arm stood up, and I wondered if he'd spiked the drinks. I ditched them on a table as I passed by.

I went looking for my friends, calling their names like a fool in the ladies' toilets, but they weren't there. They weren't anywhere. It made me feel vulnerable and lost. The room spun and faces blurred together. I felt hot. Very hot. Sweat beaded on my brow. I had to get out of this place. I got a stamp on my hand from the kiosk and stumbled out of the club into the night air.

The blast of cool air was refreshing. I could breathe. It was an instant relief.

Kiely: Gotta go. Bed. Have fun x

Standing outside the club, I stared at my phone, expecting a call or text telling me to come back, but there was nothing. I shoved it in my boot and headed up the hill. I grinned to myself, thinking of how this would wind up Murray. He'd be mad if he knew I was walking home alone and drunk.

Arizona's words from the other day sung to me: *"She's fierce and unstoppable."*

Yeah, I am!

I took the scenic route through the spa gardens that ran opposite the beach. Above, I could see the cafe Nate had taken me to the other day, and below I could hear the sea's whooshes as the waves rolled up the shore. The rhythmic beat kept me company as I followed the dark path through the landscaped gardens.

My troubles felt far from my thoughts and I'd managed an entire night without Jace crossing my mind. Maybe Fallon was right, and a good night out was what I needed. Maybe, I could get over him.

A noise behind me stole my attention. I checked over my shoulder, but nobody was there. That strange sensation of being watched crept over me. I listened more carefully.

A snapped twig.

This time I didn't look. I walked faster as the hairs on my arm stood up.

It's probably nothing.

Brad's creepy smile sprung to mind. Could he have seen me leaving? Was he following me? In hindsight, I should have waited for my friends.

My heartbeat sped up along with my speed. A prickly sensation ran through me. Something was wrong. I couldn't ignore it any longer. I stopped and turned around.

A man.

Not anyone I'd never seen before.

I ran. I didn't care if I looked stupid. Or if it was a mistake. He could be innocent, just out for a walk. But still, the hairs on my arm prickled and something in my gut told me I had to get away.

I looked over my shoulder and stumbled.

To my alarm, he was running, too.

Not innocent.

Chasing me.

Faster than me.

Gaining on me.

His eyes were yellow and glowing, like those I'd seen the other night. It couldn't be a coincidence. Had Brad spiked my drink? Maybe I was hallucinating, after all. But something told me I wasn't. I opened my mouth to scream. His hand quickly clamped over my mouth, and he forced me to the ground with the other.

Then he rolled me over and pinned me down.

His eyes weren't like any human I'd seen before. They were lit amber, a blazing gold. There was something powerful in the way he looked at me. *Unhuman.* It was captivating with a strength that was greater than his arms holding me. A liquid heat ran through my body as if pumping through my veins. The warmth saturated my body and disarmed me. I didn't want to move. My body stopped resisting, and I felt compelled to obey.

"Do you feel it?" He asked.

Was I dreaming? Was he speaking about the strange sensation running through my body? My eyes blinked, and I nodded in response to his question.

Lifting his hand from my mouth, he brushed my hair from my face. The sensation drove me wild, and I groaned with a need for more. I wanted him to touch me. He lowered his mouth to mine, and the warmth deepened. His tongue entered my mouth. I needed more. I wanted all of him.

Was this lust? Was this love? Was this even real?

His kisses trailed to my ears, creating a tingling electric current in their path. I shuddered in anticipation as his teeth nibbled my earlobes and his throat rumbled a soft growl.

"I'm sorry, Luna compelled me to come for you."

I didn't care who Luna was. My body melted into him like honey drizzling from a spoon onto hot toast. My body was relaxed and aroused all at once. I felt dizzy and my breathing felt heavy. "Don't be sorry. I want this."

A strangled giggle escaped my lips. Did I want this?

His fingers brushed against my cheek. "You look so young?"

"I'm sixteen."

He drew back.

I reached for him to pull him back, begging. "Please."

I felt confused. It was as if a spell had broken. One

moment he was all over me, and the next, he was moving away. I wanted to go back to that magical feeling. The magnetism was like nothing I'd experienced before. I wasn't sure he was even human, but my body and mind craved him. I wished to burn in the hot embers of his eyes. My mind felt fuzzy, and the stars sparkled overhead in the same way this man lit up my entire body. I wanted to forget all the messes of my life, and revel in the bliss that he filled me with.

As the warmth faded, my own feelings rose to the surface. I ached with the crushing pain of wanting Jace to want me. The man's sudden rejection was like someone pushing their fingers into my wounded heart and prising it wide open. Why, whenever I kiss someone, do they lose interest… except Nate?

"Forgive me. I can't defy her. The *amour* will help you survive. So, I'm going to kiss you again." He looked pained before kissing me deeply.

With his kiss, I fell back under his spell. My back arched, pressing my body up against his, the warmth from his lips rushing through my being. My heart sang for the sensation that drove me wild. When his lips left mine, I was panting, gasping for breath.

His golden eyes warmed my heart. He growled and bared his teeth at me. His face contorted, stretching out into a long dark fury snout with a wet shiny nose. Wolf-like. I felt no fear. Mesmerized. In a trance.

His expression darkened, baring his teeth. I wondered what had caused the sudden mood change. I knew I should be scared, but I wasn't. My head tilted to the side, and I smiled. My heart raced with anticipation of what he might do next. I laid there waiting. Eager for him to do as he would with me.

"I'm sorry." He said.

"Don't be," I whispered and licked my lips, hungry for more.

It was quick and sudden. His hand swiped across my waist, and I screamed as a burning fire tore across my skin. His weight lifted from my body.

"What did you do?" The pain sobered me.

My hand reached for my stomach, feeling the wetness of the wound. I buckled over in pain, curling up in the fetal position. The iron scent filled my nostrils. I lifted my hand to my face and saw it was wet and red. I gasped and wiped it on the grass.

He was gone. I looked around and caught golden eyes off in the distance. These eyes no longer belonged to a man. Instead, I saw a wolf with black fur. I blinked. It turned and disappeared into the night.

I fumbled in my boot for my mobile.

I felt dizzy. Who was he? What had he done to me? My hand slipped over the screen of my mobile. I couldn't see what I was doing and dialled the first number on my recent call list.

"Kiely?" Nate's voice soothed me.

"Help," I sobbed. I tried to stand, but on my knees, I doubled over and reached. Was it the drink or had I lost too much blood? My dress stuck to my body; warm, wet, and sticky. Was I dying? Was he still out there? My head spun as I laid back in the grass. Dizziness and sickness consumed me.

"Where are you?"

"Spa gardens," I croaked before I shut my eyes. My throat felt dry. My mobile rolled from my hand, but I didn't have the strength to reach for it. The soothing sea had become a pounding drum.

Nate's voice sounded distant. He was still speaking to me, but I didn't have the strength to lift the phone to my ear and hear him. I mumbled a reply. "Come quick. Help me."

I pressed my hand against my waist, trying to stop the flow of blood.

What had he cut me with?

CHAPTER 9

I CRAWLED AWAY FROM THE FOOTPATH and under a bush. My arms hugged around my waist. The warmth of my blood was wet against my sleeve. I applied pressure to the wound to stop the flow and curled up, shivering, with beads of sweat on my brow. My vision blurred in and out, and the world spun around me, making me feel sick.

My attacker could come back. Maybe he never left and is watching me, waiting to pounce. I tried to fight the nausea and look around for him. Not that I could fight him if he were there. I closed my eyes, feeling sensitive to the light, and noticed how my breath was coming in sharp bursts. Every little noise made my heart race.

Golden eyes flashed in my mind. Bright, glowing, and unhuman, like nothing I'd ever seen before.

This was stupid. I needed to stop thinking like a crazy person. *People don't shift into wolves. I must have drunk too much, or maybe my drink had been spiked.*

I tried to push myself up but collapsed again. My teeth clenched from the pain as I tried not to cry out.

The wound felt deep and serious.

I was going to die here.

Hurry up, Nate. I need you.

The sea sounded aggressive. It crashed into my head with each wave and made me clench my teeth. I pushed my face toward the dirt, finding the rich earth smell appealing. It smelt so good, so crisp and clear. I took a deep breath and found I could differentiate between the scent of each plant with their zesty, floral or herbal notes. Each one was a unique blend creating a beautiful bouquet of nature. I lifted my nose to take in more and my heart lifted as I detected the scent of someone familiar.

Nate.

"Kiely!" he shouted, his voice filling my body with hope.

I scrambled to my feet. The world swam around me, and my heart pounded in my ears.

There was a swooshing noise. I groaned and dropped to my knees.

"Kiely, is that you?"

I tried to answer, but all I could manage was a groan. I raised my arm to help him spot me. The branches scratched at my arm and made me wince.

A warm hand clasped mine. My heart pounded with joy that he'd come. My hero. He pulled me up onto my legs and wrapped an arm around my waist. His scent was a soothing ointment, and I buried my nose into his neck to drink him in.

"Kiely, how drunk are you?"

"I'm not," I croaked, my words coming out slurred. My thoughts felt foggy. We'd had strong drinks, but not enough to be this drunk.

"Tom, give me a hand!"

Oh no, he'd brought company. I wanted to shrink away and tried to slink down to the floor, but Nate had a hold of me and kept me upright.

Brad and his smarmy smile sprang to mind...

Enjoy your drink.

I gasped as another pair of arms helped hold me up. Together, they supported me down through the gardens. Tom's scent mixed with Nate's, diluting the intoxicating sensation I'd been enjoying.

Blurry path. Fuzzy trees. Why's the world so strange to me?

"Spiked it!" I spat out.

"Is that blood?" Tom asked as he helped hold me up.

"'Tis nothing," I slurred and tried to wriggle from Tom's hold and wrinkled my nose.

Smell different. Not Nate.

Fussing over nothing.

I wanna go bed. Sleep.

The summer house came to mind, and I wished I was there.

"I found her in a rose bush. Her dress looks torn too, but she doesn't look hurt. Very drunk, though."

As we passed two shapes of people.

A woman's voice said, "Is she alright? Are you alright, love?"

Go away.

I leaned into Nate, away from her.

"She will be. I'm taking her to her parents," Nate replied.

"No, they'll-be-so-mad." It frustrated me how the words came out all merged.

I heard Tom click on a key fob.

"She doesn't sound alright." The woman leaned in, smelling like fields of lavender. It made me think of my mum and holidays to Ireland to visit my grandparents.

"I miss the cottage." It was sad that we no longer went now they were gone.

"She's going to be fine," Nate snapped at the woman as he began folding me into the car.

"If she's sick, you're cleaning my car. I want a full valet service, inside and out for this."

"Yeah, no worries bro."

I dragged myself into the seat, and Nate got in beside me to do my seat belt. His scent felt like a warm embrace and chased away my fears. My sweaty head rested on the cool window as I whispered, "Don't leave me."

He brushed my hair from my sweaty head, it

soothed me as he brushed the back of his hand over my cheek. I was sure I looked awful, but even with my blurred vision, I recognised his sweet smile.

"I'm here for you. Always."

"Take me to yours?" I croaked. My throat felt dry.

"If she's been spiked, we should take her to a hospital," Tom said.

"No hospital," I said, panicked, imagining those bright lights and all the questions. I wanted to go home. To sleep and gather my thoughts. No more drama.

"Can you take us?" Nate asked.

"Sure."

I groaned. My words didn't come and they weren't listening to me anyway. I surrendered to Nate's care. He held my hand and whispered reassuring words. The dual carriageway was dark, and it felt like we were the only ones on the road. It wasn't until we got closer to the residential part that everything lit up again and I noticed my vision had already cleared.

The boys helped me out of the car and to the A&E waiting room, even though I told them I didn't need any help. Tom sat with me while Nate spoke to the receptionist. It felt awkward sitting with him as I didn't know him well.

"How are you feeling?" Nate asked as he rejoined us.

"Better, " I mumbled. It was true. The mind fog had lifted.

Nate took the seat next to me. I leaned against his shoulder, enjoying the comfort of being close to him.

"We could go home," I suggested.

"We're here now. We might as well make sure you weren't spiked." Nate squeezed my shoulder as his arm rested across the back of my seat. He looked over at Tom. "You can take off. I'll stay with her. It could be ages before we're seen."

"Thanks. Call me if you need a lift home."

Nate nodded, and Tom left us sitting on the hard plastic chairs.

As I became more coherent, I was aware of how I looked. Dried, red flakes covered my hands. It was crumbling off. *Blood!* I rubbed it against my hip, as I didn't want Nate to see. My fidgeting drew his attention.

"Are you alright?"

I nodded, my eyes widened. "I just… I need… the toilets."

I got up. Nate looked uncomfortable and stood with me. "Are you sure you'll be okay?"

"I'm doing much better than when you found me. To be honest, we could go home. You don't need to worry."

"No, we should stay and get you checked over. I'll wait here for you."

If only I had pockets to stash my hands out of sight. Instead, they remained closed in a fist to hide the blood from Nate. There were rips in the front of my dress, revealing glimpses of my torso but as it was black, you couldn't see the blood on it. But I could feel the tackiness.

Entering the toilets, I headed straight for the sink

and washed my hands in warm water. They appeared to be fine, except for a little red under my nails that I'd have to scrub out at home. Once dry, I cautiously inspected my stomach.

My dress was still damp as I moved the material, pulling at the new slits to see the wound beneath. Instead, I found wet, red smudges across my skin that I splashed water on to wash away. I was sure my attacker had cut me. There was the excruciating pain, and the blood. As my hands explored my waist, there was nothing to see. My skin looked perfect, despite my dress being torn.

Was this even my blood?

It sickened me to think the blood might not even be my own. Perhaps it was paint, and the guy had been pranking me. But that didn't explain the pain. That I hadn't imagined. I rubbed my head, exhausted by it all.

My hands were shaking, and my eyes flashed amber for a second.

That's what I thought I'd seen. It reminded me of the man who'd attacked me. But it wasn't possible. Nobody's eyes glow like that. Like an idiot, I watched my reflection, waiting for it to happen again until I accepted that I must be seeing things. *Going crazy. Or tripping?* Perhaps there hadn't even been an attacker and I'd torn my dress myself under some delusion?

My body felt cold, and I began to shake. My breathing came in short and sharp. I looked around the room, checking that nobody had noticed I was freaking out. The noise of the hospital was so loud and overwhelming. I hid in a cubicle as tears peppered my eyes. I couldn't let anyone see me like this. Crouching and tucking my head into my chest, I tried to make sense of it.

Something was wrong with me. I was going crazy. It was all in my head.

Not real.

Not real.

I repeated it over and over until my breathing calmed down. I had to get back to Nate. Maybe if I opened up to him and trusted him, it would help me heal. Maybe that was what I had to do. Then I'd handle things better and the craziness would stop.

I cleaned myself up in the sink and splashed water on my dress to clean it the best I could whilst still wearing it. I couldn't use the dryer as it was one of those machines you put your hands into. Instead, I attempted to pat myself dry with some loo roll. By the time I sat down next to him, the warm water had cooled, and it made me shiver.

"You're cold." Nate took off his hoodie and wrapped it around my shoulders.

I smiled up at him. "Thanks. If you keep giving me your clothes, you'll end up with nothing to wear."

My face flushed hot at the thought of Nate naked.

"Don't worry about me." The way he smiled felt like he could read my mind, which only made me burn up more.

They weren't kidding about the wait. We endured almost two hours of being uncomfortable before they called us through.

The nurse asked me questions about what I'd taken or drank. She sought my permission to run a few tests and explained what she needed. I gave blood and urine samples.

The nurse commended Nate for bringing me in. "You did the right thing. Some drugs are only in the system for twelve hours, and if she has an adverse reaction, then we would need to treat her."

We sat on a bed in a ward while we waited for the results.

"How are you doing?" Nate asked.

"I'm feeling better."

"I meant about Jace?" Nate pushed. "I've been meaning to ask all night."

I fell silent. This wasn't a conversation I wanted to have.

Nate stared into his lap. "Last time we hung out, you took off when you saw him and haven't spoken to me since."

"He thinks something is going on with us."

"What you do is none of his business. Do you think he's jealous?"

I shook my head. My eyes stung. "He doesn't want to know me."

"Is it true Murray punched him?"

I nodded.

"Jace says you made up being pregnant."

My shoulders dropped. Why couldn't the slash across my stomach have been real so I could have bled out in the gardens rather than have to explain myself? That lie was the stupidest thing I'd ever done and now it was going to ruin the one good thing that had come out of the breakup. "Don't believe everything he says. He said he wasn't seeing Mariah, and look how that turned out!"

"True."

It felt good to have someone on my side, but I felt uneasy. Avoiding the truth felt just as bad as a lie. I rubbed the back of my neck. The conversation had made my mouth dry. "I'm thirsty."

"I'll get you a drink." Nate got up and headed out of the room.

My shoulders relaxed as he left the room, but I felt stupid sitting on a hospital bed when I didn't feel ill. The curtain was around the bed, but I could hear someone being sick and another patient calling out in pain. I wish they'd hurry with my results so we could get out of here.

The nurse came back and told me the results had come back and showed no drugs in my system. The results shocked me as it didn't explain all the weird stuff that had happened to me.

Nate came round the curtain with two chilled bottles of water in his hand. He was frowning as he asked, "How can that be possible? She was totally out of it when I found her."

"Is there a chance someone gave you a double when you thought you were drinking singles?" the nurse asked.

"No, I knew I was drinking doubles." And I'd barely drunk them.

"Maybe, in the future, you drink less. You'll still have a great night and you'll feel much better in the morning."

I didn't feel I'd drunk that much, plus, I'd watched the bar man make the round. Even if they were strong drinks, alcohol doesn't make someone hallucinate. In the gardens, I saw my attacker. His eyes were glowing, and he'd cut me open. If it wasn't a hallucination…

My head hurt trying to think of a rational explanation. If it had really happened, I would be cut, and I'm not.

Crazy. I'm going crazy. That's the only logical answer.

I bit my lip as I contemplated saying something. But the idea of being trapped in a padded room shut me up.

"The doctor says you're good to go. Just drink lots of water to dilute the alcohol and avoid a hangover." She smiled and nodded at the bottles. "Looks like you're in expert hands."

"Thanks." I slipped off the bed. I wanted to get home, and for this bizarre night to be over.

"Let's get you home."

I shook my head. "Can't I stay with you?"

"Okay."

We left the ward. Nate felt it was too late to call Tom, so we got a taxi. I sat in the back with my head resting against his shoulder. My heavy eyes kept drooping.

The blurry lights looked beautiful as they shimmered across the ocean. The car followed the coast before heading toward town and Nate's house. I closed my eyes and relaxed.

Nate paid the driver and helped me out, although I was feeling quite capable of walking now.

"We'll go round the back." He turned on the torch app on his phone and took my hand.

My vision seemed sharper. The torch didn't seem necessary, as I could see details I usually wouldn't notice. Like the grain of fencing, or the veins on the leaves of the weeds that passed my feet. Everything felt more intense. Not like a drugged haze, but as if I was more awake than I'd ever been.

"I've got you." He slid his arm around my waist whilst his other arm reached over the gate to unlock it.

"I'm fine. I promise." With Nate, I was more than fine and wanted to let him know. To get him to see that this wasn't a rebound. I was falling for him and it no longer scared me.

"You sound better."

I leaned against the fence while he reached over to

unlock the gate. He then helped me into the summer house before returning to lock the gate.

I sat on the fold-out bed, waiting for him. He brought blankets and a pint glass of water. "You need to drink as much water as you can to flush out the alcohol."

"I didn't drink that much."

"The hospital didn't agree." He held the glass out to me.

My throat was dry, so I welcomed the drink. Plus, I didn't want to argue with him. I drained the glass in an instant.

"Kiely, you're meant to take little sips, not massive gulps." He shook his head. He pulled out some bedding and pulled out the sofa bed for me to sleep on. It looked inviting, and I was eager to get under the covers.

"Thanks," I whispered, full of gratitude.

"Wait here," Nate instructed, then left me alone.

I couldn't relax, so I stood watching for him. I looked over to where I'd once seen the wolf. Another figment of my imagination.

My gaze rose to the starlit sky, and I thought about how amazing Nate had been to me.

Starlight, star bright,

first star I see tonight,

I wish I may;

I wish I might

have this wish

I wish tonight.

The nursery rhyme popped into my head, and I suddenly wished to tell my friends about Nate. I wished they could be okay about it, and our relationship was real instead of this sneaky, secretive thing. It was complex and full of who is using who. I wanted it to be simple, like when we were alone and everything felt right. I wanted to feel that way all the time.

Nate returned and handed me a bundle of clothes and a towel. "Your dress felt wet. You need to take it off, so I got some of Fallon's stuff from the dryer."

I was grateful for the pyjamas. I peeled off the wet dress and used the towel to dry my skin. My stomach looked perfect. There was no evidence of any attack, but I was tired of thinking about it. Maybe nothing happened.

Wearing something dry felt like a warm hug. I could smell their washing powder, and it made me think of Fallon. I wondered when my friends had noticed I was gone. They'd be home by now. I hoped they were okay. Ari had drunk the whole drink Brad had given her. I was sure Fallon would have kept her safe.

"Done," I announced, to let Nate know it was safe to look. "Do you know if Fallon and Ari got home okay?"

"Yeah, I heard them chatting upstairs." He scowled. "Why didn't you stick with them?"

"Boy drama," I said, not wanting to worry Nate. I'd put him through enough already tonight, and I was desperate to get to sleep.

"With you?" His jaw twitched.

"A guy Fallon fancied liked Ari."

Nate laughed. "It'll be good for her ego to be taken down a peg or two."

I got in the bed that Nate had made for me. He tucked the blankets around me and kissed me on the cheek.

"You're too good to me."

"I'm glad you called me."

My heart raced with anticipation. I wanted him to kiss me like we had on New Year's Eve.

"Nate, I'm ready," I whispered and wrapped an arm around him, pulling him closer. My forehead pressed against his as I stared into his eyes. This shade of green was fast becoming my favourite colour. "I'm over Jace."

He untangled my arms from around him, and shook his head. His actions didn't make sense. I could see the temptation in his eyes and it made me hungry.

I reached for him. "I need you."

"You're drunk."

I shook my head and pushed my lips up to meet his. The warm passion ran through my body. I remembered my stranger, the way he'd kissed me. The way he filled me with a lust I hadn't felt before. I wanted to feel that with Nate.

"Cut it out, Kiely. Maybe I should let the girls know you're here. You should probably join them." He backed away, creating a distance between us.

"I want to stay here with you." I frowned.

"Fine." He made a separate bed for himself out of blankets on the floor. It didn't look comfortable. It gave me an idea.

"Get in with me?"

He shook his head. "I won't take advantage of you."

"You won't be." I sat up and pulled off my top, revealing myself to him.

He pressed his eyes shut and tensed his jaw. "No. Go to sleep. Sleep it off."

A deep low rumble of a growl coursed out of me in response to the rejection. Despite my exhaustion, I wanted Nate to kiss me and touch me. I wanted to fall asleep in his arms like I had before.

"If you don't go to sleep, I will get your friends and you can start explaining yourself to them."

Frustrated, I put my top back on, got under the covers and turned away from him, facing the back of the sofa, and fell asleep.

CHAPTER 10

Light streamed through the plastic window, waking me from my sleep. I still didn't feel normal, but I wasn't hungover. My skin prickled. The first thing I noticed was the fresh pine smell of the wood and the sharp chemical scent of the hospital that lingered on my skin. As I stirred, I heard two male voices outside. It sounded like Nate was speaking to someone.

I pushed myself up to listen, and as my hand pressed down on the pillow I felt something cold and hard press against my palm. Looking down, I saw that one earring had fallen out. My fingers brushed my earlobes to determine which one was missing it, only to discover I'd lost both. I scrambled through the blankets,

searching for the other one. As I found it, I exhaled a sigh of relief and held the studs while listening to the voices.

Who was Nate speaking to? Was it safe to come out yet?

I tried to put the studs back into my ear, but my fumbling wasn't succeeding at finding the hole. I froze as I recognised the other voice.

What was my brother doing here?

I hurried out of bed and looked through the glass door and saw them speaking. Murray clocked me and pushed past Nate, then pulled the door open. His brows lowered, casting a shadow over his eyes. "Can't you handle your drink?"

"I wasn't drunk!" I said for the hundredth time.

Murray tossed some clothes at me. "You're lucky Nate found you. What if some weirdo had attacked you?"

"Someone did!" I spat.

"Stop lying. Get dressed. I'm taking you home."

My jaw twitched. I felt betrayed by Nate. How else did my brother know where to find me and come with clothes? I got dressed quickly so I could leave, not wanting to spend any longer than I had to with this traitor. Any stupid feelings that had blossomed had violently had their petals ripped off.

He loves me not.

I followed behind Murray. We had to walk through the house. Fallon gave me a look of disgust as I passed her.

"Nothing happened," I begged as I passed.

Fallon shook her head. It was obvious she'd already decided on her own narrative and thought I'd broken her cardinal rule. But after his betrayal, never again. He didn't need to call Murray and tell him where I was. I could have snuck home like all those other times.

We got in the car. Murray started the engine before I'd even clipped my seat belt.

"What's wrong with you?" he snapped. "Why are you acting like a whore?"

"I'm not." I cried, hurt at the injustice of it all. My brother had always had my side. What had Nate told him?

"Just a pretend whore then." His words were laced with sarcasm. "*Pretend* pregnant. *Pretend* spiked drink. *Pretend* attack by a stranger. *Pretend* sleeping with Nate. Any other pretending I've missed?"

"Whatever!" I threw myself back in the seat. What was the point? He'd already made his mind up and wasn't listening to me.

"Pretend, pretend, pretend."

"Shut up!" I stared out the window, wishing I could disappear. I wanted out of my life and far away from all this mess.

"You need to grow up, Kiely. Stop being selfish. Did you even think about how Mum and Dad would feel when they found you missing? They were going out of their minds. They'll want the truth. No more lies!"

I growled in frustration. He was right.

We pulled into the driveway, where Mum and Dad stood on the porch, looking the opposite of a welcome committee. Dad's face was red with anger and Mum's face was pale, long, and sad. Mum hurried forward to hug me. "Are you okay, sweetie?"

"This is not on!" Dad barked. "Sneaking out! What if something had happened to you?"

"I need to sleep."

"Nate said someone spiked your drink? Thank God Nate found you. It doesn't bear thinking about what could've happened." Mum's voice wobbled as she spoke, her hand rising to her mouth.

"I'm fine."

Dad laughed with disbelief. "Why were you out? Why didn't you tell us?"

We moved into the lounge area. I sat on the futon and watched the fish swimming around in the tank. Their life was so simple.

Aero came up to me and placed his head into my lap.

"Well?" Dad demanded.

All I had was the truth. "You wouldn't have let me go!"

"Damn right, I wouldn't. You're sixteen years old! This behaviour shows exactly why you're not mature enough to go out like that."

"But if I told you…"

"No excuses, Kiely!" Dad said. "Murray told us about you lying to get that boy back. Lying about being pregnant? What sort of daughter have I raised?"

I threw Murray a death stare. He hadn't needed to tell them that.

"Did he have sex with you? Do you need contraception?" Mum asked.

I shook my head. "It was a lie, Mum! Made up! Did you miss that part?"

She looked offended, and I realised I'd lost my only sympathiser.

"Don't speak to your mum like that!" My dad placed an arm over her shoulder. "What do you say?"

"Sorry," I swallowed a lump in my throat.

"Go to your room. You're grounded!" Dad shouted.

"Use the time to revise for your exams," Mum added, as if they were helping me.

"I'll be checking on you to make sure you don't pull a stunt like this again," said Dad.

"I'm here if you need to talk," Mum whispered as I left the room.

"Don't be soft on her," Dad snapped at her. "There's no good reason for her behaviour."

I headed up to my room and threw the tattered dress in the bin. Another ruined dress.

I thought back to the one Jace had returned when he dumped me. My life had been spiralling ever since. Was it his fault that everyone now hated me, or mine for all of the terrible choices I'd made because I wasn't ready to let him go?

I stood at the post box where I usually met my friends before walking to school, but they didn't show. I waited in case they were late, but a prickly sensation ran up my back and I accepted that this was intentional.

I needed to go to avoid being late. The rush made me sweaty and out of breath. As I hurried, a relentless glimmer of hope kept me checking over my shoulder for them. The closer I got to school, the more its flame dimmed. By the time I arrived, it'd snuffed out, and I accepted that they'd dumped me.

Entering my homeroom gave me my confirmation. Fallon and Arizona were already there, and they turned their bodies away from me. I sat in my usual spot, despite my friends turning their chairs to block me out.

Slumping over the desk in front of me, I tucked my head into my folded arms. I looked to my side and behind me. I sought Jace out like a bad habit. He scowled at me and then winced with pain from his swollen eye. It was pink around the socket.

Somehow, the bruise made him appear even more attractive. His vibrant blue eyes shone through the inflamed skin. I buried my head in the darkness my arms provided and cursed my heart for its flutter. I needed to get over him.

I wondered why my friends were mad at me. I guessed it was because mine and Nate's secret arrangement had been uncovered. Or had they heard about how Jace got his black eye? Were they still pissed because I left the club without them?

I fought back a lump that was forming in my throat.

I sighed with relief when the bell rang and I could escape to class. As I walked the halls, my paranoia told me my friends weren't the only ones with a problem.

Everyone was staring and whispering.

I arrived at Textiles and found a sewing machine to continue working on my GCSE project. For my final exam, I'd designed a new school uniform and needed to stitch it together. I was eager to get on with my project without the need to talk to anyone. The constant stares made me shift in my seat and my chest tightened. Students huddled together, speaking in low voices and trying to steal glances in my direction.

The bell rang, and everybody left. The tension lifted. I closed my eyes and breathed without the tight feeling across my chest. Break allowed me a few minutes of peace until my next class. I replayed the weekend in my head, trying to make sense of how I got here.

Jace. That was where it had begun.

Nobody saw what he did to me and how much being dumped hurt. They just saw how badly I'd handled it. Since then, everything has gotten worse.

One poor decision after another.

And Nate was another issue. Why did he tell Murray where I was? He could've let me sneak home like all the times before. Nobody needed to know. He claimed he was helping me, but in one night, he'd undone everything. His betrayal hurt the most.

He'd robbed me of my safe place.

In my fury, I texted Nate.

Kiely: Why did you drop me in it?

My phone rang, and Nate's name flashed on my screen, demanding my attention. My hands sweated. I hadn't expected a reply this fast! I had to answer but wasn't ready. If only I could run away, somewhere far away from this stupid school and all my drama. I took off my cardigan to cool down before answering.

"Hi," I said as sweat prickled my armpits.

"Where are you?" Nate demanded.

"In the Textiles workroom," I answered.

"Stay there."

He hung up.

Oh my god! He's coming to see me!

I wanted to be sick. I couldn't deal with this. I switched off my mobile, tossed it into my bag, and pulled up a chair. I fidgeted in my seat, my legs wanting to run, but where would I go? Nate was about to invade the one room in the school where I felt safe. I rummaged in my bag for my deodorant to freshen up and because I needed something to do. The lid popped off and rolled across the floor, adding to my panic. I scrambled across the floor to get it back.

I preferred duels over text, where I was in control of what I wrote and could take my time reading his messages before giving a response. Over mobile, if it got too much, I could hang up, switch off my mobile, or even block his number. There was no escaping face-to-face, and I didn't have anything left to give if he wanted a fight.

Now on my feet, I paced around the room, questioning why I was even bothering to wait. Doing what Nate had told me had already got me into enough trouble. He'd forced himself on me when I was at my weakest, with his promises of help. He'd fed my vulnerability with lies to gain my trust, only to destroy everything when I needed him most. Tears pricked my eyes, and I dabbed them with my sleeve so as not to smudge my makeup.

My heart pounded in my chest when I thought I heard the door, but it was someone passing. I stared at the door, my exit.

Screw it. I was gone.

Walking fast, I fought every urge to run, as I knew that'd only attract unwanted attention. I needed to put as much distance between the workroom and Nate's impending arrival.

I had no idea where I was going. It felt as if there was nowhere safe anymore.

Nobody liked me.

I bit my lip to stop myself from crying, but more tears came. Everyone was judging and mocking me as I passed. Their whispered gossip was like the whooshing sea, taunting me as I hid under a bush and waited to be rescued.

What a fool I was to think Nate could be my hero. I should never have called him.

My tears blurred my vision, making me feel even more vulnerable. I needed to hide.

I ran to the toilets.

And straight into Fallon.

"Look who it is, Ari?" Fallon caught me and roughly pushed my shoulder, but I stepped back and bumped into the wall behind me. "Our former *friend* Kiely."

"What did I do to you?"

Her forehead knitted as she leaned into my face and shouted, "One rule, Kiely! One rule!"

"I don't know…" I mumbled.

Cutting me off with her palm toward my face, Fallon turned to Arizona. "She doesn't know! Did I not make myself clear?"

I knew Nate was a bad idea. I should never have gone there.

Fallon returned her attention to me. "My brother is off limits."

"It's not like that. There's nothing romantic between us."

"I'm not daft. I'm insulted!" She shook her head at me. "Why didn't you tell me? I've always known he likes you. But to sneak around behind my back. At my house? Who do you think you are?"

"I'm sorry."

Fallon laughed, but it was full of sarcasm. She turned to Arizona. "Oh look, she's sorry. She claims nothing was going on, but she's *sorry*."

"Can't we put this behind us?"

"It's not just that." Fallon's eyes blazed as she leaned into me. "I had your back. I always have my friend's back. I'll wear my Mega Bitch badge with honour if that's what standing up for my friends gets me. But you're not my friend anymore. Friends don't keep secrets."

"I was ill. Out of my mind. I didn't even know who I was calling."

Fallon's mouth dropped in disbelief. She looked momentarily lost for words. "You don't even know what this is about."

"Tell me," I begged. I just wanted my friends back. If I knew, I could apologise, and fix this. Maybe.

"Jace was making up this bullshit story that your brother punched him because you said you're pregnant."

My face flushed with shame.

"Oh my god! It's not bullshit, is it?" Fallon's face flushed red with anger.She stepped away and grabbed Arizona's arm. They made to leave, but Fallon stopped and added, "I defended you. I properly laid into Jace for slander. I mean, why would you make that up? Why wouldn't you tell your best friends? Then he throws at me how little I know you. Turns out this weekend wasn't the first time you spent the night with my brother!"

My face burned as I realised Jace had told Fallon about that early morning when he'd seen Nate walking me home. I felt so defeated. There was no coming back from this.

Everything had spiralled out of control and I was exhausted. So over it that I wanted to give up, but didn't know how to.

"Stay away from my brother. Seriously, what might

you lie about next?" She turned and carried on out of the toilets.

I growled with rage. I hated Jace, and I hated Nate. Boys!

Nate had screwed everything up with his stupid idea to sneak around together. His stupid mouth telling my brother we were together and getting me into trouble with my parents. All those times he'd snuck me home before they found out and when I finally had fallen for him, he threw it in my face. What sick game was he playing?

I slammed my fist into the mirror. The glass cracked and as I looked at my distorted image; I noticed that my eyes were glowing a fiery amber like my attacker's. Not that there was an attacker, I'd imagined that. This felt so real. Was it another hallucination?

I blinked, and it was gone. I leaned close and wondered if it was some trick of the light with the way the glass had cracked. At least the distraction had stopped my crying.

I let out a steady breath and inspected my knuckles. There was a deep cut where a shard of glass had broken my skin. I ran my hand under the water to ensure there was no glass in the cut. The knuckle of my middle finger kept bleeding.

I got some toilet paper to wrap around it like a bandage.

I couldn't go to first aid. Whoever was on duty would want to know how I did it and then I'd be in trouble for vandalism. If I stayed here, I'd get caught. I couldn't handle any more drama in my life. I grabbed my bag and hurried into the corridor.

At first, I felt disorientated. I had no idea where I was going. The bell rang ahead. I thought I should go to class, but my mind was spinning. I wandered around until I found myself in the sixth-form area looking for Murray.

When he saw me, he came over without me needing to call him. "Kiely, what are you doing here? What happened?" He reached for my injured hand, clocking it right away.

"Nothing," I swallowed a lump in my throat. Hearing someone care about me was hard. My walls were up and it felt like his kindness was an attack that threatened to weaken my defences.

"Doesn't look like nothing to me," he said, noticing the blood that had bled through the tissue.

I pulled my hand away. "I'm fine."

"There's a first aid kit in my car. Come on." I was thankful to get away from all the watchful eyes wondering why 'the girl that lies' was in their part of the school.

We got into Murray's car. He leaned over from the driver's side to get a little green zipped box from the glove compartment. Removing what he needed - some sterile wipes, plasters, and scissors - Murray reached over and took my hand.

He began unravelling the tissue, but as the last piece came away, he frowned. The tissue was covered in blood, but my hand looked fine. He wiped it with a sterile wipe and looked at me, puzzled.

"Where's the cut?"

"It was right there." I used my other hand to point at my knuckle.

He lifted my hand to my face. My knuckles were clean.

No cuts.

No bruise or redness.

No sign of any damage at all.

I looked at Murray and saw his disapproving look as he shook his head. "Kiely, I'm sorry I've been caught up with my own stuff and not been there for you. You need help. The lying isn't good."

"I'm not lying. It really was bleeding. Look." I pointed to the bloodied tissue.

"There's no cut." He reached over and gently turned my hand over. His face softened. "Look, I have no lectures this afternoon. I'm taking you home before you get yourself into any more trouble. You're taking a sick day and talking to Mum about all of this. She's worried about you, and rightfully so."

Murray didn't say another word as he buckled up, and I followed suit. He frowned, and I could tell he was a mixture of mad and concerned.

He was right. I needed help. I'd have sworn the mirror cut my hand. But if it hadn't, where did the blood come from? It made me think about the night with the attacker, and the vanishing wound on my stomach.

I wasn't under the influence of anything, so what was causing this?

Murray didn't take me home. Instead, we headed to the café that Mum ran.

Murray's car crunched over the gravel as he parked up in a parking bay closest to the cafe. He placed his parking permit in the window and we got out. I raised my hand up to stop the wind blowing my hair into my eyes. The air was alive with the gulls squawking and the ringing of ferry boats mooring.

The bell above the door rang as we entered the cafe. Mum looked up and frowned when she saw it was us. We took a seat by the door. I picked at my nail varnish while we waited for her to come over.

Mum pressed both hands down on the table and leaned in close. "What are you doing out of school?"

"Kiely is feeling the wrath of her lies," Murray answered for me.

Mum's brows dipped as she looked to Murray for an explanation.

"Fallon and I have fallen out." The words felt heavy, and my jaw jutted out.

Mum twisted back to Murray. "Bunking off isn't the answer."

"Sorry," we both mumbled.

Mum locked eyes with me. Her brow wrinkled. She took a deep breath and sighed, then said, "Wait here. I'll get you both an ice cream float."

Mum returned to the counter and made our drinks. The café was quiet. I guess midweek term time wasn't a busy period.

"Are you going to tell her? It'll sound better coming from you," Murray prompted.

"Tell her what?"

"About the compulsive lying."

"I wasn't lying. My hand was—"

Murray grabbed me roughly by the wrist, pulling my hand up to my face. "Does it look cut to you?"

My heart thundered as he forced me to look at my unmarked hand. When he let go, my hand dropped to the table. I didn't want to tell Mum. Telling her would be like admitting I was crazy. "Please drop it. I'll sort myself out. Promise."

"Wow, getting dumped *really* messed you up," Murray said as he looked out the window.

"Are you still upset over that boy?" Mum had caught the tail end of what Murray had said as she placed our drinks in front of us.

I stirred my drink with the straw. Was that what this was? My mind's way of coping with the pain of getting dumped. Was I visualising it as injuries to make sense of my pain? Every time I calmed down, it transpired to be nothing.

Mum brushed my hair from my face and behind my ear, causing me to look at her. "There's someone better for you. Someone you haven't met yet."

Her words felt like a warm blanket on a cold winter night and filled me with hope.

Mum had the power to bring my walls crumbling down in an undignified way that Fallon would have cursed me for. Hot tears burned down my face, and I quickly hid behind my hands.

Mum took the seat next to mine and pulled me into her arms. The smell of grease from the morning breakfasts lingered on her clothes, but underneath the soothing scent of lavender and neroli crept through. I breathed her in while she rubbed my back.

"There, there," she soothed.

I tried to speak, to apologise for making a spectacle of myself. But the sound came out as garbled nonsense.

Mum kissed my head as if she'd understood, "It's okay. He wasn't smart enough to know how lucky he was, but one day you'll meet someone who does. I promise."

Her words rubbed off on me like the salve to my wounds. As I calmed down, she released me and Murray handed me some napkins to blot my tear-stained face. I cringed as I saw black blotches on the tissues and could only imagine how ridiculous I must look.

"Can you take her home, Murray? I've got to work. I'll let the school know Kiely's unwell." Mum kept her eyes on me the whole time, stroking my hair.

"Sure." Murray got up.

Mum winked at me. "I'll cook your favourite tonight."

"Really?" Shepherd's pie wasn't quick to make.

Mum nodded. "Yeah, it's quiet here, so I'll prep it between orders. And you and I need to plan some mother-and-daughter time. Does that sound good?"

"You don't have to."

"I want to." Mum squeezed my hand.

"Thanks." I smiled.

Mum pinched my chin. "There's my beautiful girl's smile."

I rolled my eyes. I was sure that my blotchy face, puffy eyes, and ruined makeup were anything but beautiful. But she always knew how to make me feel a bit better.

Mum pulled us both into a group hug before letting us go. "I'll be home as soon as I can."

CHAPTER 11

M UM'S CHAT HAD REJUVENATED ME, and being off school had lifted some of the pressure. The need to upkeep my image, to act like everything was fine, the effort it took to pretend I wasn't breaking inside. It was such a relief to have a break from it all.

I thought about what Fallon had said. Not the negative stuff, but the stuff about work placements. I tried to figure out what I wanted to do with my life. The concept of thinking about what I wanted for a change felt very foreign. I spent so much time worrying about what other people wanted from me and doing what they said I needed to do, that I rarely allowed myself to think about my wants or needs.

Over the last few months, I'd been obsessed with boys. Fallon had me believe her crazy theory that I needed a boyfriend. Maybe that was why, without Jace, I felt so lost. I'd made myself all about him so that I didn't know who I was anymore.

Had Nate tried to mould me into someone he wanted? As angry as I was at him for betraying me, I didn't feel like he'd controlled me. He'd always been there for me. And maybe the reason I was so mad at him was because he didn't control me. He'd made me believe I had power over him.

Then, of his own free will, he did something I didn't like. Something that made no sense.

Yet, here I was trying to think about my future and somehow my mind had diverted back to boys. I collapsed on my bed. I was a lost cause.

Grabbing my mobile phone, I decided to look up 'career choices'.

Unlocking my mobile was like opening Pandora's box. My phone began displaying a ton of messages from people I barely knew. They'd tagged me in stuff on social media.

One picture of me, someone had altered it to make my nose look extended. The caption said '*Pino-Kiely*'. I knew it was a play on the name Pinocchio and to make fun of the lies I told. There was another animated meme picture of an elephant's body with my face. I didn't get the joke, but people were laughing and saying how pathetic I was for lying. I checked another app. Someone had put a toy fluffy bunny in a pan of boiling water and added the caption 'Watch out for Kiely!' It had got a ton of likes for some reason.

People were commenting on how much they hated liars, and that I should die. Someone made up that I'd claimed that Jace raped me. I couldn't ignore it and quickly hashed out a reply.

I never said that.

Someone replied with a meme saying: "*Oh, what a lie!*"

It's the truth.

Someone posted a pic from an old TV Show with the caption: "*The lie detector determined that was a lie.*"

Nasty messages started streaming in...

Just Kill Yourself!

**laughing emoji* Would you believe her if she did?*

Not until maggots have eaten her eyes lol

Someone posted an animated skull with worms wriggling in the sockets.

The bad ones never die - she's like Jason from Halloween.

Jason from Halloween gif

I tossed my phone away, unable to read anymore. My chest was tight as the room spun. My fingers ran through my hair and held clumps of my strands.

No. No. No.

How many people had Jace told? Why couldn't anyone see that he'd lied first? He said he wasn't with Mariah when he was. He hurt me. I only did it to get back at him. Nobody cared. They're making stuff up, awful stuff about me. I can't win.

I pressed my palms against my chest and closed my

eyes. I needed to calm down before I had another one of my hallucinations.

Drawing in a long breath through my nose, I counted to five before releasing it. It was a relaxation technique we'd been shown during an assembly to help us with managing exam stress. I kept repeating the technique until my hands stopped shaking.

It reminded me that high school was almost over. All I had to do was get through my exams, and then I could move away from this small-minded town forever.

Where could I go? Maybe somewhere abroad. Except, I'd never done well with foreign languages so I'd have to choose an English-speaking country. Or maybe I could stay in the UK but somewhere far away from here. I'd always fancied Scotland. The flight would be cheaper and it would be easier to travel home to visit if I wanted. The more I thought about it, the more I wished I could go now. If only I had wings.

When Mum came home, she came straight to my room to give me a hug. I could tell she'd been worried about me all day.

"How are you feeling?" She handed me a butterfly cake.

"Not great." I didn't want to mention the messages. If I did, I'd have to confess about all the lies and how out of control everything had got. I peeled the bun out of the case, and took a bite. It was too sweet for how I felt. It made me feel sick.

I discarded it on my bedside table.

"Kiely, it's okay to hurt. It's part of the healing process. It might feel hard now, but it will get easier.

Just hang in there."

I thought about how Jace had hurt me and how Nate had betrayed me. "You don't need to worry about me, Mum. I'm done with guys."

Mum pulled me close for a hug. "Good, you're all mine."

I didn't want to go back to school. Mum and Dad had already left for work, so nobody was chasing me out the door. I was taking my time, trying to stall the inevitable.

"Kiely, you're going to be late," Murray called from the bathroom, leaving his reflection to look at me.

I groaned. "I don't want to go."

Aero sniffed my fingers and let me pat his head. I crouched next to him, nuzzling my head into his neck. He was usually full of energy, but recently it was like he sensed that I needed his affection and he kept trying to be close to me and lying at my feet.

"You can't bunk off again. Mum won't keep covering for you, and I'll tell her everything."

"Don't blackmail me."

"I'm offering you a lift to school."

I groaned and lifted my school bag. This wasn't an argument I would win. We didn't speak during the drive.

The radio played, but the songs weren't connecting with me. Still, getting a lift was better than walking, especially knowing my friends wouldn't be waiting for me.

As he pulled into the school car park, he said, "Did you see the posts online?"

"Yeah, it's stupid." My chest felt tight. I crossed my arms and stared out of the window. Not looking at anything in particular, but just avoiding looking at Murray. I didn't want to leave the car. I wanted to delay facing what was waiting for me inside the school.

"I think you should tell Mum and Dad about it. They could let the school know."

I shook my head. "No. I don't want to involve them. Let me just sit my exams and be done with school."

Murray sighed. "You'll get through this. Just keep your head down low."

I picked up my bag, but my hand froze on the door handle. "I don't wanna go in."

Murray added sternly, "Suck it up. This is what you get for lying."

I tensed my jaw. I didn't need Murray to be on my case, too.

"You can fuck off, too!"

I got out of the car and gave the door a hard slam. I knew that would piss him off.

"Oi!"

I heard him yell, but I stormed off. He called after me, but I wasn't stopping to hear him berate me any longer.

I walked into my homeroom and was greeted by the chant, "Kiely, Kiely, pants on fire." Followed by laughter. It was so childish I couldn't help but roll my eyes. I tried to ignore the chants and laughter and sunk into a spare seat at the front of the classroom. As much as I tried to ignore it, it still hurt. Reacting was like feeding the beast. I made sure I didn't look toward where my former friends sat or to the other corner where Jace was. It was like wearing blinkers.

I was in survival mode, taking each day as it came. Get through today, then tomorrow, and before I knew it, I'd have made it through an entire week. It wouldn't be long before we'd sit our exams, and I'd be done with this place.

Registration was a blur, and as I walked down the corridors to my lessons, people bumped into me on purpose. A group of younger students held their fists over their noses. I guessed it was some joke to do with lying, and I pretended not to notice. To appear numb. But inside, I was struggling to hold it together.

In class, I heard the teacher speaking, but my mind was so busy it was a mumble. The words on the page were hard to read, as I couldn't focus.

With no friends, I tried to block the world out.

During breaks, I wandered the corridors, making sure I wasn't anywhere long enough for anyone to approach me. I didn't dare go to the loo in case someone came after me. The judgemental stares were everywhere. Their whispers became a constant white noise.

Although they thought they were being quiet, I caught bits of what they were saying.

Liar!

Bitch!

Their words stayed with me, running on repeat. Some I deserved. Others were cruel.

She's not even that pretty.

Jace is way hotter.

By the time I got home, I was bursting for the loo. As I relieved myself, I burst into tears. My stomach was in pain from holding it in for so long, and it exhausted me not giving them the satisfaction of seeing me cry.

Even though we'd fallen out, I'd noticed that Fallon and Arizona hadn't joined in. Fallon was never shy about voicing her opinion. Since our last fight, she'd been quiet. They wanted nothing to do with me, not even to mock me. I'd kept out of their way. But I missed them. I wanted to go back in time and undo what I did. To make it right. But it was too late. It'd become too big. There was no way to fix this.

I was relieved my parents were still working, and Murray was out. Aero laid his head on my lap as I sat on the sofa. He whined like he could sense my sadness.

"Sorry," I apologised for bringing him down. It was another thing to feel guilty about. I was making my dog depressed.

The school days were hard, but I kept attending them. The teachers were covering the final prep for our exams and top tips for passing. It was the time in between classes that was hard. It made me wish to be homeschooled. During my breaks, I walked the corridors, as it was better to keep moving than be a stationary target.

Jace approached me. His left eye looked worse than the other day, with a fresh new bruise. The dark purple made the green of his eyes look more vibrant. I wanted to touch it and comfort him. A twang of guilt for how I'd tricked Murray into punching him gnawed at my insides. I wondered who else Jace had pissed off to get punched again.

"Sorry," he said.

The simple word churned up so many emotions. It hurt me because it was too late for an apology. Too much had happened since our break up that nothing either of us could say would heal this. All that remained was anger.

He looked sad. "Now, can we just leave each other alone and move on?"

Just move on?

I felt like he'd repeatedly screwed me over, and now, with just one word, he wanted me to forget all the hurt. Forget that he'd cheated on me. Forget that he kissed me and then dumped me right after. He'd cut me so deep that those scars would last forever. I wanted nothing more than to move on and for him to never have happened, but my heart just kept hanging on to these memories. Memories where he had made me believe I was the only one for him. It was those lies that hurt the most because I believed them and wanted them to be true. He made me feel stupid.

"You've turned everyone against me. Why couldn't you keep your mouth shut?"

"The truth comes easily to me. You should try it."

"Are you serious?"

He pointed to his black eye. "Look what you did?"

"That's nothing to do with me?"

"Nate, this time. I guess he's your boyfriend now. Good luck to him." Jace raised his voice. People stopped and looked our way. My face burned up. I didn't want any more attention.

"I told you Nate and I are nothing." I lowered my voice, hoping he'd follow suit or shut up.

"You keep sending people after me!"

I wasn't sending people after him. I'd lied once to get Murray to hit him. That was it. I regretted it, too. I wasn't even speaking to Nate. There was no reason for him to go after Jace.

Jace was still acting like he was the sole victim in all of this, and that infuriated me.

"You lied about Mariah!"

He looked taken aback and confused. I couldn't stand the dopey look on his face. Without thinking, my hand slapped his cheek. I gasped as I realised what I had done.

Then I heard a voice that sent a chill down my spine. "Look! Now Princess Kiely is a man beater."

Before I turned, I knew a mobile screen would greet me. My eyes filled with tears, unable to hold it in anymore. The taunts were too much, and a fresh surge of hate was coming for me.

There was a gasp and someone else added, "Jace, did she give you that black eye?"

I couldn't survive another day of this. Tears streamed down my face, blurring my vision, but I kept running. The more I ran, the better I felt. It made me feel powerful, unstoppable, and I didn't tire. I was stunned when I arrived home in record time. It felt inhuman.

Everyone was out but Aero. He followed me up to my room. I fell onto my bed and cried into my pillow. Aero laid on the floor next to my bed, waiting for me to get it out of my system. I wondered if anyone had noticed that I'd gone. I made the mistake of looking at my phone.

The notifications were creeping up at a rapid rate. They'd tagged me in the video of me slapping Jace. I untagged myself, but within seconds someone tagged me again.

Then they posted a new version cut to show the end when I cried with the comment: *"The girl that cried wolf."*

I untagged myself and reported it. It got posted again, this time with the comment: *"The girl that cried rape."*

People were posting comments with their reactions:
OMG Jace was apologising, and she hit him!
How could she?

Do you think it's okay for girls to hit boys?
LOL that ugly crying face.
I felt sorry for you, but now you can die for all I care!

Over the next few days, I tried my best to stay out of people's way, skipping lunch to avoid staying in one place. I wasn't hungry, anyway. Although, my body didn't agree. It grumbled in class and ached, but I'd learned not to rest my hand on my stomach to soothe it. It attracted taunts like, "Who's the daddy this time?" or "Is your phantom baby kicking?"

The last straw was some year sevens throwing condoms at me. The square foil packets felt sharp as one of them hit my face. They all laughed until a teacher stepped in. "Cut that out or I'll exclude you from future Sex and Relationship Education classes."

Whilst they were being disciplined, I slunk off. I needed to get out of school fast. My hair fell around my face, protecting my face from prying eyes that might take pleasure in seeing me cry. I kept swallowing to prevent the tears and beeline for the nearest exit.

"Oi, Kiely! Wait up!" Fallon called. I looked up and saw her ahead with Arizona.

Knowing how Fallon treated her enemies, I turned on my heels and picked up my pace.

I was barely out of the building, and my phone was already ringing. Expecting it to be Fallon, it surprised me to see her brother's name flash on the screen. I put my phone on silent so he couldn't bother me anymore. Not now. If my ex-friends caught up with me and saw Nate was calling, it would only exacerbate things.

Once out of the building, I ran. Running was easy now. Was it all the pain and anger that fuelled me? I'd never been good at track or any sport that was cardio-based, but now my body loved it. It pumped me full of endorphins, and by the time I reached home, I was already feeling better.

I dumped my schoolbag on the kitchen counter and got myself a glass of cold water from the fridge. Aero came and sat next to me like I was his master. He was usually only this well-behaved for my dad, but I was enjoying being someone's number one person. I got some treats out of the cupboard to thank him for being there for me.

My mobile slid out of my bag. A text notification lit up my phone. Nate's name repeated over and over. What did he want? Why pester me? He'd called my brother and betrayed me. Ensured our secret meetings came to an end. He couldn't tell me to my face that he wasn't into me anymore, that he'd been put off. He had to go behind my back and ruin the trust we'd built. What could he possibly want? I swiped his message open.

Nate: Your parents found out you hadn't come home and were calling around.

Nate: Tom told people we went to A&E.

Nate: Murray figured you were with me and wanted to know why I hadn't brought you home.

Nate: I told Murray I was worried about you. Which is true. I am.

Nate: If it wasn't for Jace stirring people up, nobody would have thought any more about it!

Nate! Tom! Murray! Jace! Boys were bigger gossips than any girl I knew. I hated them all. Seeing their names felt like someone had poured boiling hot bubbling rage down my throat. It steamed up, rising out of me, scorching my eyes, and hot tears ran down my face. But instead of burning me, it soothed me. It felt like a pressure tap had opened and I let it go. The corset of pain that had been suffocating me all day was loose. I could breathe a little easier.

I didn't care if the school contacted Mum, or if students said I left for attention. It didn't matter because I was never going back. School was over for me. I tried. I had enough information from my classes that I was sure I could revise at home, use my study guidebooks, and pass my exams. Then I would get as far away from this stupid town as I could.

With a search engine open, I researched my options. I'd make sure that by the time my parents learned about my truancy, I'd already have a plan. There was no way

I was returning to that school full of hate, except to sit my exams. It was time to think about my future, and I didn't see this town having any part of it.

The wind was taken out of my sails when I saw someone had uploaded the condom incident and set off a new tirade of abuse. Students were now making memes about my lack of sex education knowledge. They were saying I thought I was pregnant from some other sexual act and somehow, that had spiralled into a crude debate about how I actually could be pregnant without having intercourse. Some defended me, suggesting I'd possibly miscarried. But that angered those who believed Jace and his claims we'd never had sex.

It wasn't only me getting attacked. Yes, my lies had gotten Jace punched, but he was also getting negative attention. Some people accused him of lying and dumping me because I was pregnant. The rumour mill was on hyper-drive.

What a mess! What a terrible mess. How would I ever make this right?

Reading all the accusations and theories was exhausting. The damage kept building. I tried to stop reading, but it was like a car crash and I couldn't look away. My energy was so depleted that I kept scrolling, unable to defend myself.

I felt bad for Jace. Maybe he did deserve an apology from me. If I'd gracefully accepted our breakup and moved on, I could have avoided all this. My lies had made things so much worse. He may have blabbed about how he got his black eye, but he didn't owe me anything.

I couldn't blame him. Why should he cover for me? I'm nothing to him. Nothing to anyone.

The hurtful words that people had posted swam around in my head and ate at my soul.

Hearing the front door made me freeze. I didn't want anyone to see me crying or challenge me about why I wasn't in school. I ran to the bathroom, locked the door, and got in the shower, allowing the warm water to wash away my tears.

There was a knock at the bathroom door that caused me to jump. My razor jutted sharply across my skin. It stung, and I cursed under my breath.

But the shock pulled me together.

"Kiely, is that you?" Mum asked.

It was a stupid question. She could hear the running water and figure out I was in the shower. If she opened her eyes, she'd see my school bag. But I was in no mood to speak to anyone, so I ignored her.

I watched the cut swell with blood and then flow down my leg. It mixed with the water and washed away.

I squeezed shampoo into my hand and scrunched it into my hair.

"Kiely, you can't keep skipping school," Mum began, but her voice softened when she said, "Is it that boy?"

I pretended not to hear and enjoyed letting the warm water wash the shampoo out.

She knocked again. Then her knocks became more persistent. "Kiely, answer me now."

"Yes. It's me." I hoped that would satisfy her and she'd leave me alone.

My leg was bleeding. I hobbled out of the shower to get some tissue paper to dab the cut. The bright red stream trickled down my ankle to the pad of my foot. I grabbed some tissues to dab it away, but it was bleeding fast and had already dripped onto the floor. I pressed the paper against my cut and held it there, enjoying the sting. It stung like the vicious words people had posted online about me.

The silver blade of my razor winked at me, and I had a sudden urge to do it on purpose. To just silence it all. I got back in the shower and sat on the floor, no longer concerned about a tiny cut. It was nothing compared to what I was contemplating.

Would anyone notice? Would anyone care if I was gone?

"Kiely, open this door right now!" Mum ordered with urgency.

Mum and Dad might miss me?

Murray might regret being so controlling.

Jace might regret breaking my heart.

Fallon and Arizona might see how they failed as my friends, when I needed them most.

And all those wicked tongues that had said those ugly words might see the extent of their actions.

But what hurt me the most was the thought that they might not care.

Maybe I wasn't that important. Maybe I was

nothing to them, just a waste of space that sucked up time in their precious lives.

Everyone would be better off without me. Without my stupid lies.

Some lies hadn't felt like lies, they'd been so real. Like my attacker, who slashed open my stomach. But it wasn't real. My stomach was fine. Just like my knuckles weren't cut by the mirror at school. My glance lowered to my ankle. No cut!

I was losing it. No longer the girl I once was. Insane.

Catching my reflection in the mirror, my wet hair clung to my wet body. I shivered from the cold. My hand pressed the razor against my wrist. Daring myself to do it.

End it all. Be done with this.

My eyes flashed a golden orange.

I gasped and dropped the razor.

I got out of the shower to look at my eyes more closely. They were a beautiful amber but with a slight glow, breathtaking and unreal looking. This had to be more craziness. I took a deep breath. If I could calm myself down, everything would return to normal.

Then I noticed something else. Something strange.

My ear lobes were no longer pierced. I'd forgotten all about putting the earrings back in after they'd fallen out. Now, my earlobes were ordinary, smooth, and without a hole. It was as if they'd never been pierced. They couldn't have closed up that fast. *Could they?*

Then I noticed the bloody tissue in the bin. My blood. Except my body showed no evidence of a cut.

This was impossible. Nobody could heal that fast, but what if I did?

What if I'm not crazy?

"Open this door, Kiely, or I will unscrew it!"

"No! No! I'm almost done." My voice wobbled.

I saw the nail scissors on the windowsill and grabbed them. I pressed the sharp point against my palm. I wanted to test my theory, but what if I was wrong? A few minutes ago I wanted to be dead, so why was I hesitating over this? I grounded my teeth. Why couldn't I just do it? It made me hate myself even more. This was going to hurt.

The bathroom door burst open.

"Shit!"

The scissors jutted in my hand and broke the soft skin of my palm. Red blood quickly washed over my pale skin.

"For Christ's sake, Kiely!" The fresh cut tingled as she pulled the scissors from my hand and bundled a towel around my wounded palm.

"What on earth are you thinking?"

She pulled another towel off the rail and draped it over my shoulders.

"I'm fine, Mum!" I pulled the towel tighter around me.

Mum's eyes welled up with tears. She pulled me into her arms for a hug, squeezing me tightly against her. "I'm sorry. I didn't know it was this bad. Please, don't do that. If you're hurting, talk to me. I beg you. Please. Please, Kiely."

Mum led me out of the bathroom to her room. She got the first aid kit out so she could tend to my wound. I peeled back the towel she'd wrapped around it and could see my palm was already fine.

My body bubbled with excitement. I wasn't crazy. I had rapid healing. "Mum, I'm fine."

Her brows dipped with worry. "You're not fine. Fine never means fine. Cutting yourself isn't fine."

I waved my hand at her. "Look, no cut."

She looked stunned at my clean hand. She came forward and turned it over and then checked my other hand. "But… I saw you cut yourself."

I shook my head. "Is that what you thought you saw?"

She held up the towel. "What is this?"

There were red blotches on the towel. I shrugged. "I don't know. Maybe the towel was already dirty."

Mum frowned and checked me over, but there wasn't even a scratch on my body. She let out a long sigh and sat down next to me. "I'm so worried about you. I don't know what I saw. It looked like… Maybe we should see if the school has any resources to help. You still haven't told me why you're not at school?"

My head dropped. "I couldn't take it anymore."

"Did something happen?"

I tried to think of a version suitable for my mum's ears. "I moved on from Jace with someone new. Fallon got mad."

"You fell out over a boy?"

"Sort of…" I admitted and swallowed a lump in my

throat. "I got close to Nate, and Fallon didn't like it."

"What a silly thing to fall out over." She shook her head, put her arm around my shoulders, and leaned in close to whisper, "Do you like him?"

I shrugged. "I don't know."

Mum kissed my head. "She'll come around. I'm glad you're moving on from Jace, but make sure you're ready before you start something new. You can't rush a broken heart."

CHAPTER 12

I'D WOKEN IN A COLD SWEAT. Despite my high temperature, I got the impression that nobody would believe I was unwell. It seemed rapid healing wasn't any good for a fever. Keeping quiet and out of everyone's way, I stayed off school. I also stayed offline so I wouldn't see what people were posting about me.

Once I was certain that everyone was gone, I dressed and took Aero out for a walk. I was thankful that for once he walked calmly next to me. Usually, he was so eager that he would pull me along, but tonight it felt like the dog was taking me for a walk.

Today, he understood my need for companionship and care. His tongue hung out the side of his mouth, making him look goofy, while his adorable big brown

eyes kept looking up at me as if seeking praise.

We headed along the cliff tops toward the beach. The crashing waves rolled against the shore, drowning out my thoughts. The chill of the sea air soothed my high temperature. It felt good to be outside. Despite it being winter, I wore shorts and a vest, fighting against the scorching heat of my body.

Crows lined the beach huts, keeping the seagulls at bay. They must have been migrating, as it was unusual to see so many in the area.

Although, I was sure crows weren't a seasonal bird.

Sitting on the beach, pebbles pushed into my palms as I leaned back. Spending the day here had been the right thing. I still wasn't interested in food, but I felt peaceful.

Aero ran back and forth with his ball, asking me to throw it over and over. We did this for a while until the game bored him and he settled down beside me, panting. He pressed his black fur against my leg.

It was nice not thinking about all the crap going on in my life. For the first time in ages, I felt safe. Closing my eyes, I relived happy memories that now caused me pain, like when I'd been here with Jace. I remembered the way he'd looked at me in the early days of our relationship. The way I knew he wanted to kiss me, but fear of rejection held him back.

It was the same fear that held me back; a fear that maybe I'd read it wrong, and he didn't want to kiss. We spent weeks flirting with each other, almost kissing, daring to hold hands. Those agonising moments were something I longed to experience again. But it pained me to acknowledge that all it took was one kiss, and we were over.

I remembered our only kiss. The kiss I'd waited so long for. The kiss that destroyed us.

We stood pressed against each other. My heart raced with anticipation of what was to come. The lights danced across his face. He kept looking at my lips, and I knew what he was thinking. Our bodies swayed to the music, but it was a distant sound.

As our faces drew closer, all I could feel, hear, and smell was Jace. Our lips met and the fire from our kiss raced through my body, making every part of me alert and desperate for more of him. My fingers ran through his blond hair, holding onto him and never wanting to let him go.

But he broke away.

A breeze blew between us. I opened my eyes to meet his, but he was looking off to the side. I followed his gaze to an open door. A wild wind and rain tore through the doors, blowing the heavy curtain into the legs of those standing close by.

There was my brother. Matching the storm's temperament, his shirt ripped open as he raced outside, calling her name. "Mariah!"

"What happened?" I'd asked.

"I don't know. I think he hurt her." Jace's jaw twitched.

Jace claimed to be just friends with Mariah, but they were inseparable. Even when he wasn't with her, it felt like his world still revolved around her. It was Jace's favourite topic, even when I'd confided how it made me jealous. He laughed and told me I had nothing to worry about. I should have trusted my instincts.

"Why would he hurt her?" I swallowed a lump in my throat, seeing how easily she stole his attention from our moment.

"Come on." He pulled my hand toward the door. But a teacher was already locking it and shaking their head.

"This way." Jace pulled me in another direction.

We hurried out of the hall. In the corridor, we could still hear the music, but it was fainter, almost reflecting the way I was being muted out by Mariah. We reached the main doors, still holding hands. Jace tugged me out into the pouring rain, but I squealed in disgust and resisted. I tugged him back under the shelter.

"I'm not going out in that. I'll get soaked." This wasn't any ordinary rain. It was hard hailstones, icy bullets biting my skin.

Jace looked at me, then over his shoulder, like someone was pulling him away. Torn between her and me. I willed him to stay. I knew the choice he was making, but we'd just shared our first kiss.

I begged and squeezed his hand. "Please. Let's go back inside. Wait."

Jace shook his head and pulled his hand away. "I can't. I have to know she's alright."

"You don't know where she is!"

"I'll find her."

"Don't do this to me."

He pulled a face as if I'd confused him. Like he didn't see what he was doing. I saw it. The moment he chose her.

Wrapping my arms around my body and shaking my head, I didn't want to believe it.

Now, as I look back, I see it clear as day. I wonder if he knew too. Even though he came back and rubbed my arms, reassuring me that he wouldn't be long. I begged for him to let them sort it out, my brother and Mariah. I begged and pleaded shamelessly, in a way I knew Fallon would have lectured me on.

He'd chosen her. He would always choose her.

Pulling me from my thoughts, I heard voices. I snuck between some beach huts, out of sight, and looked for another way out. I didn't want to be seen, in case word got back to my parents or the school that I was bunking. Although the fresh air had done me good, and I was feeling better, I needed more time for myself.

Aero and I headed up another set of steps and walked along the clifftops. As I reached the car park, I saw a familiar car. I glanced inside. There was his swim bag, hooded sweater, and a spare pair of trainers in the back. It was Murray's car.

What's he doing here?

Perhaps he'd noticed I was missing and was looking for me. I peeped over the edge, looking down toward the beach to confirm that it was him. My heart twisted when I saw who he was with. A girl with curly red hair. The very one that had screwed up my life.

Why are they together? I thought she was with Jace.

Does he even know they are hanging out?

If Mariah had stayed with Murray, then Jace and I would be happy. Mariah disgusted me with the way she flitted between whatever boy she wanted.

I felt betrayed by my brother. He knew how heartbroken I was because of her actions. Why couldn't he hate her with me instead of having some kind of secret rendezvous with *her!*

Pulling out my mobile, I took a snap of them together. I'd confront Murray about it later. I kept spying, trying to make out what they were saying, but I was too far away. It looked like they were arguing. Murray didn't look happy. I hid between two beach huts so they didn't spot me.

My brother's open shirt made my stomach twist. It gave their meeting a less innocent feel. They were standing so close, only a breath apart. My brother had a reputation for messing girls around. Maybe he was getting her back for me.

I hope he breaks her heart and Mariah gets what she deserves.

Oh my gosh! Her hands are on his chest!

A wicked smile filled my face as I hit record and held my breath in anticipation. A kiss was coming. As much as I wanted to punch Murray for it, it'd be the end of Mariah and Jace. They'd break up, and I'd swoop in and be there for him. Any moment now, I'd have all I needed to get Jace back. The idea made me feel a little giddy.

But my brother did something I hadn't expected. The notorious player broke away and ran up the steps. Mariah stood there looking lost and dejected. She wrapped her arms around herself and waited for

Murray to call her up before she followed.

I felt gutted. Cheated.

I hadn't got what I needed. An almost kiss wouldn't be enough.

What are you playing at, Murray?

Once again, my idiot brother had let me down. All he had to do was be himself and screw Mariah around. But no, not today. I could feel the darkness returning and all the peace my relaxing day had brought being erased.

Aero and I walked home, weaving between the beach huts to prevent being seen. I had to get home before my brother discovered that Aero was gone. If he found out I'd bunked school, he was bound to tattle to Mum and Dad.

Once in, I made Aero a fresh bowl of water. My phone was full of notifications that I was sure were malicious. I replayed the video. They hadn't kissed, but as I watched it back, it was obvious something more was going on between them. It didn't look platonic.

I made a fake account and uploaded it to social media. I tagged the biggest gossips I knew in school and hoped it would garner enough interest so I'd be old news.

My fever got worse. There was no hiding my suffering, but at least my parents could see I wasn't faking it. Mum changed my bed daily to keep up with the sweats and popped home whenever it was quiet in the cafe to check on me. The GP advised me to stay in bed, rest, stay hydrated, and take ibuprofen until it passed. Mum kept checking my temperature, complaining to the doctor, and threatening to take me to A&E. The doctor kept insisting it was just my body fighting an infection and not much more that could be done.

Even though I felt rubbish, it was refreshing to have a break from school. People shared the video of Murray and Mariah and gossiped about what it meant. It must have reached Jace, because his online status changed to single.

But it didn't satisfy me the way I thought it would. The sabotage felt sneaky. Not something to be proud of. There was relief that I was no longer *the* hot topic, but I felt guilty for hurting Jace. Browsing online was all I felt up to as I laid in bed feeling bad, scrolling through my phone.

My symptoms were worse at night once everyone else had gone to bed. I'd burn up and kick my covers off. My skin felt tight, like it was too small for my body. I kept scratching, wishing I could peel it away and be free of its confines. The dampness from my sweat sent a chill through my body despite the raging heat. I got out of bed and paced the room in my nightdress, frustrated that I couldn't sleep. Mum brought me a loose, white, cotton nightgown in the hopes that it would help keep me cool.

I opened the window to let in some air. The milky moon captured my vision, its presence soothing my mind as if it were speaking to me. My body ached as if I'd aged these past days. My muscles were stiff, my bones felt locked, and my skin was too tight. I gulped my glass of water as I paced up and down.

My bedroom felt claustrophobic. The walls were closing in on me, the space too small, and the air stale. I needed to be free. I had to get out.

I stretched out my window and climbed out onto the tiles. Clambering across, I made my way onto the kitchen roof. The house looked dark and foreboding. Everyone was asleep, which gave the impression of nobody at home.

I felt detached from everyone around me. Like I didn't belong anymore. I was no longer a part of my social circle and my family seemed alien to me. Nobody understood what I was going through. I couldn't tell them, as I didn't even understand myself.

I shimmied along the tiles to the edge and turned to crawl down the drainpipe as I'd done when I'd snuck out to see Nate. But I hesitated, gripped by an urge to jump. Fuelled by a primal instinct I couldn't deny, I leaped from the roof and landed on all fours.

The impact felt good. I felt strong as I rose from my crouched position. After days of lying in bed feeling sorry for myself, it felt good to be outdoors. There was a thrill in being bad. Doing something I knew my parents wouldn't approve of.

Aero detected my presence. He came out of the dog flap and whined for me to take him. The hairs on my arm bristled as I realised, if he started barking and woke everyone up, then I'd get caught.

"Shh! Shh! Alright, you can come with me."

Aero jumped into my arms and licked my face. I laughed at his enthusiasm and told him to hush. How did he have this much energy so late at night? I embraced him and buried my head in his neck, breathing him in.

I couldn't get his lead, but I didn't think it'd be a problem. Recently, he'd stayed by my side when I'd walked him. It was like we were in tune on a different level from everyone else. Plus, going back into the house risked drawing attention that I was up.

I led Aero out through the side gate and out onto the road. I began jogging, Aero jogged alongside me. His big, dark eyes glistened as he looked up at me.

"You're a good dog, aren't you?" His tongue hung out the side of his mouth as he panted with anticipation. "Are you ready to run?"

Back in the house, I felt like I was dying. I'd struggled to breathe, sticky with sweat, the walls suffocating me. Now my whole body was eager to move, and I needed to go harder and faster. I wanted to get as far away as I could. Aero kept pace with me. We ran up the road, stopping when we reached the Ferry.

We reached my mum's café. There was always a bowl left out on the front step for dogs to have a drink. Aero was thirsty from the run and lapped it up. I let him rest, but I was raring to go. The Ferry felt different at this hour. The boats pulled at their anchors like ghouls against chains. I saw far off a dark cloud moving, probably a storm coming inland. The way it shifted shape looked strange, but it was probably a play of the sky reflecting against the inky black sea. I was feeling restless.

My fever had lifted, and now my body buzzed as if high on drugs.

Fishing boats chimed in time with the wind and waves, sounding like an aggressive clock urging me to move. I fidgeted as I waited for Aero. The longer I stood still, the more my skin burned. When I was moving, the cool early morning air kissed my bare legs and swept up under my cotton nightdress. My feet were bare. If anyone saw me, they'd think I'd lost my mind. But I felt liberated. If I could shed my clothes completely, and run naked, I would. Only dignity and fear kept me from doing so.

"Come on, Aero!"

I moved off the road. We went across the shingle toward the sea and I followed the coast. I enjoyed the exertion as we ran up the concrete steps. Finally, I found myself at the cliff tops and knew I was almost home. I didn't want to stop. My body told me to keep going.

It was then that the sky darkened over, blocking out the crisp glow of the moon.

The hairs on my arm stood on end, sensing a change of energy in the air. I searched the sky for what had cast the growing shadow. The stormy sky moved unnaturally, as if alive. I tried to make sense of the strange mass moving toward me. As it grew closer, I realised it wasn't a cloud. It was a flock of birds. Crows.

Aero barked and nipped at my nightdress, trying to pull me away.

"Okay," I agreed with him.

There was something that didn't feel right about the birds. It filled me with a sense of dread, and for the first time since I'd left home, I wanted to get back.

CHAPTER 13

WE RAN BUT DIDN'T GET FAR. The movement drew the birds after us. They swooped down, their talons tearing at my skin, beaks snapping at me. They dived before me, flapping their wicked wings in my face. I threw my hands up and flailed around while Aero barked. He weaved between my legs, trying to protect me, but only got under my feet.

I tumbled to the ground and raised my arm to shield my face. The whoosh of beating wings in my ear, the sound of Aero barking at them. I tried to get up, but every time I raised my head, I had to duck back down.

Why were they attacking me? Had I upset them? Could I be near a nest?

My heart raced with fear. I'd never seen birds behave this way. I curled up in a ball to protect myself and show them I wasn't a threat, but the attacks continued.

Aero howled in pain.

"Run away. Go home," I begged.

He whined as he nudged me with his nose and refused to leave my side; stupid, loyal dog. It made it worse. It made me love him more. Every howl he made filled my gut with guilt. Trapped under their vicious onslaught, I cradled him. I didn't care about my pain. It was Aero's cries that raked through my body and cut deep into my heart. It was far worse than any harm they could inflict on me.

I had to get up for Aero. I pushed myself up onto my knees and tried to beat them away, but the crows' attacks were relentless. My body surrendered to the ground. For all the times I'd wished for my end, I'd never imagined this.

This was it. This was the end. Death by crows.

Confused. Delirious. Ever since Jace dumped me, I hadn't been in my right mind. It was like he'd taken a part of me with that kiss and left me broken and less of a person. I didn't feel I belonged in this body anymore. I longed for a new life. To start over fresh. I didn't want to need to lie to feel better about myself.

"Kiely?" A deep voice penetrated my head. The sound was internal, almost god-like. A masculine voice, rich with seduction and soft like velvet. "You have a choice to make."

The crows continued to swoop, but I was no longer

focused on the external pain. My body tried to shield Aero the best I could, but I felt like I'd gone into myself. The world felt far away. It was me, alone with the voice.

"Who are you?"

"That depends on your decision. I could be your king and your new beginning, or the reaper to deal your demise."

The choices were pretty poor. The pain from the constant attacks was making my mind fuzzy, and I couldn't understand what was going on or who was speaking to me. I sobbed.

I was desperate for a new start, to rewrite my wrongs and get everything right. I was tired of fighting and trying to get through the heartache and mistakes I kept making. To choose for it to be all over was promising.

I wanted my end.

"Why me?" I cried.

"A werewolf attacked you and the pack hasn't claimed you. We cannot have a wild one roaming free. We are the reapers, the keepers of our world."

"Am I a werewolf?"

I gasped as a crow ripped claws into my skin. In the blinding pain, my mind flashed to that weekend in the public gardens when a man had attacked me. His hand had torn across my stomach. The blood. Then, nothing. I'd thought someone had drugged me and I'd imagined the whole thing especially when I'd discovered my unbroken skin. Ever since then, I'd healed straight away.

"Not until you shift, but we will kill you before then."

This must be how I was healing so fast. It made sense. Even the strange fever could be connected to the attack. The way Aero was more obedient toward me, too. It felt good to have a reason for the madness. All the pieces were coming together.

"You must choose, Kiely!" the voice persisted. "Fight us and die a wolf or surrender and be reborn a reaper."

I had some idea of what a werewolf was from movies and stories, but very little knowledge about reapers. The only reaper I'd heard of was the Grim Reaper. What did it mean to be reborn? Surely that was better than certain death.

"I don't know," I sobbed.

A sudden influx of attacks from crows hit me. One after the other. Drawing blood.

"We will keep going until you choose."

The voice sounded casual, but I sensed the warning. The pain was intolerable and scrambled my brain. Did I want this to be my end, or was I brave enough to live on?

"Please stop. I can't think," I begged.

"Join us or die!" he boomed.

The attacks continued. They seemed to increase in their ferocity. Too exhausted and too weak to fight, I pulled my legs in, creating a tight ball. I wished for them to leave us alone.

If I surrendered, perhaps they'd spare Aero.

"Why are you doing this?"

"It's easier to execute a human than a werewolf. You are close to shifting. We cannot wait much longer."

There was a strange sensation, almost like a sucking sensation inside my skull. He was gone. I could hear some commotion around me. My senses became more aware of the external world, like waking from a dream.

"Kiely!" someone called.

I gasped from the shock of pain as I returned to this cruel reality. I no longer felt welcome in this world. The birds were attacking me with such frequency that I had no chance to heal.

Should I die or be reborn?

There was some appeal to dying. I could escape my existence where I'm judged and hated by everyone dear to me. There didn't feel like there was honour in choosing death, but I wasn't sure I had any honour left.

Something held me back from making that choice. Only moments ago, I'd felt how powerful my body was. I knew now that it was my inner wolf. That power had felt good. I wanted more than this and I wasn't ready to die.

Could I fight the reapers off and become a wolf? Or would I die trying? Should I surrender and join them? It could be a second chance at life. An opportunity to wipe the slate clean, to start over as a better version of myself.

The idea of sacrificing myself sounded terrifying. Would it hurt, or would it feel like a baptism with all my pain and sins being washed again? Would I remember who I was before?

Or would I be susceptible to repeating my mistakes?

I was no match for their relentless attacks, and I

sensed this was nothing compared to what they could do to me if I fought them. They were strong, and I was outnumbered. They flexed their muscles, giving me a taste of their power, a chance to consider the destruction that awaited me or the power that could be mine.

Everything was pinned on my choice.

I had a choice.

That alone held power.

The more I thought about it, the more I wanted to join them. I knew in my heart that if I fought them, even if by some freak turn of events I beat them, I didn't want to win. I was so defeated by my life that I was ready for something else.

My eyes drifted open and as I looked across the grass plain, I saw my brother. It had been his voice calling to me; he'd broken the mental hold the crows had on me. My mind was spinning, unsure I wanted to be saved from the crows and my suffering. The tempting offer to be free of my old life made me want to be saved by the crows.

Murray embraced Mariah, and they shared a passionate kiss.

My heart broke. It was always her. She was everywhere. Every guy that mattered to me was infatuated with her. My body was torn, and my blood ran soaking the soil with sticky, red iron. Yet he chose this moment to make out with the girl that had ruined my life.

My eyes burned with tears that could no longer hold and I curled up into myself. It felt like only yesterday she was flaunting her romance with Jace. Why had she ruined what we'd had if Jace meant nothing to her? She was some kind of messed up and twisted evil.

The anger boiled up like lava, filling my veins. I wanted to scream, but had no words powerful enough to destroy her. I laid there broken and hopeless, allowing the crows to rip into me. Hoping they'd finish me.

Behind Murray and Mariah was a dumpy woman in loose-fitting clothes and long dark hair; Mariah's mum. Rumour was she used a crystal ball to tell fortunes and spiked her cakes with charms and curses. They called her a witch. And I'd bet Mariah was a witch too. From werewolves to witchcraft, it no longer felt far-fetched.

As Mariah and Murray kissed, stars spun around them. Like tiny fireflies rising into the sky. The lights formed what looked like a rose made of stars. No wonder I couldn't compete with her. She was using magic. She'd bewitched Jace and now my brother.

I closed my eyes, shutting out the trio. They were the real enemy. Especially Mariah. But I wasn't powerless.

I would stop her. I turned my attention inward. Searching for the deep voice that had given me an impossible choice. I liked his voice. It sounded soothing, made me forget all the pain, and feel safe.

He could help me. He'd offered to save me from this pitiful life.

"Kiely, are you ready?" his voice filled my mind as we connected. "There's not much time. You must make your choice."

But someone was pulling my consciousness away. I felt gentle hands brushing my skin, moving my hair behind my ear. I could smell them. It was Murray. His fingers ran over my cuts and ignited the pain. What was he doing? Why wouldn't he leave me alone?

I wanted to be with the voice, my king. I coiled up tighter, trying to shut Murray out. Trying to return to make my decision.

My eyes shut tight, but when I heard the man again, he was no longer in my mind. They'd taken him from me. He spoke with them.

"Gwyn, you know better than to meddle in our laws."

I opened my eyes to see a man standing close by. Something about him oozed power. He was a dark figure from the colour of his skin to the clothes he was wearing. Where once pink had been my colour now black sang to my soul.

"The girl is innocent. There's been a mistake." My focus turned to Mariah's mother. Her loose clothing billowed in the wind.

"We make no mistakes. She is ours."

I smiled at the sound of his voice. He knew me like no other. I hadn't even answered him, and he already knew I was his.

"How can this be?" The old witch's voice made me grimace.

I willed my dark stranger to get rid of her. He could do it. I could feel it in my bones.

Finish her. I willed him.

"She is an unclaimed wolf."

As the man revealed this, my gaze turned to Murray to see if he understood. Did he now see that I hadn't been lying? Were the pieces falling into place for him, too? Was he sorry for the way he'd judged me along with everyone else? His face buried in Aero's fur, comforting our dog. It broke my heart to see Aero had been hurt protecting me.

I reached a hand out toward him and he pressed his nose against my palm.

"A wolf?" Gwyn's voice wobbled.

"One of Luna's line."

"Luna has been here? Does she know of Mariah?"

Mariah! Mariah! Why does everyone care so much about her?

"I'm only interested in Kiely. She's mine." The man walked toward me. It felt good to hear someone dismiss Mariah as nothing.

His nose wrinkled as he cast Murray a look of disgust. "Move aside, fry!"

Fry was a strange insult.

"No!" Murray wasn't small, but when he stood against the man, he looked like David facing Goliath. "You can't have her!" Murray threw his hand forward and something clear like glass shot toward the man. Could Murray do magic? Had he sold his soul to Mariah?

It bounced off my king's chest, and he laughed, a deep rumbling sound that felt like a hug. He wasn't scared of my brother.

"I am ancient. You are no match for me. Control your dog. I don't enjoy putting down animals."

The coldness of his words regarding Aero made me doubt my choice. Did I want to join a man who showed no love toward Aero?

"Murray, bring your dog to me," Gwyn said.

"No!" Murray yelled. "I won't leave Kiely."

"Come, little Aero, come to me, come sit by my side, by the power in me," Gwyn chanted.

Aero got up and walked toward her as if she were his master. I gasped as I realised my fears were true. The Turners were witches, and now they'd stolen my dog. I tried to push myself up but fell down.

Gwyn reached out her arm toward Murray. "Please come away. There are ancient laws we must follow. This is out of our hands."

"I said I won't leave her." Murray looked between the man and the witch, caught in the middle.

Gwyn waved her hands in the air in a strange motion, like a tree swaying in the breeze.

"What are you doing?" Murray cried out. His feet had disappeared beneath the surface as he began drifting away from me as if skating away.

Mariah sounded outraged. "Gwyn! You promised never to cast on me again!"

The witch continued to sway her arms as she answered, "Except for your protection."

I felt my body feel heavy and drowsy as if someone was pulling me down. Had the witch cast a spell on me, too? Was I sinking into the earth to be buried alive?

I had no fight left in me, and I gave in to the sensation.

My eyes closed, and his beautiful voice greeted me. "Are you ready?"

"Yes," I thought. "I want to join."

"As I take your soul, this will feel strange and may even hurt. You must try to relax. If you fight us, you will die for certain. Are you ready?"

"I am."

I felt an odd tugging and then a scorching fire that was burning my insides, acid running through my body. My bones broke, and my skin tore. I felt my entire body being destroyed with each agonising tug. My body fought to stay alive, but I was ready to relinquish my soul. I tried to relax, but there was still a fight left in me. I was having a battle with myself to give up, to stop living, and my body wasn't willing to relent. My defiance could kill me.

My mind pushed him out. I was fighting him despite my wishes. I was going to die, because I wasn't willing to die. The irony caused me to cry. With his absence from my mind, I was conscious again and the pain from before was now magnified. Crows swooped and were grabbing something dark around me, which they pulled at. It was being dragged across the ground.

I was bleeding out. I writhed in agony.

I felt like someone had punched me in the jaw. It was like the worst toothache ever. A blinding pain, blurring my vision. My mouth felt strange.

"Join us," the man's voice thundered.

"No!" I threw my head back and screamed. My

instincts told me to fight with a desperate need to live. I tried to negotiate with the animal within me, but it didn't understand. My body wanted to survive and fought my mind and my soul. Battling with myself, I was losing and didn't even know which side I was on.

"To be one of us is better than to not be at all," he stated.

His words were true. I was trying to join, but I struggled to relent. I tried to relax and give in to him. But it was like holding my head under water and my lungs fighting against me to breathe.

"I warned you, wave goodbye." His chilling words struck fear in my heart.

This was it. I was going to die.

"No!" I heard Mariah scream.

I didn't know she cared so much about me. Why would it matter to her if I lived or died?

I closed my eyes, trying to get back to my internal safe place so I could relinquish my soul and rid myself of this life.

"Mariah, you need to calm down!" Gwyn said.

I wished they'd be quiet. Their constant distractions were making it harder for me to retreat. Maybe it was what they wanted. Maybe they were trying to kill me.

My breath was snatched from my body as I was doused in icy water. I looked around to see what had happened. There was water everywhere. Someone had thrown me into the sea. Waves splashed into my mouth, choking me. My wounds stung like the water was acid. The sharp salty taste was foul on my tongue. My body kicked into survival mode and I was back in the world of the living. My legs thrashed out as I tried to swim.

Should I swim or do I need to drown?

My mind was a mess. There was a strong current, and I was being dragged out to sea. Instinct encouraged me to swim and to get back to land, but I was weak with no power. I could feel my body working on my wounds, and they were easing.

Or was it just the cold numbing me? I was being drawn away.

"Kiely!" I heard Mariah calling out as I bobbed under the water.

I tried to stay up above the water so she could find me, and rescue me, but the sea was rough, and I was injured. I kept gulping saltwater, making me splutter.

Raising my arm, I hoped she could see me as my weary body was ready to give in. I was about to let go when I felt Mariah pull my body against her.

I closed my eyes and let go, allowing her to hold me in the ocean.

CHAPTER 14

As Mariah pulled me from the water, my skin was chilled from the north wind. My body ached with each thud of her footsteps. She dragged me along beside her, holding me upright by my waist. My body felt like it was being ripped in two as my toes were dragged through the shingle. Mariah let me go, and I dropped, my body colliding with the hard stones on the beach. The impact forced the air out of my lungs. I rolled onto my back.

The stones crunched as someone dropped down beside me. I opened my eyes to see a blanket of black broken by tiny pinpricks of stars. The crows were gone, and the moon shone full and bright. I liked the way the night felt.

"Thank you," Mariah whispered.

"Shouldn't I be thanking you?" My throat felt dry from almost drowning.

Mariah moved so her face blocked my view of the moon. A big smile plastered across her face as her red hair dripped seawater all over me, making me grumble. Why did it have to be her of all people to save me? I didn't want to owe her anything.

She scrambled onto her legs, looking unsteady. Hauling my body out of the sea must have taken its toll on her own body. She was a strong swimmer, but the rough sea must have been more of a challenge than the tranquil pool she was used to.

With reluctance, I accepted her outstretched hand. She pulled me up onto my feet. Mariah walked up the shore to the promenade, and I followed. Much to my amazement, my body didn't ache. I gave myself a quick scan and couldn't spot even a scratch from the flock's onslaught.

"Why were you out so late?" Mariah asked.

The way she spoke felt judgemental. She was prying into my life as if she cared and had any right to know my business. It got my back up. She may have saved my life, but there was too much history between us. "Getting some air."

"Whatever," she answered, showing her true colours and dropping the act.

"I thanked you for saving my life. What more do you want? It's not like we're ever going to be friends. You stole my boyfriend. Remember that?" I said reminding her stupid arse why I don't like her.

"You're Murray's sister, so you matter. But a little gratitude would have been nice. I don't know why I bothered?"

Why did she bother? Part of me wanted to scream but being around her wore me out. My life would be so much better if she'd just fuck off. My inner wolf flared inside me and my body burned with a new strength. Every muscle in my body twitched, every sound was crisp and clear, and I could differentiate the different smells in the air. I felt indestructible, but Mariah brought my darkness to the surface, and I wasn't sure it was a good mix. To create distance between us, I hurried across the road. I'd had enough of this night. My voice broke as I struggled to stay in control of my anger as I spat out the words, "Stop bothering *about* me, and have a good night!"

"What if the crows come back?" Mariah called after me, sounding desperate.

"It won't be any of your business if they do." I wasn't desperate anymore. I no longer feared the crows, I welcomed them.

I stopped and turned to face Mariah. She looked pitiful as her wet clothes hung on her skinny frame. The smudges of mascara circling her pale blue ice queen eyes made them look supernatural. She looked like she'd been on a date. I hoped not with Murray, but that kiss suggested otherwise.

It made me so mad that I yelled at her. "Maybe I don't want to be saved."

All my drama was from people interfering, trying to help me, and not letting me live my life. A dark heat rose inside. I couldn't stand the sight of her. The farther away she was, the better. I headed up the hill. It wasn't until I was halfway up I realised she wasn't following me.

I let out a tight breath that I hadn't realised I was holding onto and looked up at the sky, wishing the crows back. If only I could call them to me.

I wanted them to take me away. It felt as if I'd died several times already tonight.

I'd suffered a fever, survived a brutal attack, and almost drowned. I didn't fear death. I was ready for it.

The werewolf in me was already healing my wounds. With every step I felt stronger. Only my blood-stained, torn, cotton nightdress stood as a stark reminder of what had happened earlier. The wet fabric clung to my body and made me appear naked. Shivers racked my cold body. But uncontrollable laughter burst from my lips as I realised I probably looked like something out of a horror movie.

Based on recent events, that wasn't too far from the truth.

I walked in the shadows, knowing that if someone saw me, I was bound to give them a fright.

I was almost back to where the battle had started. The grassy field at the top of the cliff tops was now full of mud, and the beach huts were destroyed. Littered around were pieces of broken wood and debris from the destruction of the fight and flood.

The sea must have risen. That must have been how I'd got swept up into the ocean. I couldn't help but think Mariah and her witchcraft were to blame.

Murray was gone. Mariah's mum too. I couldn't see Aero.

The only one left was the man. He waited for me, surrounded by dark figures. They didn't frighten me. They drew me toward their inky darkness. It cast down around their bodies, almost as if they were wearing cloaks made of shadows. His dark brown eyes met mine, and I felt like he was sucking me in. I made my way over, ready to try again if he'd let me.

"I'm ready," I said.

"Let us commence."

When the man touched me, I felt the darkness entering me like a chilling embrace, numbing all the pain that had plagued me physically, mentally, and emotionally.

The shadowy figures created a circle around me.

They stretched their arms out toward me, their hands fisting as if they were trying to grab me, but stood too far back. The man held me still, but my body felt like it was being pulled in every direction. I grimaced in excruciating pain as I felt my body being ripped apart.

With my eyes closed, I shut out the light. The darkness soothed me and made it bearable. I understood now, that I needed to go deeper to escape the pain. That's how I'd survive surrendering my soul. My body's instinct was to fight or run. I gritted my teeth as I fought my natural urges. It was exhausting, and I leaned my head against his shoulder. His arm wrapped around my waist, pulling me close to his body.

"I'm not strong enough," I sobbed into his neck.

"You are almost there." His voice was warm and eased my fractured soul with hope.

I wanted this.

Fire blasted through my body and I screamed with severe pain like nothing I'd ever experienced before. The blackness turned into a searing white as I crumbled, my legs giving way, my body dropping. But he didn't let go. He continued to hold me upright in his arms. With a cool wave of darkness, he scooped me up.

"You are mine," he declared.

There was utter silence. Everything was gone. Everything was still. As the world gradually returned, I heard the distant whooshing of the sea and the seagulls calling to each other. I felt well-rested, like a pamper evening with my mum. My worries felt like a distant dream and I was safe. I was so far removed from everything that had happened that when I opened my eyes, it startled me to see him.

He was real.

I looked around and saw the shadow people were watching us. A hot flush touched my cheeks, and I wriggled to escape his arms. He released me, but rested a hand on my back to hold me steady on the ground.

"How do you feel?"

I thought for a moment. "Good."

"It is time for you to find your wings, little chick."

His deep bass voice had a melody to it that almost sounded like he was cooing to me.

I looked up at him with wonder. His eyes were full of promise. I noticed the people to the side disappear into shadows that fell over their bodies like smoke. Out of the black emerged crow-like birds that flapped their wings as they rose and took flight. The shadows faded away as if they'd never existed.

"You can control the shadows and your shift. Pull the darkness and see your body change in your mind, taking shape as a crow."

I closed my eyes and bit my lip as I concentrated. I delved back to the place in my mind where I'd retreated during the fight to feel safe. The place where his voice had taken me when the crows had attacked me. I went there, and I envisioned what I'd witnessed the others do.

I imagined a cloak of darkness dropping around me, encircling my body, and transforming my flesh and bones into feathers and wings. Shrinking and taking shape, my body lifted from the floor in my new form. A chill swept over my body like the northern wind was blowing a gale against me.

The sensation stopped, and I flapped my wings; I was now a crow. I fluttered about, getting my bearings, and squawked with joy.

I can fly. I can really fly.

I beat my wings and rose to meet the others.

"Kiely?" His deep voice echoed in my mind and I knew it was him, my saviour. The one who freed me from my tortured soul. The man who brought me back to life when I was ready to die. I felt powerful and strong and like I could take on the world.

"Yes," I answered. "Can you hear me?"

I heard him chuckle. It was a glorious sound that made my heart flutter faster than my wings could beat.

"We have a long flight ahead. You must keep up."

With that, I saw a large crow pass me and take the lead, and the others followed. I joined the murder. We were like a mighty black cloud soaring above the houses. An army of wings. It felt powerful. Formidable.

My home vanished beneath me, becoming one of many rooftops, blending into a town of houses and fields and the grey-blue of the sea. I wondered when I could return home to them, but there was no time to ponder. I had to keep up. My heart was full of excitement as I set off on an adventure of a new life, a fresh start, and experiencing something I'd never thought possible.

We'd been flying for so long, the sun had risen; it was now morning. I'd seen the landscapes change beneath us; from the seaside town I called home to the wide spaces of the countryside filled with crops. I'd seen the lush green tree tops of woodlands. Then we passed over urban landscapes with high-rise buildings and the smog of traffic. I had no idea where we were, but I knew we were far from home.

Now we were weaving through mountains, gliding over large lakes and glistening rivers that cut paths through the earth. We rose above purple heather-covered spans, up toward a grey stone castle on the edge of a cliff.

The crows flew over the building and then dived into the internal courtyard. They circled as they glided down into the square. They cast dark shadows on the ground, creating a column that rose and engulfed them. As their shadows dissipated like smoke, they stood there looking like an ordinary human. These crows were people, just like me.

I glided down in the same manner, but when I reached the ground, I was too tired to cast my darkness. I tried to land but instead hopped around on feet that ached from being tucked up for so long they were almost numb. It took me a few hops to steady myself. My heart raced as I realised I was stuck in this feathered body. Tricked. A fool.

The man looked massive as he reached an arm out toward me.

"Come on, little chick," his voice sounded in my mind, but his lips didn't move. I hopped up onto his arm and onto his shoulder. I wondered if he could still hear me.

"I'm stuck like this," I wailed, but my words came out as if I was cawing.

He laughed. The sound warmed my heart. I fluffed my feathers as I shook off my fear. He looked toward the others.

"Our little chick needs to sleep. I'll take her to our guest room."

He began walking toward a door in the corner, and he spoke to my mind. "Don't panic. Once rested, your strength will return and you will shift."

We entered the building. The corridor was painted cream and flooded with light from the arched windows looking out to the courtyard with black frames. On the other side, the windows were mirrored in wood and the frames had delicate details of ivy and roses. Columns twisted up in the middle rising to a platform above, like an indoor balcony with cast iron decorative details, that looked down to where we were.

I snuggled into the man's neck as we took a spiral staircase up toward the platform. We walked along it, past many doors, breaking the pattern of archways.

The man stopped at one and pushed it open.

Inside was a bedroom with a gothic feel. The floor was dark wood, as was the ceiling. The wallpaper was dark purple with a black pattern on it. There were full-length windows with long draping grey curtains. The four-poster bed was of black wood with white silk bed linen. A chandelier hung from the ceiling. There was a mirrored wardrobe and a chest of draws. On top of the drawers was a silver birdcage with a deep purple cushion at the base.

The man slid his fingers under my feet and scooped me off his shoulder. He placed me inside the cage.

I feared he'd lock the door and chirped and flapped my wings in protest.

"Hush, little chick. I will not harm you. I will help you shift. But first, you need to rest."

My heart raced as I looked around the room, taking in the dated furniture. The room was filled with well-made antique pieces that had a gothic style I'd expect to see in a museum or stately home filled the room. This didn't feel real. Was this part of my fever? Some strange vivid dream?

He didn't shut the metal door of the cage, but he shut the bedroom door on his way out. In my bird-like state, I couldn't open the door or window. For the first time since changing, I wondered if I'd made a mistake coming here. Had there been another option, one he'd not told me? If I had fought and won, could I have been a lone wolf, one without a pack?

My head was too weary from the travel, and everything that had happened.

I walked around the cushion in a circle until I decided it was comfortable. I lowered myself down and tucked my head under my wing.

My body and brain were exhausted, and I gave in to the pull of sleep.

I woke up with a start, alert and aware that I wasn't alone. I was still a bird. Blinking and ruffling my feathers, I saw the man. He held out his hand for me and I climbed on. He placed me on the floor by his feet.

"I trust that you have had a good rest." His voice ran over me like a lover's caress. "We find our power in the darkness. You need to recall in your mind where you were when you first shifted. Go back there and come back to me as a human."

I closed my eyes and tried to remember changing.

The icy coldness that had blasted through me. The blinding white that turned pitch black. Darkness so pure it was completely void of light. Like the beginning of the world and time itself. So black and empty. A void.

I had to go into that hole and let it consume me. The icy coolness crept over my skin like Death himself was licking me with his tongue. My feathers turned to smoke and my body stretched out into a human form. It looked soft, but the pain was like bones snapping and my hair being torn out. I wanted my body back, so I went through it to be born again.

"What am I?" My voice was lighter and sounded like I was singing my words. I stood in my skin, but I didn't feel like myself. I'd changed, and I knew I wasn't human anymore.

"A reaper."

I laughed. He'd answered my question, but I didn't feel any wiser. "What's a reaper?"

"The human equivalent would be the police." He stepped forward. His stance looked authoritative, slightly intimidating. I could picture him on the force, but not me.

His power made me uneasy, but also drawn toward him with admiration. He continued. "We ensure the laws of the shifter world are obeyed and order kept."

"Why me?"

"We do not condone unclaimed shifters running wild, with no idea of the consequences of their actions. It would lead to certain chaos, with nobody to guide their shift, to tame their hunger, their satiable need to kill, to mate."

I held my arm, feeling on edge. There was an aggressive undertone to his words that made me feel uncomfortable.

I saw him smirk. He looked me up and down and brushed a strand of hair behind my ear. "The darkness suits you. Go, shower and dress. You have a lot to learn."

"I can't wear this." I held out the ruined nightdress and wiggled my barefoot at him.

"Morgan is a similar size. I shall arrange for her to bring you some of her clothes, but you will find basics in a range of sizes in the wardrobe over there." He nodded toward the wardrobe in the corner of my room. "Forgive my urgency, but time is of the essence. There are ancient conditions of your contract that we must discuss."

"I have a contract?"

He pointed to a door on the far side of the room. "Your ensuite to freshen up, and once you are dressed, Morgan will give you a tour."

He left me to shower, and when I returned to the bedroom, a slim girl with long dark hair waited for me. She had pale skin and dark eyes.

She jumped up to greet me. "Hi, I brought clothes."

I noticed that the outfits laid out across the bed were not my style. Mostly black, but also a few other dark colours. It matched what she was wearing.

"I didn't know what you'd like, so I brought a bit of everything."

"No pastels? A little pink?" My hand ran over the garments. Despite the limited colour choice, there was a range of fabrics and styles. The new me found the dark options appealing.

She blushed. "Sorry. Most of us have a soft spot for the colour black and I assumed you would, too."

I felt bad for being rude. She was kindly donating her clothes and, as I thought about it, she may have assumed right. I hadn't been into wearing black before the change, but now something was comforting about it. Was it the way my life had turned upside down, a reflection of my inner darkness, or was it because I was a reaper and the darkness was now a part of me?

"It's fine." I smiled politely and scooped up a denim skirt and t-shirt that looked the closest to something I'd wear. Part of me wanted to hang onto my former identity, even though I hated the person I once was.

On closer inspection, I realised I'd chosen a leather skirt. I went behind a screen to get changed. I didn't want to appear ungrateful or fussy.

Morgan's voice sang out from the other side. "Oh, I forgot to say, I'm Morgan."

"I guessed."

"Did Cronus tell you about me?"

"Is that his name?"

Her laughter sounded like a bell ringing. "Yeah. Did he not introduce himself? He's terrible at welcoming new recruits. You'd think after centuries he'd have got it down."

"Centuries? How old is he?"

"He is ancient. The first of our kind."

"Who made him?" I wondered, thinking of how I'd been created.

"Goddess Gaia herself."

I stepped out once, dressed.

She beamed. "You look great. Let's show you around."

Morgan opened the door, and I eagerly followed her out into the corridor. Finally, free from the confines of the room. I had a different perspective of the space now than when I'd been perched on Cronus's shoulder.

"What did Cronus say about me?" Morgan asked, twirling a strand of black hair around her finger.

"Oh, nothing much. He thought we were a similar size."

The more I thought about his name, the more I liked it. It suited him. It intrigued me how he was ancient and I wondered how old that made him, and the lifetimes he must have lived through. He held my curiosity with a complex mix of fear and fascination.

"The upstairs is our sleeping quarters and loops around the entire upper floor." We began walking down the stairs. The windows looked out to the quad where we'd flown in earlier. Morgan led me along and pointed to some doors. "These rooms are for recreation. There's a library, a games room, and a lounge. Feel free to make yourself at home in any of them. You're part of our family now."

We turned a corner and the smell of food wafted up to my nose, causing my tummy to growl.

"Hungry?"

I nodded.

"Don't worry, the tour won't take long and we'll come back here at the end. As you can smell, these doors lead to the kitchen and dining hall." She pointed out the doors as she spoke.

We turned another corner, and she explained, "The first room is the bar, then there is the cinema room, and next door is the music room."

We kept going, and I realised how big my new home was. It gave me that lost feeling that I felt on the first day of high school. Those first few days, I'd longed to get home. I felt a wave of homesickness as I thought of my family. They must have noticed I was gone by now and would be worried about me. Or accusing me of going missing for attention?

I had no idea how I'd explain my disappearance, but I needed to call my parents. They'd want to know I was safe, otherwise they'd worry.

"This is the spa area. It has facilities like a pool, jacuzzi, sauna, and different rooms like that." Morgan carried on.

I wished for Fallon and Arizona. They would love to stay here. Thinking of my friends caused a heaviness inside. I missed them both and wondered if we could ever repair our friendship.

We turned another corner, and we must have been almost back on ourselves. "This corridor is the library, meeting rooms, and a study. You'll notice they're named after birds of prey. You're welcome to use a study if you need a computer or have a private meeting, but…"

She paused as we made it to the end of the corridor. "This room is Cronus's office. Nobody enters without his permission."

Outside this room was a small red velvet couch looking out into the quad. A forbidden room appealed to my rebellious side, and I smirked. Morgan caught my sneer and leaned in.

"Nobody goes in! Alright?"

I nodded to show I understood. Morgan held my gaze and tilted her head back as she regarded me. "Come on, let's get you fed."

My stomach urged me to keep up as we returned the way we'd come.

"I need to call my parents to let them know I'm okay."

Morgan shook her head. "You can't call friends, family, or anyone from your previous life. You need to let them go. Cut them out. This is your new life, Kiely."

The cold ran through my veins and made me shiver. I couldn't abandon everyone I loved. It was too great a sacrifice.

"They'll go crazy. They threatened to call the police the last time I didn't come home."

Morgan paused and turned to face me. "Hang on. How. Old. Are. You?"

Her question sounded rude and patronising. "I'm sixteen. One of the oldest in my year group. I'll be seventeen in a few months."

"You're a child!"

"Technically." I scrambled for a counterargument to dispute the validity of that fact. Why did my age matter?

"Oh god. This is not good." The colour drained from her already pale face.

Morgan grabbed my wrist and marched me back the way we'd come. My skin prickled with panic. I worried I was in trouble for not being an adult.

Morgan hauled me outside the forbidden office and knocked.

Suddenly, I didn't want to see inside.

CHAPTER 15

I HEARD THE LOCK TURN, and as the door widened, Cronus filled the frame with his tall stature. His eyebrow and lip raised on one side as he asked, "And to what do I owe the pleasure of this unexpected visit?"

Morgan straightened up and folded her arms behind her back. "Kiely has disclosed to me that she is a minor."

Cronus frowned, and his attention turned to me. "How old?"

"Twenty-one." I smiled and fluttered my eyelashes at him.

Cronus chewed his lips and looked from me to Morgan. She shook her head and glared at me.

Her hands snapped to her hips and pressed her lips together. My blood boiled. She didn't even know me, and she was being so rude. Her stare continued to bore into me, demanding the truth.

I snapped, "Sixteen. Alright, I'm sixteen."

Cronus's face sobered as he looked at me. "This is serious."

"You seem to know everything else about me; my name, where I live, my attack. You knew when nobody else believed me. But you didn't know my age. What does it even matter?"

"You're a child."

"Barely!"

"Leave us," Cronus dismissed Morgan. He swept his arm in front of his body to invite me into his office.

Entering the room, I noticed the dark oak bookcase lined with green cloth-bound books. My finger drew a clear path through the dust in front of them and I noticed that one section was dust-free, although those books didn't look any more appealing.

This room was like stepping back in time. The laptop and mobile phone were the only modern-looking things in here.

Cronus moved around the dark polished desk and gestured for me to take a seat. Placing his elbows on the desk, he pressed his fingertips together. He leaned forward, resting the tips against his lips. He appeared deep in thought.

Waiting for him to speak made my skin prickle with discomfort. There was no window, making me feel like the walls were closing in around me.

Cronus leaned back and crossed his hands over his chest, "Well, this complicates things, but don't worry, chick, I'll fix this."

I gritted my teeth at the nickname. It had sounded endearing before, but now it sounded like he was making fun of my age.

He picked up his mobile phone and dialed a number. He got up from the desk and paced. Someone must have answered because Cronus said, "We have a human situation."

He paused, listening to the person on the other end speaking, before he added, "An unclaimed wolf joined our family, but she's sixteen."

He listened to something and then put his hand over the mouthpiece and turned to speak to me. "Are you in high school or further education?"

"I sit my GCSEs this month."

He waved his arms for me to elaborate as if this made little sense to him. "High School or what?"

"High school. Final exams." I shifted in my seat, feeling like a naughty child.

He moved to perch himself on the desk beside me and placed his hand on my shoulder. He continued with the telephone conversation. "Kiely O'Neil."

Hearing him say my full name sent a shiver through my body. It sounded like music on his lips. I looked up to meet his dark brown eyes, watching me. His gaze was warm, and he smiled in a way that made me feel like he was hugging me. He made me feel like he could keep me safe from everything wrong in the world.

He frowned at something the person on the phone said. His hand covered the mouthpiece as his attention turned to me. "Is Murray O'Neil your brother?"

I nodded and wondered what my brother had to do with this. Then I remembered that he'd been with that witch Mariah during the clifftop battle. My shoulders slumped as I realised my brother may have done more than mess with my love life.

"Yes," Cronus confirmed to the person on the phone. He listened to them and then sighed. "With immediate effect."

He hung up and turned to me. "I have to take you home."

My heart pounded in my chest, my eyes wide. "You promised me a new life."

All the drama, the hate, and betrayal, everything I'd escaped, came crashing back. It made my stomach turn, and I felt sick. As much as I wanted to see my parents again, I didn't want to go back. I wrapped my arms around my waist and bent over as I took some deep breaths. I shut my eyes, trying to block this out. But I was still here.

Cronus was supposed to be my saviour. He returned to his chair on the opposite side of the desk and massaged his temples. "In the eyes of human laws, you are a child. You can't just up and leave. Your parents will report you missing. The school will report you missing. The authorities will look for you. You will draw too much attention to us."

I shook my head. "Let me call my parents. I'll tell them I'm okay. I'll beg them to let me stay."

Cronus laughed. "You will finish high school."

I groaned.

He placed a hand on my shoulder. "Don't worry, chick, this won't stall your training and full transition to reaper. When we return, you will lay the seeds that you are leaving. Tell people that you are going to study in Scotland - a half-truth. Then cut ties to your old life without the risk of questions."

I thought about all the people I would leave behind and needed to say goodbye. I wished I was going on better terms, but everybody hated me. This could be my last chance to make amends.

"Why did you ask about my brother?"

"Turns out you are from an interesting family. Were you aware your brother is a merman?"

I laughed. He loved being the star of the school swim team. That was until he'd got kicked out for that ridiculous burn tattoo he got. Despite how good he was, it was insane to say that he was a merman.

I thought back to that strange night when I joined the Reapers. It now made sense why Murray had been there. Flashes of the night came back to me, the odd things I saw. Had that fire-haired witch made him a merman? I would have said magic couldn't exist, but now I'd been attacked by a werewolf and transformed into a bird.

My understanding of what's possible was altering but it still left me with so many questions. If Murray is a merman, does that mean being a mermaid was my fate too? Or it would have been if I'd not been attacked by that wolf. Was this why I was targeted?

"The drago will take care of your parents." Cronus got up and moved around toward me.

"What does that mean?"

"They won't be a problem anymore."

I swallowed. There was something wrong, but I didn't understand what. Cronus held out his hand. I took it, and he pulled me up to stand. The motion closed the proximity between us. My chest pressed against his. His lips were so close that I could feel his breath. All the sensation of foreboding was washed away with the dizzying thrill of anticipation.

"Can I stay?" I whispered, my eyes widened with hope.

Cronus frowned and stepped back. "Let us eat. You must be starving after your first flight, and you will need your strength to return to school on Monday morning."

I felt disappointed by him stepping away from me when we'd been so close. His hand touched the small of my back as he guided me out of his office. Once in the hall, he let go, but my skin tingled from where his hand had been.

Cronus walked me to the dining hall. There were hot plates piled with food ready for us to help ourselves. I plated up with some chili-con-carne, and then helped myself to a bottle of beer.

Cronus gave me a stern look and before I could

think, I returned the beer and switched it for a bottle of water. I sensed that it wasn't my doing. I wanted to argue but found myself unable to. As quickly as I'd switched my drink, I changed my mind. The more I thought about it, I wanted water.

The table was laid out for several different settings. Some were missing, which I guessed had been used by those who'd already eaten. I looked for an available space and spotted one next to Morgan. Although we hadn't finished the tour on the best of terms, she was the only person I knew here.

"Hi, Kiely." A guy waved to me. He was the only person not wearing black. He wore a pink collared t-shirt and navy chino. "I'm Callum."

"Hi." I blushed. It was odd having everyone know who I was when I didn't know who any of them were, but he seemed friendly.

"Wow, that was some fight your bestie put up." He grinned and leaned forward. "We almost died, except we can't. Thank god for that!" He clapped his hands together as if he was praying.

"She's not my best friend. Far from it."

He looked even more interested, and I could tell he was hungry for gossip. "Ooo tea. Do tell?"

"She stole my boyfriend, then my life unravelled, and here I am."

"Hallelujah, because this is the best thing that ever happened to you."

Cronus took the seat opposite me and I threw daggers at him with my eyes as I replied, "Except, I'm being sent back."

"Because she's a child," Morgan added.

"No!" gasped Callum. "I thought that was the wolf blood giving you a youthful glow."

"Sixteen!" Morgan added. Still salty.

"Let the girl talk, Morgan!" Callum told her. "Rude!"

I giggled at their banter. For all the craziness that had happened in the last twenty-four hours, this felt the most normal. Gossiping and bitching. Again, I was hit by how much I wanted to make amends with Fallon and Arizona. I sighed. "I fell out with my friends."

"What happened?" Callum leaned in. Something about him reminded me of Fallon and made my heart ache for her.

"It doesn't matter." I shrugged.

Callum put an arm across my shoulders. "You got us if we'll do?"

Morgan looked across at Cronus, and I noted how they exchanged a smile. It made me wonder what their relationship was.

Morgan caught my eye. "I'm sorry about how our tour ended. None of this is your fault. I'll be your friend, or sister, or whatever you need to get through this madness."

Her words made me think of Nate, and how he'd tried to be there for me. I dropped my head as I thought about how in a few days I'd soon have to find a way to say goodbye to him forever. My heart felt heavy in my chest. I could feel them all staring at me. I looked up at

Morgan through my lashes. "Can we start afresh?"

My eyes then drifted across to Cronus. I wanted to know him but didn't know where to start. If Fallon were here, she'd have his full family history and details on any scandal. I made a note to ask Morgan about him later and see what I could uncover about the Crow King.

Chapter 16

WHEN CRONUS LEFT, the energy in the room changed as everyone relaxed. Morgan thought we should get an early night, but Callum felt I should see the bar. His idea sounded much more fun, and despite her objections, Morgan tagged along. They took me to another room set up like an old English pub.

Morgan and I perched on stools at a dark polished bar that reminded me of Cronus's desk. The room had black-painted wooden beams and shocking pink accents.

Everyone appeared to be watching me, putting me emotionally back into the school corridors of gossip and whispers. I wrapped my arm around myself. I must

have made a mistake. They were a mismatched family of every race, with their inky black hair and dark eyes.

"You won't be the new girl forever," Morgan said as if she could read my mind.

Callum pushed two drinks in front of us, enjoying playing barman. He winked at me as I caught his eye. These were the prettiest drinks I'd ever seen, with a rainbow of colours and slices of orange and lemon hanging off the edge.

"Callum has spent his time perfecting the art of cocktails," Morgan said.

I took a sip, and an array of sweet and savoury flavours exploded in my mouth. They complimented each other in a way that filled me with such joy. "My compliments to the chef. Does it have alcohol in it?"

"Does a baboon have a red arse?"

I tried to smile at Callum's joke. I didn't want to be a party pooper, but I didn't want to get drunk. I didn't know these people, and I was a long way from home.

"What's wrong?" Morgan asked.

"Cronus said I've got to travel home, and I don't want to do that with a hangover."

Callum laughed. "A hangover. When have any of us had a hangover?"

"We don't get hangovers?"

Callum smiled at me. "That's right. So, drink up buttercup."

Morgan nodded in agreement. "True, but be wary if you ever go into a battle, as it can make you more vulnerable to other shifters' attacks. But you're safe here."

I sipped more of my drink and allowed myself to enjoy it. Bottles clinked as Callum put away those he'd got out.

He came around the bar to join us and raised an eyebrow. "Fancy a game of pool?"

"Come on, Callum, she hasn't even had her first lesson," Morgan scolded him.

"What are you trying to imply?" Callum's hands raised to his chest and gasped as if he'd been insulted.

"You know exactly what I mean."

"You shouldn't have come if you are going to be a bore."

Morgan rolled her eyes.

Callum gasped. "Don't roll your eyes at me."

Their banter made me giggle, especially Callum's animated responses.

"Behave yourself then, and bring more cocktails."

"Yes, queen." He saluted her and returned to the other side of the bar.

It didn't take many more drinks for Morgan to loosen up, and soon we were dancing on the dance floor like we were the best of friends.

We weren't the only ones dancing. Others hung around the jukebox, deciding what tunes to play. Lounging in the chairs surrounding us were others chatting amongst themselves. They played pop music that was easy for us to dance to, including some old classics like 'Come on, Eileen', where Morgan got me doing the can-can with her.

I was about to suggest we sit down when Morgan

grabbed my arm and wiggled her way off the dance floor with me in tow. She dropped into the seat of a nearby booth.

Her eyes sparkled. "I can't keep up with you."

I shook my head. It felt like it was the other way around, but I didn't say so. I felt like I'd made a ton of new friends, but one person was absent. "Where's Cronus?"

"He likes to keep himself to himself in the evening," one guy answered.

"Is he single?"

The guy laughed as he slid in beside me. "Don't even go there."

I blushed. "I'm not. I just…"

"He's mine," Morgan added.

"You wish." Callum laughed as he placed two more drinks down in front of us. "Cronus keeps himself to himself."

"That's what he said," I pointed to the other guy.

"I told ya!" He laughed.

"Do you think he's hot?" Callum asked, making me blush.

Morgan shook her head and threw him a look.

Callum moved closer to me. "Okay, here's the tea. As our maker, he has a certain draw over us."

"It's not just compulsion for me."

"Compulsion?" I'd not heard that word before.

"It's the warm feeling you get when you're around him. Cronus can make you feel devoted to him, safe, and loved. Some people are delulu and think it means something more." Callum elbowed Morgan, and she shoved him back.

I questioned the attraction I'd had toward Cronus. It made me feel sick to think he was messing with my autonomy. The more I thought of our interactions, the more oddities I saw, like at dinner when I got the water. That hadn't felt like my choice. The more I thought about it, the more I wondered how much control Cronus had over me.

"How are you settling in?" Morgan asked, pulling me out of my thoughts.

"A lot has happened." I wasn't sure I could tell them how I was really feeling.

"It's a miracle you're alive. No child has ever survived the sacrifice before."

I screwed up my face. It annoyed me every time someone referred to my age.

"Most don't make it," Callum added.

"You must be strong, and now you're even stronger," Morgan said as she rubbed my leg.

"What is a drago?" I asked.

Everyone shivered and looked away. When Cronus had said that word something had felt off. Their reactions made my heart beat harder in my chest. I asked again with more urgency, "What is a drago?"

"They're vile snake-like beings that slither into your mind, steal your free will, and suck your memories dry," Callum said, wrinkling his nose.

He must have seen the shock on my face as he added with a shrug, "Don't worry. We're safe. These days, they only attack humans."

Morgan added, "Their methods are harsh, but like us, they play an important role in keeping order in the world."

"Except we are way cooler," Callum added.

"Cronus said they are contacting my parents." My voice shook.

Seeing Callum's face void of a smile was quite chilling. We'd only known each other for a short time, but I knew it meant this wasn't a good thing.

I begged, "Tell me what it means?"

Callum shook his head and fidgeted. It was clear he didn't want to answer. I glared at Morgan, and she sighed. "It probably means they'll possess your parents. As long as they don't fight it, they'll be fine. No coma; no death."

"No coma? No death? I have to call them! I have to warn them!"

"It's too late!" Morgan said. "If they've already made contact, it's done, and it's for your protection. For all of us, to protect our world."

"What threat were my parents?" I yelled at Morgan.

She leaned back and shrugged. I felt bad. It wasn't her fault. She hadn't sent them. Cronus had. That's why he'd made the phone call. The evening's mood soured.

I got up from the booth, ready to leave.

"Kiely, where are you going?" Callum asked.

"I'm tired." Anger caused me to storm out of the bar. I was worried I'd lash out and say something I'd regret. I hurried up the stairs to the guest room. As I created distance, I could feel tears pricking my eyes. I slammed the bedroom door shut and threw myself onto the bed.

I'd thought that things couldn't get any worse, but I'd made another terrible choice. Now my parents were in danger. I hated to think of them possessed by snake-like creatures, or worse. Acid burned up my throat at the thought. I should have chosen death.

Tears peppered my eyes.

Maybe they were wrong. Maybe my parents were safe. The idea allowed me to breathe a little easier.

I still wanted to call them. I felt so lost without my mobile. But I knew where I'd seen a phone.

I snuck out of my room and hoped I could get there before anyone spotted me. The corridors were empty, and when I reached Cronus's office, I pressed my ear to the door, but all I heard was silence.

My heart thumped in my chest, and my palms were sweating as I pushed open the door. Even though I was sure Cronus wasn't there, I was relieved to be right. My skin still prickled at the thought of being caught. I slipped inside and shut the door behind me.

The phone was lying there in the center of his desk. It felt too easy, like it was left there on purpose, as a trap. As I looked around the room, something stole my attention.

The heavy bookcase had moved, and there appeared to be a secret door. The rug had wrinkled up, revealing scratches across the wooden boards. The walls of the hidden passage were made of the same grey stones as the exterior ones.

Morgan hadn't mentioned secret rooms in her tour, and I wondered whether she or any of the others knew about its existence. As I got closer, I looked through the entrance and saw stone steps leading down. It had the look of an old castle.

I could hear voices below. Cronus wasn't alone. A woman screamed, and then there was a loud oomph, like she'd received a heavy impact blow. I heard crying and mumbling. They were too far away to make out what they were saying.

There was a clang of metal followed by footsteps getting louder.

I can't be here.

I tiptoed out of the room and edged the door shut. Once back in the corridor, I let out a heavy breath. My heart was pounding in my chest, but the danger wasn't over.

The door handle moved. I needed to get away, but I couldn't go too fast. That would look too obvious. It took all my self-control to slow myself down.

With the glass windows looking into the quad, I felt too visible. Cronus would see me as soon as he stepped out the door. I prayed that I didn't look guilty. I didn't want him to figure out that I'd been snooping.

"Kiely!"

His voice left me frozen in my tracks. I kept my eyes cast down, worried that if he saw my face, he'd know where I'd been. "Cronus."

It was barely two strides for his long legs to join me.

"Are you lost?"

"Yes." I beamed with too much enthusiasm. I threw my hand up in despair. "I can't find my room."

Cronus smirked, amused by my dramatic performance. He held out his arm for me to take. "You will need your strength for tomorrow. Let me take you to bed, little chick."

His eyes were so dark that they were almost black. They drew me into him and soothed my tortured soul. I forgot all my worries, but my heart didn't steady. It beat with a whole new danger. A danger I wanted to embrace and be held by all night. I'd sworn never to allow another man close enough to break my heart, but my body craved it despite my good sense.

There was something not right here, like he'd drugged me to be armoured to him. This didn't feel safe like when I was with Nate.

This had to be the compulsion Callum had mentioned.

"What's the plan for tomorrow?" I asked, my voice breathy.

"There are steps you must take in your transition to join us. You must complete an ultimate challenge."

"What sort of challenge?"

The challenge didn't concern me. I felt a need to impress Cronus and was willing to do anything he asked of me.

"Don't worry about that. First, we must get you home so you can sit your exams."

I frowned. My exams weren't appealing, but if it

meant I could see my family again, I'd go along with it.

Cronus rubbed my hand. "Don't worry. We will bring you back here to complete your training as soon as possible."

"I love it here." I bit my lip to prevent myself from confessing why. My desire for Cronus was overwhelming. In his presence, the world felt fuzzy, but somewhere deep down, I knew it wasn't real. I remembered what Callum had said about Cronus's ability to draw us to him. I blinked to clear my head.

"You have an eternity to enjoy this." He pushed open the door to my room and entered with me. "Tonight, you must sleep."

Scotland was a million miles away from my troubles. Returning home reminded me of the mess that awaited me. I wanted to stay here and party with my new family, and enjoy an eternity with them.

Being around Cronus filled me with a strange warmth. I guessed it was the compulsion that Callum had mentioned, but it felt good and I never wanted it to end.

My fingers reached out for him. "Can you stay?"

He frowned. "What do you mean?"

I blushed as I thought of Nate and the way he'd comforted me when I felt broken. So much had happened and changed. I wanted someone to hold me the way he did. I missed Nate, but it was Cronus standing here now. If only he could read my mind like he did when we were in Crow form, so I didn't have to say it out loud. Or was this feeling because I was falling prey to the compulsion? If only I knew how to pull myself out of it.

Cronus laughed, a deep rumbling sound that filled me up with a need to be part of making him smile. "You have so much to learn, chick."

"Teach me."

"I will, but now you must sleep."

"Please," I begged with a desperate need that felt like if he left, I would die.

A shadow cast over his features. "Take off your clothes."

I felt small, like prey to a predator. My cheeks flushed at the thought of standing naked in front of him. My hands trembled, not wanting to fulfill his command, but I did it. I shed my clothes along with my free will, discarding them into a pile on the floor. Standing in my underwear, the cool air made the hair on my arms stand up as I shivered. I felt exposed. My hand trembled as I pushed the strap of my bra off my shoulder.

"Stop!" Cronus commanded.

I froze. My bra strap hung limp off my shoulder. Folding my arms across my chest, I dared to look at him through my eyelashes. Despite feeling violated, I had a strange desire for his approval. Part of me wanted him to want me.

"Get into bed."

My mind was screaming at me to stop, that I wasn't ready for what was about to happen. This was wrong. There was something alluring about him, but he was ancient - who knew how old that was? But I couldn't disobey.

Into bed I got. With the covers off, I lay there waiting for him to join me. I wanted to run. I wanted to scream. But my body wasn't listening and the words wouldn't come. I was compliant and unable to stop what was happening. Deep down, I knew I didn't want Cronus, but my will was being overridden. A strange urge to please Cronus in any way was strangling me, like an invisible rope holding me to his bidding.

"Now, sleep." His eyes turned an electric blue. He swept his arm, and the blankets moved up the bed of their own accord, covering my body. He turned toward the door.

"Aren't you joining me?" I said, confused.

"I don't think so." He went to leave the room.

The rejection washed over me, and I felt deflated. "Is there someone else?"

"No." He shook his head. "I have no interest in that. It serves no purpose."

He left, and as the distance between us increased, I felt more in control of myself. My body and mind were my own again. He scared me with the power he could wield over me with such ease.

Although I was free, I still felt trapped.

I struggled to sleep. The sound of the screaming lady haunted my dreams, and objects moved that should have been stationary. I dreamt that I crept into the dark and discovered a hidden room that looked like a dungeon.

A woman made of light was expecting me.

Everything around us moved with a life of its own. The feeling of dread turned my stomach and made me sweat...

CHAPTER 17

I'D FORGOTTEN TO SHUT THE CURTAINS and woke to sunlight streaming in and a knock at my door. I threw on a dressing gown and went to see who it was.

Morgan stood there with a tray. It had a glass of orange juice and toast. "There's more downstairs, but I thought you might like a little something to get you going. I wasn't sure how you were feeling this morning."

"Thank you." I took the tray and walked over to a small table by the window that looked out over the beautiful mountains and valleys below. "Considering how much we drank, I feel good."

"We can handle drinking better than most because

of our rapid healing, but I worry about you being young." She smiled.

Fed up with my age being used to judge my capabilities, I frowned at Morgan as I sat at the table where she'd placed the tray. My stomach grumbled with hunger as I washed the toast down with the orange juice. I mumbled thanks in appreciation between bites.

Morgan sat on my bed whilst I ate. "You'll find clothes in various sizes in the wardrobe, and a selection of toiletries in the bathroom. Feel free to help yourself."

"Thanks."

"No worries. Cronus has asked that you meet him in the Eagle Suite to discuss your transition plans."

"Okay." My cheeks flushed as I remembered our last encounter. A sour taste filled my mouth, and my stomach felt heavy at the thought of seeing him again. The piece of toast trembled in my hand, no longer appealing. I put it down on the plate so Morgan wouldn't notice.

"I'll leave you to get ready." Morgan got up and left the room whilst I gazed out the window, calming myself with the beautiful view. A strange prickling sensation ran over my body, causing the hairs on my arm to stand up. I felt the urge to shift. I wanted to spread my wings and soar over the landscape, but I knew I couldn't be late for Cronus.

I washed and checked out the basic clothing options. The selection of black clothes looked like a uniform, each item with two crossed scythes in the corner, like a crest. Others had a small crow logo. I found my size and slipped on a T-shirt and jersey shorts.

As I passed the mirror, my reflection took me back. I still looked like a stranger, my skin now deathly pale and my hair an inky black that matched the dark feathers of my crow form. I looked through the wash bag Morgan had supplied. She'd included a little makeup. I pulled out some red lipstick and applied it to add a little colour to my face before heading down for my meeting with Cronus.

The meeting rooms were a few doors along from Cronus's office. I read the brass plate on each door until I reached the Eagle Suite. I pushed the door open and entered a grand-looking vintage lounge. Cronus sat on an emerald couch, waiting for me to join him.

I blushed as I remembered how things had ended last night. "I'm sorry…"

Cronus cut me off. "Don't worry about it. We have more important things to discuss."

I sighed with relief.

"Your transition contract."

I nodded, not because I had a clue what that was, but to show him I was listening and pleased the topic wasn't about last night or my age. I was trying to behave as grown up as possible to show I wasn't a child, but a woman.

"First, I thought it would be nice to show you the grounds."

My face lit up as I remembered the view and how eager I'd longed to explore it.

"Shall we?" Cronus offered me his arm in the same

way he had the previous night and I took it. He led me down the corridor and out the large double doors.

We stepped out the front, which looked out over a cliff edge.

The North Sea glistened below us in the morning sun, a vast twinkling plain. My hair blew back in the wind. It reminded me of the glorious sensation of it running through my feathers as I glided through it.

Cronus slipped his arm out of mine and placed his hand on the small of my back. He guided me down some stone steps cut into the mountain that looked like they'd been there for centuries. The old path was hard to walk down, but I took in the scents and smells of the pretty purple colours of heather and thistles. Cronus led me down to the shore below. There were patches of long grass as the soil turned to sand.

You couldn't see any houses or buildings of any kind, except the mansion we'd come from at the top of the cliff. Grey rocks and mountains framed the beach. It was so different from the shingle beaches back home, with the bustling promenade and rows of beach huts. This beach was desolate, like a lost island.

Cronus took my hand as we walked along the shore. I caught him watching me and blushed. I could feel that strange sensation washing over me, and wondered, "What powers do we have?"

"We collect the lost souls by taking their shadows. As the wolf that marked you didn't claim you, we came for you. It is our most important power. To join us, you will show us you can be part of the murder by taking the shadow of the wolf that marked you."

"He'll join us?" My mind flicked back to the wolf and the way he'd seduced me that night. I wondered if I'd have that power, and could then have anyone I wanted. No more being rejected for someone better, or for nobody at all.

"Join us?" Cronus tipped his head back as he let out a deep-throated laugh.

"What?" I squeezed his arm to demand his attention.

"You will use your powers to hunt him down and seek your revenge."

"Revenge?"

Cronus shrugged. "He will cease to exist. Dead."

I gasped. "I don't think I could kill anyone."

"You will if you want all this." He waved his arms around, reminding me of the freedom I now had from my past life. The setting was beautiful and despite not yet mastering my powers, I knew I was stronger. The price for this life was too steep. I wasn't a killer. "No. There must be another way."

"I was afraid of this, what with you being so young..."

"It's not my age!" I snapped.

He smirked, which annoyed me further.

"I'm not killing. And I want you to stop the Drago going after my parents. I've had enough of this secret world!"

Cronus laughed. "You relinquished your soul to me. You have no choice. If you don't, you'll cease to be part of my flock. Stuck as a bird forever."

Anger bubbled inside me. My skin prickled, and I felt the wash of darkness. I cast the shadow down, engulfing my body. I became a crow and beat my wings.

Rather, a crow forever than a murderer.

I needed to escape this madness and get my old life back. My friends, my family, and my undeniable need to see Nate again. I wasn't sure which way to go. Just as far away from this island as possible. Anywhere across the ocean would do.

A strange sensation gripped me. It flipped my stomach, and I found myself flying backward. I pushed my beak forward, beating my wings harder, trying to free myself from the strange force overpowering me. No matter how hard I tried, my body was returning to the island. I crashed to the ground, black feathers scattered around me. My breath was knocked out of me with the impact and sand coated my feathers. My screams came out as angry squawks. I tried to fly, but a fire-like pain burned through my wing every time I tried to lift it.

I twisted my neck to see Cronus. His arm reached toward me. I gave in, defeated and aware that I was no match for him. Pressing my head down into the wet sand, listening to the waves rolling toward me and unable to move.

Strong hands lifted me up close to his mouth, almost as if he was going to whisper a secret.

"Sorry, little chick."

He carried me back up the path we'd come down

and returned me to the little cage in my room. This time I didn't look to him for safety or guidance. I thought about how he wanted me to kill, about the crying woman, and how he laughed at the Drago going after my parents.

Cronus wasn't a good person.

Conflicted by a desire to be with Cronus, and to satisfy him; a desire that wasn't my own. My stomach turned, and my mind screamed that I needed to escape. I was powerless to do anything. My body wasn't mine. I felt sick by the invisible bars his powers had over me, which felt more real and restrictive than the slender golden bars of the little cage he'd placed me in.

I shook with fear as I watched Cronus's rage grow. He stood in the centre of the room, waving his arms around wildly. Just like in my dream, objects were lifted from the floor untouched and flew around out of control. He trashed the space I'd come to know as mine. They were just things, but it felt like a direct attack on me.

The others must have heard the commotion because Morgan ran in. She begged him to stop. Asked him what had happened. He looked like he was going to turn on her. She flung her arms around his neck and kissed him.

His arms dropped. His body melted. It was like she was sucking the anger out of him with that kiss. Cronus pushed her back and stormed toward the window, and I feared he was going to start again, but he pointed to me.

"She's a liability."

Morgan shook her head. "She's a child. A frightened little girl. She never should have been dragged into this. Don't punish her for Luna's crimes."

Cronus clenched his fists. "It's all a mess. We should have killed her and let her parents report their daughter missing. She wouldn't be our problem."

Morgan approached Cronus with caution and rubbed his arm. "What happened?"

Cronus looked at me. "She tried to leave."

I began chirping, as I lied. Begging Cronus to free me and promising I'd never attempt to leave again. The thought that he could kill me if I didn't do as he asked forced me to beg for a second chance.

I was good at lying and for once I hoped it'd save me from the trouble I'd got myself in.

Cronus hadn't entered my head as he'd done before. I didn't know if he or Morgan could understand what I was saying.

Callum entered the room. His eyes widened as he took in the mess, finally resting on me in the cage. "Is everything okay?"

Cronus pointed at him. "You! Coax her to shift and bandage her arm up. She can't fly. I'll have to take my car."

He held out his arm to Morgan, who took it and left the room with him. Despite all that had happened, I felt an odd pang of jealousy that it wasn't me on his arm. Choosing her felt like another rejection, another blow, and all I wanted was his forgiveness. My heartache mixed with relief that he'd gone. I wondered if I'd ever be free of his influence.

Callum unlocked the cage door and lifted me out and placed me on the bed. "Shifting back won't be easy with an injury. It's gonna hurt. But once you're in human form, I can treat it."

The need to have my voice back urged me to do as he asked. He was right. As my body changed, I felt the fire of my broken bones blaze through me as they took on their new shape. By the time I was back in my human body, I was screaming in pain.

My body fought to fuse my bones back together, but they wouldn't. It felt like they were breaking all over again.

I surrendered, covered in sweat and panting. My eyes screwed shut, blocking out the pain. Shifting had used more energy than before to achieve, and I felt miserable. The god-like feeling of flying and being superhuman was gone.

I jumped in response to Callum's hand on my face and called out in pain as he moved my arm.

"It's okay. I'm going to help you," he soothed.

I relaxed a little and took in his kind face as he held a cool flannel to my forehead.

From the way my arm laid gingerly across my waist, Callum could tell which was injured. He moved closer to inspect it and lifted it up. I flinched. Although he was tender, it still hurt.

Callum reached to my side table and picked up some pills and a glass of water I'd not noticed. He must have fetched them when my eyes were closed. He offered them to me. "Pain killers."

I leaned on the elbow of my good arm, but the pain still raged through my body in response to the slight movement. I washed the pills down, desperate for them to work, and took in the state of my room. It looked like a tornado had hit. It was a miracle the bed was still in one piece.

With caution, I settled myself back down onto the bed. Every slight movement impacted my arm, whether I felt I was moving it or not.

Callum tried to help me by placing pillows to prop me up.

Callum said in a dull tone, "There are things I need to get. Stay here. I'll be back soon."

I nodded. Where would I go anyway?

This beautiful home, set in a beautiful landscape, no longer felt safe. It was a prison.

I thought about telling Callum about Cronus attacking me, or about the crying woman, but I realised he hadn't asked how I got injured. It didn't matter to him. He likely knew and was okay with it. He was devoted to Cronus and would do his bidding.

As I laid there waiting for his return, I realised I couldn't trust any of them.

Callum returned and although he talked through what he was doing, he confirmed my theory. He didn't once enquire about how my arm got broken.

Callum spoke only of the plans for our upcoming journey. He'd been told I'd be riding with Cronus and the others would fly and meet us there. The only comforting words he gave me were that my body would heal faster than when I was human. It made the pain more bearable to know this agony would be over soon.

CHAPTER 18

ORGAN ENTERED MY ROOM. "Everything is prepared. Cronus has requested that you join him in the Eagle Suite."

I didn't want to go as my mind flashed back to how our last meeting had ended. Morgan came to my side and helped me onto my feet, but I didn't welcome her assistance. I felt betrayed by them all.

The sling kept my arm close to my body like a hug.

The walk to the suite felt different from the previous morning. There was a strong foreboding like I was being taken to trial. My arm ached as I thought of the harm he could inflict on me. Morgan knocked on the dark oak door. Dread ran cold through my body, and I closed my eyes and prepared myself to face him.

Cronus opened the door with a smile. The smile was so unexpected that I tripped as I entered the room. He looked different from the man who'd caused me to break my wing on the beach. Or the madman who'd unleashed their rage in my room.

He waved his hand to encourage me to take a seat.

The warm welcome threw me off guard. It scared me more, knowing how unpredictable he could be. I fidgeted with the edge of my sling and kept watch of him as I took a seat.

"We have less than thirty days to train you to use your powers, to enable you to take revenge on the one that marked you."

"What if I'm not ready in time?" My voice was a weak croak as I approached the topic with caution.

Cronus leaned back in his seat, one leg across his lap. He was relaxed and confident in knowing he had control over me. "There is no extension on the full moon. Once it is here, you will not fail me. You will complete the transformation and prove that you are a reaper."

My heart longed for another option. I didn't trust Cronus, and I didn't dare disagree with him. I strained against the urge to shake my head and pressed my lips together to prevent myself from speaking out.

Cronus waved his fingers in the air. Like a puppet with strings attached, the coffee pot lifted. But there were no strings, no contact from anyone or anything. My eyes widened as I watched it float across the table and tip. The hot liquid poured into my cup. With a similar motion, the milk jug lifted into the air and followed suit.

Ghosts?

I recalled how he'd tucked me into bed, the way he'd willed the blanket up over my naked body without touching it. The scene of him raging in my room as if he commanded a poltergeist to carry out his destruction. My heart thundered in my chest and my skin prickled. I knew Cronus was doing it. Was he using a telekinesis-type power or was he a type of necromancer controlling the spirits of those whose lives he'd taken?

He had a casual expression on his face, a gentle smile, but his eyes were lit a bright blue like when he'd seen me naked. With a casual wave of his hand, he lifted the mug. It came toward me.

"You look like you need a strong drink," he said with a smug look on his face.

My hands were shaking as I plucked the mug from the air. I inspected it. It was an ordinary mug. I took a sip. It was a strong coffee with nothing unusual about it.

My voice trembled. "How did you do that?"

"Shadow kinesis. It's one of our abilities I will teach you to use." He smiled.

It excited part of me to learn about my new powers, but another part of me knew what I was supposed to do with them. I still didn't think I could go through with killing someone. But I got the impression that I didn't have a choice. Cronus wouldn't allow me to live out my days as a crow. I had to fulfill my transitional contract.

I looked at his powerful hands wrapped around his mug and imagined what they'd feel like clasped around my neck.

I knew it wasn't only his physical strength that I needed to be wary of.

"We will start your training once you are home."

"Why must we go back?" I wanted to keep him and his kind as far away from my family and friends. I was aware of the way his voice coursed through my body and made me feel calm, in complete contrast to his true nature.

His smile dropped, and his eyes glanced down at my broken arm. "You know how dedicated I am to protecting the avatar world. A missing child will cause too much attention. If I'd known your age, I would have killed you then and there. I should have offered you no choice."

A chill ran through my body. I knew he meant it.

His award-winning smile was back. "But you are here now. You are mine to keep. And keep you, I will."

Although he appeared friendly, I felt the undercurrent of his words. The subtle warning that trading my soul for a new life had put me at his mercy. He owned me. Were the other crows even aware they weren't free?

If I was going to free myself from him, I needed to become stronger. Which meant I had to allow him to teach me about my powers. A plan was forming to learn from him and surpass him. I'd find a way to break the soul contract.

"Can I have some milk?" I smiled, pleased that I sounded more relaxed this time.

Cronus raised an eyebrow and then complied. A little carton of milk rose from a basket in the corner. It floated toward my cup; the lid peeled back and it poured. I saw the way his hands moved and planned to practice as soon as I was alone.

"That's amazing. Will you teach me that?"

He smiled at the compliment. "This, and so much more."

There was that draw again like his words were causing the world to disappear, creating a bubble that was only for us. I pulled my gaze away to break the spell and gulped my coffee. It wasn't as sharp now, since the milk had sweetened it.

He reached out to tuck a strand of hair behind my ear, pulling my attention back to him. "We'll leave as soon as you've finished."

The air felt thick between us, full of unspoken words. For a house full of people, it was too quiet. Cronus's hand trailed down my back and rested there. I wanted to tell him not to touch me, but I feared his retaliation. I feared him listening and not touching me too, but that contrary thought had to be the compulsion.

The coffee was hot, but I drank with haste in the hope that once I'd finished, we could go. He couldn't touch me if his hands were on a steering wheel.

I prayed that my return home wouldn't endanger my loved ones. I worried about the harm the Drago may have already inflicted upon them.

Cronus walked me out to a yellow sports car. He walked me around to the passenger door and held it open for me. Getting in was difficult without the use of my arm. The car was low, and I was forced to allow Cronus to help me. Once I was in, he walked around the car and got in the driver's side. The car rumbled to life, and we took to the winding roads.

Not long after, we reached a ferry crossing. Those operating it appeared to know Cronus well and allowed us to board. They didn't wait for anyone else, and we were soon crossing to the mainland.

I looked back at the island; there was no denying its beauty. I mourned that I hadn't had the privilege of visiting under different circumstances.

The man sitting beside me had warped my time here.

My chest tightened, and the air felt too thick. I opened a window and let the fresh salty air gush in, reminding me of home. With that, I thought of my family and feared for their safety. This road trip would feel longer with the constant foreboding.

I needed to break the silence so I coughed to clear my throat and attempted a minor distraction with small talk. "So, what's the plan?"

"During the day, school and exams. In the evening,

you train to kill."

A chill ran through me at the ease he spoke of me killing.

"Is there no other way?"

I saw a vein in his neck twitch as he clenched his jaw. He didn't answer.

"This will be a long trip if you won't speak to me."

"It will be a short eternity if you won't accept your fate."

We reached the mainland and there was some commotion as they prepared the ramp to allow us to drive off. Cronus turned the engine on and the rumble of the powerful engine shook through me.

I leaned back in my seat and shut my eyes. Maybe I could sleep through the journey.

I knew I wouldn't sleep. It wasn't the loud engine keeping me up or my busy mind; it was the dread. I didn't feel safe. My whole body was as tight as a coil. I constructed an invisible wall to keep me safe.

I thought my old life was behind me. But tomorrow, I'd face the judgment of my peers and spend my evenings training with a man who owned me. If I'd thought my life was a mess before, I'd proven that it could get worse. A tear dampened my eyelashes, and I hoped Cronus was too busy to notice me wallowing in self-pity.

"Many give up." His voice startled me.

I flinched and looked over to see if he was looking at me, but his focus was on the road ahead.

"Many cannot survive becoming one of us. But you

made it. Despite your age, you survived the first test. You're strong, and should be proud of yourself."

I groaned. "Why are you all so obsessed with my age? It doesn't define me."

Cronus smiled. "I like your spirit."

I twirled a strand of hair around my finger and chewed my lip. I wanted him to like me, despite hating him. His voice seeped under my skin, warm and inviting. It made me eager for his approval and instead; I teased him.

"I bet you say that to all the girls."

Cronus's laugh rumbled over the engine. "You assume too much."

"What does that mean?"

"Maybe I do not seek the pleasure of women."

"I saw you kissing Morgan."

"Is that what you saw?" His eyebrows raised.

"Yes! You did it in front of me."

"I believe what you saw was Morgan kissing me. The desire was one-sided. As stated, I do not seek the pleasure of women."

"Oh…" I'd not expected that, but it made Cronus appear more human. "So, guys are your thing?"

Cronus chuckled. "Not that it is your business, but I've no interest in either."

"I have a friend that's never had a boyfriend."

"You place too much value on boyfriends."

"I don't. I'm so over my ex." I cringed. My professing sounded so childish, like Jace still bothered me. He *did* still bother me, but I wasn't into him like that. Part of me hung onto wanting to go back to before we broke up, but too much had happened that we never could work. My pride wanted us to end on my terms, not his. I wanted him to want me so that being over him mattered.

"Is he the reason you were so willing to sacrifice your life?"

It was my turn to grind my teeth. "Why are you so judgemental?"

"Comes with the job. We are the enforcers of our laws. We are the judges, and we deliver the sentence. Killing the one who marked you is your first job. It is why we are the most feared of all our kind. It's why we are the rulers. And I am your king."

I smiled. "More powerful than Mariah?"

"If she breaks our laws, I promise she is yours."

"What laws?"

"The most important laws are about protecting our world. If she revealed anything about us, like using her abilities in front of a human, we would punish her. The Drago would silence the human."

"How do they silence someone?" I shivered as I thought of my parents.

He moved his hand to change gears and then returned his hand to the steering wheel. The fields whooshed past outside.

"They have various methods, but don't worry about your parents. The possession went well."

"They're possessed." My eyes widened and my heart thundered in my chest. That didn't sound good.

"But they don't know anything."

"They were a liability, and you must prefer it to them being dead."

"You speak about death as if it is nothing."

Cronus laughed. "When you have lived as many years as I, you will see it as a blessing. I have lost all my primary family and their existence is marginal to the long-term bonds I've formed as a crow. You will see them soon and can decide for yourself. If you would prefer them dead, I can arrange it."

I choked. "Of course, I don't want them dead. Did you always lack empathy, or did it just vanish over the years?"

Cronus laughed. His laughter bubbled inside me until I couldn't help but laugh with him. How did he do that? Was it a skill I would learn?

Seeing my home again felt surreal. The same girl who had taken her dog for a run in the middle of the night was no longer the girl who returned. This no longer felt like where I belonged. I had to sit my exams and get out of town before I endangered anyone else.

Cronus entered my home with me. My parents were there ready to greet me with big smiles on their faces. A wave of relief coursed through my body and I flung my arms around my mum to hug her, tears streaming down my face.

"You're okay! Thank God you're okay."

"Of course we are," Mum said.

I sensed how stiff her body was. Her hug felt different, more like someone patting me on the back. I stepped back.

I took them both in. Something was off. "What's wrong with you?"

"Nothing is wrong with us," my dad answered.

Their expressions didn't change. They were stuck with this strange over-the-top smile that didn't reach their eyes. They'd not worried about where I'd been all weekend, or that my arm was in a sling. There was no relief regarding my return as if this was an ordinary day. My shoulders sunk as my body felt heavy.

I turned toward Cronus. "Where are my parents?"

"There." He swept his arm toward the two figures in front of me.

They looked and sounded like my parents, but instead were empty shells. The spirit of who they were as people had vanished.

I shook my head. "They're different."

"They will be. They're operated by a Drago," Cronus said, his tone matter of fact.

"Where's Murray?" I asked.

"He has left for an incredible, sponsored placement as a marine biologist," Mum said, like a proud parent.

"What about his A-Levels?"

"His new sponsors are taking care of that," Mum said, and exchanged a smile with Dad.

Dad reached for her arm. "I think it's okay to tell

Kiely the truth."

"Yes! Where is he?"

"He's a Merman. He's with his people. Just like you are with your people." Mum gestured toward Cronus.

The room spun. I put my hand on the counter to keep myself steady. Nothing made sense. I couldn't be certain that the truth really was the truth.

I wanted to check in with Murray. For once, I wanted him to interfere in my life and get me out of this mess. His absence reminded me how alone I was in this.

A lump rose in my throat. "Where's Aero?"

Dad shrugged. "He was struggling to adjust, so he's outside."

It was out of character for Dad not to care about Aero. It was confirmation that he wasn't *really* my dad.

I ran through the house, and out into the garden. Aero jumped up, happy to see me. I buried my face into his neck and drank in his scent, a smell like fresh rain and long walks mixed with his meaty breath. I looked into his dark amber eyes that sparkled like gems.

"I'm so sorry, Aero, for the mess I've caused."

His tongue licked the tears from my face, and I laughed. "I love you, too."

It was then that I noticed his injuries were gone. I ran my hands over his body and marvelled at the miracle. He'd appeared in a terrible state when I'd been swept out to sea. I'd worried about how my brave pup was doing. I could feel my eyes welling up with the relief that he was good.

"I arranged for a healer to visit him." Cronus's voice interrupted the moment I'd been having with Aero. "As I stated before, I don't like harming animals."

I stood to face him but enjoyed the warmth of Aero's body against my leg. Aero let out a low growl and bared his teeth at Cronus.

"I'm not a monster." His voice was deep, warm, and inviting.

But I knew better. Aero knew it, too.

I led Aero toward the house to take him in.

"I don't think that's a good idea. Dogs have a tendency to attack Dragos, and the two inside are hosted inside your parent's bodies."

"Aero will be fine. We are going to bed. We have had a long weekend," I replied.

I took Aero inside and shut the door behind me. He growled as we passed the room with my parents, but I took him up to my bedroom. I let him on my bed. My parents hadn't let Aero in our bedrooms before, but I didn't have my parents anymore.

Only Aero and I were left.

And Murray… somewhere…

CHAPTER 19

LAYING ON MY BED, my pillow was damp beneath my cheek. It felt exhausting and liberating to cry. I thought I'd been at rock bottom before, but now I had nothing, nobody, and it was all my fault. Aero lay beside me, trying to comfort me by reminding me that he was still there for me.

As I cried myself to sleep, night crept into my room. It was so dark that it didn't feel natural as if someone had sucked out all the light.

A gradual light glowed on the floor. It started as a pin prick dot and grew bigger. Getting out of bed, I reached down to touch it, only to feel something cool and hard. My fingers closed around it. The object pressed against my palm, and when I opened my hand,

I realised it was a key.

A strip of light appeared at the base of my wall. It stretched up the wall, forming a door. As it became part of my room, I recognized it as the door to Cronus's office. I bit my lip as I wondered if this was a trick by Cronus. Was he in my mind again, and would he hurt me if I didn't do as he wished?

I was hesitant as I pushed the key into the lock and turned it. The door opened, but his office was empty. The bookcase was already pushed aside, revealing the secret passage.

As I made my way down the stone steps, the smell of moss and mud got stronger. It was dark, but I could see a light at the bottom. I placed my good hand against the damp wall and crept down the uneven steps to the room below.

The room was lit by a small candle flickering in an old-fashioned dish. I lifted it to look around the room.

In the corner was a large cage like a prison, and I noticed a woman curled up, sleeping in the far corner. She was easy to see as her whole being lit up as if made of light. She reminded me of an angel with her pure white hair that was pulled back into braided locks.

"Hello," I called out to her.

Her violet eyes opened. She stood and approached the bars of the cage. "Kiely, I've been waiting for you."

I stepped back and stumbled onto a table.

"I called you here to warn you."

"Who… who are you?"

"Darcia. It is an honour to meet you." She wore

a tatty white gown, torn and covered in stains. It reminded me of the nightgown I'd worn the night Cronus took my soul.

She gripped the bars as if she needed them to hold her up. She pressed her face into the gap, but it was too small for her to fit through. "This must be our secret. Tell no one we spoke."

I nodded. "What are you doing in there?"

I could see her better now. Her bones jutted out as if the skin that covered them was too small for her frame and her lips were chapped. I noticed the bruises scattered across her body like the markings of a cheetah. Her head moved as if she was trying to look at me from every possible angle. She was whispering to herself, "Is she like me? Not yet. When will she be? We'll see."

"Did Cronus do this?"

She blinked and jumped back upon hearing my voice. She said, "He made her tell him. He forced her to tell him about you."

"Who?"

She shook her head. "Not long. I never have long. He keeps me weak, so I have little power."

"What are you talking about?"

Her eyes were wide, and she kept looking over her shoulder as she spoke. "You will see. He will turn on you. Be safe. Don't get trapped like me."

I wanted to tell her I knew how dangerous he was, but her glow flickered like a bulb going out. She looked so vulnerable and yet still so beautiful.

"I'm going to free you," I promised.

"I'm counting on it." She smiled. "Keep it secret. Keep it safe."

The room went dark. The candle, cage, and the girl were gone.

I woke, my cheek damp from my wet pillow. The dream had felt so real that I wasn't able to shake it. Was it possible to meet someone in a dream? Is that what Darcia had done?

I moved my broken arm and smiled. It felt a tad tender, but it wasn't unbearable. I took off the sling and wriggled my fingers. Aero snuggled his head up against me, lifting my spirits. I'd forgotten he was here, but I was so glad he was. He was the one constant in my life.

I ran my fingers through his fur as I thought about Darcia and tried to make sense of what her powers were. I thought about all the others I'd learned about and their powers.

Cronus was a dangerous enemy with his shadow kinesis and the ability to manipulate people. I shivered as I thought about the Drago and how they'd taken control of my parents. I wished I could speak to Murray and ask what abilities he had.

When Mariah had rescued me from the sea, had she been a mermaid?

I headed to the bathroom to get ready for school. Instead of picking up my toothbrush, I stared at it in the cup. I willed it into the air, pulling the object's shadow in the same manner I'd seen Cronus do it. It felt like I was lifting an incredible weight.

I strained as I brought it over to my hand. Sweat ran down my brow. As soon as it was close enough, I snatched it from the air. It felt satisfying to hold it. I panted from the exertion as if I'd just completed an intense workout.

Okay, now for the toothpaste.

Again, I used my power to lift it up. It was hard, but not too hard. But trying to hold it steady over my toothbrush was trickier. It reminded me of when someone challenges you to rub your tummy and pat your head, and you lose control over your arms.

I needed to move my toothbrush toward the paste to make it easier. Then I flipped the cap using my shadow kinesis. I wanted to cheer at my accomplishment, but I wasn't done yet. I gave the toothpaste a squeeze. Paste shot out all over my brush, the sink, and my pyjamas.

I laughed with joy and dropped my toothbrush and the paste into the sink. Grabbing a damp flannel, I cleaned up the mess. I was certain that if I kept practicing, this would get easier. It was like learning a new yoga move. With practice, I would master it.

I dressed for school and headed downstairs. Mum stood wearing an apron like a robotic Stepford wife. My dad sat at the dining room table and straightened when I entered the room, a smile plastered on his face that wasn't genuine. They had laid a selection of breakfast items out on the table.

"Orange juice freshly squeezed for you. It's packed with vitamin C." Mum poured me a glass and handed it to me.

"Thank you."

"It's a pleasure." The forced smile seemed sarcastic.

I gulped the juice down. They both watched me, unblinking, and my skin prickled with an eerie discomfort. I had to get out. I grabbed some dry toast and headed out of the door.

Seeing my parents in their strange zombie state was unnerving. It felt odd to attend school, considering everything that had happened this weekend.

Home no longer felt like home. It was a dystopian world. I wondered if there was anything I could do to save my parents and if anyone could help me.

They were continuing their normal routines, but anyone who knew them would sense something was off, even if they didn't figure out that they were possessed.

Attending school felt like stepping back in time. Nothing had changed, yet I was no longer the girl from last week. The taunts and sniggers didn't bother me. They were about someone else.

As I marched down the corridor, I took pleasure in waving my hand down by the side of my waist and watching the locker doors smack open into the faces of those who dared to mock me. I kept my head dipped, conscious of the fact that I had to conceal my eyes when I was using my power.

I swapped books in my locker and heard a girl refer to me as The Oscar Queen. Hiding behind my door, I took glee in shooting her books out of her locker and catching her in the jaw. My aim was off and one book hit her friend, but it served her right for laughing.

I headed to my form room for morning registration. My eyes zoned in on Jace. I kicked myself for the old habit. I was acting like a homing pigeon when I was a death crow. After all that had happened, I still wanted him to notice me. The old Kiely still lurked inside.

Arizona and Fallon moved as if they were encouraging me to sit with them, but I wasn't stupid. I knew it could be a trap and I no longer needed friends like that. I took a seat at the front and gazed out the window.

Our teacher hurried in late and began handing out slips of paper. I looked and realised it was our exam schedule. Once seated, the teacher rushed through the register, completing it before the bell rang and we were dismissed for class. I was happy to go, eager to get through the day so I could start my training.

"Kiely," Fallon said in a gentle voice that sounded too close. I glanced over and discovered her matching my pace. "Can we talk?"

"What do we have to discuss?"

"Nate."

"There's nothing going on between us." I sighed.

"That's a shame because he really, *really* likes you."

I shrugged. "Well, your problem is with him, not me."

"Kiely, I hate what's gone on between us." Fallon's voice broke in a vulnerable way I'd never heard before.

"Whose fault is that?"

"Please, Kiely. My parents are getting divorced."

I stopped. As angry as I was for the way she'd treated me, and as desperate as I was for her to apologise, I could hear the pain in her voice. "I'm sorry to hear that, but what's it to do with me?"

"Nate isn't speaking to me or anyone. He's heartbroken over you. Now he's messed up about our parents. I'm worried about him. He needs someone, and I ruined that for you both."

"That's not your fault."

"I hate how people are treating you," she continued. "I was mad at you, but we're best friends."

"Were," I corrected her.

Fallon's shoulders slumped. "Please, I can't stand by and watch the way people are jumping on the bandwagon to make fun of you. They're like a pack of hyenas."

"They'll get bored." It felt easier knowing my days in this town would be over soon.

Fallon reached out to touch my hair. "I'm loving the new look."

"Thanks." I'd gotten so used to my black hair that I'd forgotten it was new to everyone else.

"Please hang out with Ari and me. If you like Nate, you have my blessing."

"I can't."

Fallon's lips twitched as she tried to sound a

counterargument.

With no choice but to lie again, I added, "I'm still not over Jace."

It sounded more believable than the truth. I couldn't tell them I was a supernatural law enforcement officer who shapeshifted into a crow with dark, uncontrollable desires for the worst monster I'd ever met. Or that my involvement with the shifter world had resulted in my parents being possessed by a strange snake creature, and for Nate's safety, it was best he stayed away regardless of any feelings either of us may have had.

Fallon groaned. "Move on."

We both laughed. The comment felt so normal. So like the old us. She squeezed my arm, and I knew we'd taken the first steps to repair our friendship.

I wanted to tell her about the crazy weekend I'd had. The fact I'd almost drowned. I'd died and given up my soul. Now, I was reborn as a crow and could fly anywhere in the world. My trip to the Scottish Highlands. My new family. The terrifying and alluring Cronus.

But the image of my parents behaving like complete strangers made me shiver and bite my tongue. If I told Fallon, the Drago could come for her, too.

My eyes caught a flash of red hair and I knew it was Mariah.

"We can catch up at lunch. I have to do something," I told Fallon and raced off before she could stop me.

Catching up with Mariah, I pulled her into an empty classroom and slammed the door shut by moving the shadow. I could feel my anger for her rising inside me, consuming me in a way that made me feel powerful.

For a long time, she'd stolen the attention of the men in my life and turned them against me. I'd done nothing wrong to her. The injustice infuriated me.

"Kiely, are you alright?" I saw the alarm flash across her face.

I reached for her shadow, holding her wrist in my hand, twisting it, and causing it to burn. Her squeal of pain warmed by bitter heart. She knew I was doing it but couldn't work out how.

"I'm the law! If you slip up, I will be there to make sure you suffer." My hands flew forward to grab her neck. As she choked, I kept my distance. I wasn't touching her, but she felt my hands tighten and panic flared in her eyes as she struggled to breathe. "Do you understand?"

Mariah nodded. Her curls bobbed around her flushed face.

I loosened my hold. "Promise you will never tell Jace. Promise you'll keep him safe."

I wanted to make demands about Murray too, but I was still unclear on the situation as I didn't believe everything I'd been told by Cronus. Before I could figure out where I wanted the conversation to go, the classroom door opened.

A girl I'd never seen before entered. She appeared too old to be in school uniform, but I saw the family resemblance to Mariah. "What's going on here?"

She waved her hand and a forceful wind pushed

my arm away. Her eyes flashed silver, and I knew she had powers. Outnumbered, I stood down. "Just making sure Mariah doesn't break any rules."

"That's my job," she said sternly. "Now piss off, death crow."

I wanted to punish her for interfering, but she knew what I was and I had no idea who she was or the extent of her powers. She had the advantage of knowledge.

"I was going anyway," I said as I sauntered past them both. I threw Mariah a warning look over my shoulder and saw her eyes flash silver, too.

I met Arizona and Fallon for lunch. Arizona threw her arms around me for a hug. "Are you alright?"

I nodded.

"I might have to create a new polish shade and name it 'Dark Kiely'. This look is really different. What made you dye your hair?"

"I love it," Fallon stated. "It's so edgy."

"Call it 'Soul Reaper'."

Arizona's eyes widened. "Yes!"

Fallon gave a sceptical look. "Whose soul are you reaping?"

That was a good question. Cronus had mentioned that I would need to kill my maker. I pictured the guy who attacked me, the way he kissed me, the way he touched me. He'd violated me and I'd enjoyed it. That was so messed up. Of all the men that had wronged me, he deserved comeuppance the most, but killing still felt too far.

"It's a joke. 'Dark Kiely' is fine."

"I can't wait to start making it. It's gonna be dark and edgy." Ari grinned.

"Well, if Kiely is getting an entire line of shades, I should too!"

"I'll work my magic." Ari giggled, enjoying us getting excited about her products.

I turned my attention to Fallon. "So, what happened? Why are your parents—"

Fallon's face twisted with discomfort. It was odd to see her squirm. The sudden shift in her character was telling. I placed an arm over her shoulders. She shrugged me off and whispered, "Don't."

"Sorry, I shouldn't have asked."

Fallon reached over and placed a hand on mine. "It shows that you care." She jutted out her chin as she nodded and added, "I don't want to cry, and I'm not ready to talk about it. Okay?"

"Fair enough." I wanted to reach out and hold her and show her how much I cared, but it wasn't her style. She didn't like to let her walls down. "I'm here when you need me."

"We both are." Ari put her hand on top of Fallon's.

"Us three forever." Fallon smiled. Ari nodded, and I copied her, despite feeling a lump in my throat, knowing I'd soon be saying goodbye forever.

CHAPTER 20

I WAS ONE OF THE FIRST to leave the school. I hadn't gotten far when I passed a parked car. The window wound down and a familiar voice called my name. It was Nate.

I sped up. Part of me was mad that he told people where I was and about our trip to A&E, but that wasn't what drove me to create distance between us. I cared for him. More than I dared to admit. Above all, I couldn't cope with any more casualties because of who I was now.

I heard the engine of the car as his friend fired it up. Soon, the car was level with me again.

"I know you're avoiding me."

I ignored him. Fallon thought I was what he needed,

and I wanted to be there for him like he had been for me, but I had my reservations. Knowing his feelings towards me complicated things, and scared me more than Cronus. I wasn't ready to trust anyone and be vulnerable.

"Where were you this weekend?"

A chill ran through me. He was the only human who noticed that I'd been gone. I wondered how he knew, how much he knew, and hoped he wasn't in any danger. The more distance I could create between us, the safer for him.

"Leave me alone or I'll call the police and report you for harassment."

There were a few mumbles between Nate and the driver that I couldn't make out over the sound of the radio. He leaned back out the window. "Kiely, just give me five minutes."

I pulled my mobile out of my school bag. "Nine-nine-nine. It's only three numbers. I'm calling it."

"You wouldn't."

He was right, I would never do that. Deep in my heart, I wanted Nate to get out of the car, hold me, and force me to listen. I wanted him to make me feel safe again. But it was for his own sake; I had to convince him that I would call.

I held the mobile to my ear, pretending it was ringing. "Police, please." I pretended to wait for a reply as I continued walking. Then I heard the car engine rev up, and it was gone. Leaving me to walk home in peace.

Nate needed to move on and I hoped he'd got the

message, but if not, I hoped his friend was giving him an earful. I wanted to avoid him asking questions that might attract the drago's attention, afraid of losing him to a similar fate as my parents. It pained me to know that we could never be more because of the choices I'd made.

Cronus was waiting for me at my house. He stood casually on the doorstep, shrouded in shadows that were thicker than anywhere else. When he saw me, he walked over. "We have checked into a local hotel."

He clicked the key fob for his car and again opened the passenger car door for me to get in.

I raised an eyebrow. "Can't we fly there?"

Cronus laughed. "This car is better than flying."

"I doubt that."

"Okay, you have a point, but I want you to conserve your energy for training."

I got into the car. He shut my door, then walked around to the driver's side.

I wanted to fly. I could feel my wings flap beneath my skin in frustration that they wanted to be free to soar, but I did as Cronus said. The heated leather seats were comforting, and I relaxed into them as they stole the cold from my bones. The low seats caused my school skirt to ride up, and I had to readjust it. Where I'd once wanted Cronus to notice me, I now recoiled at the thought of his touch.

We drove in silence and I thought about when we'd first met and how trusting I was with him. I thought about every time someone had told me what to do, and how I did it without question. The way he knew me before we'd shared anything made me feel like it was my fate to follow him. The way he'd given me the release from my inner demons and pain when I was at my lowest made me feel I owed him.

But I wasn't a killer.

We drove through town and when we got to the end; he pulled into the car park at the Deben Hotel. I'd heard a story that this hotel had once hosted the royal family. It was an old hotel that had kept a lot of its original Victorian and Edwardian features and décor.

We walked through reception, and Cronus waved to a member of the staff. He took me into the lounge. It was a large room with green and red leather sofas. There was a piano in the corner and a fireplace with a painting of a nobleman in a gold frame. There were dark redwood shelves full of books that looked like first editions of classics. Hanging from the ceiling were chandeliers with fake candles. It reminded me a little of Cronus's own home. He took a seat on the long, green leather couch as if this was where he belonged.

I sat in the small, red leather armchair, and the guy Cronus had waved at hurried in and placed a silver tray on the small coffee table. The tray held two small teacups, a little teapot, and a milk jug. There were scones, clotted cream, and jam.

"Please make sure we're not disturbed," Cronus instructed the guy and passed him some folded money.

The guy nodded as he left the room. He carefully shut the door behind him, almost bowing as he went.

Cronus smiled at me. "Are you ready to start your training?"

I nodded and slid to the edge of my seat, ready to pay close attention.

"We shall have cream tea without physically using our hands." Cronus waved his hand at the teapot. It lifted gently and tipped with precision. The tea poured out of the spout as he filled his cup with ease. He nodded at me. "Now, it's your turn."

I stared at the pot and identified the shadow. I moved my hand. The pot rattled before it lifted. It shook like it was being held by a shaky hand as it drifted toward my cup. I focused harder as I tipped it. It tipped quicker than I expected and splashed into the teacup. I tried to correct it, and it spilled over the edge and onto the saucer.

Cronus burst out laughing, and the teapot dropped to the table with a clatter. That made Cronus laugh even harder. He wiped a tear from his eyes. They sparkled with merriment as he lifted the milk jug by its shadow and added it to his cup. He placed it down and, with a snigger, he said, "Your turn."

I was aware my movements were more obvious than Cronus's. His hand gestures were discreet. Plus, I was clumsy.

I was determined to do better and lifted the jug. It was easier. Almost like my telekinesis could tell this object was lighter. But I still needed to focus. I slowly tipped the jug, pouring milk into my cup. I was concentrating so hard that a bead of sweat ran down my forehead as I lowered it back to the table. I grinned with triumph, proud that I hadn't spilled a drop.

"Well done," Cronus said, wearing a smirk, one eyebrow shooting up. "Have you been practicing?"

Guilt caused my cheeks to flush, and I feared that he might know. I shook my head as my throat locked up. There was something in the manner he asked that made me feel like he didn't want me to be practicing alone. I could tell Cronus was a man who liked to be in control.

"This should be fun." He then flipped his scone onto its side and the knife lifted into the air and sliced it in two. He added the clotted cream to one half, then spooned on the strawberry jam. The scone lifted in the air and floated up to his face, where he took a bite. Crumbs showered down. His tongue licked his lips to retrieve some cream that had been caught there. "Let's see how you do."

I forgot to tip my scone on its side. Instead, I lifted the knife and moved it back and forth in a sawing motion. My scone was hacked in half. I dropped the knife, causing it to clatter against the plate. Cronus laughed causing me to sigh.

I lifted the top of my scone off, turned it over, and laid it down beside the other half. I then attempted to spoon the clotted cream, but it was hard to lift the spoon, which was stuck against the cream. I tugged, and it shot up into the air and catapulted the clotted cream. It splattered on the posh painting across from me.

"Oh no!"

"Don't worry," Cronus said with a chuckle. "Try again. Try to envision how it feels and go with that motion."

This was much harder than flicking a switch or knocking things over. I was feeling frustrated and wanted to reach over and use my hands. But when I looked at Cronus, his eyes sparkled at me, full of encouragement. This was supposed to be fun. I tried to remind myself that if he wasn't taking it too seriously, maybe I shouldn't either.

I tried to relax and tried again. I felt a slight resistance, but once the spoon lifted with the clotted cream, it was easy to move over. It refused to drop off the spoon, and I resorted to spreading it onto the scone using the back of the spoon. I then attempted the jam and achieved it without too much trouble. I lifted the remaining half and put it back on top.

I realised that I would have to lift it. I checked to see if Cronus was really making me do this the hard way.

"You can do it," he said, as if reading my mind.

I glided my hand as if reaching for my scone and lifted the shadow toward my lips. As I took a bite, the scone crumbled in my mouth, mixed with the cream and the fruity jam. It tasted like success. I sent the scone back to my plate.

"I did it."

"I told you."

"So you did."

"Tomorrow, after school, I want you to come

straight here for practice."

I nodded.

We continued to enjoy our cream tea, practicing my powers until it was time for me to go. Cronus walked me down the road to the nearby woodland, where I could shift and fly home.

Hanging out with my friends again felt amazing. But I was cautious not to let them be too close for fear of the repercussions if they discovered my new life. I was well aware of how Fallon loved to snoop into other people's business, but now that hobby could get her killed. I prayed the drama with her parents was enough to keep her distracted.

Everyone was making plans on how to celebrate finishing school after the final exam. It was strange to get involved with plans that I had no intention of keeping. Not that I didn't want to go, but I knew Cronus had other plans for me. Those plans were far away from this simple life, and it made me feel like a stranger amongst my friends.

"Hey, wait up!" Fallon called.

I'd attempted to leave school without Arizona and Fallon. Cronus had asked me to meet him at the hotel and I wasn't sure how to explain to them that I wasn't walking home. There would be questions. Questions I couldn't answer.

They chatted about the end-of-year party they were planning, but as the hotel neared, my palms became sweaty.

I needed to lose them, but there was no polite way of telling them to go.

"I've started piano lessons."

The words felt thick in my throat.

Fallon's eyes squinted. "Why start that when you have exams to sit? You should have waited and done it over the summer. You've never been interested in music before - why now?"

My back knotted as she saw right through my lie. "My mum said it helps to calm exam nerves."

Arizona smiled. "I hadn't heard that. I wish I was learning piano too."

"What's your teacher like?" Fallon asked.

"Nice. I should go, I don't wanna be late." I waved over my shoulder as I walked onto the hotel grounds. Their eyes bore into my back and I sensed the questions already brewing. Once I was free of them, I could breathe more easily.

That was until Cronus met me.

His eyebrows dipped in the middle in a deep frown. "This way, Chick!"

"What did I do? I came here straight from school, like you told me."

The sweating returned, and my heart raced as I feared what unknown law I could have broken and what the punishment could be.

He didn't answer but clenched his fist. It felt as

if he'd gripped my wrist. He marched off down the corridor and an invisible hand yanked my arm forward and forced me to run to keep up with his big strides. My cheeks burned with humiliation. I must have looked odd to anyone watching us, but nobody could see how Cronus was hurting me.

We were back in the lounge we'd occupied the previous day. Cronus stood in the centre of the room and swung his other hand. The door slammed shut as if blown by a gust of wind. "I've been informed you have been abusing your power!" His eyes bulged and his forehead creased with his frown.

"W-what do you mean?"

"Did you or did you not attack a mermaid? Princess Mariah, to be exact."

I had to laugh. Mariah was a fucking princess. Of course she was. She couldn't be an ordinary girl who stole my boyfriend, stole my brother, and god knows what else she wanted. No, she had to have it all. She was a princess. Mother fucking royalty.

My blood boiled with the injustice of it all, and the room darkened as it filled with my sarcastic laughter. "And what about it?"

Cronus growled. "You can't do that. As the law, we must uphold the standard expected. We are role models to the whole hidden world, entrusted with a great power, to do what is right."

"Sounds frigging boring to me." I snorted. What fun were my powers if I couldn't use them against my enemies?

The air slammed out of my chest as my body was thrown into one of the mahogany bookcases. The dusty books toppled from the shelves on top of me. Stunned and scared, I sucked on my lip. A fresh cut stung as my tongue traced the wound and tasted the iron.

"Do you want to fight me? I am ancient. I have had forever to master my power, to become this formidable authority. You are nothing but stupid if you want to take me on." He rubbed his temples as if speaking to me wore him out. "This is why we should kill children rather than recruit them."

Dust caught in my throat with the chill of his bitter words. He began walking toward me. His fists clenched by his side, his eyes lit an electric blue. I sensed another onslaught.

I waved my hands to lift the books from the floor and threw them at him.

Cronus laughed as he dismissed the books with a wave of his hand, sending them flying off in different directions.

"Cut it out before you get hurt."

"Isn't that what you want?"

"No, this is a lesson. I am order. You are part of my order. Obey our laws. What possessed you to attack Mariah?"

I felt juvenile as I admitted, "She stole my boyfriend."

Hearing the reason out loud made me cringe. It sounded like an affirmation of all the judgments he'd made of me based on my age. I wasn't even into Jace anymore. It was my wounded pride. Jace had destroyed my trust, but I wanted to punish Mariah for being the reason I got hurt.

Cronus lifted me from where I cowered on the floor. His laugh rumbled and filled the room. I drifted across the room as if cradled in invisible arms, and he placed me down onto the sofa. "Remind me not to get on your bad side."

I offered him a timid smile. But his sudden shift in mood did nothing to ease the tension in me. He was unpredictable and could turn at any minute. The surrounding air buzzed with energy, and I knew it was his power.

Cronus waved his arms, and the books lifted off the floor. They hovered for a minute before returning to where they'd come from. "You need to grow up, chick. I don't mean to sound condescending, but there are much bigger things to deal with than love. It's a human construct that leads to poor choices. Case in point."

I sat rigid where he'd placed me. It took all my willpower to prevent myself from bolting.

"Thankfully, you are still in training. You couldn't have known our ways, and this is the defence I gave the council to get your pardon."

"What would have happened if I hadn't been pardoned?"

"Death. We can't have that." Cronus smiled. "We need to seek revenge on that wolf that marked you. You need to kill him so you can achieve your eternal transition."

Whenever Cronus brought up the subject of murder, I felt sick, but this time, my near death made me feel like I had no choice. I didn't know the rules of this world and I had to trust Cronus to stay alive. I felt like a cat with nine lives when I thought about all the near deaths I'd had of late.

"I thought you said we cannot die."

"Do not fear, it is rare," he said and moved on to the next subject. "You impressed me today."

His compliment caused me to sit up a little straighter in the chair. I liked the feeling, and I wanted to know what I'd done right. But I couldn't relax following his little display of power. I couldn't shake the feeling that he may turn on me at any moment.

"I did not think you had it in you. I had to think fast."

"Thank you," I said with caution, worried the wrong response could trigger him.

"I need you to be stronger. We have wasted enough time this evening dealing with your misdemeanour. Let us return to your training."

Cronus moved his arm, and the bookcase righted itself. The last books lifted closed their pages and returned to the shelves. Other than my fresh bruises, there was nothing left to signify that a disturbance had taken place.

CHAPTER 21

CRONUS KEPT ME UP, training until late. He'd used his compulsion to ease the fear I'd felt after our fight. That was after he'd bought me dinner and made me cut up my food and eat without using my hands. It was challenging and a little messy, but by the time dessert came, I was getting the hang of it.

When he finally let me fly home, it felt like the attack had never happened. Even the bruises had healed. He'd promised that I could hang out with the other crows tomorrow night.

At school, we began sitting out exams. I wasn't too worried about my lack of revision, as I knew I had forever to resit them if I wanted to.

But there wasn't a GCSE for soul snatching.

The bullying had fizzled out. People were cowards or sheep. Whatever they were, they were fickle. Seeing my friends had forgiven me for my lies encouraged others to move on. Passing them in the corridors, they'd cast fake smiles in my direction. But they didn't fool me, as I couldn't forget the awful things they'd posted online.

It takes great courage to stand up to others, and I admired Fallon for her tenacity. She was like a warrior queen telling people to back off, get a life, and leave me alone. She stood proud as my friend, and it empowered Ari and me. If anyone dared to challenge her, she gave them some home truths, causing them to scurry back to the hole they'd crawled out of.

After school, I enjoyed taking my detour to the hotel. With each lesson, I was getting better at controlling my powers. But I hated going home.

It was eerie to see my over-happy parents, a reminder of all I'd lost. My brother's absence weighed heavily on my heart. I was ready to forgive all of his interference in my love life. Murray had wanted to protect me. Under Cronus's eye, I felt vulnerable, and I'd give anything for my brother to be back. Even if it was only so, I wasn't alone in all this.

Cronus's regime left very little time for me. In the mornings, I avoided breakfast and stayed in my room until I had to leave. On my own, I practised using my powers. I couldn't see myself ever being strong enough to take him on, but I couldn't relax. Time was running out, and I felt trapped and compelled to do what Cronus asked.

In addition, since our fight, I was scared of him. He was stronger. Wiser. Unpredictable.

He wanted me to kill the werewolf that made me, but I wasn't okay with that.

It made my future feel bleak. My days were numbered, with no way out, and I felt hopeless as I tried to figure a way out.

When the last bell rang, I tried to leave without my friends, but they saw me leave and hurried to catch up with me.

"Wait up, Kiely," Fallon called out.

As they drew up beside me, I could hear their breathing was heavier. Fallon grabbed my arm, pulling my attention. Her eyes narrowed as she pinned me with one of her looks. "What's the rush?"

"My piano lesson," I lied.

"Again?" Arizona's eyebrows raised. "Is it every day?"

"Yep, I got a special deal for a batch of lessons, but they all have to be taken in one month."

"That's intense." Fallon frowned. "Who *is* teaching you?"

"Um…" I couldn't think of a name for my piano teacher. "You don't know him."

"Try me," Fallon pushed. She gestured to Arizona. "Ari is interested in lessons, too."

"He's not that good. I think I'll give up after the month-long trial. I wouldn't recommend him."

"Why bother going, then?" Fallon pushed. "You'd be better off focusing on your exams, actually revising."

"I dunno." I shrugged. Her interrogation was unravelling me. I thought I was good at lying.

"Give me a name?" Fallon demanded. "Stop being so weird about it."

"Cronus. He moved here from Scotland."

"Interesting," Fallon said with a smile. "Let us know how your lessons go. And if Cronus offers discounts for recommending a friend."

"I will." I nodded.

"You'll ask for me?" Arizona sounded happy. "Find out how much and if he does a twin discount, in case Phoenix is interested, too."

I nodded. "Okay."

I waved them off and ran across the road. I heard Fallon laughing as she told Arizona there was no way Phoenix would want piano lessons. Their happiness made me want to cry. They didn't realise their interest could put them in danger. I feared how mad Cronus would be if he knew they had his name. He had a thing for keeping his world secret.

Cronus had me practising my shadow kinesis again, but he promised that tomorrow I could have a respite and we would all go out together for a bit of fun. I was keen to hang out with the others again, but I was wary that the atmosphere would be different with Cronus around. I was sure I wasn't the only one to see his ugly side.

I knew the routine. Get through school and then head to the hotel for training. Today, I was extra excited as this evening we were going for a night out, on a school night.

Cronus sent Morgan to meet me at the reception. We hurried up the stairs to her room, where I was able to get changed out of my uniform and borrow some of her clothes. She'd been shopping, and there were store bags everywhere.

"You didn't hold back." I chuckled as she pulled the tag off a black sequin dress for me to wear.

"There aren't many shops here. This has been a lot of hard work to collect."

Once in her dress, Morgan got me to sit on the foot of her bed. She gave me a smokey eye and a red lip. It was the sort of look that Fallon would say was too much, but around my new friends; it was perfect.

"Beautiful," Morgan said, admiring her work.

I smiled at my reflection. "Is it okay if I agree?"

"Of course it is," Morgan said. She dipped her head to face me head on. "Love yourself and don't give a damn what anyone else thinks. Be you."

"Thanks." But I had never felt less like myself.

We headed out of her room and down the corridor to Cronus's room. I was surprised that the room wasn't more extravagant. It was decorated in the same style as the rest of the hotel and looked exactly how I'd seen it in the brochure. Part of me thought that Cronus would have somehow managed to bend the rules to make the room his own.

Cronus opened the window, and we all shifted into crows. It felt good to be in my crow form. We hopped onto the window ledge, one by one, and flew out. Cronus led the way, and we followed him. We sailed through the air, past my school, and up the dual carriageway. We flew into the centre of Ipswich.

I'd always wanted to go out in Ipswich with my friends, but we'd worried about not getting home if we missed the last bus or train. The amount of trouble we'd be in with our parents if we got caught. But here I was, and I had no worries about how I would get home or what my parents would think.

As we walked in, I noticed how guys turned and noticed me. I loved the way the dress shimmered. We headed to the bar and Cronus ordered a round of drinks. He carried the tray over, but on closer inspection, I saw how brazen he was being. The tray was hovering in front of him. It glided down to the table, undetected by the regular punters that anything unusual was happening. Well, all except one guy that was slumped in a chair across the room as if he'd drunk too much. He rubbed his eyes and, after what he'd seen, got up, scratched his head, and stumbled out of the establishment.

To my disappointment, everyone had fancy cocktails. Cronus slid a Coke in front of me. "You're not old enough to drink. There are laws before our own."

Callum began choking on his drink. Cronus gave him a serious look. He tried to explain himself: "Come on Cronus, do you think she hasn't ever had a drink?"

"Not without my say so." His eyes flashed electric blue and Callum slid down in his seat.

Once Cronus was distracted chatting to some punters at the pool table, Callum whispered, "Please don't tell him about the other night."

"I won't." I saw the flash of fear in his eyes.

The bar had pool tables, and Cronus challenged two young lads to a game. Cronus slipped on some dark sunglasses, and his eyes lit up electric blue as he eyed me over the frames before pushing them up his nose. It didn't take me long to figure out he was hustling the lads. With the sleight of hand, he could cause their balls to curve and miss the intended pockets. Whereas his own shots tapped multiple balls into the pockets.

"You must be a pro!" one lad demanded. "Nobody is that good."

"Are you cheating?" the other lad asked. "That was magic, man!"

Cronus casually responded, "I used to play way back."

"What's your name?" the first lad asked. "Maybe we've heard of you."

"Doubt it. You weren't even a twinkle in your father's eye."

"Oh, come on, man," the second lad said, waving

his mobile phone at Cronus. "I'll google it."

Cronus laughed. "Beat me and I'll tell you."

The guys gave up after being beaten three games in a row. Then, Cronus suggested they play against me. The second lad bowed out claiming he was done losing. The first lad checked me out. I saw the way his eyes ran up and down my body, and he nodded.

Cronus passed me his cue. As I chalked up my cue, his voice tickled my neck. "Beat them and I'll get you a cocktail. I know you want one."

I did. I'd been watching the other crows enjoy fancy drinks all evening whilst I drank coke. The guy that had accepted the challenge was older than me. The sort of guy that would pique Fallon's interest.

"You can break." He stood back and watched me lean over the table to take the first shot. The triangle broke, and the colours spun around the table. I saw the black racing toward a hole, my heart fluttered, and I waved my hand in front of me. The ball took a sharp change in direction and shot across the table.

"Woah, I've never seen that before," he said, stunned.

"Me neither," I gasped, and then giggled. "Must be my guardian angel."

"Don't be too obvious." Cronus's hot breath tickled my neck again.

He wasn't too bad a player and for the next shots; I let him pot a ball. "So, I'm yellow," he confirmed like I was some kind of novice who'd never played pool before.

I wanted to pot a red to show him I was no novice,

but Cronus's words echoed in my ears. I had to make it appear that I was playing and not cheating. When I didn't pot a ball, he laughed. "You need that guardian angel to come back."

I mouthed to Cronus, "*Help*," but his nose wrinkled in amusement and shook his head. I was on my own and realised this was another test. It was hard to manipulate the table and keep my movement slight.

The guy took his shot and potted two. I was going to lose if I didn't figure this out. I leaned over the table, eyeing up the ball and figuring out my shot. Realising the guy was checking out my backside, I came up with a way I could win. I wiggled my bum to distract him and took my shot. Using my powers, I encouraged four reds down holes. When I spun round to face him; I grinned. "I guess she's back."

His jaw dropped as he took in the table. He hadn't been paying attention and now the playing field had levelled. As the guy took his shot, I strolled around the table, and as I passed Cronus; I reached up and swiped his glasses. Now, I didn't need to worry about distracting the guy. I could look him straight in the eye and use my powers.

Cronus chuckled as I had fun cleaning the table with my next shot. The guy watched in silence as I strolled along with the table, stroking the wood but encouraging the white ball to keep rolling into the black and then guiding the black into the pocket, right before his eyes. I did it gently, slowly, so it wasn't obvious. I grinned at the guy when I won.

He shook his head. "I'm glad you said just for fun!"

Cronus walked up to the guy and shook his hand. "I never play for money. That is a poor man's game. You are good. We are just better."

The guy scratched his head. He couldn't believe it, but he couldn't deny that after being beaten four times he'd lost.

Cronus slid an arm around my waist. "I'm going to get this little chick a drink."

Cronus walked me to the bar and ordered me my first-ever Daiquiri. As I sat on the stool and took a sip. I loved it. This was winning. Cronus smiled at me and I was conscious of the fact his presence made me feel warm and safe, which was a complete contrast to how I knew I should feel in his company.

We were all merry from the evening, diving into the River Orwell. The water sprayed up on both sides around me, like a beautiful watery curtain. The moonlight blinking off the water, sparkling like the stars in the night sky, making it look like a majestic carpet. We played all the way home and when the river opened up to the sea, we finally beat our wings. The water sprayed off us as we rose to the sky.

"You head off, Kiely," I heard Cronus's voice in my head. "You have school in the morning."

I groaned. He was right, but I didn't want to go as

we were having fun. But I knew better than to disobey him. I departed from the murder, heading across the cliff tops where I'd first met them. I recognised the familiar territory of my neighbourhood. When I reached home, I landed in my backyard and transformed. I walked into my house and made a note to myself that in the future I should leave my bedroom window open so I could glide in.

I slept well, and morning came too soon. My friends were talking about their last exams, our futures, and how we'd celebrate.

Fallon shook her head. "It feels like only yesterday we were those fresh-faced year sevens."

Arizona hugged us both. "I'm so glad we became friends."

"Next year is going to be so different. I'm kind of scared. What are you guys planning to do?" I asked, with a nostalgic need to imagine I could have a future with my friends. I wanted to imagine I wasn't leaving without a goodbye after my exams. Or the fear that if I couldn't find another way to complete the trade of my soul, then I'd become a crow forever.

Arizona answered, "I'm going to college as they have better science equipment than our school."

"I'm still undecided," I shrugged.

"Well, isn't anyone going to ask what I am doing?"

"What will you be doing, Fallon?" I laughed.

"Of course, I'll be going to sixth form to do my Law and English A-Levels. But here is the juicy part," she squealed with excitement and leaned in closer like she was going to tell us a big secret. "I've secured a summer work placement at a local law firm. Not only that, but they've agreed that if I pass my A-Levels they'll take me on as a trainee paralegal."

"That's amazing, Fallon!" I gushed.

"Congratulations," Arizona added.

I envied how my friends had futures full of dreams. If I killed my maker, I wasn't sure I wanted a life in Skye. As beautiful as Cronus's home was, and the stunning views, I couldn't stop the sound of the woman's cries ringing in my ears.

It caused this nagging fear inside me, that I could one day be that woman.

"With school finishing this week for home revision, we should definitely celebrate," Arizona stated.

"I'm one step ahead of you," Fallon said. "My house, tomorrow night."

"What about Nate?" I asked. I still wasn't ready to speak to him.

Fallon's face screwed up. "He's my brother. I can't turf him out. This is why you don't date your best friend's brother. You went there, now you need to deal with it. I'm your best friend and it's my home. Please don't make it awkward!"

"I'll be there," I said through gritted teeth. She just didn't get it. Nate wasn't the issue. Cronus had insisted I train every night. The thought of asking him to bend the rules for me made my arm throb with the memory of his attack. My heart ached as I realised even once I'd killed my werewolf maker, Cronus still wouldn't let me hang out with my friends.

Cronus was waiting for me at the hotel reception. He smiled and led me away to the lounge without saying a word to start tonight's training session. It was hard to focus. I longed to be at the party with my friends but knew it would be awkward to see Nate. My heart screamed for a chance to say goodbye, even if I couldn't let them know I was going. I wanted to savour these last days as they were all I had left of them.

Asking Cronus for permission filled me with dread. It sat heavy in my stomach as I prepared myself to bring it up. Although I anticipated how the conversation might go, I needed to ask despite the repercussions.

Cronus signalled to a staff member at the hotel to bring us whatever he'd ordered.

"So, I'm almost done with school," I began but could feel the next words lodging in my throat.

"Good. When is your final exam?"

"In two weeks," I admitted, and swallowed a lump down.

He grinned. "That's made my day. You can hunt and kill with no one worrying you are gone."

I fidgeted in my seat. I saw Cronus clock my discomfort and my body burned as I began to sweat.

"Don't worry. You won't even have to get your hands dirty." Cronus's laugh filled the room. It was a beautiful sound that was out of sorts with our conversation. It reminded me of how cold he was, and made me more fearful to make my request.

He noticed I hadn't joined in laughing and added, "You know, because of your shadow kinesis. Don't you get it?"

"Yeah," I snapped. "It's not that."

"What is it then?" The room darkened.

"My friends have invited me to a party to celebrate finishing school." I blurted out and swallowed a lump in my throat.

Cronus sobered up. "I hope you told them you can't go."

"Actually, I said yes. Why wouldn't I go?"

Cronus groaned and rubbed his temple. "Typical teenager wanting to waste time with silly parties. Your days are numbered if you don't train and kill! Life or death?"

"But I can't tell them that."

"No, but you can lie. Tell them you are washing your hair. I don't care. But you are not going to that party with people you won't even remember several centuries from now."

That idea was chilling. I thought of everyone I loved in my life and how one day, I would outlive them all.

The young lad came in carrying a silver tray with food on it for us. He placed it down in front of us and then left the room. I went to use my powers to lift the pot to pour my tea, but Cronus reached out and took it and poured my cup. "Save your power. Today, I am going to teach you to track."

Cronus and I finished our tea and cakes in silence.

It was a novelty to use my hands, but there was an atmosphere between us since I'd made my request. I got the impression, Cronus expected this meeting to go differently. Afterward, we walked together to a local woodland called Abbey Grove. It wasn't far from the hotel, and we found a secluded spot on the trail.

"Close your eyes," Cronus instructed.

I did as he said. I could sense Cronus moving around me, getting closer. The coolness made me shiver.

"Think of the last time you saw your werewolf. Remember the way he made you feel. His smell. The way he tasted."

I thought back to the night in the gardens, and the way he struck fear in me, but then warmed my heart. His eyes lit up a warm gold-like fire and the heat coursed through my body.

I remembered the way he kissed me, the way I wanted more. The earthy scent surrounded me as he pressed me down onto the ground. The way he touched me and made my skin crave more. I wanted to be burnt all over by him. For the searing fire from his slash across my belly to ravage my whole body. I wanted him to have me. I remembered that desperate need for him.

My breathing became heavy as my need for him consumed me. I felt Cronus's breath on my neck.

"Oh, you liked it."

My mind swirled with confusion. Was I not supposed to have enjoyed it? It had felt so good and he'd been so handsome. His firm jaw, his dark hair. I groaned from a carnal need to have more of him.

I saw green, blue, and purple lights. Like a breathtaking electric ribbon. It reminded me of the northern lights, but it moved and stretched out into a straight line. I gasped at its beauty.

"Do you see it?" Cronus asked.

I nodded.

"You can open your eyes now."

I opened my eyes. The world swirled around me. Cronus put a supportive arm around me. "Are you okay?"

I shook my head. "I came over dizzy."

The colours still stretched out in front of me, rippling like water made of lights.

"Did you and this wolf," Cronus waved his hand in a circle as he searched for the right word, "have sexual relations?"

I blushed. "We didn't have sex."

"Okay," Cronus said, and laughed. "You appeared very keen about him."

"What do you mean?"

Cronus shook his head as he laughed. "Most people are gripped with fear when they think of their attacker. You moaned like he was pleasuring you."

I blushed.

"A masochist?"

"No!" I gasped.

Cronus laughed. "Well, it's between you and your soon-to-be-dead werewolf."

"What does this have to do with the lights?" They

were already fading and part of me was sad to see them disappear. They called to my heart, and I had the urge to follow them and find out where they went. Like following a rainbow in search of a pot of gold.

"You have a bond with the wolf that created you. You need to sever those ties. Set yourself free to live eternally with us and harness your crow powers. He left you for dead. It is justice that you deal him his death."

Every time he talked casually about murder, it made me shudder.

"I'm not sure I can do it," I confessed and braced myself for his blow.

"You must find a way. It must be done by you. It's your first duty as a reaper."

CHAPTER 22

"COME GET READY AT MINE," Fallon chimed as we walked home together.

"I'll have to go home and get my stuff," Arizona said.

"Me too," I lied, with no intention of going.

"I'll come with you, Kiely. It's on my way home. We can get your stuff and I'll help you carry it to mine."

"Sorry, I have to go to my piano lesson first." I lied.

"Who are you kidding? Piano with that hot-looking teacher?"

Oh no! She hadn't.

"W- What?"

"We followed you into the hotel yesterday," Fallon said. "We saw you not playing the piano. What was she

doing, Arizona?"

"Eating cake."

My face grew redder. I knew they were outing me. They'd figured out I was lying again. After our recent fallout. This wouldn't end well.

"We waited at the bar to confront you, but you and your pianist went for a romantic walk," Fallon said.

My heart thundered in my chest. I feared what they may have seen. I wanted to cry at the thought of the danger their curiosity put them in. How close had they been? What had they heard or seen?

Fallon continued, "Why are you lying about it? Who is he?"

"Nobody."

"Well, he isn't a piano teacher, is he?" Fallon said. "Is he why you're not interested in Nate? Is he your boyfriend?"

"No!"

"Are you coming to my party tonight?"

"Of course," I lied, and cringed.

Fallon saw right through me. She coughed out a short laugh, one that was empty of joy. Her face was a picture of disappointment. She shook her head, her eyes pink as if she might cry. "You're such a liar! You've no intention of coming. You're going to sneak off with Cronus – if that's even his real name."

"It's not like that." I felt sick that I'd given them his real name. Now they had a face, too. They knew too much.

"Oh, like how it wasn't like that with my brother?"

Fallon spat. She didn't give me time to answer. "Come on, Ari."

Fallon tugged Ari's arm, and they crossed the road to walk on the other side.

As Fallon reached the other side, she called out to me, "We only finish school once. If we matter to you, you'll be there."

"That's not fair." I wanted to cry. Cronus wasn't someone to mess with. Once I'd killed the wolf, this would no longer be my life. But they would never understand that.

I ached to tell my friends the truth, but I knew I had to keep them safe. I swallowed and held my chin high. Better for them to hate me than for a drago to possess them.

My eyes stung with tears I couldn't let flow. This was goodbye, and they had no idea.

When I entered the hotel, Cronus could tell something was wrong. He walked up to me and pulled me into a tight embrace. Right there in the reception, for all to see, I burst into tears and collapsed. He lifted me up into his arms and carried me to the lounge. He sat in the armchair and rocked me. A warm sensation ran through my body. My muscles unravelled. The room fell into a pink haze, almost dreamlike. My world melted away and I forget everyone that mattered.

As I came around, I felt silly for making a show of myself. My head rested on his broad chest, and as I looked up at him through my lashes, I saw a gentle giant. He was nothing like the man who'd thrown my body against the bookcase. Here, he felt like my protector.

I uncurled myself and blushed as I acknowledged that he'd probably used his compulsion to control me.

"Sorry about that." I rubbed my cheeks dry with the palm of my hand and hoped my skin didn't look too blotchy.

"What was that about?" He sounded sincere, like he might care.

Did he?

My voice wobbled. "I fell out with my friends. I won't be going to the party."

Cronus smiled. "There will be other parties, and more important people to fill your life."

My shoulders slumped. He didn't get it.

"Tonight, you will fulfil the contract of your crow soul. Avenge your death, or your death will become final."

"But..."

"If I hadn't taken your soul, your body wouldn't have survived. You had no pack for strength. Joining us was your only choice. Killing him is your only option. It's his fault that you are in this situation."

My head dropped as I felt out of options. Cronus ordered me a three-course meal to preserve my strength for the journey and fight ahead, but I wasn't hungry. I pushed my food around the plate with my fork.

"You need to take his soul. Pull his shadow. Just as we did with you. Then cut it free and the deed will be done. Your bond severed."

I nodded to show I was listening, but I had nothing to say.

"If you will not eat, we may as well go now."

I pushed my plate away, but then the feeling of dread overcame me. Now was the time. Now, I was going to head off to rob a stranger of his life.

We returned to the spot in the woods where we'd been the previous day. The walk had felt like I was on my way to my execution.

Except I am the executioner.

In the clearing, Cronus searched the surroundings to make sure we were alone. Then he levelled with me. "First, I must give you something."

Instinct made me glance at his hands to see what he was holding. It wasn't an object, but a dark cloud that cloaked his fists, swirling around as if moved by the wind.

I stepped away.

Cronus smiled. "Don't be afraid. It is an honour to be bestowed with our weapon."

I saw something shimmering in the darkness. Light reflected from it like sunlight on metal. The darkness cleared, and I saw Cronus holding a large scythe with two hands.

"Is that what I think it is?"

Cronus held the scythe out to me. The black shadow still rippled up and down the pole and over the hooded blade. "The Soul Scythe."

My hand closed around the cool pole. When Cronus released it, I felt its full weight. "What am I to do with this?"

"It is to reap the wolf's soul," he said, and chuckled as if what I'd asked was ridiculous. He sobered up and looked me dead in the eye. "When you shift, you cast your shadow out. What I want you to do right now is draw the shadow in. Pull the darkness that engulfs the scythe into your being."

It felt strange to pull the shadows into me. The smoke ran from the metal and up my arm. It seeped into my skin, turning my veins black. As I drew it in, the scythe went with it. I shivered, having it inside me felt like a cold had set into my bones.

"Well done."

I liked Cronus's praise. It drove me to want to impress him more. The ice inside me tingled under my skin and stimulated a deep pleasure. I bit my lip as I thought about how good it would feel to kill for him and the praise he'd shower on me. A pink haze tinted my vision.

He's doing it again.

Snap out of it!

There was no time for me to pull away from this control. His velvet warm voice was irresistible to disobey. "Close your eyes and connect with your maker. Find his signature, the tether that binds you to him."

It was easier this time, now I knew what to look for. They lit up my mind as they whirled around, giving the effect of a high-speed merry-go-round. I opened my eyes and waited for them to stretch out to show me the path to take.

"Now you have connected with him, you can track him," Cronus said. "Shift and fly. Be swift or die."

I allowed the darkness to drop around me, to change my mould and form me like a bird. My wings spread out and lifted above the canopy of trees. I followed the lights like I was travelling through time. The colours whooshed past me, like diving through a rainbow tunnel. At first, I thought of nothing but following his signature. The more I flew, the more I felt desperate to find him. I had a sense of belonging and needing to be with him. My wings beat in time to my heartbeat. Rapid. Frantic.

The lights got thicker and denser the further I flew. It was almost a dizzying blindness. I felt as if I was flying with blinkers and all I could think about was that I had to reach him. It felt like some strange instinct. Maybe my body knew what Cronus was telling me was true. It was me or him. This bond made it harder. It made me want to choose him.

I could smell fumes in the air, and I knew I was somewhere urban. The sounds of traffic were louder and I could see a city lit up with lights. I was approaching a building that looked like three massive towers of windows. I saw the building's name, *Birmingham Hospital*.

A heaviness filled my stomach.

Why was he here?

I hoped he wasn't hurt or in any kind of trouble. It was ironic that I was worried that he might be harmed when I'd travelled all this way to kill him.

I took flight and flew around searching for a sign of him. Nothing. I dove behind a dumpster where I could shift out of sight. In the darkest of shadows, I transformed and emerged as a human. I shut my eyes and searched for the man. I sensed that he was close by.

"Are you alright?" A man's voice forced me to open my eyes. I was startled to see someone in a high-vis jacket. "You're not allowed to be back here."

"Sorry," I apologised, and stumbled forward, my head bowed as I hurried off before he could ask any more questions. I darted down a footpath, walking toward the main entrance, but there was no point going in. My footsteps slowed with the realisation. I couldn't ask if he was here. I didn't know his name. Who was I to him?

His victim?

His soon-to-be killer?

Something caught my attention. Two people I recognised from school were standing at the bus stop. The new girl, Briar, and Kaden, the outcast boy. What were they doing here? We were miles away from home.

I looked back the way they'd come, and my heart fluttered. There was the man - my werewolf. My speed increased with each step as I tried to catch him up. He was with a woman and I wondered if she was the infamous Luna. Should I be cautious?

I followed them, taking care to not draw attention to myself. My heart pounded as I prepared to fight. As I gained on them, I searched for his shadow, but I couldn't see it. The only visible shadow was that of his companion, a slim woman with dark features. She looked over her shoulder. I froze and my breath caught in my chest. Her eyes met mine and flashed an unnatural green. She wasn't human.

She took his hand and gave it a squeeze. There was a silent exchange between them. Their pace increased and once they reached a busy road, they ran. I chased. I felt a darkness inside me, like a predator after their prey.

The next thing I knew happened so quickly. She whipped him off his feet and into her arms. In a flash, they raced through the traffic to the other side of the road, moving faster than anyone I'd ever seen.

I tried to keep up, but in my human form, I couldn't. She was using powers. Surely, she was breaking an ancient law by using them in public. Any of the drivers could have seen her. They could've been caught on a dashcam. Maybe, once I dealt with my wolf, I'd be tasked to take care of her, too.

If I was going to catch them up, I needed to use my powers as well. I searched for somewhere to shift and ducked beside a low-level barrier, hoping it would provide enough cover. I cast myself in shadow and rose as a crow.

Taking to the air, I searched for them. It wasn't clear which way they'd gone, but I flew across the traffic, tracking the way I'd seen them go. Exhaustion was taking over, and I struggled to bring back the light to track them.

I continued down the road in pursuit of my wolf

man and his companion, but they were nowhere to be seen. They'd vanished. How would Cronus react when I returned and confessed I'd lost him?

I felt sick to my core. If I didn't complete it tonight, I was going to die.

I saw a small woodland. It reminded me of Abbey Grove back home, where Cronus had conducted my training in tracking my maker's signature. In the woods, I felt a buzz in the air. It reminded me of being with Cronus, the way he got under my feathers with his deep voice and warm breath. The way he got me to think of my wolf. The feelings mixed and brought forth the colourful ribbons of light illuminating the way.

When I saw the man-wolf alone by a lake, I flew down and shifted back into my human form so I could take his soul. Instinct told me to cast out the scythe. I pushed the icy darkness from my system. The smoke unravelled out of me, and the whispers of smoke twirled and went from air to solid. I felt the metal harden against my palm, and the weight of the weapon made my bicep tense. I dragged it behind me, letting the blade cut a trench through the dirt. "Wolf, I've come for you."

The world quietened as he stood expectantly before me. My heart pulsed at the sight of him with his scruffy dark hair, his blue eyes, and the gentle stubble on his chin. I thought of how it had felt when he'd kissed me. The craving for his touch stirred up. He was the first to use compulsion on me. It made me sick how these shifters could manipulate my emotions. My anger helped me reclaim my control.

He didn't appear scared. "I'm sorry for what I did. I was under Luna's influence, but I'm free from her now."

"It's too late. It's you or me. Kill or die." I tried to sound fierce, but my heart felt heavy. I'd felt the compulsion from Cronus and knew what it was like to lose your free will. This wolf was as much a victim as me.

He bowed his head. "Please, forgive me. I didn't mean for it to turn out like this."

My hand touched his cheek. I felt the roughness of his unshaven face against my palm and I knew how it felt against my body. Our bond was still intact. I leaned close. "Why didn't you claim me?"

"We're both pawns in a war we didn't know of."

"What war?"

"It wasn't by chance you were chosen. It's because you are Mariah's lover."

I laughed. "That's the most ridiculous thing I've ever heard."

"You're not her lover?"

"Definitely not." I had to laugh. Lovers – ha! Luna couldn't be further from the truth. Yet, Mariah had saved me from the crows and dragged me to the shore after the tsunami. Maybe one day we could be friends, but never lovers.

"But, that's why she wanted me to target you." He frowned. "I didn't want to, but I couldn't say no. Please forgive me." He dropped to his knees, clasping his hands together, pleading.

He looked so frail, and mortal. It felt cruel to do this when he couldn't even fight me. Despite everything, I wasn't mad at him. "I forgive you. I promise to make this quick."

I raised the scythe, ready to take his soul. I wouldn't drag it out like when the crows took mine. With one quick swipe, it would all be over.

His head bowed as he accepted his fate.

The icy darkness flooded my body, urging me to bring down the blade on his neck. Yet, my hand trembled with the resistance from my conscience. "I'm sorry."

I closed my eyes.

I didn't want to see him die.

I took a deep breath. Here goes –

A powerful force slammed into my chest. I gasped for air, my eyes strained as I was flung backward. Spit showered my face, and I met sharp teeth framed in the black face of a panther.

On instinct, I pulled the creature's shadow, throwing it from me.

As I scrambled to my feet, the panther found its paws and growled in response. I held the scythe between us.

I thought Luna was a wolf, but this creature was a large black cat with green glowing eyes. It had to be the woman I'd seen earlier. Whoever she was, she was guilty of breaking many laws. Perhaps, I could take her soul instead and avenge my wolf and myself.

Perhaps that would be enough to sate Cronus.

She growled as we circled each other. The scythe was heavy as I dragged it behind me, trying to calculate what I should do. She had that look in her eye like she'd killed before and wouldn't hesitate to add me to the count.

"Please. Don't hurt her," his voice sounded far away.

The rest of the world had zoned out. It was just us. Predator to predator. I lifted the scythe into two hands and held it across my body, ready to strike or defend, whichever came first. She lowered her body, never taking her eyes off me. I could see her muscles tightening.

She pounced, all teeth and claws, her massive paws honing in on me. I ducked and swiped the scythe. It caught her underbelly as she flew over. A spray of red blood splattered my face. Before I could react, fiery flames tore down my back. I wailed as I fell forward. Blood ran down my back and the scythe slipped from my fingers and as it descended, it dissipated into a dark mist. "No!"

I rolled over and backed away from the snarling beast. Her lips had curled back, revealing her dark gums.

My fingers trembled as I tried to summon the scythe. Unarmed, I was going to die. The panther prowled slowly toward me, well aware that she'd won. I felt sick.

She was drawing this out, enjoying every moment.

She wanted me to run. She wanted a chase, but I wouldn't give her the satisfaction.

Searching for a weapon, I found her shadow. I grabbed it and flung her backward. Her body smashed into a tree, knocking the cat form from her body. Now I saw the woman from earlier gasping for breath. Her bright green eyes were wide and full of hate. Now it was me that prowled toward her.

As I got closer, black fur ran down her arms, forming into paws with the claws out. My stomach tensed as I recalled how it'd felt when my wolf had cut through my stomach. I shook my head. I wouldn't let her swipe me.

Holding her in place, I turned my attention to the wolf.

"Please. Please. Let her go," he begged.

She'd attacked me. She wasn't going to let me go. It was me or her, with only one way to end this.

"This will be over soon," I promised.

This was the part Cronus hadn't taught me. Instinct made me stretch my hand forward and feel for a shadow that was inside him. He collapsed, as if I was causing him pain, even though I wasn't even touching him. My hand felt warm as my fingers flexed and explored the air before me.

The moment my hand felt something that pulsed, he gasped. It was full of life. I clasped hold of it and pulled. He screamed with pain. My heart shattered. I didn't want him to suffer. I had to move quickly, to get this over with. Tears ran down my cheek.

I gasped as I saw a black wisp flick out of his chest. I drew it toward me. Pulling it into my palm, weaving the dark strands into a lump of darkness in my hand. It looked like a beating heart made of shadow. A thin tendril stretched back to his body like the soul's placenta wouldn't let go. This was what the scythe was for. This was what I had to cut.

My hands were full with the soul in one, and the werecat's shadow in the other. She didn't need to see this. I lifted her body and summoned as much strength as I could, before catapulting her away.

I knew I didn't have long before she would be back. My hand tingled as my veins turned black.

The darkness took form, the cold metal forming. The scythe was ready to fulfil my mission.

I was a reaper.

His soul beat in my hand, and the tears rolled down my cheeks. "I'm sorry."

"It's okay," he sobbed. "I'm ready."

I raised the scythe. This time I would do what was required. My lips pressed together. My body felt heavy. I couldn't face him so I kept my eyes on my weapon. This felt wrong. He didn't attack me out of malice. He attacked me because Luna compelled him. I was here to take his soul because Cronus was compelling me. We were all puppets in a war that wasn't ours and there was only one way to stop this…

I cast the scythe back into my body and let go of his soul.

He gasped, taking in big breaths like he'd been held

under water. I collapsed to my knees.

What have I done?

What would happen to me?

A bright light filled the forest. My arm rose to cover my eyes. It was all-consuming and warm. So blinding that I couldn't see a thing, like I was in the centre of it.

As quick as the light came, it was gone.

What was that?

"Are you alright?" he asked.

"Are you?" I replied. The forest seemed to darken as our eyes adjusted to the night.

"I don't think you took my soul?" He was shaking.

I got to my feet and stared at the floor. Cronus was going to kill me for this, but I wasn't going to make my wolf pay. I held out my hand to help him up. "I forgive you."

He took my hand as we heard a growl from behind me. My body tensed as I turned to see bright green emerald eyes glowing out of a bush.

I'd forgotten about her. She still wanted to fight.

"Eve, don't!" he said.

The growling stopped and the panther stepped out of the bush and laid down. She looked as if she might sleep, but kept one bright green eye fixed on me.

"Eve?" I asked.

"Eve's my fiancé. Luna has a long-standing feud with the shifters for sacrificing her lover, Darcia, to the crows. She wants the families that survived her blood lust to know her pain."

Darcia? The name sounded familiar…

A street lamp shone through the trees creating long shadows on the ground. The knitted pattern of a metal railing ran across the ground behind them. The shadows of trees stretched forward across the ground towards me. And, I noticed the panther's shadow blending in with her fur, but no shadow came from the wolf-man. "How come you don't have a shadow?"

"I think it's because I sacrificed my soul to be with Eve. I'm not a wolf anymore."

A chill ran through my body. What had I almost severed with the scythe if it was not his soul that I had held beating in my hand.

He rubbed my arm. "One day, you'll find a love like ours."

I felt the warmth of his words as he spoke. There was no malice in them. The panther moved toward him and rubbed herself against his leg. Now that we weren't fighting, I took in how majestic this enormous cat was. Her green eyes pleaded with mine. I reached my hand out toward her. She lifted her head up into my palm. She made a rumbling purr. I crouched down and buried my head in her neck like I would Aero. She wasn't wild; she was human. She knew what I was saying, and she loved this man. From where I crouched, I could feel the love between them, even with her in her werecat form. It buzzed in the air between them. "I'd love that."

He smiled. "Are we good?"

"Yes. But Cronus is going to kill me for letting you live."

"He won't. Tell him you did it and my soul is no more. Eve and I are going into hiding, and the only person who can find us is you."

I nodded. I ought to be getting back. "One last thing. Your name?"

"Leo."

"Leo, please keep a low profile."

Leo reached out to touch my arm. "We will, and if you ever need anything, we owe you."

It was a strange feeling to return home, knowing I hadn't fulfilled my contract. The threat of my life ending didn't scare me. Leo also caused me to doubt Cronus's words. He wasn't the only one. The warning from Darcia was feeling more real every day, and less like a dream.

I felt satisfied with my choice. Forgiving Leo had been like lifting a weight off my shoulders. His words ran through me like a healing light, chasing out the darkness that had been consuming me. I'd been carrying so much hate in my heart. I felt like everyone had done me wrong. I'd been so focused on what I thought I'd lost, I couldn't see my future. But Leo had filled me with hope. I hope that one day I will have something similar. Something real. Somebody who loved me completely. I couldn't help but think of Nate.

The crows followed Cronus without question, and I

wondered if it was that same bond and connection I felt to Leo for making me. The same bond that had enabled Luna to control Leo. I wondered, if I killed Leo, would I have become compliant to Cronus, his spell over me completed? Would it have cost me my free will or my life?

It dawned on me that Cronus may be a better liar than me.

Leo and Eve would have their happily ever after. I would tell Cronus I took Leo's soul, that he was no more. I would lie like my life depended on it, because it literally did.

As I got closer to home, I felt stronger. There was closure in not fulfilling my contract, like the burden of the task no longer hung over my head. I sailed through the open window of my bedroom and cast my shadow down.

Stepping out of the darkness, I was human again.

With every shift, it was getting easier. I spun around, feeling elated, liberated and free of my contract, only to discover I was not alone. Staring back at me was someone I wished to keep safe from all of this.

Chapter 23

"Nate, what are you doing here?" I could feel the blood draining from my body. My hand shook as I pushed back my hair.

Nate stood statue-still, his eyes wide and his jaw lax.

"You can't be here. You have to go," I whispered so my snake-controlled parents wouldn't hear me. I could barely move or think. Maybe he didn't see anything, or maybe I could convince him that he hadn't. I needed a plan to keep Nate safe.

He blinked. "What was that?"

"What was what?"

"What are you?"

I hurried to the window to check the rooftops and backyards to see if there were any crows who might be watching. Cronus may have asked someone to monitor me. Relief washed over me as I detected noone or any birds, I slammed my window shut and drew the curtains to prevent any would-be spies seeing in.

Nate barely moved. He remained frozen, except for his eyes shifting as they followed me around the room. He acted like I was the predator, and he was a small, helpless animal.

"Why are you here?" I asked desperately.

"You didn't come to Fallon's party."

"So you broke in?"

"The window was open."

My throat felt dry as I swallowed. "Nate, trust me, and don't ask questions. Anything I tell you puts you in danger."

"What does that even mean?" Nate eyed me as if I were dangerous. I feared what would come of him for simply being here.

I shook my head. I felt jittery as I paced back and forth in complete contrast to Nate who was pale and stood statue still. Only his bright eyes moved as they followed me. I threw my arms around him, hoping to protect him if it came to that. His scent returned me to the summerhouse; my safe place with him. Now it was up to me to keep him safe. I was worried that if he left, someone would spot him.

"Can you stay the night?"

Nate nodded. The hug had returned colour to his

face. Relief washed over me.

"Wait here," I instructed, before sneaking out of my room. I wasn't sure what my zombie parents were up to. Even though they were in la-la land, I knew a human boy in my room wouldn't be permitted. The reason would differ from why my actual parents would be against it. Mum and Dad would wish to protect my dignity and my heart from getting broken. But the drago would do anything to keep our world secret, and what Nate had seen would put his life in danger. Not only that, but I was also certain they'd tell Cronus.

I got some PJs from Murray's bedroom for Nate. When I returned, I was relieved to find Nate still sitting on my bed. He looked shocked. His eyes were still wide, his body frozen.

"Here." I tossed the clothes to him. Catching them broke the stiffness of his body and his laugh lit up his eyes, and warmed my heart.

I got a nightie out of my drawer so I could finally get out of my school uniform. "Turn the other way and get dressed."

"How do I know you won't peep?"

"You won't know." I smiled.

One side of Nate's mouth lifted in a half-smile.

Once changed, I asked, "Are you done?"

"Yeah."

I turned around and saw that Nate was sitting on my bed, facing the wall. As I walked toward my bed, he looked over his shoulder at me. "How are we doing this? I can sleep on the floor. Have you got some spare pillows?"

I thought about sneaking out to get some extra bedding, but the thought of leaving him made me feel sick. He wasn't safe here, but it would be dangerous for him to leave. He'd have to sleep in my bed. "It's fine. You take the bed."

Nate frowned. "Where are you going to sleep?"

"I'll be fine. I like sleeping on the floor."

Nate laughed. "Don't be ridiculous. It's your bed, and I shouldn't really be here."

I reached over and grabbed his arm. "Nate, please don't go."

He sobered up and nodded, "Okay, but…"

"If it's not weird, we could share my bed. I promise to behave myself."

Nate's lip rose up on one side and his eyes twinkled.

"What?" I asked, wanting to know what the joke was.

"Get in and stop making it weird." Nate held the covers up. I got in and he quickly joined me. "This wasn't my intention when I snuck in, but I'm not complaining." His voice sounded a little higher than normal. Almost as if he was intimidated by our proximity despite all the times we'd fallen asleep together in the summerhouse.

I worried about the questions that may follow and knew I wouldn't be able to answer them. Was he already in danger from what he'd seen, or could I swear him to secrecy? I didn't want to lie to him, but I'd have to convince him it never happened. I had so much to learn about the laws. The more I learned, the more I feared Cronus. The biggest rule was to be discreet and keep our world hidden from humans. I didn't want to discuss what he'd seen. I hoped if I could keep away from the topic, he'd doubt he ever saw it.

"Did Fallon tell you about my boyfriend?"

Nate's smile dropped. In a broken voice, he asked, "Is it true?"

"No, Fallon made an assumption."

"Who is he then - this Cronus?"

I hated that she'd told Nate his name. "You need to stay away from him. I'm fine, but he'd hurt you, Fallon, and Ari. I have to keep you guys away."

He tucked hair behind my ear and whispered, "You don't need to be afraid. I'll protect you."

Nate didn't know the people he was challenging. I shook my head. "I need you to trust me to protect you."

"Why are you so scared of him? Just walk away. Tell your mum and dad."

"It's complicated and late." I stroked his face. "Please, stay out of it."

"Kiely, I've missed you."

I've missed you too.

The words were caught in my throat, held back by the guilt of keeping secrets from him. I wasn't even human anymore. It would be best to push him away, but I didn't have the strength in me. I didn't deserve him. My hands covered my face. "You shouldn't."

He reached out to move my hands. "Kiely?"

"Please let me handle this my way. I know I've got you if I need help."

"I wish you'd let me help."

My breathing deepened, and my skin prickled. I

knew what I wanted, but feared how he might respond. I held his gaze and whispered, "Help me forget the way you do."

I touched his face and allowed him time to understand what I was asking. The distance closed between us, but he stopped. My heart pounded. I wanted to beg him, but didn't want to scare him. I placed a gentle kiss beside his mouth and waited with bated breath.

Nate turned his lips to meet mine. He kissed me gently, hesitant with each kiss, almost unsure, like he didn't know if it was what I wanted. I kept kissing him back, reassuring him. Each kiss lasted longer than the last. His hand reached under my top and touched my breast. I gasped into his mouth, letting him know that I liked it, and encouraging him to continue exploring.

Nate groaned, and the sound of his pleasure excited me. My hands reached for his arse, pulling him closer, feeling his hardness pressing against my leg. His hands circled my waist and then moved down into my knickers. Energy and excitement rose in my body. I'd wanted this for a long time, but had held back because of my heartbreak.

The darkness of the room heightened as I tried to fight the memory of my pain. I wanted to stay in this moment with Nate. He made me feel good; so good. Yet, now the fear of getting hurt mixed with the lust and I felt like my emotions were spinning inside me.

Thud!

My lamp fell onto the floor. It was on the other side

of the room. Nothing had been nearby to knock it over. The window was still shut.

I shot up.

My heart was pounding.

I watched my door, worried my parents heard the crash, and might come to investigate.

Nate was probably wondering how the lamp got knocked over, but I knew. My mind had thrown it to stop what was happening. I grabbed his wrist. I wasn't ready. My body was crying out for him, and my breath was raspy. "Not yet. I'm not ready."

Nate groaned. He pulled his hand back and kissed my neck. He groaned again before retracting. Lying on his back, he called out in the dark, "Oh Kiely, you're killing me."

I closed my eyes tight. My eyelashes crushed my tears. He didn't know how true his words were. I was thankful for the darkness. I didn't want to explain.

"It's okay." Nate rolled over and put his arms around me. "I can wait. I promised you I would."

His arms felt good around me, but I couldn't sleep. I was alert and aware of the dangers of Nate being here. My mind raced with the evening events. I'd still not processed the reaping, or lack of.

I kept seeing Darcia, her ghost-like appearance coming out of the darkness. I could hear her hushed whispers, getting louder and louder. Like the sounds were ocean waves, crashing and rolling around me, dragging me down into the darkness. Like the bubbles as I drowned, her words rumbled past my ears.

Like calls to like.

He will see.

Find me!

Kiely!

Darcia's words made little sense, like parts were cut off. I could see her coming in and out of focus in rippling waves of light. The sensation of drowning was all-encompassing, and I called for Mariah to save me. It made sense knowing she was a mermaid.

I calmed down and floated in the water of light. I felt safe. The whispers grew louder, like the taunts of the students in the corridor.

Darcia's face was on mine, screaming.

Get up!

My eyes flashed open, and there was Nate. I cursed myself for falling asleep.

"Are you alright?" Nate asked.

I scanned my room. My heart drummed in my chest. Was it a dream, or was Darcia warning me again?

Being cautious, I went with the latter. I couldn't take any risks with Nate's life.

"Stay here. Stay hidden."

I got out of bed and had just made it to the stairs when I bumped into Cronus.

"What are you doing here?" I prayed Nate wouldn't get curious or stupid and brave. I hoped his good sense and ego would let me protect him and stay put.

Thank you, Darcia.

The dreams were something more than a coincidence. If I hadn't woken from her demand,

Cronus would have entered my room and discovered Nate.

"I heard you were back." He raised his eyebrows. He turned and returned down the stairs, with me following behind him. "Let's enjoy your parents' hospitality one last time before returning to Skye."

"They're not my parents."

"Then you'll find saying goodbye much easier."

When we got downstairs, the table was set for breakfast. We never did this. It was too much. They had a selection of cereals, spreads, pastries, and fruit. My parents stood to attention beside the table, like servers waiting for our orders.

Cronus took a seat and poured himself a glass of orange juice. "How did the reaping go?"

I shrugged. "I don't really want to talk about it."

"You'll feel better once you have. Do tell me?"

No longer under Cronus's spell, I didn't feel obliged to do as he said. I felt no need to please him. The fear for myself had gone. It was Nate I feared for now. Nate was a real person, with genuine feelings for me, and if I let myself, I knew I felt the same toward him.

I couldn't let Cronus know I had my self-control back, that I had disobeyed his order and let Leo live. I had a strange feeling that the contract was another manipulation of their laws, and if I'd gone through with it, my soul would have been owned by Cronus. Every crow before me had complied. They were all his.

Only I was free.

"I need to go for a walk to clear my mind. Do you

wanna join me?" I hoped the invitation would entice Cronus away from my home.

Cronus smiled. "I'd be honoured to join you."

"Wait here. Enjoy breakfast. I'll get dressed and we can take Aero." I excused myself and hurried upstairs to throw some clothes on.

As soon as I got to my room, I saw Nate standing there looking uncomfortable. I pressed a finger to his lips.

"Say nothing. He's here. When we leave, sneak out. Don't let anyone see you."

"Will you explain?"

I shook my head. "Forget last night ever happened."

"I can wait, but I can never forget."

My finger dropped from his lip and hurried to get dressed, pulling on clothes in front of Nate with no time to worry about nakedness. My only wish was to get Cronus away from here as quickly as possible. There was no knowing what he would do, but it wouldn't be good for Nate.

Wearing a sweater and joggers, I put on my trainers and hurried down the stairs. I fussed over Aero before putting on his lead and then left with Cronus.

We looked like any ordinary pair walking a dog. To those who passed us, they'd have no idea of the dangerous man they passed or the dark topic of our conversation.

"Where was he when you found him?" Cronus asked.

"Birmingham," I said, trying not to be too specific.

"Wolves like cities," Cronus shared. "How did you attack him?"

"He knew I was coming."

Cronus frowned. "Who warned him?"

I shrugged.

"Maybe Luna. Was she there? Long blonde hair?"

I didn't want to implicate Eve, so I shook my head. "He was alone. I shifted into my human form. He recognised me and apologised for what he did."

Cronus laughed. "Too late to repent."

"I told him it was me or him. Of course, I chose me."

Cronus smiled at me with pride.

"He continued to plead for my forgiveness, but I left him shadowless, soulless, a wolf no more." This was easy to say, as there was some truth to it.

"Good." Cronus reached for my hand and lifted it to his lips to place a kiss. "Now you are officially part of the family."

"Thank you." I knew there was an ice cream hut ahead, and I wanted to be sure Aero had a good walk and Nate had enough time to escape. "Can we get an ice cream to celebrate?"

"Of course. Kiely, I have to tell you that you have the makings of becoming a wise bird. I foresee an exceptional future ahead of you."

I smiled back at him. We got a classic Whippy and sat on the shingle beach, listening to the gulls. I wanted to change the topic from Leo's murder before I said something that made it clear that I hadn't gone through with it.

"Not so long ago we were here fighting over my soul. Why did so many of them come for me?"

"Your fight with your wolf is between the two of you. But an unclaimed shifter is all of our business," Cronus said sternly. "With no guidance, you would have run wild with blood lust."

"Why couldn't you offer me guidance to live as a wolf?"

Cronus laughed. "I'm not a wolf."

"You know what I mean. Why did I have to become a crow?"

"It's our way."

I knew I wouldn't get any more from him. He was set in his old way, and I still didn't know enough to challenge him on it. But I knew he was wrong. I could feel it in my bones. That feeling you get when you sense the weather changing. The dread I felt toward my future with the crows was like watching a storm rolling in on a sunny day. It was all going to change, and I couldn't be certain, but I sensed Cronus was still not being genuine.

We'd almost finished our ice cream when Cronus said, "I may have been too hard on you regarding your friends. I didn't want them distracting you from your mission. If you promise not to tell them about our world, you can see them one last time."

"Really?" I asked. Cronus nodded, and I added, "I promise."

Cronus smiled like a parent who had just rewarded a child. I couldn't wait to visit Fallon and apologise for not being there last night. I'd make amends for missing her party.

"Try to say goodbye without making it obvious. Once your exams are done, we are gone."

My heart dropped. I knew his offer was too good to be true. My friends and Nate were the only ones I trusted and knew were loyal to me. I needed to see Nate and to know that he'd gotten home safe, but prayed that he wouldn't ask questions I couldn't answer.

Cronus walked me back to my home. "Meet me for dinner at the hotel. We'll celebrate together as one big happy family."

I agreed, and once inside; I hurried up to my room to check Nate was gone. The window was open, and the breeze eased my worries that he'd escaped. I silently prayed he'd made it home without being seen. I wanted to call him, but I didn't want to draw attention to our relationship. Once again, we were in hiding, but this time for his safety.

I called Fallon.

"What do you want?"

"To apologise about last night."

"Don't worry about it. I didn't expect you, anyway. Did you have fun with your boyfriend?"

My cheeks burned as I initially thought she knew about my night with Nate. Then I remembered she was talking about Cronus. "He's not my type."

"That's worse, Kiely," Fallon snapped. "You dropped me for a guy you're not even that into. Have you thought about what that says about you?"

"I wasn't with him."

"It doesn't matter. We had a great time without you," Fallon said lazily into the phone, but I sensed the undercurrent had a bitter taste of poison.

"Can I come over?"

"What? Now?"

"If that's alright?"

"If you want," Fallon said. "I've not got anything better planned. Let me check with Ari." I heard Fallon speaking with someone, and I guessed Ari had stayed over. "Would you mind picking up some croissants from The Bakery on the way over? I like them warm."

The Bakery wasn't on my way to Fallon's house. It was a test to see how willing I was to make up to them for not attending the party. "Sure. I can do that. See you soon."

I got changed, did my hair and makeup, and set off for The Bakery. I got a box of croissants for us all and some lattes to sweeten the deal. When I arrived at Fallon's, she opened the door and looked pleased to see me, and also surprised that I'd got the requested goods.

We sat in the conservatory on the couches. I figured this was their breakfast. I noticed Arizona's dark purple and glittery nails. "Your nails are lovely."

"It was for you," Ari said. She pressed her lips together in annoyance before continuing. "It's Dark Kiely. I wanted to surprise you with it last night."

"I'm sorry." My eyes moved back and forth between her and Fallon. "I really am."

"Why do you always bail on us?"

"I don't always."

Arizona and Fallon exchanged a look, and I could tell they'd talked about this and were in agreement.

Fallon took a deep breath. "I know I'm ballsy, but I'm your best friend. If you want to say no, you can. I just insist you come because I want you here. But you give some lame excuse instead of telling me the truth and that's insulting."

"It's like we don't even know you. You're never real with us anymore," Arizona added. She usually avoided confrontation, but she was clearly upset about this.

"I'm sorry," I said again and shrugged my shoulders. "I don't know what else to say."

"The truth," Fallon said. "It's simple."

I felt like a deer in headlights. "Can we start over?"

"Start over?" Fallon spat and laughed. "Didn't we just do that because of your gigantic lies before?"

Nate stepped into the room. "She was with me."

I dropped my head into my lap. This wouldn't help with Fallon or Cronus. How was I supposed to keep him safe if he was going to tell everyone we were together? He didn't know that the saying 'a little birdie told me' could be literal.

I sat up and checked out the window to see if I was being watched. My heart sank when I saw a crow sitting on the fence with its beak pointed at me. My eyes peppered with tears. If anything happened to him, it would be my fault. Why hadn't I checked the room before shifting? I got up to run, although I didn't know where I was going. "You promised not to say anything."

Nate caught me. "Can we talk?"

He opened the door to take me outside. I shook my head, not wanting to go outside to talk. Those listening were dangerous.

Fallon slammed her hand on the door, shutting it. "No, she wasn't."

Nate and I were dumbstruck. Fallon glared at Nate, "You were at the party hoping to see Kiely. You waited almost all night."

I didn't know what to say. My wings beat under my skin, urging me to shift and fly. I glanced away and saw my eyes lit a bright blue in the window's reflection. I shut my eyes so they couldn't see and lied.

"I was here, but left. I had a panic attack."

"It's true," Nate said, putting an arm around me. "She started having them after her breakup with Jace. It's why she ran out of school. That's why I offered to help her and why we've been spending time together."

His ability to lie was impressive, but I was still on edge, fearing who might be out there watching us.

"I'd no idea," I heard Arizona's soft voice and her arms closed around me.

"I'm so sorry," Fallon said and added her arms around me.

The massive hug made me choke on more tears. These were my people. I wouldn't let the crows break our ties, and I would be damned if I let the drago wipe their minds.

"Thank you," I whispered to Nate. He knew those words were for him, but I knew they'd pass my friends' ears undetected and wouldn't rouse the suspicions of any enemies listening.

He nodded. "Just take a deep breath."

I inhaled his spicy cologne mixing with the floral and oriental perfumes of my friends. A few more tears ran out as I thought about those I'd lost and still could lose. I wanted my parents back, for them to notice when I was gone all night, hunting a man for his soul. I wanted my brother to interfere and scare away any guy that was stupid enough to put himself in danger by loving me. Taking another deep breath, I squeezed my friends back, allowing their support to nourish me. They had no idea this was a goodbye.

When I'd calmed down enough, I opened my eyes, and their arms unravelled.

"You should've told me." Fallon's voice sounded weak and broken. I turned to see my friend, who never cries, welling up. "I'm pleased my brother was there for you and I'm sorry I gave you a hard time over it."

"Come here." I pulled her in for a hug.

"Oh god, no." Fallon pushed me back. "I need to pull myself together."

Arizona reached over and rubbed Fallon's arm. "It's okay to let your walls down sometimes. You've been through a lot recently."

"Thanks," Fallon said, and smiled at Arizona. Fallon dabbed at her face to wipe away her tears without smudging her makeup. She stuck out her chin. "I love you guys, but I need a glass of water. Anyone else?"

I shook my head and so did Arizona.

Nate rubbed my arm. "Are you going to be okay?"

"Yeah, I just need to be with my friends."

Nate nodded. "Just don't forget me."

My fear was him forgetting me. I screwed my face up, unsure what he meant and puzzled over the cryptic message that might be behind his words.

"Do you want me to paint your nails?" Arizona asked.

"Yes, please."

We sat at the table and Arizona began painting my nails in my very own shade of *Dark Kiely*.

CHAPTER 24

IT WAS HARD TO LEAVE MY FRIENDS, knowing we'd never hang out like this again. Fallon and Arizona were unaware of how final this was. Their smiles and cheers made me feel alone and isolated. Our school days were ending and our lives were changing. I wanted to say goodbye properly, but the secrets between us created a distance that was greater than any miles.

Fallon was broken over her parents' divorce while focusing all of her energy on passing her exams and pursuing her career in the legal profession.

Arizona was struggling to focus on her exams. She was feeling creative and distracted with prototype products and draft logos for her business. She wasn't settled on the name of her company, but she was excited

and making it happen.

Neither of them asked what I was planning to do. They probably assumed I'd do something with nutrition or physiotherapy, as it was what I'd always said I wanted to do. But that girl wasn't me anymore. My goals had changed. Not that they knew or would ever understand that.

I was determined to bring my parents back and bring my brother home. I would find a way that I could keep my friends in my life and maybe even trust someone enough to fall in love again without putting them into danger.

When I arrived at the hotel to meet Cronus, Callum greeted me. He took me through to a large dining room where everyone was seated around a long rectangular table.

Entering the room gave me an odd sensation. It was like my head was underwater. I tried to act normal, but sweat prickled my skin as I feared something was wrong. Maybe I was about to pay for not killing Leo as I was supposed to.

Cronus was late. It just added to the sense of foreboding. I fidgeted in my seat and kept checking the door. I tried to listen to the surrounding chatter. They were smiling, laughing, and clinking drinks. It looked like a celebration, but my mind felt fuzzy. The whooshing in my ears got louder, making it hard to hear anything at all.

Then I heard Darcia's voice, and it made me sick to my core.

He got him!

I didn't need to know who. I knew.

Goosebumps trailed up my arm. The silence after hearing her message was almost deafening. I pushed my chair back so roughly it dropped to the floor. I got my mobile phone out of my bag.

"Are you okay?" Callum asked.

I nodded, but my body was shaking. "I need to make a call."

As I left the room, my hand was shaking so much that I dropped the phone as I got Nate's number up. I picked it up and clicked his name, my breathing coming fast. The phone rang and rang. I waited impatiently for his voice, desperate for him to answer.

"Come on!" I begged and began pacing.

A feeling of sickening dread told me it was too late. He couldn't answer.

The air was being sucked out of me, and the room spun.

I ran down the corridor, my hand trailing along the wall to keep me steady. I burst out through the double doors into the gardens. The cool air chilled my skin and cleared my head.

I shifted and flew to Nate's house, beating my wings as hard as possible, trying to push myself to fly faster than my physical capabilities. It felt like that nightmare where you run but don't seem to get anywhere fast. I felt so hopeless.

I landed at the summerhouse. There was no time to check if I was out of sight before shifting. I ran up the garden path and found the back door locked. I banged on the door like a madwoman, tears streaming down my face as I called for Nate.

I almost toppled in when the door opened.

"Kiely, what are you doing?" Fallon stared at me like I was crazy.

"I need to see Nate."

"He's in his room," Fallon mumbled. I shoved her aside and barged my way into her home.

She chased after me, following me up the stairs. She was yelling, but her questions were a faint mumble as blood pumped in my ears with the urgency to get to his room.

I pushed open his door and saw him lying on his bed, fast asleep. He looked so peaceful, and I breathed a sigh of relief. Perhaps I wasn't too late. Perhaps it wasn't Nate who had been *got*. Whatever *got* meant.

"Nate?" I asked, my voice wobbling.

He didn't stir.

The panic returned.

"Nate!" I yelled louder. I ran to his bedside and collapsed on my knees. I shook his shoulders, crying his name over and over, and begging him to respond.

My panic infected Fallon. She ran forward, calling his name and shaking him, too. "Nate, wake up. This is not funny!"

Her eyes were wide with alarm. "What's wrong with him?"

I shook my head. Fear gripped me, as I thought he was dead. Fallon tipped his head back and hovered her cheek by his face.

"What are you doing?" I asked.

"Checking if he's breathing!"

"Is he?" I squealed.

"Yes."

We both sighed.

Fallon reached across the bed and grabbed my arm, getting my attention. "I need you to help me. Fold that blanket and raise his legs!"

I did as she said whilst she pulled her mobile phone from her jeans pocket and dialled a number. She waited for someone to answer and then said, "Ambulance please."

"You're calling an ambulance?" I took a deep breath to calm myself. I knew this was my fault and there was nothing a paramedic could do. I had to figure out how to help Nate myself.

"He's unconscious, and we don't know why," Fallon snapped. She pressed the button to put it on speakerphone so she could hear when someone answered. "Do you know?"

"No," I squeaked. I really didn't, but I couldn't share with her the awful possibilities running through my head of witches, reapers, wolves, and snakes.

"Can you see anything that's restrictive?" Fallon asked, but she didn't see me shaking my head. She was already patting Nate's body down. She unbuckled his trousers and then opened his mouth and looked inside.

"Hello, where are you calling from?" A woman with a gentle voice came on the phone.

Fallon gave her address and postcode.

"What's the nature of your emergency?"

Fallon's voice sounded wobbly. "My brother's not responding."

"Where is it happening?"

"At my house, in his bedroom."

"Is that the address you already gave me?"

"Yes. I'm with him."

"Thank you. I'll send somebody along, but stay on the line."

Knowing an ambulance was coming appeared to relax Fallon. She let out a sigh and her shoulders loosened.

I held Nate's hand. "I'm sorry this happened."

"How old is your brother?" the call handler asked.

"Eighteen," Fallon answered.

"Does he have any medical conditions?"

"No."

"You said he's not responding. Is he awake, conscious, or breathing?"

"He's breathing, but unconscious."

"Can you see any bleeding?"

"No."

"Could he have been experiencing chest pains?"

"I don't think so. We found him like this."

"Is he injured?"

"No," Fallon said, her voice wavering.

"Do you know what caused him to become unconscious?"

"No, we just found him like this in his bed."

"Is there anything nearby that might indicate what has happened?"

Fallon checked around the bed, the floor, and then her eyes found mine. I saw the accusation as she frowned at me. "Nothing obvious."

"Can we call you back on this number?"

"Yes."

"Call us back if his condition changes. An ambulance should be with you shortly."

The line went dead, and Fallon shook her head. She locked on me and her expression darkened. "Get away from him."

"What?" I stayed, holding Nate's hand.

"How did you know?"

"I had a bad feeling, and he wouldn't answer his phone."

"If you've hurt my brother," she growled at me.

"I wouldn't." My eyes stung with tears at her thought that this was my fault.

Fallon slumped to the floor and took Nate's other hand. Her voice was barely audible. "I can't lose him."

"I know." I whispered back.

"No, you don't!" Fallon wailed from her position on the other side of the bed. "You haven't been there for me. My parents are all over the place, trying to drag us into their mess. My older brother and sister are away at university, removed from the drama. Only Nate is in this with me. I need him."

"I'm sorry, Fallon." I couldn't tell her how much her words resonated with me. My parents weren't present either, not really. And my brother had gone to live his new merman life. I'd never felt so abandoned.

There was silence as we took a moment to process what had happened. Fallon's voice was quiet as she said, "It's not your fault. You've had your own shit to deal with."

I closed my eyes tight. Fallon only knew half of it, but it felt good to have someone acknowledge that these past months hadn't been easy for me.

We waited for the ambulance. It felt like forever. My mind was loud with a thousand thoughts, gushing so fast that it took me back to when I'd been drowning. The water whooshing past my ears and feeling like it was over. There was nothing I could do then.

And there was nothing I could do now.

Mariah had pulled me out. She'd used her powers to save me. Now I had powers, but I was still useless. It broke my heart to see Nate lying there, knowing I couldn't help him after all he'd done for me. It was Fallon, a regular human, that had taken control of the situation.

Even with all the drama in her life, she was still strong.

"Hey, Fallon. How did you know what to do?"

"I didn't do this to him!" She shot up onto her knees and glared at me across Nate's body.

"I wasn't accusing you. I'm impressed. You handled it like a pro."

Fallon shook her head. "Sometimes I volunteer at St John's. I thought it would look good on my CV." She laughed. "Guess we all have our secrets."

"Yours may have saved your brother's life."

"I hope so," Fallon said, and let out a heavy breath. We heard a knock at the door. "Will you let them in? I don't want to leave him."

I nodded despite not wanting to leave Nate either, but what good had I been? I ran down the stairs so fast that I missed a step and fell missing the last steps. As I hurtled forward, wings sprouted from my back. Like an angel of death, I glided to the door. I quickly drew them back into my body.

My heart thudded as I checked over my shoulder. Thankfully, Fallon was still with her brother and nobody had seen anything. I opened the door.

"Where's the patient?"

"Upstairs." I flattened myself against the wall to let them hurry past with a stretcher. It wasn't long before they came charging down the other way and out the door with Nate. Fallon came down behind them. Her cheeks were stained with tears.

"I have to go," she said.

"Do you want me to come with you?"

"Only one of us can go with him."

"I'll get myself there." I hugged her. "Tell him I love him. I should have told him before."

Fallon whispered into my ear, "I think he already knows."

I watched the ambulance go and listened to the sirens fading as they raced to the hospital. Fallon's words lingered in me, and I prayed they were true. I needed Nate to know how much he meant to me.

Making my way back through the house and into the garden, I shifted into my crow form and flew to the hospital. There, I found a secluded spot to shift back.

The A&E entrance was clearly signposted. Being here made Nate's absence weigh heavily on my soul. The last time we'd been here had been when all of this craziness had begun. He'd come right away when I called and rescued me from the gardens. He'd brought me to the hospital when I needed treatment for an attack that left me without a scar. It'd been a miracle, and now I prayed for him to have a miracle too.

The receptionist gave me directions, and I found Fallon crying in the corridor. The moment she saw me she broke into tears and flung her arms around me. She sobbed, "He won't wake up. They're running tests to find out what happened."

"Have you called your parents?"

Fallon nodded. "Yes, but I don't want to see them. I can't deal with their drama."

We got coffee from the cafe and found somewhere to sit and wait for any news. Once their parents arrived, I said goodbye and asked Fallon to keep me updated. Her dad checked that I was okay getting home, and I told him I was.

Questions raced through my mind. What had the others thought about me leaving the meal, and how might Cronus retaliate?

Flying around searching for somewhere to shift gave me a chance to clear my mind. Finally, I landed on a lamppost in the car park and watched people running around, caring for one another. I saw the ill and injured struggling with their ailments and the way they tried to hide their struggles from loved ones that worried about them.

From my spot, I watched and waited until I saw Fallon and her parents leave. They were crying, huddled together, united in their pain. I feared the worst and flew to the roof of the hospital, shifted back into human form, and checked my mobile phone.

Kiely: How is Nate doing?

Fallon: He's in a coma. We won't know more until the results come back.

I wondered if the results would tell them anything. If I was right and the supernatural world was involved, then the cause would be unknown. Guilt riddled me as I feared they'd found out about Nate witnessing me shifting.

I needed to see Nate. Remembering how I tracked Leo, I closed my eyes. This time, I thought of Nate; the way he'd held me when I was broken; how he kissed away my tears.

I thought of the way he smelled when he lent me his sweater. His hungry eyes when he looked at my lips. How Nate had dared me to love again after Jace had broken my heart.

The more I thought of him, the more the colours

filled the air and swirled around me. The bright lights stretched out into a steady line. I opened my eyes, and the light was still there.

I opened the door that led out to the roof and hurried down the steps and along the sterile, white corridors. It was hard to stay focused on Nate when this place was trying to bleach out any trace of anyone within their walls.

I held fast to the warmth that Nate filled me with and followed the light.

It led me to a closed door. Pushing it open, I saw the light streaming toward a bed by the window. Nate was lying there, sleeping like an angel. I walked up to him and drew the curtain shut around us. They'd linked him up to a machine to monitor his heart rate. I sat on the chair by his bed and took his limp hand. Placing a kiss on the back of his hand, I waited, but there was no response.

"Can you hear me?" I whispered, half expecting him to smile and reassure me that there was nothing to worry about, but he didn't.

He was still. The room was eerily quiet.

Pressing my head against his chest, I listened to his heartbeat over the mechanical beeps of the machine. I wanted to hear that he was still human. I wanted confirmation that he was still in there; my Nate.

"I'm here, Nate," I sobbed, and kept my voice low for fear I'd get found and thrown out. I didn't want to leave him, even though being with him was probably what put him in this predicament.

My fingers ran through his hair. His golden curls crushed into the pillow. He looked so peaceful, but he wasn't sleeping. This coma was unnatural. "Sorry, I never wanted this for you. I wanted to protect you and keep you safe. It didn't matter. They still got you."

My teeth grounded together. "I should have told you when I had the chance, but I was a coward. I feared getting hurt."

My heart ached, and a tear trickled down my cheek. I couldn't keep the words locked up inside me any longer. "I love you."

Nate didn't respond. His hand was warm but loose in mine. I kept waiting for him to wake up. Thud-thud, thud-thud. The gentle rhythm of his heart and his soft, sleepy breaths were all the reassurance he could give me.

I got on his bed and laid down next to him. The moon poured light in through the window. The thin clouds moved over it, revealing a perfect circle.

I felt a change, a shift within my body. Being with Nate felt like I was being filled with warmth and light, the darkness being flushed out. It soothed me and I shut my eyes, drifting off to sleep with the only person who made me feel whole. He may be human, but he was the most powerful being in the world when it came to making me feel safe, truly safe, unlike the illusion that Cronus used on me.

"K… i… e… l… y…" a female voice whispered to me, over and over again. Sometimes loud, sometimes quiet and distant. It sounded like the way sound carried when the wind

blew on a blustery day, whirling everything around.

Then, silence.

Darcia stood before me. A woman formed of light with large white wings protruding from her back. She reminded me of an angel.

"Have you come for Nate?" I asked. Fear and heartache peppered my eyes. If the crows took the souls of a shifter, did she come for those of humans?

"I do not have long. I came to say, use your light to create. Do not allow him to bond his powers with yours. He will take it all. Kill you. Kill us all...."

Her words got lost in the wind. Occasionally, I'd decipher the odd word.

"Unstoppable..."

"Bond..."

"Key..."

As she faded out of my mind, her words dissipated into nothing. I fell into a troubled sleep, where my dreams were full of fear for those I love.

I saw snakes coiling around my parent's bodies, tightening so much that their eyes bulged in their sockets. I tried to free them, but crows flew out of the shadows, beating their wings in my face.

Once they passed, my parents were gone, and I stood with my friends by the clifftops. I saw the snakes grab their ankles, whipping out their legs from under them and dragging them away. I ran after them, but a wolf with amber eyes came out of a bush, snapping at me. Its barks echoed in my ears as if it wasn't one lone wolf, but a whole pack.

I stepped back and fell over the edge.

Plummeting down into the sea. I screamed, but no sound came out. The salty sea filled my mouth as I plunged down below the surface. My lungs burned as I kicked my way back up. The waves were rough, tossing me around like a rag doll, and I saw Nate on his hospital bed, floating not far away.

I swam toward him and noticed he was tied down at the wrist by snakes. I tried to swim closer, but the sea was wild, and mermaids made of shadows appeared and started pushing my head underwater.

I would fight to get back up, gasping for breath and coughing up seawater, only to be pushed under again. When I turned towards the land, there was a horizon of amber eyes watching me, waiting for me to surrender. Nate's bed drifted further and further away.

"You didn't kill him," a deep voice startled me awake.

I scrambled to my feet in alarm. My body was coated in sweat from the nightmares.

"Cronus?"

"You're the one." He licked his lips as if he might devour me, making me shiver.

My heart thundered in my chest. If he was here, he must have tracked me. I wondered how he'd found out that I'd not killed Leo.

"Did you do this?"

Cronus shook his head. "Does this look like my handiwork? I told you, the dragos handle human business. We handle shifter business."

"Was it because he knew?"

Cronus came and put an arm around me, but I

shook him off. I felt uncomfortable having him touch me whilst Nate lay in the bed before us, fighting for his life. I didn't have it in me to pretend I was still under his influence.

"Did you tell him and put him in danger?" Cronus asked sweetly, as if he cared, but his words dripped with poison.

"No!" I shook my head. I'd tried to keep him safe, to keep him away. He'd come looking for me. He'd found out by mistake. Still, I felt it was my fault. I'd failed at keeping them all safe. The guilt was crippling.

"Do you understand now why we must leave our old life behind? This is why you must push away those you love."

"I tried." My voice broke as the words made their way out past the lump forming in my throat.

Cronus kissed my forehead. "It'll be okay."

I cringed at his touch. I didn't trust him, or even like him. Part of me suspected that he had something to do with Nate's condition. But I didn't know what else to do. I reached for Nate's hand. "How can we help him?"

"The best thing we can do is pray he is strong enough to recover."

No shadow came from Nate's hand. I remembered how Leo had the same thing. He said it was because he'd sacrificed his soul for love.

My hair fell around my face and I noticed it was no longer black, it was pitch white. My fingers lifted it up to inspect, "What the…"

"It is a sign that you are destined to be my wife."

I shook my head and laughed. "I don't think so."

"There is a prophecy that the crow whose hair turns white as snow is the one that I shall take as my queen. She will sire the true blood crows, and together we will create our dynasty."

"No." A chill ran over my body.

Cronus's features darkened. "Do you need me to erase your past so that you may embrace your future?"

Cronus's hand struck forward like a viper. Nate's torso rose as if possessed, his head fell backward and pink marks appeared on his neck. Nate's body was limp. He was helpless. There was no fight in him, making him appear even more vulnerable.

"Please, don't." Hot tears ran down my cheeks as I begged and watched Nate's face turn pink.

Cronus's free arm reached across the bed, and he rubbed my arm. "I know you have been through a lot tonight. Go home and sleep and we can talk in the morning, my love."

My eyes stayed fixed on Nate. Frozen to the spot. It petrified me to leave Cronus with Nate. But I feared that if I disobeyed him, he'd crush his windpipe.

My hesitation angered him. His eyes lit up in blue. "Your past or your future?"

"I will marry you," I wailed in desperation and swallowed the bile rising in my throat. "Please, let him go."

Cronus let Nate's body drop back into the bed as if he were nothing. My anger was suppressed by my fear for Nate's safety. One wrong move and this powerful enemy could destroy Nate to punish me. His body lying unconscious in the hospital bed was a reminder of what they were capable of, and Cronus was threatening to do worse.

"Don't be sad. If he recovers, he won't remember you anyway. It's no loss. Your future is with me." Cronus spoke as if he was attempting to be comforting, but he was angry and I knew he wanted to upset me.

To know I would be nothing to him if he woke up broke my heart, like hearing Jace say, '*It's not you, it's me.*' Nate and I hadn't had a chance to be anything, and it hurt more, all the wasted time and missed opportunity.

I took a deep breath and forced a smile. If I loved Nate, I would make sure he lived.

If Cronus saw me crying over Nate, he could harm him to punish me.

Cronus took me by my upper arm and led me out of the ward. It took all of my strength to keep my composure. It reminded me of the school days when I'd been the target of wicked words, and I bled internally because I couldn't allow anyone to see my pain. Now, Nate's life depended on it. I tensed my jaw and raised my head in defiance of my own emotions.

We returned to the roof.

My white hair flew around me. I didn't believe his prophecy. There was no way I would marry him. I had no desire to sire his children. The mere thought made bile rise in my throat. His use of language grossed me out like I was a prize pig.

"Fly home. Rest. We can talk more in the morning." Cronus leaned into me and kissed my cheek.

My skin itched. The feathers beneath were eager to break free and fly away from him. I didn't want to leave Nate. Cronus has already shown me how quickly his temper could flare. For Nate's sake, I had to show that I was compliant.

I cast my shadow and shifted. I flew away from the hospital. My love for Nate felt like he'd captured my shadow and was reeling me back. It took all my strength to fight against my will and return home. Nate's presence called me back whilst Cronus's presence drove me away. I was torn and tortured as I departed.

Gliding in through my bedroom window, I shifted back. Stripping off into my bra and knickers, I flopped into bed. There was too much to think about.

I tossed and turned as I thought about all I'd lost.

Losing Nate hurt the most. His condition wasn't natural. Someone had taken his soul. As much as Cronus said he wasn't in the business of humans, it felt different from what the drago had done to my parents. It seemed someone else was behind it, not them.

I got out of bed frustrated and met my reflection in the mirror, trying to adjust to my new look. My hair was as white as snow. I'd only seen hair like this one place before. Darcia, the girl from my dreams. The girl whose voice had warned me of danger and sent me to Nate. She had visited me with a strange message about light and power. I knew what I had to do and it couldn't wait until morning. Throwing on some clothes, I shifted. I had to get to Scotland before the others.

I was sure Darcia was the person I'd heard crying from the secret room. It had to be.

She'd already tried to help me, and she knew stuff.

I was sure she was on my side and could help.

CHAPTER 25

As I landed in the quad, I knew I didn't have long before the crows would discover I was missing. And shortly after that they would figure out where I'd gone. I hurried to the office and found the door locked.

I ran to the next room and took a heavy chair, dragged it out into the hall and tried to swing it at the door.

The weight prevented me from getting enough momentum. I couldn't smash the door open.

I ran through the house in a frenzy, not knowing what I was looking for. Anything that might open the door. In the kitchen, I grabbed a knife from the rack. Perhaps I could pick the lock? As I was weighing up

whether it was possible to pick a lock, I spied the emergency fire equipment. Next to the extinguisher was an axe. I snatched it as I raced back to Cronus's office.

It was better than the chair, but no matter how hard I tried, I couldn't break the door. I collapsed on the floor in defeat. Cronus would punish me when he found me. Worst of all, his punishment could involve harming Nate.

Then I remembered the broken message from Darcia when I'd slept at the hospital. The word I'd heard was 'key'. Had she tried to tell me where it was? If Darcia could contact me, maybe I could contact her. Being in closer proximity might strengthen our connection. I focused on the light and tried to picture her in my mind, and what I needed to know.

Where is the key?

I repeated my message over and over in my mind, but it wasn't Darcia I saw.

As I searched for her, I saw a glowing light in my hand. It shone bright white, like a hot metal. My eyes were shut, but I could picture it and feel the weight of the object developing in my hand. It was cool and heavy against my palm. I opened my eyes and gasped to see the key I'd envisioned was now in my hand.

I slipped it into the lock. It was a perfect fit. When I turned it, I was relieved to hear the satisfying click as the door unlocked. I paused. I had no idea what might be on the other side. My hands felt clammy, and I wiped them on my clothes.

I looked around, expecting someone to appear and stop me, but nobody came.

This was it, I was going in.

I entered the room and opened the secret passage.

The stairwell was difficult to navigate in the dark, and the stone steps were worn and uneven. As I tried to focus, my body lit up like Darcia's had been. The glow aided me as I descended.

The room opened, and I knew I was under the building, in a cellar-type room. My hand lifted to cover my nose at the unpleasant damp smell. Curled up in the far corner was a woman that glowed with light.

"Darcia?" I called out, but knew in my heart it was her.

The woman sat up. I felt a prickle of nerves across my skin as I wondered if I was right to trust her after all the mistakes I'd made. The woman approached me, but stopped. She was in a cage; the bars were made of shadow and with no door. She held the bars and pressed her face toward a gap. It might look like shadows, but the bars were solid, like the key I'd manifested.

"You came." She smiled.

I touched her hand. "Can you help me?"

Her laugh rang out like a little bell as she stepped back, waving her arms around. "Do I look like I am in a position to help you?"

"I thought..." I stared into the dark emptiness, and the hairs on my arm prickled. My heart thundered at the thought of Cronus catching me here. If he came down those steps, there was nowhere I could run. The space closed in on me, and my chest felt tight.

I'd convinced myself that Darcia would help me out of my mess, and now I was alone with no idea what to do next. A stray tear rolled down my cheek, and my voice wobbled. "He wants to marry me."

Darcia threw her face against the bars. Her eyes bulged, the smile gone. "You can't! He wants to steal your power."

I leaned toward her and whispered, "Tell me what you know."

Darcia stepped back, keeping her eyes pinned on me. Almost as if she wasn't sure if I was someone she could trust. She strolled back to her bed and sat down. "I fell in love with a shifter. We wanted to be together, but her family would never approve. I still love her, you know."

Darcia's eyes glazed over as if she was remembering her lover. Then the dreamy look vanished, she stood up, and slammed her hand on her chest as she said, "When they found out I'd been marked, they locked my lover away." She shook her head, her voice raised in pitch as she recalled what happened. "They didn't want me to be claimed beneath the full moon. They hated me. Wanted me gone."

Her fists dropped to her side and clenched, and her eyes flared. Her tone changed and her words came out from behind clenched teeth. "Dragged me away. Tied me up to the highest point of a home belonging to the mer."

She turned away, and took a deep breath. Her

shoulders dropped as she looked over her shoulder at me. "They knew the crows would come."

Darcia walked back towards the bars to where I stood. "Join or die. You've been there. You know. As I was restrained, they bet on my death. Nobody thought I'd survive, but I did, and they feared I'd come for my lover's soul."

Darcia's features softened, and her head tilted to the side. "So they hid their princess away. As if, as a crow, I couldn't track her and take her soul. But if they knew my love for her, they needn't have bothered. I would rather die than kill my love. My Luna."

"Luna was your lover?" All I'd heard about the she-wolf were bad things.

Darcia nodded. "Everyone thought if I didn't kill the one that marked me, I'd die. Everyone believes it is the rite of passage for crows. But when I didn't, it caused problems for Cronus. Instead of dying, something new happened. I became a dove."

"What has this got to do with Cronus and I getting married?"

"Cronus didn't want the crows to know there was a way to be free of his control. My very existence threatens his power. But I am stronger than him - doves are greater than crows."

I had to laugh. "So how come you're in this cage and he's gallivanting around?"

Darcia shook her head. "Don't underestimate the power of knowledge. Cronus has been around for centuries. He has studied ancient magics, and figured out ways to bend it for his own advantage."

She wrapped her arms around her body. "He pretended to be my friend, then trapped my soul inside an urn. As the owner of the urn, he can control me. He has spent centuries trying to learn how to absorb my power into himself, and finally, he found a seer. She told him he must free my soul and marry me to unite our powers. Once united, he can kill me and my power will transfer to him making him unbeatable."

Darcia smiled at me and said. "There's a problem with this plan. He knows I'd never agree to marry him. My soul belongs with Luna." Darcia reached through the bars for my hand. "He cannot force you to marry him. You cannot allow him to bind your soul with his. He will take your power as his own."

I shook her touch away from me. "He's put Nate in hospital, and threatened to finish him if I don't marry him."

Darcia frowned, "If you find my urn and free me, I can help you."

"How? How are you going to help me? You can't even help yourself. Plus, how do I even know you're on my side?"

Darcia bit back words that fell silent on her lips. Everyone lied to control me. I was sick of it. I stormed out of the dungeon and up the steps. I couldn't get out of Cronus's office fast enough. My shaking hands fumbled to lock the door behind me and return to my room. I needed somewhere to hide the key and decided to stash it on top of the bathroom cabinet.

From my balcony, I saw a strange black cloud in the dawning sky. They were returning. My white hair swirled around me, and a coolness washed over my body as it urged me to shift. I stood my ground, only allowing my wings to protrude from my back like an angel. Breathing in the crisp, Scottish air, I watched as they neared.

They flew overhead, and I realised they'd be landing in the quad to shift.

I felt sick as I waited for Cronus to find me. The minutes felt like hours, but I held my head high. I wouldn't let him know that he had any power over me, especially not fear. I heard footsteps ascending and knew someone was nearing my door. The closer he got, the faster my heart beat. My throat dried and almost felt like it was choking me.

Cronus entered my room. He frowned, and I braced myself for an attack. "I ordered you to go home."

I swallowed a lump and held my head high. "This is my home now."

A wide smile filled his face, but his eyes were empty of joy. "Very true, chick!"

"Don't call me that!" My muscles tensed. He was going to attack me. I could feel it in my bones, but I didn't want him to see my fear.

"Do you prefer *fiancée*?" He drew nearer, closing the gap between us. The air thickened, infused with fear. I refused to surrender.

My eyes narrowed in response. If he wanted me as his wife, I would present myself as his equal or more. "I prefer my name, Kiely."

"There's no need to be like that." He trailed his fingers down my face.

I pulled away and could feel hot acid rising in my throat.

Cronus laughed. "Eternity together is going to feel very long indeed."

"Then why?" I spat.

Cronus grabbed my throat like he had Nate. Spit sprayed my face as he spoke. "You know why, you intolerant child."

He thrust me back by my throat, causing me to stumble back onto the bed. I rubbed my flesh where he'd held me. His eyes flashed to my bedside table, where he spotted my mobile phone. Other than a frown, I barely saw any movement from him other than some slight twitching of his hand. My phone levitated, and the SIM popped out and snapped in half.

He gave me a chilling smile. "There. We wouldn't want any more of your friends or family to become casualties of your stupidity."

He said it like he was trying to be kind, but I knew better. He was cutting me off. Making sure I was isolated from the outside world with no way to communicate. Little did he know that I now had a key to his office, and could access the old-fashioned phone. That thought made me look him dead in the eye and pretend I had no fear.

Cronus stepped forward so that he towered over me. His face softened, and he held his hand out to help me up.

I refused his help and got myself to my feet. I walked

toward the balcony, glad I'd not closed the doors. The fresh air felt good and soothed my nerves. The salty sea air reminded me of home and gave me strength. Creating a distance between us calmed me.

"Why do you hate me? We could rule side-by-side and take pleasure in our nesting."

Nesting! My body shivered at the thought of what he meant. I'd lost so much and all I had left was my free will. I felt I was hanging on to that by a mere thread. "You have a woman in your dungeon!"

I saw the colour fade from his face. His eyes widened as he realised I knew more than he thought. He licked his lips and rubbed the back of his neck. "What makes you say that?"

"I've seen her."

"Have you told anyone?" His words rushed out.

I laughed. The others didn't know. I ran my tongue over my teeth. This information was power over him.

Cronus's nostrils flared. Using his shadow manipulation, he grabbed my hair and yanked my head backward. "Are you so vain? Do you think I would have chosen you? This is a marriage of convenience. There's nothing romantic about it. You will bear my children, and, out of respect, I will make you a queen. Unless you'd prefer to be my whore, kept in the dungeon with that poisonous bitch."

Tears pricked my eyes as he twisted my head back to face him, despite him not touching me. He overpowered me so easily. My body shook against my will. Sweat prickled my brow and my breaths came in short, sharp bursts.

He loosened his fists, and I stumbled back. Cronus ran forward and caught me in his arms.

"I'm sorry, chick."

The way he said *chick* sounded like a cuss. I closed my eyes, feeling too humiliated to argue over the nickname. Tears rolled down my cheeks as I surrendered.

He'd won.

"Our wedding will be fit for a king and queen, and you'll be more beautiful than ever."

I felt sick. He lowered me down, my feet gently meeting the floor. I swiped the tears from my cold cheeks. He wasn't being kind. I could see the wickedness in the way he watched for my reaction. I was on edge, waiting for the knife in my back.

"After, we will consummate every night until you've satisfied my need for a brood."

"I hate you," I spat the words out as bile churned inside me.

The corner of his lip rose. "But you love that boy more."

The remainder of his threat caused my back to straighten. He noticed, and a sinister smile spread across his face. He knew I'd do anything to keep Nate safe, and that put Nate in danger.

"Behind closed doors, you can hate me all you want. But if anyone sees through our arrangement, I will erase your past. Do you understand?"

I swallowed a lump in my throat and nodded.

Yes, Cronus. I understand perfectly.

I would have to play along until I figured out how to get Nate somewhere safe, somewhere Cronus and his friends couldn't reach him. Then I would be in a position to make him pay!

Cronus jutted his chin out toward me. "Be convincing, little chick."

I nervously reached forward to touch his cheek. I looked up at him through my lashes. He felt bigger and more powerful as he intimidated me. He no longer had any charm over me. I took a deep breath and kissed him.

Then I waited for his appraisal.

Cronus laughed and turned to leave my room. "Try harder when we have company. Now, make yourself pretty for dinner, and meet me in the lobby."

He left the room.

My legs folded beneath me, and I slumped against the bed, dropping to the floor. Feeling defeated, the last thing I wanted to do was to dress up for him. I didn't even want dinner. I'd rather starve than eat with him.

My knees were pulled in toward my chest as I pulled myself back together. Feeling calmer, I went to the ensuite to tidy myself up. I needed to figure out how to escape this life without anyone else I loved being harmed.

A knock at the door made me jump. All the muscles in my body tensed, as if the person in the hallway could hear my thoughts and knew I was plotting. I gave myself a quick once over at the mirror and splashed cool water on my face to make it less obvious I'd been crying.

Satisfied, I returned to the bedroom and opened the door.

It was Morgan. She stepped into the room, with outfits draped over her arm. She dropped them onto my bed and some shoes tumbled onto the floor.

"If I knew he liked blondes, I'd have dyed my hair decades ago."

I bit my lip to prevent myself from saying what I thought of Cronus. She gestured for me to sit on the stool in front of the mirror.

Morgan picked up a brush and began styling my hair.

She sighed. "So, how did it happen?"

I wasn't prepared to answer questions about my non-existent romance with Cronus. His threats rang in my head to make it believable. I thought back to the occasions before I feared him, when he'd used his powers to seduce me.

"Come on, I want all the deets."

Be convincing… Cronus's voice echoed through my mind.

"We were training, but not really, if you know what I mean."

"I'm so jealous," Morgan groaned. Her eyes flashed wide as she realised she'd said it out loud. "Sorry, I'm super happy for you both. I will be the best head bridesmaid you could ever wish for."

I laughed. It felt like a joke. If this was a real wedding, I wouldn't want anyone as my bridesmaids except Fallon and Arizona. My dad would give me away, and my mum would have been by my side through all the planning. My heart ached for them to be here for me, but it wasn't safe for them and Cronus would never allow it.

"I'm sure you will be." I smiled at her through the mirror.

"Tell me more," Morgan coaxed.

The fear of angering Cronus caused the hairs on my arm to stand on end. This felt like a test. Even though he wasn't here, I felt he was watching. It was hard to be convincing when everything about him repelled me.

"It happened so fast. I'm still trying to make sense of it."

"You will have an eternity together." Morgan gave me a warm smile through the mirror. She believed I was having my fairytale happily ever after. She had no idea how what she'd said sounded more like a threat to me and filled me with dread.

I couldn't help but let out a sigh.

Morgan noticed my nerves and moved around to face me. She rubbed my shoulder and said. "We're all here for you. You will be our queen."

I swallowed a lump in my throat and wondered how she'd feel if she knew I planned to destroy her king. I forced a smile.

"Everyone sacrificed their soul to be here and would do it again for Cronus's hand. As his queen, that devotion extends to you. You're living the dream." She returned to finish my hair with a dreamy look on her face.

It was sickening how they were all under his spell

and couldn't see the monster he was. I was sure their extended devotion wouldn't include betraying their king.

Morgan had back-combed and plaited sections of my hair. She'd dressed me in an off-shoulder top and black wet-look leggings. I had a rock-chic feel to my outfit. She'd done my makeup and given me a few gold accessories.

Even though I didn't care whether Cronus appreciated how I looked, I liked the way Morgan had styled me. I grabbed my mobile and took a selfie. I wanted to send it to my friends for their approval, but knew I couldn't, so I saved it. Maybe one day, I could share it. An alert on the phone told me there wasn't a SIM and the internal data was low.

Morgan led me down to meet Cronus before I could agonise over my predicament any longer.

Cronus stood in the foyer waiting for me. He'd made an effort and, despite my hatred for the man, he was hot. I felt bad for Morgan. She'd have loved to have been in my shoes, minus the manipulation and control. Cronus wouldn't have needed to force her. People had gathered to see us off like we were celebrities. I heard whispers that took me back to the high school corridors. I didn't want to be the centre of attention.

Cronus offered me his arm, and I accepted. I was keen to get moving and away from the watchful eyes. I wondered if any would follow and whether I could keep up our pretence for an entire meal.

We got into his car and set off along the roads. The

last time I'd been in this position, we were heading back to my home. So much had happened in that short time the memory felt like forever ago. No longer was I the girl that belonged in 'Stowe.

My eyes dropped to my lap. I wasn't sure I was the girl that belonged anywhere anymore. Could Cronus be my fate, and this was my comeuppance for the lies?

We headed in a different direction from the day he'd taken me to the beach. I looked back in its direction and remembered the first time he'd shown how little he thought of me. The shock and betrayal mixed with the strange charm he'd had over me.

He focused on his driving. He had a firm jaw and rippling muscles, but I didn't care. The awe had gone. It was as if by not killing Leo, I'd broken the spell he'd had over me. I realised that was why he was so invested in us completing our contract.

We didn't become crows forever unless we did it. By not doing it, I'd become something else and was free of his control.

Cronus pulled over, and we stepped over a small wooden stile and followed a trail through some woodland. I cursed Morgan for making me wear heels. I stumbled over a grey rock, moss, and wet mud, and clung to Cronus's arm for support.

The trees were flushed with green and yellow leaves, and the air was wet. I could hear a loud noise in the distance. We were moving toward it, getting louder.

Finally, we came out into an opening. It was a secluded enclosure created by nature. Surrounded by thick trees climbing a wall of grey rocks, decorated in crisp green moss. The centrepiece was a waterfall cutting through the mountain and a shimmering pool at the bottom. The sound of the gushing water thundered in the space, echoing around us. The air was wet, fresh with the scent of foliage, like cut grass. It was spectacular, like a grand temple in the middle of the forest. As the river hit the pool, it foamed up, splashing across the rocks that tried to restrain it. It followed the path that cut through the green.

Cronus's hand slipped down my arm and held my hand. He had to shout over the thunderous roars of the waterfall. "Beautiful, isn't it?"

I had no words to answer him. My eyes were wide, taking it all in. I'd only seen places like this through screens and never imagined it to be so magnificent in real life.

I beamed at him. Despite my situation, I couldn't help but be taken in by this moment. Even my hatred for Cronus couldn't spoil this.

We stood on the edge, holding hands, admiring the sight before us.

"Come, I have another surprise for you."

Cronus led me along another path of trodden dirt, and we moved through the trees. This path was overgrown, and I had to step over roots and branches that made the footpath uneven. Cronus had to duck as the trees crossed overhead, creating a low tunnel.

We stepped out into a clearing and I could see that someone had prepared the area for our arrival. There were storm lanterns lit, casting a soft glow, and in the centre was a picnic table.

"Is that for us?"

"Yes, my queen."

My skin crawled at the new nickname, begging to return to 'chick'. I wouldn't give him the pleasure of knowing that it bothered me. I sat down on the bench, ready to entertain this meal. A bucket of ice and a bottle of champagne had been prepared for us. He poured me a glass and handed it over.

I took it and squinted. "I thought you were against me drinking?"

His eyes narrowed. "Don't be so critical."

I sipped the crisp champagne. My nose wrinkled from the sharp taste that I wasn't accustomed to. The aftertaste was refreshing, though. I sat back, enjoying the rustle of branches and birds singing their songs. We were far enough away from the waterfall for the sound to be soothing. I could hear it like a whisper, rushing down the rocks and crashing into the pool. The air smelled pure, awash with nature.

Cronus encouraged me to taste a strawberry from the platter. They were bright red and the perfect shape. I needed little persuasion. They tasted even better following the champagne.

"I have begun a schedule for the preparations, so we may be married as soon as possible."

"What's the rush?" I laughed, feeling relaxed by the setting and his demeanor.

"You struggle with making hard decisions, like

killing when required. I have taken the liberty of making these choices on your behalf."

"Thanks," I said with sarcasm, and took a generous gulp from the glass, enjoying the way it tasted more with each sip.

"Behave, and this doesn't have to be difficult. I have resources you couldn't imagine. Don't think I haven't toyed with the idea of locking you up in a tower and only visiting when you are in season."

"Wow! Romance is not your strong point."

Cronus laughed and waved his arm around. "Is this not romantic?"

"Is it not for show?"

Cronus reached forward to clink his glass against mine. "You're not what I expected."

Cronus rested his chin on his hand as he appraised me. His eyes wandered over my body in a way that made me feel disgusted. He spoke of me as if I were cattle, and I was sure that was his intention.

We sat in silence sipping champagne and eating strawberries, whilst shooting daggers through narrowed eyes. It was exhausting always being on guard.

I sighed. "Is this fun for you?"

"I'd hoped we could be reasonable to one another."

I choked. "How? You are constantly making threats."

Cronus licked his lips as he thought about what I'd said. "I need to make sure you won't deviate. You have already proven incapable of following simple orders."

I gripped my seat to prevent myself from fidgeting. I didn't want him to know he intimidated me, but I was aware of the danger of being somewhere remote with him. He'd proven already that his power was greater than mine, despite what Darcia claimed. He'd lost control over me, and I refused to allow his intimidation to give him power over me.

I held my head high. "I am well aware of what you'll do if I don't comply. The reminders are tedious."

Cronus nodded. "Noted. Now, let us enjoy this meal in such beautiful surroundings. At the very least, we should be civil, mother-to-be of my children."

I wished he'd shut up. It was hard to swallow the food down with him, reminding me of his disgusting, perverted plans for me. I groaned, but got through the rest of the meal without any more conflicts. Cronus entertained me with fascinating tales about how the island had once been inhabited by the fae folk and that was why it was rich with life. He told me how they'd played tricks on visitors, leading them astray with lights and kidnapping them into their realm.

As the evening set in, I stared into the darkening woods, willing a fae to light up and lead me away from the nightmare I was trapped in.

The only light here was the storm lanterns and the stars above.

Once we'd had our fill, we left everything there. Cronus said he'd send someone to clean up. He helped me along the uneven paths back to the car. If the date had been with Nate, it would have been perfect.

But thinking of Nate only reminded me of how careful I had to be to keep him safe. I agonised over how to do that, and yet not fulfil Cronus's sick plans for me.

CHAPTER 26

THE DAYS BECAME A BLUR of appointments and plans for the wedding. Cronus played his part well as the dashing fiancé, and if I played my part, he didn't deem it necessary to remind me of the threats. Whenever I was in his presence, I feared doing something that might anger him and worried for Nate. There was always a crow nearby watching me. It made me feel more trapped than if I were behind bars like Darcia.

Cronus was playful when we were tasting food and choosing our cake. We created moments like a dreamy couple in a movie. It was fake, and I couldn't shake off the shiver that crawled over my skin whenever I was around him.

If I ran, he'd hunt me down, but not before he killed Nate.

I was a prisoner without bars or chains, held only by my fears. It kept me compliant in his roleplay. On the inside, I was powerless and tortured by the illusion of an open door, yet knew I could never leave.

Some days, pretending felt like a pair of hands tightening around my throat, choking the air from my being. Not being myself was disorientating.

Still, he paraded me around whilst everyone celebrated my good fortune at being chosen. The lies sat heavy in my stomach and made me feel sick.

It was when I tried on dresses that it got too much. They had me stand on a podium while the seamstress circled me, pulling and tucking the fabric, and adding pins at different points. I stayed still, barely breathing, as a tear rolled down my cheek.

I didn't swipe it away, fearing that any movement might draw attention to it. If I failed to be convincing as the blissful bride-to-be, there would be consequences, and those consequences were a price I didn't want my loved ones to pay.

I couldn't shake the longing for my mum to be here. It ached inside my chest. This wasn't how I'd imagined my bridal dress feeling.

But I couldn't escape it.

Right in front of me was a long mirror that forced me to look at myself.

I kept thinking of how my mum should be here, but memories of my parents were warped by the robotic drago that inhabited their bodies. Although Morgan was trying to be my head bridesmaid, she wasn't my best friend. Everything was fake. The loss of my family and friends built up in my throat as a lump I couldn't swallow. I was preparing to marry a man I hated, with no idea how I'd escape our arrangement.

I was exhausted from worrying about everyone I loved.

"Hey." Morgan hurried up to me and dabbed my eyes with a tissue.

My body went rigid as I realised she'd caught me crying.

She dismissed the seamstress, who was here for my fitting. "Give us a moment."

Morgan helped me off the platform and we sat on my bed. She rubbed my back, and I finally surrendered and let the tears flow. It was a mix of relief letting it go, and exhaustion and worry as I feared what was to come.

"There, there. What's the matter?"

I took a deep breath as I thought of Cronus's reaction if he found out I'd been crying. "It's nothing."

"It doesn't look like *nothing* to me. I can tell this is more than wedding jitters. You can tell me."

That was a lie. She was Cronus's most loyal lackey, but it was hard to deny my breakdown after Morgan had witnessed it. I cursed myself for being so weak whilst she waited for me to share. My brain raced through different ideas of what I could say to appease her.

"I miss my friends and family," I admitted, knowing a partial truth was easier to tell than a full on lie. My shoulders dropped as I let that truth go. More than hating Cronus, I wanted them. "I wish they could be here."

"You can't invite humans, but your parents might be able to come as they are under the drago influence. They'd not quite be themselves, but they'd be here physically."

I shook my head. The thought of my zombie parents here would make this event more torturous. "I'd rather not."

"What about your brother? Isn't he a merallo?"

I sat there, stunned for a moment as I tried to make sense of what she'd said. Then my heart filled with hope. Murray could come. He was part of this crazy shifter world, and yet he was still himself. I could have someone. Someone who was on my side and I could trust, that loved me and was safe.

"I'd love that." I beamed at her. "If you can make that happen, you really will be the best bridesmaid ever!"

"I will get it sorted." She squeezed my hand. "Let's get this dress fitting finished and then have some drinks. I heard Cronus has lifted the ban now that you are going to be our queen."

Queen? Not if I could help it.

Knowing Murray was coming filled me with hope. I began counting down the day until his arrival. Every morning, I'd stroll down to the beach to see if he was there. My mood improved when I realised I wouldn't be alone in this new world.

I was standing on the shore with a thermos flask in my hand when Murray stepped out of the sea like a mirage. I'd suffered a drought of needing someone I loved and trusted, and there he was, glistening in the morning sun.

Light shimmered down his body and he transformed his scales to human flesh. As his skin dried, a black t-shirt formed around his torso.

I knew he could shift as the others had told me, but seeing him do it was more bizarre than hearing about it. I pulled my arms tight around me; the flask digging into my left side. I wasn't sure where we stood after everything that had happened. I needed him, but I was still mad at some of the things he'd done.

"Hey there." He approached me and raised an eyebrow.

"We have a lot to catch up on."

Murray frowned. "Yeah, I left you for five minutes and now you're getting married?"

I swallowed a lump in my throat. It didn't feel safe to talk, but I didn't want to lie to him. Flashbacks from last time crashed into my mind. It'd ruined my life, and now the stakes were even higher. It wasn't my life on the line. That was exactly why I needed to tell him the truth, but I had to make sure we were alone.

"What?" Concern washed Murray's face.

"Nothing," I shrugged. "Come on, I'll show you the house."

"Tell me about Cronus? King of the Crows?" Murray asked. I could sense the subtle dig behind his words. I led him up a trodden path, away from the shore and up the side of the cliff towards the house.

"Sounds like you're well informed."

"Barely."

"Come on." We carried on up the hillside, passing the purple thistles and heather that decorated the edge of the path in splashes of colour amongst the green. The building towered up above and cast a shadow over us, blanking out the summer sun. The wind chilled my arm, and dread set in the pit of my stomach.

Murray had stood up to Cronus the night I'd been taken. But I saw how he was overpowered by Cronus's ancient magic. I feared I was leading my brother to the slaughter. I knew how protective he was of me, and worried that he'd put himself in danger when I revealed to him the truth of my situation.

We walked up the driveway. The front door was wide open, ready for our arrival. Crows and shifters were hanging around to glimpse at my brother like he was some kind of celebrity. Some said hello, but most stayed back as if they were wary of his presence or waiting for a reason to snatch his shadow. Their stares made my back prickle with sweat. Their presence confirmed my suspicions that I was being watched by his feathered spies.

"Cronus has requested that you join him in the Eagle Suite for afternoon tea."

Murray followed. When we entered the Eagle Suite, we saw Cronus had prepared a tray of teas and cakes. He was prepared for Murray's arrival, and this show was a statement of his intel.

Cronus stood up to greet us. He held out his hand to shake hands with Murray. "It's a pleasure to meet you."

"Likewise," Murray said with his arms folded across his chest.

"Although we have met before," Cronus reminded him. "How is your mermaid mate?"

"She's fine." Murray's face screwed up at Cronus's choice of words.

"And their fairy?" Cronus pressed as he poured our teas without showing off his powers.

"Gwyn is, unfortunately, in a deep sleep."

"How unfortunate." Cronus's smile filled his face as he finished making tea.

I shuddered as I wondered if her deep sleep was anything like Nate's. It didn't feel like a coincidence that they both were suffering the same fate after close proximity with Cronus.

Cronus moved our drinks toward us. "Will you and Mariah postpone having fry until you have a guardian to raise her?"

Murray narrowed his eyes and began to tap his foot. "We've not discussed children."

Cronus smirked and reached over for my hand to squeeze it. "Kiely and I cannot wait to consummate and grow a large family."

A shudder crept through me at the thought. I tried to tug my hand free, but Cronus's grip was tight.

Murray choked and sprayed tea everywhere. He composed himself and added, "Kiely has fantasised about having a baby."

I rolled my eyes. I didn't know what was worse, Cronus's or Murray's passive attacks.

"It's been a long time since two humans of the same family have joined our world. How are you finding the mer?"

"I'm learning a lot about the shifter and spiriter clans."

Cronus lifted my hand to his lips to kiss. "Kiely is my favourite student."

The feel of my feathers ruffling under my skin coursed through my body. I wanted to be free of his touch and a million miles away. Instead, I took a deep breath and wished the time would pass quicker.

Murray and I sat at the little table on my balcony, looking out over the cliffs toward the glistening ocean. We were enjoying chilled cans of Fanta, and were finally alone.

Murray leaned over and lifted up a portion of my

hair, "What made you bleach it?"

The way he asked sounded a little like a dig at me. "It's not bleach. It seems our hair turns black when we become crows, and white if we become doves."

"Interesting." Murray leaned back in his chair. He had one eyebrow raised that told me he was processing a question he wanted to ask. His quizzical look felt familiar like my typical brother that wanted to know all my business.

Sitting out here reminded me of being away for the summer holidays, where my biggest concern was getting a great tan before returning home. I was enjoying the moment, but Murray's being here was my opportunity to solicit his help. My throat was dry as I plucked up the courage to speak. I coughed to clear my throat.

Murray turned to me. "Spit it out."

"I need you to do me a favour…" I pulled a face. I didn't know how to ask this. "Actually, I need to ask—"

"What is it?"

"It's Nate. I think Cronus did something to him. I'm sure of it. This romance, Cronus and I, isn't real."

"What are you talking about?" Murray leaned in, a vein pulsing in his neck. "Why would Cronus attack Nate?"

"You can't let on, you know. He's dangerous."

"I already know that. Has he hurt you?"

I bit my lip. I knew Murray would get mad if he knew, but I had to tell him.

Before I could find my words, Murray got up so abruptly that his chair fell backward. I reached around to grab his arm. "Please, Murray, you've gotta keep your cool. I need your help, and whatever you're thinking won't help."

Murray paused. His jaw twitched. "You better tell me the truth, Kiely. I can't take any more of your games."

"Cronus has made threats against Nate. Until I know he's safe, I can't leave. Is there anywhere we could take Nate? Somewhere that Cronus and his kind wouldn't be able to reach him?" I clutched his arm out of fear that if I didn't, he might hunt Cronus down. "He will kill Nate if I don't go through with this wedding. It's fake, but you need to play along because Nate doesn't have powers like us. He's just human."

Murray relaxed. "Why Nate?"

I rubbed my temples with my fingers and took a deep breath. "I like him. Really like him. And Cronus found out."

Murray nodded and sipped his can before speaking. "I'll speak to Mariah."

I threw my arms around Murray's neck. "Thank you, thank you, thank you."

I felt Murray relax. Tears of relief ran down my face as a new hope bloomed. If the plan worked, if Nate was safe, Cronus wouldn't be able to use him to manipulate me.

Murray wiped his thumb over my cheeks, sweeping away my tears. "You know I hate crying."

I chuckled. "Sorry."

Murray shook his head. "I'm going to kill that bastard the first chance I get."

"Not if I do first." I laughed. "But first, Nate must be safe."

Murray nodded. I reached over to rest my hand on his. It felt good to have him close; to be able to touch my family and for them to be themselves.

"Have you seen Mum and Dad?" I asked, swallowing a lump.

"I dropped by the other day." Murray frowned. "I don't agree with it. There must be another way."

I bit my lip to prevent myself from crying. It felt good to have someone on my side. I thought about our zombie parents, and somehow that was more chilling than Nate sleeping in his hospital bed. Nate was in there, and as soon as he woke up, he'd still be Nate.

My mum and dad were strangers, their bodies possessed vessels.

Murray jutted his chin up. "We'll help them too."

They had summoned me to the courtyard for the wedding rehearsal. Black roses and blue thistles decorated the area, interwoven with fairy lights. They went around the columns and over our heads. It looked hauntingly beautiful, like a gothic magical wonderland.

The choice of decor had been done by Cronus. Sometimes, he'd give the illusion that I'd picked something, but he'd guided me on what he wanted, and I didn't dare challenge him with an alternative.

As I'd requested, Murray was to give me away. I hooked my arm through his. We walked along a pathway marked out by a rope. Morgan had told us tomorrow the pathway would be decorated with dark blue petals.

We passed rows of wooden benches as we walked toward the front to join Cronus and the officiant. The young girl was frail and bony. Her movements were fluid like a ballet dancer's. I suspected she was another victim of Cronus's. I saw the fear in her eyes, the way she checked back to him for confirmation that she was doing as he bid. She wasn't under his spell, but he had control over her somehow.

She went over what we'd be doing, that she'd bind us to one another with the silk ribbon and we would exchange our vows. I cringed as I'd still not written mine. I'd been so focused on escaping that I'd not noticed the wedding creeping closer. Now the thought of everyone watching me with nothing to say made me feel sick with nerves.

Murray still hadn't heard from Mariah that she'd extracted Nate. I'd rather marry Cronus than see Nate harmed. It felt like Murray was here to witness my doom.

I was relieved when Cronus said we could go.

"Why don't you enjoy your last day as a maiden with your brother," Cronus suggested, but I knew very well that it was an order. Cronus gave Murray a wicked smile. "Soon she'll no longer be an O'Neil."

"What will I be?" I asked, wide-eyed. It'd never

crossed my mind that my family name would be gone. Even though there was no law to say I had to take his name, I knew Cronus wouldn't stand for it.

"Mrs Reaper, of course." He leaned forward to press his lips against mine. My eyes remained open, and I looked at Murray. My feathers prickled under my skin, begging me to shift and fly away.

My shoulders dropped as soon as I knew we were far enough from the house to be alone. I was going to show Murray the island, but I could feel my skin prickling and wanting to shift. I was desperate to fly from this island that had become my prison.

Pretending to be in love with Cronus was sickening.

As time passed and the day drew closer, I felt more and more hopeless.

We jumped over a running brook and crossed a field. I led him far away from the house. We settled together beneath a large tree that stood alone. The view would allow me the advantage to see if anyone, even a crow, tried to spy on us.

I leaned back and saw a rainbow in the sky. I'd always loved them and it didn't fail to make me smile. "Look. A rainbow."

"You know what that means?"

I shook my head.

"It's done," Murray whispered.

He said it so quietly that I wasn't sure if I'd imagined it. I was scared to believe it. I wanted him to say it again, and louder, but I knew he was being cautious. His expression told me it was true; I'd heard right. The corner of his lip was turned up in a conspirator's smile. A look I recognised from when we'd been kids and up to mischief.

"We can go," he added.

"I'm not going."

"Kiely, what are you playing at? You can't be serious. I can't leave you with him."

I shook my head. "You have to let me take care of myself. My greatest weakness is you and everyone else I love. I'm stronger if I know you're safe. I need you to go and be with Mariah."

Murray got up and started pacing. "Kiely, I know I've made mistakes, but all I want is to protect you."

"I know, but I don't need you to."

Murray grimaced. "I can't."

"You must. If Cronus discovers Nate's gone, it's Mariah that'll be in danger."

Murray frowned. "You think she's in danger?"

I shrugged. "I dread to think what Cronus is capable of. You'll be safest together. You're most powerful in the ocean, and I'm most powerful in the sky. We must play to our strengths if we are to beat an ancient. Help Mariah keep Nate safe."

Murray rubbed the back of his neck. "I feel like if I go, I'm leaving you to your funeral, not a wedding."

"I know, but I need you to go."

Murray chewed his cheek. He stopped pacing and stared at me. He slowly let out a sigh and nodded. "I'll go tonight."

I shook my head. "No, we'll walk back along the

coast, have an argument, and you'll leave now. You're not coming back to that house. The sooner you leave, the better."

Murray let out a groan, but nodded. I threw my arms around him, relieved he wouldn't argue this. I didn't have the energy to fight his stubborn arse.

I held onto him for longer than usual. We were secretly saying goodbye. I didn't want him to leave, but I had to let him go.

"What will you do?" Murray asked. "You're not really going to marry him."

"No way, but I can't just leave. I'd be forever looking over my shoulder. I've got a few details to figure out."

"The wedding's tomorrow!"

"Don't remind me."

I could see Murray's face was starting to worry about me again. I reached for his arm. "Please trust me. For once, Murray, let me do it my way. I can take care of myself."

He raised an eyebrow but didn't argue. We walked back toward the house and detoured along the beach. Seeing the sea weighed heavy in my heart. Tears pricked at the nostalgia of wishing I could return home with him. I wanted to enjoy the sea without all of the drama that had become my life. With every step, I knew we were getting closer to Murray leaving. It made me slow down, trying to hold onto as much time as possible.

If I failed, this would be our last moment.

We stopped at the shore.

"Ready?" Murray asked.

Not really.

"Yes."

Murray turned on me and began yelling, "You're so selfish, Keily. You're never thinking about anyone else. It's always me, me, me!"

I was stunned by his sudden outburst that it took a moment for me to realise he was doing what I'd asked.

"Me? Selfish? What about you and taking off without even a goodbye?"

"Says the girl who is marrying some guy she didn't even tell her family about."

"It's not like we planned it."

"Yet you plan to spend the rest of your life with him. It's double standards, Kiely – you want me to accept him, but you don't accept Mariah."

That last bit sounded too personal. I choked on my words.

Our history made it difficult for me to like Mariah, but so much had happened. I'd been so wrapped up in my own problems that I hadn't thought about how he might be feeling.

It made me see myself as selfish. Tears pricked my eyes.

The fight felt too real.

"You want my blessing?" Murray stepped into the ocean and looked back over his shoulder at me. He tilted his head and pressed his lips together. "I just can't give it. I love you, Kiely, but I can't watch you marry him."

Murray dove into the crashing waves. I saw a white

light flash over his body, and a large fishtail flicked out behind him. I gasped. It was the first time I'd seen him in his mer-form.

All his harsh words washed away and I knew that, at the heart of it all, we loved each other.

My body tingled with adrenaline as I realised I now was going to have to fight Cronus. I'd save Darcia first, and then we'd face him together.

He wouldn't let me just leave. Not marrying him, not giving him his brood, would injure his pride.

He would want my blood.

If I just ran, I'd be forever looking over my shoulder, and everyone I loved would be endangered.

I returned to the house. As I approached, I felt like a traitor sneaking into the enemy's camp. After all, I was plotting their king's demise.

My body was tense as I mentally prepared myself for the war. I waited for someone to notice Murray's absence and readied myself to lie.

CHAPTER 27

I COULDN'T SLEEP. I waited for the house to go quiet. Many had stayed up drinking in celebration of the festivities to come. Once the house was silent, the sound was deafening.

My heartbeat in my ears sounded like a war drum.

I slipped the key off the top of the bathroom cabinet where I'd hidden it. My heartbeat erratically as I scanned the room fully expecting to be discovered.

They were always watching. I was never alone.

Except now I was, and I didn't trust it.

Perhaps it was the silence that bothered me. Everything was too still. Too quiet. Building up like a black panther hiding in the grass and ready to pounce. My muscles tensed, waiting for my shadow to be

snatched out from under me.

I crept across my room toward the headless woman standing in the centre, wearing my wedding gown. The delicate crystals sewn into the fabric sparkled in the moonlight. It wasn't the dress I would have chosen, but it was beautiful. I picked at the seam down the side of the bodice, needing a hole small enough to slide the key inside, between the layers of fabric.

My teeth gritted together as my nails scraped away, trying to pull a thread loose. One finally came free, like a whisper of light. I tugged at it to make the hole big enough for the key.

I returned to my bed. Waiting to be dressed and made up for a wedding that would become a battle. I feared for my life, where only months ago I'd not cared to live. I wondered how warriors slept, knowing an impending battle was on the horizon.

I must have fallen asleep because Darcia visited me again.

"Kiely…"

"Kiely, are you there?"

"Kiely…"

Her voice grew louder.

"Darcia?" I answered.

"Kiely, Cronus doesn't want to marry you."

"I know. He just wants heirs."

"No! That's a lie."

I felt so bitter about the situation that all I could give was sarcasm. "Unfortunately, it's true. Our big day is tomorrow. Yippee!"

"It's a trap."

"A trap?" Everything had felt dire before. I was planning to attack him and one of my advantages was the element of surprise. It hadn't crossed my mind that he was planning to attack me, and this display was all an elaborate ruse.

"The ceremony isn't to bind you as lovers; it's to bind your powers to him. Once he has light and dark, he will be invincible."

"I won't let him. I'm going to fight him. Kill him if I must!" I shuddered at the thought of taking a life, even one as dark as his.

"He is the King of Death. He cannot be killed."

A tear ran down my cheek as my fighting spirit waned into hopelessness. "What am I to do?"

"Find my urn. Free me, and lock his shadow inside."
"An urn?"

"Cronus studied Djinn and uses an urn like a lamp."
"Djinn? Like a genie."

"He cannot be killed, but you can become his master."
"Where's your urn?"

"I don't know. Find it before the ceremony. Wake up!"

I sat upright in bed. Darcia's words were still ringing through my head.

I scrambled out of bed and flung open my door to begin searching, but I was greeted by the entourage. They swept me back into my room and started styling me for my execution, under the pretence of a wedding.

I'd never felt more beautiful, but my delicate appearance was nothing compared to what was brewing beneath my skin. My newfound power was burning so brightly inside me that my body glowed. The bridesmaids Cronus had chosen lifted my train to help me down the stairs.

I entered the courtyard garden where fairy lights weaved between the arches and I could see Cronus standing at the far side. Wooden pews were set out for his guests, who twisted in their seats to stare. Pale faces framed with pitch black hair watched me as I walked down the aisle, decorated with black roses and blue thistles.

The sky was a warm red, waiting for the sun to rise and start the day. Cronus had insisted that the wedding be held at sunset. It was to represent our new beginning, but now I saw it as part of a ceremony to steal my powers.

The young girl with dark features stood at the front. She wasn't like the others. She was scared, eyes wide, as if she was screaming with her mouth shut. Instead of her look instilling fear in me, it fuelled my anger.

Today, I would put an end to this.

I began my slow descent to the front, not sure when to attack or how. I thought I'd have freed Darcia by now, and that we could face Cronus together. Ever since she'd made me aware of the urn, one of Cronus's minions had supervised me.

Murray was gone, so I was walking alone. I prayed they were somewhere safe hiding Nate. The sick feeling was starting to feel normal as I approached the front.

"You are glowing, my love." He licked his lips.

I ignored him and spoke to the officiant. "Are you okay?"

Cronus answered for her, "She is our fae to perform our ceremony. Let us not waste a second."

He returned his attention to her, and she shivered. "Begin."

Our guests hummed a song I didn't know. It sounded dark and foreboding, not something you'd expect at a wedding. In contrast was the slender girl who began to dance with fluid movements. Her dress lifted and floated around her as if she were underwater. It pooled like soft white clouds and flowed after her.

Rising and falling, rising and falling, like it had a life of its own.

Her body glided with the grace of a ballet dancer.

I knew she was using magic.

As she moved, a ribbon manifested, tracing her movements. She spun around and swept it up in her hands. The humming stopped and she dropped to her knees and bowed before us. Her arms were outstretched, and the blue ribbon draped across her palms.

Her sad eyes met mine, and her mouth opened as if she wanted to say something, but turned to Cronus and thought better of it.

She took my hand and wrapped the fabric around my wrists. "I bind you, Kiely, one of light. I bind your powers to the night. The one you give your all, your soul. Consent to Cronus, surrender and fall."

Her voice was like a sad song, and I felt almost hypnotised by the magic.

Cronus broke the moment with his deep voice I had once loved and now hated. "This is when you say I do."

The girl was now binding the material around Cronus's wrist, and I knew I didn't want to say those words. It wasn't the haunting expression of horror on her face or the idea this was more than being tied to him forever. This wasn't about Cronus wanting a dynasty. There was more. I could feel it in my bones.

I was out of time.

At my bleakest moment, I cast my eyes up to the sky, begging for help. How could I go through with this? But if I didn't consent, I was sacrificing Nate.

There in the sky, I found hope. Blazing across the castle was the most perfect rainbow I'd ever seen. My heart filled with hope. It reminded me that I wasn't alone and I had to fight for everyone I loved.

I pulled my hand away. "I do not consent."

The ribbon unravelled from my wrist, freeing me from this union, and dropped to the floor. Our audience gasped and every muscle in my body tensed as I prepared for his retaliation. The frail girl's eyes lit up, and she bit her lip to stop a smile. She swallowed and backed away until she found herself up against the wall.

Darkness poured from Cronus, a dark cloud forming around him, but he didn't shift. His lips pressed together, and his eyes bulged. His voice boomed, "You must!"

A nervous laugh escaped my lips as I stepped away from him and shook my head. He couldn't make me. He had no power over me.

His jaw tensed and his hand shot forward. I expected to feel his shadow grab my throat as he'd done before, but instead a painful sharp tug on my heart. My chest thrust forward and I saw a pool of pulsing light seeping out of me and travelling toward his outstretched hand.

"You can't!"

"Surrender to me or die!" he bellowed.

I pulled against him. The resistance felt like a rope tied around my chest. My ribs constricted, and I struggled to breathe. I released my wings of golden light and flew upward.

At first it reminded me of the day at the beach when I couldn't move, but then his shadows snapped, like an elastic band breaking.

I was free, but the win was short-lived.

Cronus released large, dark and feathered wings and joined me in the sky. This time he struck out both hands and black tentacles shot forward, wrapping around my arms and legs and pulling me toward him. I wrestled against their hold, but they only grew stronger. My appendages felt as if they were going numb as the tightness cut off circulation.

"Is this what you want?"

I couldn't answer. One tentacle wrapped tight around my throat, making me cough and splutter as tears blurred my vision.

Cronus passed the tentacle leashes to one hand

and gave them a sharp tug. The movement threw my bound body. My stomach lurched, and the world spun around me.

He caused my body to jerk as he shook the shadowy strands. His musical laughter rang out as he enjoyed my agony.

He slammed my body down. My face impacted the stone slabs, cutting my lip against my teeth. The copper taste of blood filled my mouth, and my head rang.

The world whooshed past as he yanked me back up into the air. He spun me around him like I was on a lasso. He hovered in the centre of it all, the only one I could see clearly.

A chill ran down my spine as his free hand summoned his scythe again. The dark, thick shadow snaking out and taking shape.

"I liked you, Kiely. Really, I did." His words didn't match the sadistic smile on his face. He shook me again.

I flopped around like a rag doll with my bones breaking. The shooting pain raked through my body. Then I healed. And he did it to me again. A vicious cycle of pain. I felt foolish for thinking I could take on an ancient.

"Think what I'll do to that boy I don't even like." Cronus laughed.

He raised his weapon, now fully formed, ready to sever my soul from my body.

But bringing Nate up was his mistake. It reminded me that he didn't know Nate was safe. I burst into a blinding light, and the tentacles vanished. My light cancelled out his dark. I reached my hand out like he had and tried to create a scythe, too, so I could take his soul.

Strings of light raced over my hands, like when I created the key. Cronus shot out his tentacles again, trying to reach me, but I dodged them. The strings were welded together, creating a perfect circle that looked like a burning sun, and as it formed into a glowing, gold, hollowed disc, I threw it. It sliced through the shadow. The tentacles reflected off my weapon and sent them back to him.

"Help me, you fools!" he raged, causing a sea of shadow to consume the people below us as they shifted into their crow form.

He swallowed hard. The simple act had betrayed him, for it told me I had a chance. Fear fuelled his anger, and my power incited it. Cronus raced toward me, sweeping his weapon. I caught the disc as it returned to me and deflected his blow.

The metal of his weapon clashed against mine.

The sound rang out like a chiming bell.

Metal against metal.

Silver and gold.

Blow against blow. Evenly matched.

Then the sound of a hundred wings thundered in the surrounding air. The summoned murder had come. I backed away to create some distance and threw my weapon. I cut through the black clouds, but there were too many. They began swooping and clawing. My mind returned to that fateful night when I'd first surrendered and joined them.

Everything Cronus had told me was a lie. They were just as much a victim as I was. I couldn't stop their attacks. I couldn't get them to see the truth.

They were too far under his spell.

Now I would have to take them on along with Cronus, pitifully outnumbered.

The distraction enabled Cronus to latch onto one of my wrists with his tentacles. He pulled me back toward him, and I wrestled against him. Catching my disc, I cut myself free and threw it to take out some of the nearby crows.

Cronus's confidence grew with every crow that joined the fight, and his tentacles shot out more rapidly, trying to grasp me. The constant attacks made it impossible to focus on my light. I was in defence mode. Wings flapped in my face, talons tore at my skin, and I blindly lashed out at them. Their distraction was giving Cronus an advantage, and another tentacle took hold of my body.

Blood mixed with tears.

He had me. Every limb. Holding me steady as he allowed his crows to torture me.

Their beaks and talons were vicious and cruel. My dress was soaked in my blood. I was thankful Murray wasn't here to witness my death.

This was a battle I couldn't win. I'd failed those I loved.

Cronus crashed me back onto the floor and I laid there defeated on the altar. Hot pain racked my body from all the gashes. Feathers, blue thistles, and black roses scattered across the ground and their floral scent filled my nose.

Cronus dropped down beside me. His feathered friends cast shadows behind him and took human form as our guests. Everybody was tired and sad.

"Let's try this again."

He reached out and the young girl stumbled out from where she'd been hiding with no control over her legs.

"Say the words!" he demanded.

The girl lifted the ribbon from the floor. She knelt beside me where I lay and wrapped it around my wrist. My blood stained the fabric.

Her voice quivered as she said the words, "I bind you Kiely, one of light. I bind your powers to the night. The one you give your all, your soul. Consent to Cronus, give your all."

A tear rolled down her cheek. The air was silent as if everyone had stopped breathing, waiting for me to make the ultimate surrender. The corner of his lip rose in a cocky smirk.

He'd won.

He'd beaten me.

Or so he thought.

His smug face made me sick, but he wasn't going to get what he wanted. I'd fight him until my dying breath. I recalled that moment I'd seen the fear in his eyes and he'd needed to call for backup. It sparked hope in me. Right now, his guard was down, thinking the battle was over, and he had won.

I pushed up onto my feet, and my body lit up as I started healing myself and returned his smile.

My wounds closed. The pain faded.

I didn't have to be bound as his mate and live in his servitude.

I knew what I had to do.

I would master him.

I sent out my tethers of light. They wrapped around his body, binding him. He tried to cast out his shadow, but he couldn't access his power.

Darcia was right, I was more powerful than him. He was helpless in my light.

His people cast their shadows down, trying to shift and save their king. I would struggle to hold Cronus once they began their attack. The first of the crows began their descent, swooping down, raking welts down my arm with their talons. My hold weakened. The pain pulled my focus, and I knew I needed something stronger. I needed to create something to hold him without drawing my full concentration.

"You cannot kill me. I am already dead." He laughed, but I detected a trace of nervousness.

I wove strands of light from the floor up. I pictured the cage he'd placed me in when I'd first arrived, but this one was big enough to hold him in his human form. The space illuminated in a blinding light, cancelling out his power. He was trapped within the birdcage and I could release the strands that bound his arms.

I shot out a ball of light, knocking the crows from

the sky. It was only a small portion of the many that darkened the sky.

Cronus laughed. "It's cute that you think you can beat me. I hope our chicks have your fire."

I was spinning to keep up with the assaults. My hands flew out in every direction, trying to take out my feathered assailants. They were getting through, and blood ran down my bare arms where their talons had found success.

I refused to surrender like I'd done the night on the cliff.

The priestess hurried to my side. "Let me help you."

She waved her arms around, and the thistles lifted into the air. They moved in tune with her dance, and when she slammed her hands down on the ground, they shot out. Like purple-headed arrows, the thistles flew into the unsuspecting crows, knocking them from the sky. Black feathers and black petals swirled around us. Her attack had balanced the scales against Cronus.

"Thank you," I told her.

It was just me and him now, and I knew how to end this fight.

I snatched my hand out and reached for his dark soul. It wasn't warm like Leo's. It chilled my palm as it pumped in my hand with its icy coolness. I tugged and saw a flicker of uncertainty wash across his face.

Confidence fired my belly as I taunted him. "Don't worry, I won't kill you."

I placed my hand on my chest as strings of light came to life. I thought of a way to lock up his soul so he couldn't harm me, my friends, or his family. The creation from my mind was inspired by an object Darcia had told me of. However, my creation would be different.

The object took shape under my hand, wrapping itself around my neck.

"What is that? What are you doing?" Cronus's words rushed out, and I felt him pulling furiously against my hold.

A locket of my own design now hung around my throat. A filigree heart with a small crow charm. I grabbed his soul with both hands. The muscles in my arms pulsed as I pushed them to the max. Sweat dripped down my brow. I could see his shadow wrapped in my strings of light, pulling him toward my locket.

"Stop her!" Cronus wailed full of desperation.

Cronus screamed as he realised his fate. I yanked his soul from his body. The moment it came free, I stumbled back. It became lighter.

His body was no longer a force against me. His jaw dropped as he gasped. Even in those last moments, he hadn't thought I could ever beat him.

I felt the rush of his power combined with mine, but I didn't want that darkness. I pushed his soul into the locket and shut it. The corner of my lip curled up in the same smug way he used often with me.

His crow army returned to their human forms.

There was no king to fight for.

Their bond was now broken.

They sank to their knees and folded over. I thought

they were grieving until I heard the small girl address them.

"All hail, your gracious queen." She turned to gesture to me. "Kiely of the Light."

I laughed. Just when I thought my life couldn't get any crazier, I was made a queen. A vision of bowed heads filled the space before me.

I took in my subjects, and felt overwhelmed with duty. I wasn't prepared for this responsibility.

I paused when I saw Cronus. He was hunched over like the others, but his body appeared heavier. At that moment, I felt sorry for him. It must be hard to have come from a position of such great power to become ordinary.

Powerless.

"Cronus?"

He lifted his head. I saw his sadness.

"Get up," I ordered. I felt uncomfortable seeing him in such a submissive position.

He did as I asked.

"I suppose we should plan your coronation."

"My what?" I blinked.

Cronus sighed. "A ceremony to make it official. You get a crown."

"I know what a coronation is, but I—"

"Defeated the Crow King," the fae girl interrupted me.

Cronus's head dropped on hearing her words. The crowd stared at me, expecting something. I had no idea what I was supposed to do, and it made me jittery.

"Why are they staring?" I whispered to the fae girl.

"They're admiring their queen. Compelled to love, honour, and obey."

I didn't feel like a queen in my blood-soaked bridal gown. My wounds had healed, but I looked a mess.

"I need to freshen up."

"That you do," Cronus replied from within the cage of light.

"Can I just leave, or should I say something?" It irked me that I'd turned to him for advice without thinking. This was a habit I'd have to learn to break.

"I'd recommend a speech, but you can just dismiss them," Cronus said.

I waited for him to follow up with a smirk or snarky remark, but it didn't come. The sea of faces made me uncomfortable. It felt eerie to have them under my control. This wasn't what I wanted, but with them under my control, at least my loved ones were safe.

"You're dismissed," I shouted.

To my surprise, they all rose and made their way back inside. As the space opened up, my body softened. Watching them leave, I shivered in my gown, keen to follow them inside and rid myself of this dress. Instinct told me to stand tall and appear stoic. I had to bury my nerves, because now I was their queen.

Queen Kiely of the Light.

CHAPTER 28

UNDER THE SHOWER, I stayed for an extended amount of time to allow myself to process what had happened and figure out my next steps.

There was still the matter of Darcia. She had helped me, but her soul was still trapped somewhere in an urn I had yet to find, keeping her a prisoner under Cronus' control. If I had charge of Cronus, could I demand he free her?

An image of Cronus on his knees filled my mind, making my heart feel heavy. It felt unnatural to have control over him, but he had forced my hand by giving me no other choice. Even as his master, I wasn't sure how much I could trust him. His vast knowledge made

him a valuable asset, and I hoped we could figure out a way to work together that could allow him some freedom without putting myself at risk.

Then there was Nate. I was desperate to see him. My heart fluttered with wings, wanting to soar my way back to him. I had to have faith that he was safe and that's what the rainbow had signalled. But I needed to see for myself, to know without a shadow of a doubt that he was okay. Although, I still had no idea how to wake him from his coma.

I returned to the courtyard. Cronus was sitting on the floor in his cage of light. I used my powers to flip the latch and swing the door open.

"Take me to Darcia's urn."

"This way." Cronus rose to his feet. His steps were heavy, slow, and reluctant. I could tell he had no choice but to do as I bid.

He took me back into the house and to his office. He pulled the top drawer out as far as it would go and reached his arm in. I heard a pop sound and the back of the desk dropped away. Cronus came and moved it like he was opening a door and lifted something out.

"Here." His face paled as he placed a glass item in my hands. It was shaped like a vase with a lid on top. Inside was something floating like liquid light.

I opened the bookcase and hurried down the steps to Darcia.

"Is that…?" Darcia's eyes were wide, and her finger jabbed toward the glass lamp.

I nodded. "How do I free you?"

"Grant it. Just say you set me free."

"Darcia, I set you free."

The light in the lamp swirled and lifted, rising out of the glass. It whirled around me before whooshing across the room into Darcia. Her body burned brightly and the bars of her cage vanished. In a flash, Darcia had thrown herself across the room and wrapped her arms around me.

"Thank you," she sobbed.

"I told you I would free you," I said.

"How can I ever repay you?"

I shrugged. "You helped me too."

She grabbed my face and kissed my cheeks. "Thank you a hundred times over."

Cronus huffed behind me.

Darcia turned her attention to Cronus. "Where's Nate's?"

"Nate's?"

Cronus shrugged. "I don't know what you are talking about."

Darcia turned to face me. "He did the same to Nate, but with him being only human -"

"That's not possible. Only Drago is involved in human business." Cronus turned to face me. "Queen Kiely, you see why I had her contained. She is dangerous, and not to be trusted."

My head spun. Whenever anyone referred to me as queen, it sounded bizarre. She might be dangerous to Cronus, and he might not trust her, but I didn't believe that was true for me. Plus, Nate's coma had never felt like the drago's handiwork. In my gut, I suspected Cronus. He could lie to Darcia, as he wasn't under her command, but he couldn't lie to me. My heart filled with hope. If Darcia was right, I could wake Nate from his coma.

"Bring me Nate's urn," I ordered.

Cronus' jaw twitched, but he had no choice. He led us back to his desk and reached back into the drawer. When his hand emerged, he passed me another urn. This one was almost identical to the one Darcia's soul had been trapped in. My heart thudded like I now held the most precious thing in the whole world. Tears filled my eyes. Please let this work. My voice was a whisper like I was making a wish. "Nate, I set you free."

The light swirled and lifted out of the lamp. It rose toward the ceiling, then out of the office. I followed it into the corridor and chased after it. It raced into the courtyard and shot up. With my wings extended, I ascended into the sky, but as I hovered above the castle, I couldn't locate his soul. There was nothing to follow.

I lowered back to the courtyard and prayed Nate was somewhere safe. I needed to get home and find him and make sure this crazy world didn't put him in any further danger.

The urn in my hand now was plain. Lifeless. It was a symbol of what Cronus had done.

I glared at Cronus and smashed it on the floor.

Cronus flinched.

I turned to Darcia. The brightness of the morning was too much for her eyes. It must have been forever since she had seen sunlight. She raised her arm to shield her face, but couldn't hide the huge smile. Cronus' people, now my people, were confused by who Darcia was. It was clear they'd never seen her before. I heard the whispers like those that had taunted me in the corridor, but this time the sound was empowering. The sound buzzed, and I knew it was the sound of the beginning.

I turned to Darcia. "I need to head home. Can you keep an eye on *him* and make sure *he* doesn't do anything stupid?"

"I am sorry, I cannot. I have waited so long to be free and I need to find Luna. It is what has kept me going all these years and finally, I can -"

"No. You don't need to explain. I understand. You go to her."

Darcia's eyes teared up. "Oh Keily, I will forever be in your debt."

Before, I could assure her it was okay, and she didn't owe me, light rippled down her body. Then out of the white came a beautiful dove. She flew around the courtyard working her way up and over the top of the building.

"Good luck, Darcia!" I called after her and watched until she flew out of sight.

I returned my attention to Cronus. "You are to stay here and you will not do anything that would piss me off. Do not use your powers whilst I am gone."

I brushed my hair back and strolled out of the castle. I had to do this on my own.

I shifted and took to the sky. High above the Isle of Skye, I looked down at the castle that was now mine. The sea that circled the island sparkled in the sunlight, and the little coves called to me and I remembered the day Murray had arrived. I saw the rolling green hills and the woodlands where Cronus had told me tales of fae folk. One day, I'd love to share this with my friends, parents, and Nate. The beautiful island disappeared behind me as I made my way over to the Scottish mainland and neared closer to entering England.

I'd flown back home and through my bedroom window. So much had happened since I'd left that it no longer felt like my room. The vanity mirror was cluttered with bottles of sprays and makeup tins, hair accessories, and jewellery. It seemed crazy that those things had once felt so important to me, and now they were just a mess.

Stuck to the mirror was a pale pink heart-shaped post-it note. On it was Murray's handwriting.

Come to the beach where Granddad always took Aero. Murray x

I knew exactly which beach Murray meant. He had written it cryptically enough that if I hadn't read the note, nobody else would have known where he meant. My wings ached from the flight, but I couldn't wait. I shifted back into a dove. Flying out the window, I followed the coast to Nacton Shores.

The woodlands were a vast green and when it broke into yellow sand; I knew to seek out my brother. The beach here was more secluded. Although it appeared empty, I hid amongst the trees to shift back. I ran along the surf, hoping when I found Murray he'd have Mariah and Nate with him.

"Murray!" I called.

The seagulls answered with screeching screams overhead. I sucked in a shaky breath. My chest was tightening as I feared the worst. My body shook as I stared out over the sea. It went on forever, a long plane of blue, but nobody was there.

I was too late.

I thought I'd won, but somehow Cronus had got to them first. My fists pulled at my hair. I kicked at the stones. I should have known. Nothing ever works out for me. What was the point of my power if I couldn't even save the ones I loved?

My legs felt heavy. My heart longed to hang on, wishing for them to appear. It was hopeless. I dragged myself away before collapsing onto my knees in the sand and let out a loud sob.

"Murray!" I cried begging for a miracle.

The sea bubbled like it was boiling. Something was happening. My breath caught in my throat as I scrambled to my feet.

White foam gushed across the waves a few yards out. I wiped the tears from my face with the back of my hand.

Part of the ocean was rising and forming into a

sphere of water. It was moving slowly and steadily towards me. I stepped back and faced the sea, waiting, my heart full of hope.

The closer they got, the clearer it was to see. I couldn't believe it. I didn't dare to believe it, but it was him. Nate.

My hand went to my mouth as I gasped. He stood inside a watery orb. The ocean lifted him and opened like a blossoming flower. It was as if he were surfing on the waves without a board. The wind whistled around his body, whisking him dry. It was gentle and controlled. He landed in the soft wet sand and I ran forward. I threw my arms around his neck. He spun me around and I was engulfed in his smell mixed with the salty ocean spray.

"Nate," I gasped. "How?"

"Mariah."

It didn't matter how he was here. I needed to touch him, to hold him, to appreciate that gorgeous smile, green eyes, and… I pressed my lips against his, trying to communicate everything I was feeling about him. My fingers ran through his golden curls, and when he pulled me up against him, I knew my body was glowing. I didn't care to hide it. I was a queen, and he was forever under my protection.

"I love you, Nate." The words gushed out before I could filter them. Part of me didn't care if my big feelings scared him. I was more scared of another disaster preventing me from letting him know how I truly felt.

His lip cocked up on one side, and his eyes lit up. "I've been waiting for you to be ready to say that. I love you, too, Kiely."

We embraced each other and shared another deep kiss. His warm lips tasted so good, and I couldn't get enough. My fingers ran through his hair and I never wanted to let him go.

A loud cough came from behind.

We broke away and saw Murray standing on the shore watching us. My cheeks heated. His arm looped around Mariah, who leaned into his body, gazing up at him with that goofy look I once despised. They were so happy together and I found myself pleased it had worked out for them. It was difficult to feel any hate when my whole body was consumed with love.

"Thank you," I said to Mariah. She had rescued Nate when I hadn't been able to, despite our chequered past.

Mariah shook her head. "No need. It was the right thing to do."

Murray broke away and pulled me into his arms for a hug. "I've been worried sick about you going up against that monster."

"He won't be a problem anymore."

"No more drama, okay?"

"I'll try." I half promised, but I had a feeling that this new world we were part of wouldn't be drama-free.

I squeezed Nate's hand, "Are you okay."

"Well, I'm not in a coma anymore."

"About that. Where does your family think you are."

Nate looked at Mariah when he answered. "Something about dragos possessing doctors and telling them I've been transferred to see a specialist."

"Mum and Dad called in some friends to help," Murray said.

I felt cold and rubbed my head. It felt wrong that we'd had to lie to the Rein family to keep Nate safe and that some innocent medical professional had been possessed in doing so. Nate squeezed my shoulder and I melted from his gentle smile.

Mariah said, "It is a temporary solution. We need to get Nate's immunity. I found a book in my family's library and there's a law that a human can know about our world if at least one representative from each family agrees to it."

My heart dropped. Mariah's words reminded me that Nate still wasn't safe. Worry wrinkled my brow.

"It's okay. I get it. You can protect me until we get this sorted." Nate rubbed my arm as he reassured me.

"Who do we need to find?" I was eager to make sure Nate was safe.

"The six; a mer, a reaper, a drago, a werewolf, a werecat, a Kitsuné." Murray listed. "Between us, we cover two of them, and I've spoken to our parents, and the drago inside has no issue with granting this." Murray took a deep breath and I braced myself for the bad news. "The problem is the last three. The werecats are old-fashioned in their ways and despise humans.

The only werewolf is Luna and she hates everyone, plus she wiped out all the Kitsunés."

"But, we'll find a way around it. There has to be another way." Mariah added.

I smiled. There was a way. "Luna may no longer be our enemy, but that's another story I need to follow up on. As for the werecats, there's one that's in love with a human. I'm confident Eve will help us, as she'll probably need our help for the same reason."

"What about the Kitsuné?" Nate asked.

"Maybe Luna didn't get them all?" I suggested but their expressions were all uncertain.

Nate's hand slipped into mine, and it felt good. "Maybe."

Something in my heart told me there was still a Kitsuné out there. If everybody thought they were extinct, nobody had even looked. With my new powers, I was confident that if anyone could find the last Kitsuné, it was me. Until then, I had a whole murder of crows under my command to keep Nate safe.

THE END

AUTHOR NOTE

Dear Reader,

I know this book covers some tough topics. During my teens, I struggled with my mental health and feel it is important to raise awareness so people know they are not alone. If you are struggling, the best thing to do is talk to someone. This can be a friend or family member, or a professional like a teacher, doctor, or a mental health champion at work. There are also lots of charities with resources to help. At the time of writing this, some examples are Mind, YoungMinds, Samaritans, and many more.

Thank you for reading *Sky Heart*, I hope you have enjoyed it. Reviews can help books get discovered by their ideal reader. If you can spare a moment to write a review for *Sky Heart*, I'd really appreciate it.

Visit my website www.allyaldridge.com to discover how you can connect with me on Social Media.

All my love

Ally

Acknowledgements

Thank you to you, the person who is reading this. I can't express how much I appreciate you taking the time to read my novel. I hope you've enjoyed it and will continue to be part of my author journey. If you are interested to know who else helped me get where I am today, keep reading…

As usual, there are parts of me and those I know that went into the making of my main character. At times she was hard to write because of the dark places Kiely's mind went and having to remember how that felt. As a Scorpio, I really don't like liars and although this negative trait was important for the plot and her character growth, I didn't like it. I feared her lies were unforgivable and readers wouldn't connect with her. My beta readers gave me insightful first impressions and helped me improve the story.

My husband has continued to support me. He often challenges my plot holes before anyone else, and works with me to develop the powers, and encourages me to add more magic wherever possible. We spent a lot of time discussing shadowkinesis and what the dove powers might involve. My son is now old enough to be impressed that I wrote a novel. Seeing him being proud of me has been a huge motivator, and he often asks how I'm getting on with finishing it. My youngest fancies herself as a director of photography and tries to help me with my social media posts.

My writing started as fan fiction at the early age of five. My first teacher is responsible for telling me what an author is and, from that moment on, I knew that was what I wanted to do. Another influential teacher was Mr Macy from my high school. He gave me extra notebooks for story writing so I could create my novels.

I want to thank my parents for establishing a love of fiction in my siblings from an early age. Now I have my own kids, I know how challenging it must have been for my mum to keep three excited children under control at the library. When I look back, I still cherish those special moments when I'd snuggle up with my dad at bedtime and he'd read to me. Thank you to my cousins, who enjoyed my storytelling skills and constantly demanded I make up more. I must thank my little sister, Heather, and her best friend for reading all those early attempts at novel writing and for continuing to believe in me.

I need to thank my best friends for being part of my adventures growing up. I remember sleepovers watching Stand By Me and Jo saying, "You could write about us one day, Ally. If you ever run out of ideas..." I don't think I'll ever run out of ideas, and some of our real-life adventures are stranger than fiction. Thank you girls for supporting my writing, and being excited to get your hands-on book two after loving book one. A big thank you to my husband's best friend Dale for reading all my drafts, offering feedback, and being my companion on trips to Book Festivals.

Thanks to Felixstowe Scribblers - my local writing group. It was good to know that I wasn't the only one with a crazy imagination in Felixstowe town. You've always made me feel welcome no matter how long I've been gone. To all the online readers whose kind and encouraging words helped me to improve and believe in myself, I thank you too.

A special thanks to everyone at World Indie Warriors and founder Michelle Raab for bringing together creatives to share and support one another. A special shout out to my author friends J D Groom, and Cassidy Reyne. You've been important to my author journey and your continued support and encouragement has kept me going, especially when my imposter syndrome has kicked in. Thank you to Rachel Churcher for introducing me to Bury and Beyond and the Foreword Festival, and all your advice and tips. Thank you to Roxy Eloise for giving me the confidence to do my first ever Book Festival, Herts Book Fest, and for being the most amazing Beta Reader I have ever discovered. A big thanks to all the Book Festivals that have allowed me to share *Ocean Heart*, promote *Sky Heart*, and take part in their author panels.

Thank you to my editor, Avery McDougall, for the way you've made me laugh at my mistakes and how you've taught me to become a better writer. Thank you to Kara S Weaver for stepping in as my editor. And, a big thanks to April Grace, who edited the final draft of *Sky Heart* and her sweet motivational comments at the end of each chapter to keep me going. Thank you to Natalie Narbonne for taking my ideas and creating a beautiful cover design. Thank you to Julia Scott for making the inside as special as the outside. You guys helped turn my manuscript into the book I envisioned.

Sky Heart has been very challenging to bring to publication. This book has taken longer than anticipated to bring to print. I've been fortunate enough to have a special online friend cheering me on, and helping me overcome obstacles. Thank you Tarot for always being there for me.

Also, a special mention to Aiki, a young reader that not only loves this series but is writing her own series with her own character art. Her enthusiasm often has picked me up when I've most needed it.

There are so many people to thank as this has been a dream I've chased for several decades. If I've not mentioned you, please know it was not intentional. I love you all.

About the Author

Ally was born in London but grew up in Suffolk which is where most of her YA Fantasy novels are based.

She is happily married to her high school sweetheart, and together they are raising their son, daughter, and two cats.

When Ally is not writing (or at her day job), she loves spending time with her family at the local beach, in the forest, or watching way too much Netflix.

Ally loves a cup of tea and has been known to order one on a night out.

MORE BOOKS BY ALLY ALDRIDGE

THE SOUL HEART SERIES

Ocean Heart (book 1)

Sky Heart (book 2)

Forest Heart (book 3) - coming soon

Flame Heart (book 4) - coming soon

SOUL HEART NOVELLAS (STANDALONE)

Summer Heart - coming soon

Dark Heart - coming soon

I also have plans for more books and more series...

I can't even count how many other stories are in my head but if you want to be the first to hear what I'm working on and future releases, please sign up to my newsletter and follow me on social media. All links can be found on my website.

allyaldridge.com

www.ingramcontent.com/pod-product-compliance
Lightning Source LLC
Chambersburg PA
CBHW050851210726
48290CB00004B/1179